Checking Boxes

Checking Boxes

Magdoline Ward

Checking Boxes

This book is a work of fiction. Names, characters, places, and incidents are either products of the author's imagination or are used fictitiously. Any resemblance to actual events, locales, or persons, living or dead, is entirely coincidental.

Cover Photography: George Favios
Editor: M. J. editing
Proofreader: Angela Pruden
Cover Model: Lucas Facchini
Formatting: Alt 19 Creative

magdolineward.com

To the girl in the shadows
I'm trying

CHAPTER ONE
Grace

HAVING A ROOMMATE has its ups and downs, and listening to Shelia and her flavor of the month having wild sex is definitely one of the downs. I put a pillow over my face, wishing I could escape their moans and noises. It's just a reminder of how lonely I am.

A moment passes, and I open my mouth in shock. *It can't be!*

Shelia is not having normal sex—or at least normal by my standards.

There are two different male tones. There are two men in her room, and I gasp as the reality sinks in. I know she's a little adventurous when it comes to men, but that girl doesn't slow down.

My feet hit the floor. I cannot take this anymore. They're too loud.

Soon, I won't be complaining about it. Shelia is thinking of offering Jack, her on-and-off-again boyfriend, a chance to rekindle their relationship. I think she wants him to move in with her, and I don't want to be an obstacle when she makes her decision. However, I wonder if it'll work. She wants an open relationship while Jack doesn't.

I wish Shelia the best, but now I have to think about *me*. Where will I go?

Well, it's right there. Just a step away from this apartment.

The guy who moved into the apartment next to ours is seeking a roommate. There's a sticky note on his door where he asks for one.

I put on my coat and leave the room, heading out to the hall. I need to check if it's still there. I close the apartment door quietly, then turn and walk the little distance to —maybe—my new place. I tilt my head to the side, reading his note. He isn't specific about gender, but he has some rules.

"Cook dinner every night, and I'll grant you a rent-free stay."

He wants someone to cook for him. It's like he needs a maid, not a roommate.

I bite a nail till it hurts, thinking about the advantages.

Rent-free means I'd save lots of money, means I'd move my plans forward to have a place of my own, and I'd be on the right track to having the stable life I've always wanted.

And I don't mind cooking.

Every night? I don't think so. He's probably going to have dinner over the weekends with someone—a girlfriend, his family, or some friends—so it wouldn't be every night exactly.

Suddenly, I'm excited. Then the elevator dings, and I immediately turn. The doors open, and heat strikes my face and every inch of my body.

Ian Skene strides out of the elevator impatiently, as if he had a bad day, but that doesn't affect the aura of authority radiating from him, labeling him as a leader without mouthing a word.

I haven't really given his offer any serious thought. It'd be embarrassing to explain my late presence at his apartment door. But as his scent starts to invade my space, I truly think of bolting.

Turn and run, Grace

But I don't get the chance. His eyes are faster than my feet. He spots me, and we lock gazes. Too late to escape, I hold my ground.

"Is everything alright?" He pauses, two steps away from me and a little too close for my comfort. The icy look on his face says he's not worried about me but probably wondering what the hell I'm doing in front of his apartment door.

We've bumped into each other a couple of times where he politely introduced himself, so did I, and that's all the interaction we've had so far. Fortunately or unfortunately—I feel it's kind of both.

"Yes." I clear my throat. "I was reading your offer...." Needing something to hold onto, I hide my hands in my pockets. "I'm really interested."

"You are?"

Though it's a bit dark, I can feel the amused smile he's trying to hide. "I know it's late to talk, but you know... you've just walked out while I was thinking about it and um, you know...."

What is he supposed to know?

"Do you wanna continue this inside?" He inclines his head toward the door. He's taking pity on me. I don't think we're off to a good start.

"Sure." I shrug one shoulder, a bit reluctant.

He unlocks the door, and I'm overthinking it again. "I'm sorry, but maybe it's too late to talk. I mean, you've just arrived. I'm sure you need some rest."

His entire body freezes for a moment before he pulls the key out of the lock. He turns to me while pushing the door open with his shoulder. "It's totally fine. But if you're not comfortable, we could discuss it tomorrow."

I take a step back, my eyes taking him in. This guy is tall and ripped. "No, it's fine. I just...you know."

Again, what is he supposed to know?

He's fighting laughter, I'm pretty sure, but he's keeping himself in check. He gives me a nod, then turns to open the door wide and walk inside.

I'm still at the door while he gazes at me over his shoulder. "Please come in."

Not quite sure if it's a wise idea, I step inside, wondering if I should shut the door behind me. I don't get to dwell on that as he turns and shuts it himself, making the tiny distance between us slightly uncomfortable again. I instantly step back. My hand reaches for the handle while my back meets the door.

He folds his arms, staring down at me. "Do you wanna leave?"

Awkward, awkward me stays mute. As a twenty-three-year-old woman, I should have grown out of this awkward stage a long time ago.

"Please do if you feel uncomfortable," he says, but I bet he's wondering what the hell is wrong with me.

I push away from the door. "No, not at all. I wanna hear about your offer."

Gazing down at me, I try to hold eye contact with him. His eyes are unreadable, but I feel like he's enjoying this a tad too much.

"I need to take a shower," he says casually, hiding the amusement that's starting to show in his eyes. "So, make yourself at home. I won't take much time."

"Oh, please take your time," I whisper only to myself. At the moment, doubt is taking control over my mind. That's typical. I'm not an impulsive person who makes quick decisions. But maybe I need to make one tonight.

Shelia is entering a new era in her life, and even if she doesn't invite Jack to move in with her, her lifestyle is still a bit chaotic for me.

It's time for a change of scenery before I have a place of my own. But now, I need to check out this place. I cross the narrow hallway and walk directly into the living room.

There's a vast TV hanging on the wall, an oversized couch, and a couple of armchairs here and there. It's a typical guy's living room with not much mess, so I guess he's kind of neat.

My eyes take everything in, looking for more insight into his personal life. I catch a photo of a couple placed on the shelf under the TV. I reckon they're in their fifties. That's a good sign of character; being close to your parents would top anything for me.

Another point for Mr. Skene, which makes the idea of rooming with him plausible, is how he interacts with Shelia and me. Okay, the way he interacts with Shelia whenever we bump into him.

I've known Shelia for two years, and I've never met a guy whose eyes didn't run over her body. She is gorgeous and sexy, and Ian Skene keeping himself in check around her tells me what a gentleman he is. But I don't think he's not affected by her beauty. I don't believe he didn't check her out in his own way, but not showing it and making her feel uncomfortable, as most guys do, is a plus.

"Hey..."

I half spin as Ian walks out of the bathroom facing the living room while drying his hair with a towel, wearing black pajama bottoms and a dark blue T-shirt. This outfit makes him reachable, unlike the dark blue suit he wore earlier. But he's still out of my league. Ian Skene is all sorts of physical perfection.

And I've tried, every time we bumped into each other, and even earlier, I've tried not to stare, but my eyes are now renegades against my mind. They're staring and taking their time.

My eyes register what my brain refuses to dwell on. He's tall, slightly over six feet, with broad shoulders topping a very muscular body. His face is all sorts of male beauty. He has dark blue eyes, a strong nose, and a firm jaw. Very masculine indeed, and I need to look away and gather myself before he notices my inspection.

Entering the living space, he throws the towel on the floor carelessly as if he's used to that. Not as neat as I thought him to be. But that's the least of my concerns right now. I'm seriously keeping my hands in check. I want to pick up that towel and dry his hair appropriately. It's started to drip, making little spots on his shoulders.

"Would you like something to drink?" he asks, his eyes a bit skeptical. And I get that. I can be a little awkward sometimes.

"No, thank you." It's late, so I need to get through with this. "I'm ready to hear about your arrangement."

"It's pretty simple." He looks at me for a second before settling on the armchair next to the couch; then he gestures for me to take a seat.

I take the left corner of the couch and adjust myself to face him. "I'm listening."

"I don't spend a lot of time here. I leave around seven-thirty for work, where I often stay past nine, so I wouldn't be in your way that much, but I've got a couple of rules if you don't mind."

I smile, his self-assurance and practical approach making me comfortable, but then his eyes are intent on me. Um... he probably wants to figure out what kind of person I am before considering the idea of letting me live with him, so I keep my smile. "You own the place, so it's quite fair if you have rules."

"If you've read the note, then you know I expect a meal every night." He pauses, gauging my reaction before adding, "A home-cooked meal. *A healthy* meal. If this works, I'll give you a list of the things I don't eat. You don't have to pay for any groceries. It's all at my expense, but you have to cook."

I didn't give the idea of moving in here much thought, but I guess it's time I do. "I can cook a meal every night and pay for my part of the groceries. I don't expect you to pay for me."

He waves a firm hand. "I won't take a dime for the groceries. My terms are non-negotiable; you either take my offer or leave it."

It's kind of weird, but I need to know the rest of his rules before making my final decision, that's if he approves of me. "So, are there any other rules?"

He nods, taking a moment to gaze down at the floor, not shying away from discoursing his rules. I don't think there's any bit of shyness in him. "I don't allow partners, friends, or family members to stay the night. Or to hang out here."

I clear my throat. I don't know what to say to that. I don't have a partner or friends who might stay the night. "But they would be staying in my room."

"They?" he exclaims, his eyes not approving. "I thought your roomie is the one who's the adventurer, not you!"

So Shelia's wild sex life does get to his ears. Usually, she's pretty loud. I've wondered if anyone complained about her.

"Well?" He's kind of pissed as if he wouldn't be approving if I were.

I try not to gawk at his rudeness. I couldn't get my head around his remark for him to push it even further. "That would be none of your business, even if I stayed here."

"It is my business," he says with a bit of boredom like he's heard this before. "Your lifestyle would affect mine. But be sure, I'm not interested in your private life outside of here."

Gathering my wits, I don't want to be judgmental. Look how Shelia's lifestyle is affecting me. "If I moved in here, you wouldn't have to worry about me not following the rules."

He rests back into the chair, though his expression is blank; I can feel he's not pleased with my comeback.

Placing two hands on the armchair, he says, "Then, I think you would fit very well with my lifestyle. Now it's up for you to decide."

"I could move in right away?"

Just like that, like he's not the least bit upset about me evading his question, he wants me to move in with him. I try to hide my sudden surprise, not wanting to look too eager and lose this opportunity.

"Tonight, if you like," he says calmly as if he's inviting someone he truly knows to move in with him, not just a person who's bumped into him a couple of times.

"Do you even remember my name?" I'm grateful to my impetuous tongue for expressing my doubts while my brain doesn't approve. It might cost me this chance.

"Grace Edwards." He stares intently at me, assuring me he has no doubt that this is my name. And I'm glad he does remember it because, for some odd reason, his name has been imprinted in my brain.

"Do you wanna take a look at your room?" He stands, smiling down at me with a welcoming invitation. He's won this. He's that sure of himself. Of his offer, I guess.

"I'd love to." Though things are moving fast, I stand. There's nothing for me to lose.

Following him out of the living room and into a narrow hallway, he pauses at the first door. "That's my room." He turns slightly, gesturing toward the opposite door. "That's yours. Feel free to check it out." There's a moment of silence where I smile like an idiot before he says, "I'll grab a drink and be right back."

This, moving fast, should have rubbed me the wrong way, but it doesn't as I walk into the room. My room. I'm eager to make it happen.

Inside the room, the beautiful dresser catches my eye. It's an antique. I smile standing before it. Then I inhale a deep breath before looking into the mirror. I'm not panicking as I would have been six months ago.

Mirrors used to make me panic, but not now. I have healed.

Mirrors and thinking about Sam don't make me panic as they used to.

Sam.

I sigh this dear name to my heart. It's only a name now, nothing more.

I guess death belittles our dear ones into names and memories. But with Sam, it's only a name for now. I cannot deal with our memories.

For the last six months, I've followed a path. I've chosen numbness. I've decided not to feel anything anymore. I will get on with my life, hoping for the best. Hoping one day I will remember Sam and smile.

Now, back to my reality, I touch a hand to my hair. I've completely forgotten that I marched out of bed. My long black hair is all kinds of messy. It's pretty gorgeous when it's combed, though. It contradicts beautifully with my white skin. I try to tidy it a bit, thankful that I've put on a coat because the PJs I'm wearing are like a thousand years old. I should have thrown them away a long time ago.

Closing the last button on my coat, I make sure they're well hidden. It's enough he's seen my hair. I'm about to check out the antique closet when I catch his sight in the mirror. He's holding a beer while leaning against the door frame, watching me.

"So, what do you think?" He waves his beer around, not deterred by the fact that I've caught him watching me. It's his apartment, after all.

I turn; my hands, again, are deep in my pockets. "Great."

He's blocking my exit, and I don't know where to go from here. I don't feel threatened by him, but I need to be cautious. He's practically a stranger who has offered me his place.

No, I'm the one who started this. I need to be fair, even if he controls this whole thing now.

He sips a little from his beer. "You know, either you're nervous about all of this, or you lack some social skills."

I don't know why I get these whispers of worries around him. He seems like a decent guy. I try to smile. "I had them once."

"The social skills, you mean?" He's a little skeptical.

"Yep. But I guess I have changed," I say without hiding my bitterness. I wish I could have them back and stop my parents from worrying about me. But right now, I don't need to think about that. I need to move forward, hoping for the best.

"I beg to differ." He takes a step inside, then turns and walks till he's half seated on the bed. "Some people change and keep on changing, but the lucky ones," he pauses, raising his calm eyes to me, "the lucky ones just find themselves."

I like that. Finding myself is way better than being lost. "And some are very good at uplifting people."

"I wasn't trying to uplift you. I would never do that." He grins.

I fold my arms, leaning into the dresser. "Why?"

"I've learned it the hard way. You burn yourself out trying to ignite another soul. It's not worth it, trust me."

"I feel there's a sad story." I don't mean to intrude or push him to reveal something, but I'm intrigued by him.

"You know," he says, a bit uncomfortable that I've put him on the spot, "We all have our share of bad luck and sad stories. I believe it's a universal thing."

"Even if you've found yourself and know what you want in life?" I throw his words back at him, sensing he was just saying them to uplift me.

"Especially if you've found yourself. By then, you know what makes you tick, what you can tolerate, and what you can and can't live with, and there's where all the battles begin."

"Then, finding ourselves doesn't make us so lucky!"

"Again, I beg to differ." He's a bit surprised. "When you find yourself, you knock down so many walls you have to go through. You'd be lucky to have only one miserable barrier to get through or at least try to get through to find this happily-ever-after or a motive to keep pushing yourself day after day."

I make a face, trying to lighten this conversation and erase the sadness that has rested in his eyes. "I thought you were uplifting me."

He does laugh, but nothing reaches his eyes. They're weirdly staring at some point beside me. He's staring at my left arm.

I start to panic. I need to act.

I hide my left hand in my pocket, hoping he'd missed the scar. The testimony I had given up on life. That I had given up on *me*.

Not that I'm not used to people staring at it, but for some reason, I'd find it hard not to try and justify my case to him. Something I'm sure I wouldn't be able to do.

"So, do you think we're going to be roomies?" He stands, and I dread looking at his dark blue eyes. I cannot tolerate any look of pity in them, but if he's going to give me that, I need to know, so I can abort this whole thing about moving in with him.

I raise my eyes to clash with his careless ones.

Thank God he missed my scar.

"I understand if you need to think about it more, but I won't be waiting forever," he adds amid my silence.

"You're right," I say, a bit apprehensive. "I need to talk with Shelia first, and that won't be happening tonight. So, is it okay if I give you my final decision, like...tomorrow night?"

"I can wait until then." He gestures toward the door. "I'll walk you back to your place."

"Oh, you don't have to," I say, lurching toward the door, but he's following me. I guess he's determined to walk me back!

He's still by my side when I unlock the apartment door. I think it's time to say something, so I turn to him, but he's faster with his words. "I need to have your number if that's okay?"

I haven't given him a decision yet, so I wonder why he needs my number. But I don't mind him asking at all. I put the keys back in my pocket. "Give me your phone. I'll just type in my number."

He points back. "It's in the apartment."

"Okay, I'll just bring mine out then." I turn to push the door open. I make it inside and look over my shoulder. "You can come in if you want." I offer out of politeness, but I don't expect him to follow me inside.

"I'll wait here," he says, resting his back against the wall. He's sensed I don't want him here.

I smile, wanting to play the polite hostess. "Oh, no, please come in."

And I sure need to think before offering something I'm not comfortable with as he pushes from the wall and follows me to the living room. But as soon as my eyes view the naked man lying on the couch with a naked lady pressed to his side, both sleeping,

I reckon Shelia has invited her friends to stay the night. The rest are probably spread across my room.

I've only been gone for ten minutes.

Ugh... Shelia

I raise a hand, then drop it back to my side. Shelia is the sweetest thing on earth, but she has no clue about boundaries. That's why I need to move out of here.

"I guess you didn't see that coming?"

"That's pretty much why I need to move out." I sigh. "Just a second, I'll bring my phone."

"I think I'll walk you there too." I move, and he's walking by my side.

I don't say anything until I reach the bedroom door, and there they are, three on the bed and two on the floor, occupying my room.

"What the hell?" Ian is a little pissed. "She didn't tell you they were coming?"

"She never does!"

"Then that's it," he says in a tone a bit disturbed and judging, like why the heck I've been tolerating that.

"What?" I ask, folding my arms and daring him to articulate these judgmental thoughts lurking in his mind.

"You're moving in with me, case closed." He walks into the room. I watch as his eyes travel everywhere before he gazes at me over his shoulder. "Do you have a small bag?"

I reluctantly step inside. "What for?"

"To grab some stuff for you to stay the night." I can see his stare fixated on the bed where the male zombies are probably drunk. "I can't let you stay here. My dad always says a girl shouldn't spend the night under the same roof with a stranger, not to mention a bunch of them-"

"But how is it different from spending the night at your place?" I retort, cutting him off. It seems he lost some logic recalling his father's words.

He gives me this soft look, unlike his assured self. "You didn't let me finish."

I gesture with my hand, challenging him. "Please do."

"My father also says, the worst strangers are... the—friends of friends. In that case, you let your guard down. But I'm not a friend of your friend, so your guard would be on point. See, I'm the lesser of the two evils you have."

I touch a hand to my neck, my eyes calculating the scene. It won't be the first time I've stayed the night with Shelia's friends occupying the place, but now I've got a choice. A safe one. A lesser evil, he claims.

So, should I bring the small bag he's asking for, or politely show him to the door?

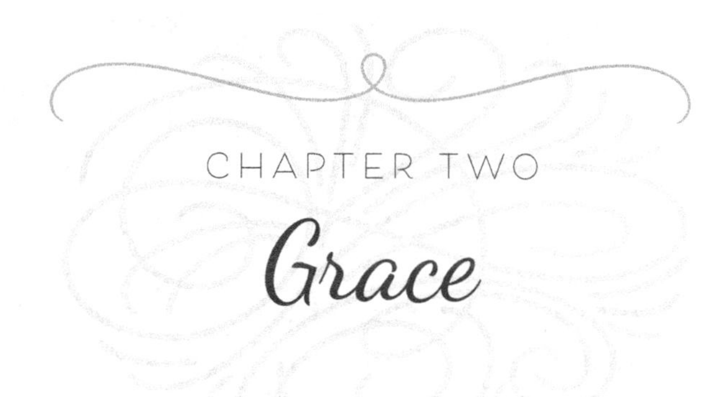

CHAPTER TWO
Grace

I THINK WAKING UP in a new place is quite thrilling, even if it's in a room resembling the one I left behind last night, because it's not about how things look around me but how they feel.

For instance, the bed, though very comfy, is igniting the rebel in me. What if I do invite someone to spend the night here? I'm sure the bed wouldn't object to that, but Ian Skene sure would. I think he has a tremendous amount of passion and fire despite his calm demeanor, and I'd like to wake up to that!

Wait. What?!

I flip the covers back and swing my legs around, hopping out of bed.

What the hell has gotten into me!

Thinking about spending the night with someone, something that hadn't even crossed my mind for the last couple of years, then wishing it was Ian Skene.

That would be catastrophic. The quiet, dashing looker is a heartbreaker. I don't need to spend another minute with him to know that. And I don't need to analyze the intense stares he kept giving me the night before.

He was studying me, of course. That's it. He needs to be sure of his roomie.

I shrug off my doubts and open the door to nip my way to the bathroom. I'm not aware if he's even up yet, or asleep, and I shouldn't care. I have a business to take care of, and I need to get going.

After brushing my teeth and splashing my face with cold water, I grab a towel and head out of the bathroom.

I barely close the bathroom door behind me when I sense his calm presence. I move the towel away from my face and turn slightly to ensure he's there, standing with his feet crossed while leaning against the wall.

"Good morning," he greets, and I feel there's something unusual about his greeting. Like he's been practicing the words.

I mentally shake my head; I'm overthinking. "Morning," I say and pause, sensing he wants to say something. Maybe there's another rule he forgot to tell me about last night. "Is there something I need to know?"

Sighing, he rests his head against the wall, his eyes seeking mine. "I thought of making it more comfortable for you, but I'm making things more awkward."

I smile at this vulnerable moment of his. I didn't think I would witness one, considering how self-assured he is. "Awkward isn't bad, but…." I raise a finger, feigning a serious face. "It pains me to tell you, you're right." I look down, then gaze up at him while running two fingers up and down my body. "Especially when I'm wearing my favorite ratty PJs."

He cracks a little laugh. "Right. But I was thinking that the sooner we get this out of the way, the better."

I do need to get going. I have a shop to open, but I cannot abandon this, whatever it is. "Get what out of the way?" I don't need to ask, but I'm asking. I guess I like the sound of his sleepy voice too much. I like the less assured guy in front of me.

"You know." He spreads a hand. "You seem a little nervous around me. I'm just trying to make you less nervous, that's all."

"You don't need to worry about me." I like that he cares, but he doesn't have to. "We'll figure it out. But you can't change things this fast, from total strangers, into comfy friends."

He distances himself from the wall, discomfort clouding his face. "Is that what you think? I'm a stranger?"

"One of the best strangers I've ever met." I smile, but he's not smiling back. He barely nods and turns, heading to the kitchen. I follow him there. I need something hot to start this cold day.

Feeling I have disappointed him, I try to explain. "I just thought you were one of those guys who keeps to himself. I mean, your rule about not letting anyone stay the night kind of gave me that impression."

"Does it bother you?" He turns, and oh boy, all the concern in the world is gathered in his eyes. I don't know if that's how his eyes usually are, or if it's just for me. The latter thought makes butterflies flutter in my stomach.

I stare down at the floor. I don't need to be thinking that way about my roommate. Or anyone.

I need to be on solid ground before dragging someone into my mess.

Feeling his eyes still waiting for an answer, I lift a shoulder. I don't know if it's bothering me or not. Other than the fleeting moment this morning, I haven't thought of being in a relationship for a long time.

Being intimate with someone means I have lots to explain. For instance, why did I try to end my life?

I don't think I have it in me to explain. Or to even talk about it. Though I'm healing, it's still raw for me. Because if I have to face it, then I have to face all my actions prior to that. This thought terrifies the hell out of me.

"It does bother you. You are not making eye contact with me," he says, then turns and walks into the kitchen.

"Coffee," he offers, his face carefree. Like we didn't semi-argue a second ago.

"That would be great." I hope my face resembles his, but I doubt it.

"So, what would you like for dinner tonight?" I ask while he gives me his back, busying himself with the coffee maker.

"Anything is fine. It's your first night after all," he says nonchalantly, still giving me his naked back. Once again, I try not to concentrate on it. But he has a lovely, strong back that I would probably wake up to every morning.

After a while, he joins me at the counter after telling him how I like my coffee. "I think I'll make mac and cheese tonight."

"Sounds good," he says.

I jump to ask, "But is it healthy?"

He smiles. "Mac and cheese is so awesome it could be anything it wishes to be."

I cannot help but giggle while his eyes are still on me. I feel he's going to ask something before he even utters, "So how did you and Shelia end up living together?"

That's a safe subject for me. I turn in my seat to face him. "I met Shelia two years ago. One day she walked into my shop, and we just clicked. The next thing I knew, she was offering for me to stay at her place. She'd signed with a big modeling agency and was able to afford to buy her own apartment, but she needed the company."

"Why two years?" he asks, and I know what he's really asking. Why didn't I move out earlier? Why did I tolerate her mess for two years?

Well, the building is close to my shop, a ten-minute walk, and these apartments are a luxury, and I like that, but that's not the only reason that's made me stay. "You could say I was a little apprehensive about starting from scratch with someone else. But recently, I felt it was a must."

"So you've been thinking about moving out for a while."

"I love Shelia, and I didn't want to break her heart or cause a rift between us. Right now is a perfect time for both of us."

He doesn't ask for more details; he continues drinking his coffee with a busied look on his face. Like he's thinking about the day ahead of him.

"I need to get going," I say, then hop off my chair. "Thanks for the coffee."

"No problem."

I turn away before my eyes rest on his moving neck. He's got a beautiful and manly neck. Just long and masculine enough. I wonder how a hickey would look there. It's so strong; one would have to bite deep into it.

Yeah. I should keep having these thoughts about him!

I roll my eyes and head out of the kitchen to my new room.

Opening the bag I brought last night, I pull out the ensemble I packed for work: a long black skirt and dark red sweater.

In front of the mirror, a concealer is a must to hide the dark circles under my eyes. I apply enough, so the tone there matches my fair skin. Nothing on my dark brown eyes; they're big enough that anything more would be too dramatic for the day.

Ten minutes later, I grab my coat, bag, and phone and head out of the room. Shelia is probably asleep, so I'll just text her this afternoon and suggest lunch to talk. I'm a little nervous about it, but I'm hoping she'll understand.

What I don't quite understand is why Ian is leaning against another wall. This time the one near the front door as if he's waiting for me, *again.*

Smiling and a little nervous because this has become kind of weird, I make it to the door. "Going somewhere?" I ask while my eyes register the hoodie he's wearing over trainer pants and sneakers. Maybe he's going out for a run. He wore that while I was heading to the shop the first time we met, so I reckon it's his ritual.

"Running," he says, his eyes quickly assessing me, just for a fleeting moment. If I weren't so focused on him, I wouldn't have noticed it.

"I'm walking you to the shop." He doesn't offer. He states.

I shouldn't hang my mouth open.

Somehow, in front of him, I cannot hide anything. I'm an open book, and he either chooses to read it or close the cover, but I hope he won't tear any pages.

Or, I'm totally overreacting toward a gorgeous guy.

He rubs his neck. "You know, to kill the awkwardness a little between us."

Great. I've made him uncomfortable.

I adjust my bag over my shoulder. It's a good thing he's acknowledging the awkwardness. "Um… I'm famous for that. Making things awkward, but once you get used to me, you'd get used to that."

He chuckles and pulls something out of his pocket. "Here's your key."

"It's pretty official then." I smile, then take the key, and my skin ignites after the light contact with him.

Ugh. Shelia is right. I need to get laid.

But I won't. I'm not that girl who would settle for a casual thing. I want the whole thing, but I'm not ready for it.

"As official as it can be." Ian smiles big at me.

He's an intense kind of guy, but his smile is boyish and gorgeous.

Stepping into the elevator, I know I'm not the brightest person on earth. "How do you know I walk to my shop?"

"While running, I've passed your shop a couple of times," he says, his eyes searching mine for a moment, in which I fail to give him the response he foresees. He exhales a troubled breath before continuing, "I saw you there, arranging flowers. There's something about you that's hard not to notice."

Unease mixed with excitement is baffling me. I don't know if Ian Skene is just a guy with excellent lines, or if there's something more to his words. My body pushes me to believe there's something more, but the way he talked then stared nonchalantly back toward the elevator doors assures me he's not.

As we step out of the elevator, it hits me. Ian didn't answer me.

Okay, the shop is close to the building. Maybe he's figured it out. He, for sure, is not stalking me or anything of that kind.

Drawn into my thoughts and unnecessary doubts, I don't notice when we hit the sidewalk or our complete silence. It's a comfortable silence. My eyes dart to the side to check if it's the same with him. I notice he's put up his hood, his hands in his pockets, and his eyes in another world. A world I'm so intrigued to know everything about it. Yet, I don't want to know anything about it. I cannot decide.

I clear my throat, wanting his attention, weirdly jealous that he's forgotten about me, engrossed in his world.

When I know he's back to earth with me, I say, "You should have stopped by, said hello, picked some flowers, or hung out. We're neighbors, after all."

He stops in his tracks and turns to me. "Roommates," he corrects with a playful tone. "We're roommates now, and I wanted to stop by, but..."

We stand facing each other. He draws circles on the curb with his foot. "You seemed so lost in the flowers. Like it was a tranquil moment for you, and I didn't want to disturb you."

I'm the one drawing circles on the floor now. I don't want to read much into this, but I am, as my eyes meet his intense ones. Everything seems fervent now, so for my sanity, I need to break the spell. I turn ahead and walk. "You wouldn't be disturbing anything. So, whenever you feel like it, just stop by."

We walk side by side in silence until he stops and smiles down at me. "I feel like it now, if you don't mind."

With his dashing smile, I don't think I'll ever mind anything Ian Skene asks. "No, I don't mind at all," I respond casually, trying to hide my excitement.

After he gives me another soulful look, we turn to the road, and I cannot keep my mouth shut. I'm so intrigued by him. "So how about you, what do you do for a living?"

"Marketing," he answers curtly, which gives me the impression he doesn't want to divulge more about himself, making me regret asking him in the first place.

Reaching my shop, a thin line of unease stretches between us, but that doesn't stop him from offering to open the front doors for me. I don't want to argue, so I hand him the keys, but I feel like I'm giving him more than just the tiny object. I feel like I'm handing him the lead in all of this. I cannot help but feel this thing between us, and I don't know how to label it yet.

"After you." He holds the French doors for me. I smile and step inside, turning on the lights. It's a bit dark this early.

It's seven-thirty. I need to arrange two bouquets and photograph them to upload them on my social media accounts. I look sideways at Ian, who's still at the door. He's standing peacefully. His eyes travel slowly from one corner to the other.

I take lots of pride in my shop, so I wonder what he thinks. "I need to arrange some stuff first. So, feel free to take a tour."

"I will." He smiles, his eyes taking in my shop. For a moment, I don't like that he's oblivious to my presence and so lost in the flowers, but that's not a bad thing. They're *my* flowers.

I head to my design table, where I do all the work. My eyes dart to Ian instead of the usual roaming around the flower displays. Maybe I'll get my inspiration from him. He's still standing at the door, folding his arms. I don't know if he's admiring my flowers or if it's a private moment of his. I feel like he has conquered something. Like he has been yearning for this moment, and as it has finally arrived, he's determined not to take it for granted. Which makes no sense at all, but that's what my stupid heart is urging me to believe.

"What a beautiful sanctuary you have," he says, catching me watching him. I don't feel embarrassed he's caught me in the act. I'm enjoying his take on my shop. In some ways, it's a sanctuary for me. Surrounding myself with all this beauty is a defense mechanism against any dark thoughts that might attack me at some point.

I'm lost in him, in his quietness while multiple ideas are running through my mind. He's my inspiration today. But then, he glimpses down at his watch. "I need to go."

"Please don't."

Oh My God

I didn't say that aloud. The surprised look on his face says it all. I certainly did!

CHAPTER THREE

Grace

WHAT HAS GOTTEN into me? Ian is standing with a 'what the hell?' look on his face.

And yes, I did beg him to stay. I did say PLEASE!

Racing to save face, I say, "Um… I mean, wait till I arrange you a bouquet." I shrug one shoulder. "Consider it a thank you for letting me share your apartment."

"You don't have to thank me, just fulfill your part of the deal," he states, his voice calm, but his eyes alert. Like I've crossed some boundary of his.

I don't know why my hands are shaking. Earlier, I thought he wanted us to be friends or at least get along, but I'm starting to doubt it now.

It's just a deal for him. It should be for me too!

"Of course I will," I mumble as I busy myself again, arranging the flowers.

I feel him walking toward me. A moment, then he perches himself on one of the seats around the table.

His presence envelops the place. There's too much of him, making me suddenly nervous. I gaze at him from the corner of my eye as I pick up one of my favorite flowers. I bury my nose in the red petals, inhaling deeply, and instantly my mood is more joyful and less nervous.

"What is it called?" he asks, making me smile. I love to talk about my flowers.

"Fire Lily," I answer, locking my eyes with his for a second. "It's one of the rarest flowers in the world. They say it can heal a wounded heart."

"So, do you think I have a wounded heart?"

"Um…." I'm caught off guard by his out-of-nowhere question.

He doesn't seem to have a broken heart. On the contrary, I think *he* might have broken a couple. "No, why would you assume that?"

"Well, you're arranging it in my bouquet."

There's a hint of discomfort in his voice, or I'm just overthinking everything.

I clear my throat before turning to him. "It just happened to be here. I didn't mean to imply anything by it, honestly."

"Good."

Good.

So, he was annoyed!

For a moment, I stare at him. I want him to know he's acting over the top. I want him to feel a little embarrassed or something. But he just stares back. His eyes are calm; I cannot figure out how he truly feels.

His phone rings while I try to arrange his bouquet as quickly as I can, relieved. Maybe someone, somewhere, is asking why he's late? Funny thing, I didn't want him to leave earlier. Now that's my ultimate wish for the day.

He doesn't pick up. And I'm becoming so nervous I almost cut myself while trimming the flowers' stems.

"Careful," he says, his voice holding so much concern, it forces me to glance at him. And I have to face the truth. I'm drawn to him. Seriously, anything he does or says is making me attracted to him. He takes me out of my numbness. In the short moments I've had with him, I've experienced many different emotions other than the numbness I've lived in for the past six months.

"Don't worry. I've done this a hundred times," I say, tying a red velvet ribbon around the stems. Done.

"Here..." I proffer the bouquet to him. I want to avoid his eyes, but he doesn't even move a muscle until I meet his with a forced smile.

His phone rings again, and as I think that's it, he's going to leave, he turns it off. "I think I'll hang here after all." His eyes searching mine, he adds, "If you don't mind?"

"Sure." I don't sound excited.

He doesn't get my discomfort, or he simply doesn't care. Setting his bouquet aside, he gives me a genuine smile. "Everything is so beautiful here. But..." his lips press into a thin line before asking, "does it do well? There are lots of flower shops around the city, with bigger spaces and bigger names."

I have tons of things to arrange. But here I am, sitting perplexed by this guy and his out-of- nowhere inquires. Does he really care to know? Or is he just a bit inquisitive? He works in marketing, after all. Maybe he's looking for some tips.

"I inherited the place from my aunt," I find myself revealing amid the genuine concern in his eyes. "She had very loyal customers. So when I reopened it again, they started to come back.

You could say I had a good start, but the breakthrough came through social media."

He rests a little in his seat. "Did you hire a marketing team?"

I wave a hand. "No, I couldn't afford that."

"So?" He crosses his arms. "What did you do?" he asks casually, but something in his posture gives me another impression. I just get the feeling that he's sort of upset.

"I got lucky," I say nervously, regretting saying too much. But this guy can make me relaxed one minute only to make me nervous the next. I kind of like it. I like that he's breaking my numbness, even for these fleeting moments.

"How did you get lucky, exactly?"

He becomes very rigid, and though he tries to hide his discomfort, somehow, I have no doubt now. He's upset. Maybe he's wondering what kind of person is going to share his place? He has every right to be cautious. I would, too, if I was in his shoes.

"It's a long story." I'm not sure it's a wise idea to share with him.

"Why do I think it's a sad one," he says carefully. I know without a doubt that he wants me to share, but he's trying his best not to seem so eager.

He's trying too much, and that's how I've figured him out.

I want to lessen his worries. After all, we're going to be roommates, and him, being on edge because of me, would be an uncomfortable thing to go through every day. "It was a bittersweet moment. But in the end, it helped me to get where I am today. So, I wouldn't say it was deplorable."

"Why don't you let me judge for myself?" he pushes, not ashamed to seem eager to know. I've read him wrong. He's the kind of man that doesn't care what other people think as long as he gets what he wants.

I take a second to gather my thoughts. I want to be as calm as him, or more accurately, pretend to be as calm as he seems to be. Or maybe he's genuinely calm. I don't know. But I don't want to jeopardize my chances with him. I mean... rooming with him. It's a pretty good opportunity.

"I was wearing a red coat," I start, my eyes staring back at him. "Perching myself on one of the seats outside, when I noticed someone watching me."

The worried look that suddenly appears in his eyes makes me, for some reason, a little excited. What the heck!?

I clear my throat. I don't want my voice to sound hoarse. "When I looked closer, I noticed someone was taking pictures of me." I smile. "But, I got scared for no reason."

"Well, you had every reason to be," he interrupts. "Seems he was a stalker."

My smile grows bigger. "No. It was Theodore."

"Oh, really?" he says, mocking me, and he has every right to be. He doesn't know Theodore. So just mentioning Theodore doesn't explain anything to him.

"Of course, you don't know Theodore. He's street famous, though." I giggle.

"Are you gonna tell me who this Theodore is?" He's impatient, and that makes me feel victorious. It's way better than his 'don't give a damn' attitude.

"Theodore is a journalist." I unconsciously drum my fingers on the table, wondering how much I should tell him. "He reports local stories on his social media accounts. He has lots of followers. So, when he approached me for an interview, I had nothing to lose, not to mention it was very comfortable talking to him."

He's drumming his fingers too. There's another question coming, but he doesn't ask anything. He stares at me like he's disappointed. "I see."

"And what is that exactly?" I push my chair back and stand. I won't let him judge me as viciously as he's doing right now.

"Do you really want me to say it?" He shrugs like he has no care in the world, but somehow I know otherwise.

"Say what?" I cross my arms, daring him.

He points a finger back and forth carelessly. "You two exchanged favors. He introduced you to his followers and you... you know..."

I've read this guy completely wrong. He's one of those pathetic judgmental assholes. I want to kick him out, but the sadness in his eyes catches me off guard. Like he's sad for me, for what he thinks I've done. Maybe it resembles something he went through. There's more to his words than just him being a jerk.

Suddenly my heart is aching for him, so I pick up my phone, searching until I find the article. "Here," I proffer it to him. "That's the interview he had done with me. You could read the other ones too. There are hundreds of them. Theodore has made a community for people to support and help each other without expecting anything in return."

I stop explaining as I notice the shock on Ian's face. He's reading my story, the one I shared with Theodore. I hadn't told much, but it was a raw moment for me. And when the responses came back, when his followers started to write back to me, commenting on my story and encouraging me, I felt relieved. It was good to share.

"'I don't want anyone to feel sorry for me'," Ian starts to read aloud from my phone, and I still. What the heck is he doing?

Hearing my own dark words is making me on edge.

"'I don't need anyone's pity," he continues while I've become very rigid. "'I just need someone to tell me these exact words '"It's okay, you will not commit that horrible crime again!'"

I'm hardly breathing. He's hardly breathing. His eyes stay glued to the screen while I frantically wait.

I'm waiting for his verdict. People always have something to say to me or about me.

"I wish I could tell you that." Finally, Ian lifts his eyes from my phone's screen. And they're void. Nothing is there. Just emptiness, and that makes me shiver. He isn't sympathizing with me like most people do or even judging me. He must have gone through so much.

One thing I know for sure now, I'm in front of an honest person. He says it like it is. With him, there's no pretense, just the raw truth.

And for an unknown reason, he doesn't believe I will not try to kill myself again. That terrifies me.

I shake my head. He's a stranger who doesn't know a thing about me.

"It's okay," I say calmly. "You don't have to say anything. I don't need to hear that anymore. I know, without an ounce of doubt, that I would never do it again."

I sense he doesn't quite believe me, so I find myself adding, "Back then, when I met Theodore, things were still raw for me. But now I'm in a steadier place."

He hands me the phone back, and resumes his careless attitude. "But he's not showing your picture."

I didn't allow Theodore to show my face. Only the scar on my wrist, and a tiny part of my shop showing in the background.

"Or mentioning your shop or anything to showcase your identity?"

I know what he's asking. He wants to know how Theodore helped me. "True, but what you're not aware of is this community Theodore has created. Someone must have recognized my shop. It was in the background, after all. And these people are very online-close, so by word of mouth, my shop has become popular amongst them."

I don't want him to think they keep coming because they feel obligated, so I add, "At first, they came to support me. We would exchange a word or two about the interview. But after a while, no one was mentioning anything. But new faces keep coming to my shop. So they must like what they get here."

"I'm sure they do." He holds my eyes for a second, then inclines his head to the side, his fingers looping around the bouquet. He's going to leave, finally.

With a hint of a smile, he stares back at me. "You know I shouldn't have assumed that you and this Theodore guy, you know..." He pauses for a moment. "I hope you're not upset about it."

Is that an apology? But where's the five-letter word—Sorry.

I shouldn't make this easy for him, but, damn me, I cannot stand the sadness in his eyes. I jump to say, "Well, I understand that people like Theodore are rare to meet these days. I'm just lucky I did. So maybe I can understand why you'd assumed that."

"Good." He gives me a genuine smile. "And thanks for this lovely bouquet. Suzan is gonna love it."

Wait a minute, Suzan who??!

This bouquet is for you, not Suzan. I want to object, but Mabel, my assistant, walks in.

I'm an expert on flowers, love them, breathe them, and arrange the best bouquets, but Mabel is a great help with everything else. She's also very talkative and cheerful, which helps with customers, especially the indecisive ones.

As usual, there's a smile on her face, but as she spots Ian, she pauses for a moment. And Mabel doesn't pause or hesitate. So far, I haven't seen anything that fazes her. Apparently, Ian does.

Maybe she has a valid reason. No one hangs around my design table. Definitely not customers. I inhale deeply, readying myself for Mabel's nosiness or delight! I don't know what's worse.

"What a lovely morning this is," Mabel says as she approaches us. Her eyes are fixated on Ian. She wants to know all about him. And God, help me. She's teased me nonstop about the lack of men in my life. I don't think she'd lay it easy on me now. Her dancing eyes tell all. She's going to get the best of this situation.

Through the last two years, we've become close, despite our contradicting personalities. She's like fire, and I'm, well, kind of relaxed compared to her. But we have each other's best interest at heart.

I abandon watching Mabel and glimpse at Ian. He's smiling. He likes what he sees. Why not?

Mabel is an attractive woman. Her off-white dress highlights her gorgeous skin and lovely curves; she looks like she's in her late twenties, not early forties.

She flips her hair as she stops close to Ian before extending her hand. "I'm Mabel."

She's taking charge of this, and I don't want to be a part of this conversation. Though, I know it's going to be about me.

Ian looks at me sideways before shaking Mabel's hand. "Nice to meet you, Mabel."

"And do you have a name?" Mabel says as Ian lets go of her hand.

"Why don't you guess?"

Oh, he's flirting with her! Right before my eyes

I shake my head. He can flirt with anyone. I don't care.

"If that includes dinner at a fancy restaurant, then burn up the sheets later," Mabel looks over at me, winking before looking back at Ian, "Then, I'd definitely guess."

Ian laughs out loud, then quickly recovers. "I'm Ian Skene."

"Of course he's an Ian," Mabel says, looking at me again, her eyes dancing. "Lucky you, I don't do Ians. I cannot keep up with them. But you, *mi amiga*, Ians can do you wonders. It's about time you heat up your tatty sheets."

I hear Ian burst out laughing again while I try hard not to commit a violent act against Mabel.

"Seriously," Mabel addresses Ian, ignoring my discomfort. She's tried so many times to set me up with guys, and she's not going to waste this chance. She spills her theories, "If you want anything to happen between the two of you, you should flat out say it to her. She's ridiculously inept around guys."

"Oh, is she now?" I feel Ian's eyes on me. But I'm not eager to witness the amusement in them.

They both ignore me and talk like I don't even exist, but I'm a little flattered inside. Ian is giving all his attention to Mabel. He wants to hear things about me.

"Maybe next time, I'll tell you a story or two." Mabel finally has mercy on me. "But now, if you'll excuse me, I have tons to do."

With Mabel disappearing inside the shop, I have to face the amused Ian. I gaze up at him then point back, where Mabel has disappeared. "She once told me about a hard fall she had. So sometimes her stories get mixed up."

Ian nods, still amused, and I nod myself. "Totally. Like she isn't stable. You shouldn't believe a word she says."

"I get it." Ian cannot keep a steady voice. "You don't have tatty sheets, nor are you inept around guys."

"Exactly," I say, way too cheerfully.

"But..." Ian holds up a finger. "I believe I can do you wonders. So, she's not that unstable."

"What is that supposed to mean?" I gawk at him. I cannot believe he's said that.

"Handsome boy." We both turn our heads where Mabel's yelling from somewhere inside. "I told you, you have to flat out say it to her. Like, I want to fuck your brains out or something."

Don't look. Don't look.

But I look back at him anyway. He's shaking with silent laughter. He's even resting a fist on my table; he's that out of control. And I'm seething as my eyes rest on his bouquet.

If he wanted to give it to this Suzan, he should have kept his mouth shut about it.

And I need to keep my mouth shut. But I'm pissed. "Who is Suzan?"

CHAPTER FOUR
Grace

IT'S BEEN A week since I've moved in with Ian, but I haven't been able to tell Shelia yet. When I texted her to meet for lunch that day, she couldn't make it. She was leaving for L.A. to shoot some ad, but I'll talk to her as soon as she gets back.

The week has been a good one. I succeeded in getting more than a thousand stems of Peony on short notice. It was upon a customer request, a very loyal one. She's a friend of my late aunt who wanted to surprise her daughter with a dream wedding. And knowing she could have gotten those Peonies anywhere in the city made me more determined to get them on time. There's nothing I wouldn't do for a loyal customer.

As for Ian, I haven't seen much of him during the last week. Other than when he would go out of his way to invite me to share the dinner I've made for him. He arrives too late, so we don't share dinner since I've eaten already. But he makes sure to ask every night, and that's it. I don't see much of him. Well, I see his naked back every morning, not his chest. I cannot stare while he's facing me, so I only take a glimpse at his six-pack and delicious V. But when he gives me his back, I stare, admiring the strong view. That's if I wake up early enough to drink the coffee he makes. I try to wake up early to enjoy his less assured self. Not like that morning at my shop.

I don't know why I cannot move on from that.

I shouldn't have asked him about Suzan.

I squeeze my eyes shut, gutted by embarrassment. He had this smug smile when I asked. "Suzan is my assistant." He looked me up and down for a long, taunting moment, the smugness never leaving his eyes. "She's very fond of flowers."

Then he turned to leave, but as he reached the door, he looked at me over his shoulder, his eyes a bit indecisive. "Only an assistant. Nothing more."

I won't lie. I sighed in relief afterward. Not that I'm interested in him, it's just I like that he's not the kind of guy who mixes business with pleasure. I've heard enough stories on how some employers take advantage of their female employees. A point for Mr. Skene there.

I don't know why these thoughts run through my head at five in the morning. I don't know why I'm alert this early, either. Maybe it's the new place and the things I still need to do.

Though everything is going smoothly between us, I still haven't moved all my stuff here. I need to talk to Shelia first, and as always, I'm cautious in case Ian changes his mind.

I'll give it another two weeks; then I will move everything here. Now, I need to get out of this bed and start my morning routine. Wearing new PJs, as I cannot risk Ian seeing me in those ratty ones another time, I head to the bathroom.

After doing my business and brushing my teeth, I half turn from the mirror to return to my room when my heart sinks.

I freeze in place, scared. This cannot be happening. It's been six months since I've seen one. Since I've stopped going to my therapist, thinking I'm over that. Mirrors are safe for me now.

I put a hand to my chest. I want to be as calm as possible when I recheck it. I silently count to ten, and with my breathing calming, I cock my head slightly to the side and gaze at my reflection in the mirror.

I sigh in relief; there's nothing there. But as I half turn again, I catch it there, out of the corner of my eye. The tiny red drops start to rain over the glassy surface.

God, please... Please... Not again.

My heart isn't functioning anymore, my mind isn't in a better place either, but I'm not going to panic. I'm too scared to turn my head and face the mirror. But I need to be sure.

I inhale deeply before gazing back at the mirror. It's only me. My panda eyes and pale skin. My panicked eyes. I don't need to panic, though. Nothing is there. It's just a flash—an out of nowhere incident, nothing to make me worry.

So, assured now, I turn from the mirror, but the tiny red drops start to rain again. I only catch it sideways. When I look back at the mirror, they disappear. Only my panicked eyes are staring back at me. I cannot stand the sight of them. I don't know what's bothering me more, their dark circles, or the horrified look in them.

I let out a soft cry and face away from the mirror, and the vicious play begins. I look back into the mirror, then turn my head away.

I look, then turn. I keep looking then turning away.

I turn away from my panda eyes, only to see a more horrifying scene. Each time I look away from the mirror, I see the blood drops dancing against the glass, taunting me. As soon as I turn to catch them, they disappear. They keep playing with me.

When I face them, they're not there. Like they know better. But when I sway my head, they're dancing and spraying against the glass.

I cannot let this continue.

So, I turn, and this time I stare. I stare at my reflection in the mirror. I dare them to show. To face me. I stare and wait. My hands grip the shelves on each side of the mirror tightly, my legs start to shake, and my breathing is out of control. But I have to face this and end it. I won't let it haunt me again.

I count to one hundred before I'm at peace to walk away. But damn these tiny red drops, they're showing in the background spraying on the glass.

This cannot be happening.

I close my eyes, then open them and stare back, but now there's no more dancing around it. The blood drops are facing me. They're spraying with such force into the glass.

They're back to haunt me.

I let out a scorching cry before I reach for the closest object my hand can get. I hold it up, take a step back, then throw it against the mirror. I'm not going to wait till I see myself there, cutting my vein. I'm not going to see that again.

But as the mirror shatters into so many tiny pieces, I still catch my sight there, through the shattered glass. I'm broken and bleeding.

I don't want to see that. I'm over that. I have healed.

But I'm bleeding to death, and my eyes cannot stand it anymore. I reach to tear out these shattered little pieces with my hands. I want it to stop. I don't want to see it again. I want this mirror to disappear.

"Fuck… Jesus. Fucking fuck."

I'm staring at what's left of the mirror when I hear his shocked voice, then I see Ian's reflection in the little broken pieces. He's at the door, his eyes filled with terror while his body is indecisive. He wants to step further, but he keeps himself in place as if he knows better.

"Stay still. Please stay still." There's urgency in his words, but his voice is firm and calm. Terrifyingly calm. Like he's giving orders to defuse a ticking bomb.

He carefully steps closer, his eyes gazing into mine through the broken pieces, until he's right behind me. "Please don't panic."

His presence is strong, assuring, and warm. I'm not going to panic. I feel a little at peace.

Our eyes hold in the broken mirror, and I don't miss how he's breathing rapidly before his eyes shift to my hands, still pressed to the glass.

Holding my eyes again, he exhales a long breath. "This way, you're going to hurt yourself, Grace. So just please take your hands off the glass."

I nod. I don't want to be here anymore. I don't want to see this mirror again or any mirror for a long time.

"That's it," he encourages while I slowly pull my hands away. They sting a little, but it doesn't bother me as it should. I just want to be out of here, away from this mirror.

I pull my hands away, but I don't know what to do with them. I just hold them in front of me, covered in my blood.

I'm shaking all over when I feel his hands grip my arms and slowly drag them to my sides. Then, without registering when or how, he lifts me from the floor. My shocked eyes lock with his assuring ones. "I'll fix this, I promise."

But I don't need to be fixed. I have healed. Or is he talking about the mirror? I don't want him to fix it. I'm back to hating mirrors again.

I mumble an objection. I cannot control my tongue.

"I'm gonna carry you out, okay?" he asks, sensing my discomfort. Though I feel he's going to carry me out whether I like it or not. He only wants me to relax.

"Okay." I push myself to mumble because I feel how rigid he's become.

With urgency, he walks us out of the bathroom and into the kitchen. "It's nothing we cannot handle. I promise."

"It's nothing, really," I whisper. I don't need him to worry about me or drag himself into my mess. There's no *we* here. It's only me. I have to face that again. But I don't know if I can handle it.

He sets me on a chair, his arms still around me. His face is close when he says, "I wanna check your hands first, so just lay them over the table."

I nod. I will listen to anything he says to end this. I lay my hands where he guided me. They sting, but that's all I feel. I'm surprisingly calm. Like I'm enveloped by my mother's hug, or is it his warm breath?

Ian leans close to inspect my hands. "Thank God, there are no glass fragments here." He tilts his head to look me in the eye, but I just stare ahead. I'm calm, but I cannot function right.

"I'll wipe the blood and see if you need any stitches," he adds, his voice a little wary. Maybe my calmness is evoking his nervousness. I cock my head and gaze at his blue eyes. I hope that's enough to ease his nerves. I want him to know I'm aware of what he's doing because I cannot force myself to speak yet.

"It's gonna be okay," he tells me in a soothing, assuring voice, but his eyes are full of doubt. He doubts me as he did that day. He has no faith that I won't try to harm myself again. But I wasn't even trying to harm myself. I only wanted to preserve the calmness I've been living for the past six months.

I turn my head away. I don't need to see doubt.

I hear him opening one of the cabinets, then water running.

He settles in a chair next to me. "It'll sting a little," he says, then starts wiping the blood off my hands.

I try not to flinch. I don't need him to worry about me. I don't even need him to clean my cuts, but I'm only sitting to make him calm again. To let him know I will be okay. And to be honest, I don't want him to doubt me.

I'm not okay. I'm not going to try to harm myself again. I know that for a fact, but that doesn't mean I'm not shattered at this moment.

The tears I've been holding in start to take over. I feel them rain silently down my cheeks. I can't cry out loud like I want to while he's here. But I'm barely able to take in any air or let it out.

"The bleeding stopped, and lucky you, they're just tiny cuts, nothing serious," he pauses, and I feel his eyes on my face. I hear a troubled sigh before he pushes his chair back, then he picks me up and puts me on this lap, one arm around my waist, the other soothing up and down my back. "Just let it out."

I try to break from his embrace. But he puts a hand at the back of my head and holds it to his chest. "I heard someone saying.... Just cry, even if it's the millionth time you do. Cry, because the more you cry today, the less you will tomorrow. So, just let it all out, Grace. I'm here till it's all gone."

I'm still stiff in his arms, but when my mind registers how sad his voice sounds recalling those words, I let my cries out. I don't know if I'm crying for myself or him. I haven't heard such a tormented tone before. Like it's a close one to his heart who've said those words. I'm crying now. I cry and shake in his arms. Like I've known him my whole life, not just a guy I met days ago. I know I'll be embarrassed later, but with his strong arms, warm breaths, and gentle hands, I feel safe to let it all out.

A minute or two have passed before my cries subside, but somehow, it feels longer.

"Um..." I try to pull a little from him, and as his arms loosen, I catch a point on the opposite wall and say, "I'm so sorry. I didn't mean for this to happen."

I know I need to explain more, but at this point, I'm happy I have my talking ability back. I'll try later, maybe when I leave his lap.

I feel his finger on my chin, urging me to look at him. But I cannot handle any pity at this moment. The hot breath he exhales over my skin tells me how troubled he is but thank God, he gets me. I need more time. He slowly sets me back on the other chair.

"I'll bring the first-aid kit," he tells me, and in a second, he's out of the kitchen.

Without being asked, I lay my hands on the table, barely able to take a deep breath to calm myself, before he's back again, holding the first-aid kit.

"You're lucky you didn't harm yourself." I can see him shaking his head before dropping beside me and edging his chair closer. He opens the kit and picks up an ointment. "It'll sting but bear with me."

I clear my throat. I'm a little embarrassed as I notice his bare chest and messy hair. I've woken him from his sleep.

"I think I'll take it from here." It hurts, but I manage to put a hand over his.

Instantly, he gives me two firm eyes. "I think I'll keep handling it myself. They may be small cuts, but still, you need to be careful for a couple of days."

Our eyes lock for a second: his unfathomably calm, mine eager and searching. I wonder what he thinks of me.

Does he think I'm a total disaster and want me out of his place? Sure, he doesn't want to room with a crazy thing like me. He can get anyone to cook for him.

"I would never judge you or think any less of you. So far, you're the best roommate I've ever had," he says nonchalantly while applying more ointment on my tiny wounds. The breath I've been holding bursts out of me. He knows what's lurking in my mind.

I remain speechless while he finishes treating my wounds, but I'm aware of every breath he takes. He chuckles a little before giving me two playful eyes. "I once roomed with this pothead guy. He'd... um, have sex with himself." He chuckles again like he's fighting laughter, but if he means to make me at ease, a story with sex and a pothead guy is not the story to tell, but he continues, "I don't mean masturbation. I'd hear him having sex as if a girl was there. And guess what... he would change his voice tone to play both parts, and I don't need to tell you how many times I've heard about how big he is. 'Cause at that stage, he'd be screaming his lungs out."

I don't know if it's me who cannot enjoy this, or it's just a disturbing story, but his genuine laugh finally affects me. I smile. "I'm sorry you had to go through that."

He chuckles again. "So you'd never top him. You could go and break mirrors, punch walls, and you'd never top that pothead."

"I hope you didn't room with him long."

"Oh..." He shakes his head and keeps on chuckling. "Just a day with him is too long. Trust me. But I tried to put up with it, he was decent in some ways, but one day I couldn't take it anymore."

I glance where he puts a hand over his stomach, keeping the laughter in check. Instantly, I know the best part is coming.

"His step-mother crashed on the couch one night. He said she had been visiting for a week. And each night, I'd get worried he might start having his imaginary sex, because I didn't know if he was aware of what he was doing. I thought he'd get into some weird state… but everything went well till the last night. I woke up mortified. He started his imaginary sex while his mom was outside on the shitty couch. I had to stop it, so I stumbled through the dark to his room, wanting to put some sense into him. But when I opened his door, the pothead was finally having real sex." He lets out a big laugh before he reveals, "With his mom."

I gasp. "But how is that funny?" I'm starting to berate Ian as he cannot keep still.

"I know it's not," he keeps on laughing. "But see… the joke was on me. For a whole week, I was in knots about his mom. I didn't know if he's even aware of what he's doing, afraid she might know how fucked up her son is while she was probably the reason why he was a fucked-up pothead to begin with."

"Still, it's not funny." This story is disturbing.

He gives me one soulful look. "See, you break mirrors and try to take them out of walls, and I find this story funny. We're both kind of wrecked."

I give a little laugh. I love how he's trying to make me comfortable and not ashamed of what I've done.

"I think we both need something hot to drink." He stands, still giving me his soulful look.

I cannot agree more. I need something to drink.

In no time, a cup of hot tea is in front of me, and one is in his hand. Before I even thank him for his help, I blurt, "I'll pay for the mirror."

"What?" He utters like he cannot fathom what I'm saying.

"The mirror," I repeat. "I'm so sorry I broke it, and I'm so sorry I've disturbed your sleep. But I'm gonna pay for everything and clean everything." I'm finally able to give him a decent apology.

He carefully puts his cup down, his eyes studying me in outrage before a cloud of mystery fogs them. He rests back in his chair. "Yes, you are," he says firmly. "You're gonna pay for that mirror, and..." he raises a finger, "I need a disco lamp in my room."

"You need a disco lamp," I repeat, amused.

"Yep, and guess what? You're gonna pay for that too," he adds playfully, making me giggle.

"Actually, I'll give you a list of all the weird stuff I'm ashamed to buy."

I cannot help but burst out laughing. He's trying his best to put me at ease, and I'm so grateful for him, making me comfortable to talk about it—a thing I cannot share with anyone but my therapist.

I inhale a deep breath. I don't know how he'll react. "I didn't know how that happened. I mean... I've been calm and fine for almost six months." I connect my eyes with his careful ones, they're not playful or at ease anymore, but I don't care. I need to talk. No, I need to tell *him*. I don't know why, but I do. "I'd even stopped going to my therapist, thinking I'd never have these flashes again. You know..." I exhale a troubled breath. I don't know if I can reveal more, but I try, "You know, I've been seeing these um...."

"It's none of my business," he says firmly amid my reluctance, and my eyes snap to his. His eyes are wary. Like he doesn't want me to tell him even if I can. I won't lie to myself. It hurts that he doesn't care about me in a sense of being more than just his roommate, and he has to give me some help.

"Well." He pushes his chair back, standing. "I've got to get ready for work. So, do you need anything else? Do you want me to call someone?"

After all his tender treatment, soulful looks, and doing his best to make me feel at ease, he gives me this cold and distant voice. I cannot believe he's the same guy who has been trying to make me laugh.

"No, thank you, I'm fine. Thank you for everything."

Walking away he pauses, to gaze at me over his shoulder. "Are you sure you're fine?"

"I thought it was none of your business." I know I sound hurt and pissed, but I cannot help it. I feel a little betrayed.

I catch the pissed look in his eyes before he turns to face my timid anger. He takes a step forward, his fists clenched at his sides. "Don't sweat about it. You're lucky I'm not making it my business." He lets his calm words hang between us for a while before taking further steps inside till he's hovering over me. He reaches to run the back of his hand over my cheek. "You know why, Grace," he says, his voice is lethal, his eyes intense. "'Cause if I make it my business, trouble would be written all over it."

I'm shivering under his touch as his hand travels to cup my chin, his thumb presses against my lower lip, and I squeeze my thighs together in shame.

His eyes gaze down. At the evidence of how he's affecting me. "Yeah. It would be trouble," he whispers, pressing another touch to my lip before he drops his hand and turns to walk away.

CHAPTER FIVE
Grace

I ASKED SHELIA TO meet me at Serenity, my favorite coffee shop. I like how tiny and warm this place is, while Shelia is kind of *meh* about it. She likes places that scream excitement and adventure. Maybe I should have opted for one, as I need to tell her my big news. When she texted me to pick her up this morning, I couldn't find it in me to tell her after arriving from her flight. So, I hope now is a good time to break it to her.

As usual, she's a bit late. I asked her to meet me at five-thirty, it's almost six now, and I have a meal to cook. I want to carry out my part of *the deal* as best as I can. I don't think Ian trusts me to, and I need to prove him wrong; especially after my mirror breakdown. I'm still a little embarrassed about it, even after a week, but Ian has been great with me. He acts like that incident has never occurred. But he has become a little more attentive to me. He checks on me every night while I'm sleeping or rather, pretending to be asleep. I know he does. He asked me if he could check on me if he had the urge. When I asked him about the urge, he pointed at his heart, saying it would be something there he couldn't explain. And to be honest, I like the idea of someone checking on me. I won't lie to myself; I haven't entirely healed. I'm just taking a break to gather myself, but soon I need to see my therapist and break out of my numbness.

With that in mind, I try so hard not to fathom why I'd be trouble for him.

I take a needed sip of my coffee. If only I could forget how he looked at me.

After a minute of thinking about my roomie and what his actions mean or don't mean, I lift my eyes to the glass doors and see Shelia walking into the shop. Spotting me, she wrinkles her nose. Without giving her any heads up, she's sensing it's going to be a serious talk.

"Hey... hey... hey... I missed talking to my favorite girl," she says, reaching the table. I smile. I love how full of life she is.

"I missed you too." I stand to hug her. She runs a hand up and down my back, maybe sensing how nervous I am about this talk.

We pull away from each other, giggling for no reason. She plops herself on the opposite seat, dropping her large bag onto the floor. As always, she's effortlessly beautiful. She's wearing a simple shirt over jeans. Her caramel curly hair is left wild, and her hazel eyes shine as beautiful as her earthy-brown skin. Then I catch how messed up her shirt is.

Neat me points a finger. "You've mistaken the third button in the second buttonhole. The fourth one isn't in place either."

Shaking her head, she starts to fix it. "Ah... Lucas."

"You were with Lucas?" I'm already sick of this Lucas. He's a wealthy, married man, in his late forties. "I don't need to tell you how I feel about that."

She rolls her eyes. "I'm in my twenties. If I don't live today, when will I? Besides, his wife is totally okay with it. They have an open marriage. Something I'm sure you have no idea about."

"Yeah. You really know how to live." I smile. "I mean that night before your L.A. trip, there was some serious living going on."

She grimaces for a second. "Did you hear that?"

"Hear it!" I yell. The whole building might have heard. "It was like I was in the front row."

She giggles. "I was drunk. Really drunk."

"Oh..." I touch the base of my throat. I shouldn't have left her alone.

"No, no, no." She waves a hand. "No one forced me to do anything. But you know, liquor gives us the courage to make our lewd dreams come alive. Otherwise, I wouldn't have had the guts to do it." Her eyes dancing, she leans forward. "I mean... do them!"

I laugh, and Shelia joins me before she's stable enough to ask, "So girl, what's this all about?"

"I'm moving out," I blurt. "I found a new place, and I'm moving out."

"Shit." Shelia is taken aback. "Tell me you're kidding?"

"I'm sorry." I reach to take her hand in mine. "It's an opportunity I couldn't pass up. I want to have a place of my own, and this new place is rent-free."

Shelia gives me her pissed eyes. We've talked about this a couple of times. She's offered me to stay for free, saying her finances are pretty good, but I've consistently declined. I don't want to change our friendship dynamics or take advantage of her.

"So you're leaving me!" She untangles her fingers from mine. I hate how unhappy she's become. But maybe I should tell her about the bright side now.

"Yes, and no," I beam. "We will be neighbors, so I wouldn't be really leaving. We'd bump into each other all the time."

"Neighbors?" Shelia has a suspicious look in her eyes, then she opens her mouth, disbelieving. "You're moving in with the new guy?"

I nod. "Yeah. His offer is pretty awesome." I try to convince her, and at the same time, dispel my worries after how I've become intrigued by him.

"Yeah, I guess." She narrows her eyes.

"What? If there's something you want to say, just say it, Shelia."

"I don't know." She huffs. "He's kind of intense, and then there's the way he looks at you-"

"What do you mean?" I interrupt. I don't need her to put things in my head. I'm already baffled by my unhealthy infatuation with him.

"Are you telling me you haven't noticed?"

"Notice what?"

I won't tell her about the mirror incident. Or that look.

Shelia shakes her head. "He's... like, fucking you with his eyes."

Before I interject how ridiculous this is, Shelia adds, "But that's not the issue here."

"Issue?"

Shelia takes a moment, maybe to gather her thoughts before explaining, "I don't know. But like, if he's that interested in you, why doesn't he act upon it? You know, ask you out or something. I don't think he lacks any self-confidence to do so."

I swallow. *Again*, remembering that look.

"I'll tell you what, ask him out?" Shelia blurts what I won't admit to myself. Since I laid my eyes on him, I've had this feeling. This delicious unsettling feeling that makes butterflies sprint down my stomach, pushing me to reward them with their awaiting satisfaction.

Shelia giggles. "Girl, you wear your heart in your eyes. You do like him, and he likes you too. So, isn't it time you spice up your life a little?"

"Even if." I cannot pretend in front of Shelia; she knows me very well. "He's gonna be my roomie, and I don't want to complicate things or mess this up."

"Or you're still hanging onto the past." Shelia looks at me soulfully. "Still feeling guilty and blaming yourself."

I rub my fingers back and forth over my forehead. I don't want to have a headache, but I feel one is coming on as Shelia continues, "I don't think Sam made all these sacrifices for you to go through life without really living it."

Sometimes, just sometimes, I regret opening up to Shelia about Sam and what happened because of me. But maybe that's the push I need to start moving on. To start living. I don't want to go back to that dark period of my life when I felt the need to cut my vein. I need to live, but easier said than done.

I'm not living my life to the fullest. I don't want the guilt to consume me again.

Guilty, that I'm the one who got adopted and had a safe, loving home and wonderful parents, and not Sam. I'm the one who's living now, while Sam isn't here anymore. I have all these beautiful things, and not Sam. Not the person who sacrificed so much to keep me safe and protected.

I exhale deeply. "I know. It's just… I'm finally stable, focusing on my goals, and creating the life I've dreamed of having. I'm afraid things will get complicated, then I would have to face more demons."

"Then, let's take baby steps." She reaches for my hand, gently squeezing. "Lucas is throwing a party at his mansion tonight. Why don't you come and invite this guy to tag along? Don't make it sound like a date, just something to test the waters."

"But I sensed you have a bad feeling about him."

She waves a hand. "Not a bad feeling. I feel… like he has lots of baggage, and I don't want that for you. But since he's the only guy that got your interest, you need to start somewhere."

He said I'd be trouble, but I don't mention that to Shelia. I have to figure this thing out on my own. Shelia has a point. I need to start living. Or break out of numbness—the mirror incident kind of changed things a little.

Back at the apartment, I've already made mac and cheese. Since Ian likes it so much, I plan to make it every week.

I pull the apron over my head, toss it on the table, then hightail it to my room. I need to get ready. It's almost seven, and we're leaving at eight.

Being besties with a top fashion model means I could borrow lots of beautiful outfits. Shelia gave me two ensembles. Both are black leather and show lots of skin.

I pick up the one with the strapless crop top and mini skirt. I want to blend in. I'm sure the females at Lucas's party will be showing all kinds of skin, and I'm not in the mood to be different.

Putting the outfit on, I'm thankful for my biological mother's genes. I have the same flat stomach as hers. It doesn't matter what I eat; I never gain a pound there. And this crop top needs a very flat tummy. Luckily it doesn't require large breasts, and I don't have large ones. But somehow, they're sticking out weirdly. I shake my head. It doesn't matter; the girls at the party will have more enhanced assets than mine.

It's seven-thirty now. I'm done gathering my hair in a messy bun and putting on some light makeup. I pick up my small purse and head out, a little disappointed. Ian hasn't come back yet.

But walking by the kitchen door, I see him there, sitting at the kitchen table, eating my mac and cheese. He didn't even bother to say hello. Or ask me to join him for dinner like usual.

A little gutted, I stand at the kitchen door. He's so engrossed in my mac and cheese, I get the chance to stare. I love to stare at him. He's all sorts of male beauty, the kind I like the most.

Ian Skene has good posture, broad shoulders, narrow hips, and strong muscles. Then there's his 'don't give a damn' attitude that has made me so damn interested, so I'm going to stare.

His dark brown hair is wet, which means he's been here for a while. He's so weirdly serious, but I don't get the chance to enjoy my inspection as his eyes suddenly clash with mine. He's about to say something, but when his eyes take me in, whatever is supposed to come out of his mouth doesn't.

His eyes leave mine, but they are on me. Roaming up and down, with disbelief, though I don't know why. Then something changes. His eyes darken, traveling over me a bit slower and lingering in places.

As he hardly swallows what's in his mouth, my heart pumps so hard, so loud.

He's fucking me with his eyes.

I touch a hand at the nape of my neck. Shelia has put these thoughts in my head. I need to end this. I need to breathe again. "I didn't know you were here."

His eyes narrow, like he's annoyed, then they meet mine again. Gone the heat, gone the passion, they don't care anymore. "You're going out?"

"Yes," I say, bringing a hand to my stomach. I don't know why the sudden need to cover up. Maybe it's his eyes. They're back to staring again.

He's not fucking me with his eyes. It's only Shelia's influence.

"On a date?" He gives me his eyes again, his fork stabbing back into my mac and cheese, but instead of raising it to his mouth, he moves it in circles.

"No," I say as calmly as I can. I still need to invite him to join us. "One of Shelia's friends is throwing a big party." I hide one foot behind the other, and I hope my voice doesn't sound hoarse when I gather my courage to offer, "If you feel like it… you could join us."

There, I've said it. Now I need some strength to look into his eyes.

I let out a long breath, readying myself to face his eyes.

I don't like the way he looks at me. Like he's trying to find the right words to decline politely.

"Um…" I'm trying to let him off the hook as he puts his fork aside, but before I get the chance, he pushes his chair back and walks toward me.

"Turn around." He motions with his finger, and I nervously smile. "What?"

"Trust me on this, just turn."

I'm really perplexed, and a bit embarrassed right now. What the heck!

He shakes his head before walking out the kitchen door. I think he's fed up with me or annoyed that I have asked him to tag along, but then comes his voice, "You're wearing black lace panties."

My hand shoots directly to my ass before I turn around and glare at him. "What the heck is wrong with you?"

He's fighting a smile. "It shows. Your skirt, if that's even a skirt, is not covering um..." he raises a fist to his mouth, playfully clearing his throat, "is not covering your modesty."

I'm pissed at him. "And?" I raise my voice, more pissed that he's ignored my timid invitation.

He shrugs like he has no care in the world, like he's not even a tiny bit invested in this. "You don't want to walk around announcing your panties to the world."

He's so amused. I know my face has reddened with heat, so I walk past him and clump to my room.

He doesn't try to stop me, or even call after me, or anything. He doesn't think he needs to fix this. Or even give me a polite excuse why he's not coming.

I return, defeated, to my room. I need to change out of my outfit. Pissed at him or not, I don't want to show my panties to anyone. And yes, this outfit is too short.

I pick up the other one. It has a similar crop top with spaghetti straps, and instead of the mini skirt, it has short shorts.

Done, I turn my back to the mirror and inspect my behind. Then it hits me. My panties were not showing as he claimed. I remember checking my back before heading out; the skirt did cover my behind very well. I was just too nervous to think straight.

I shake my head. I've walked right into his trap. For some odd reason, he doesn't want me to wear that outfit. But *Mr.-Pretends-I-Don't-Care* doesn't want to show me how much he cares. As a matter of fact, he exhaled a breath of relief as I walked back to my room. And silly me, I thought he felt relieved of *me*. And as for figuring out what kind of panties I'm wearing, it was just a wild guess. With a black ensemble, what are the odds?

Ian Skene, what kind of game are you playing?

Shelia will knock soon, so I don't have time to change back into my first outfit or figure out his game. So, again, I walk out of my bedroom.

I don't want to face him, and I'm very thankful he's nowhere in sight, but as I reach the front door, there he is, leaning against the wall.

He's nursing a habit now.

I don't dwell on that. He has changed into an elegant black suit. And I suck in a breath. I want to move, take my eyes off him, but I don't have the will to do that.

Instead, I'm mesmerized. This guy has enthralled me without even trying. It's not even about how good he looks. It's not about his obvious actions either. It all has to do with the hidden meaning behind them.

"How's that any better?" he grumbles as I settle close. Finally, he's showing his discomfort. Because this outfit is indeed not any better, it's just the same.

Lightly, I spin around. "I'm not announcing anything now," I say, gazing at his pissed-off blue eyes.

He shakes his head, then asks, "Do we have a ride? Or should I call Rick?"

Who's Rick?

Before I utter my inquiry, it dawns on me. He's in a suit because he's coming to the party. He has put in an effort for me. I haven't given him any details about the party, or if it's a must that he wears a suit. But he's wearing one just in case.

He has done it for me.

I swallow my sudden nervousness. "Shelia's friend is sending us a car."

He nods his head, then gestures with his hand to the door. I walk timidly, till I'm standing by his side, facing the door. I turn my head slightly. "Who's Rick?"

Do I need to ask about everyone in his life?

He steps closer with that smug smile. He's so close, just a thin sliver of air separating us.

"Rick is my driver," he answers casually. Like it's a normal thing to have a driver.

I wonder what other private persons he has.

A thought crosses my mind, and I make a face.

"What has gotten into you now?" he asks, concerned.

"Do you consider me your personal cook? Or one of your employees?"

He opens his mouths, then shuts it again. He's fighting a big laugh.

"You're my roommate," he finally says, narrowing his eyes. There's a bit of reluctance in them before he adds, "I would like it to stay that way. It's a great deal we have going on."

This is so embarrassing. He must have interpreted my invitation in the wrong way. Like I want to go on a date with him or something of that sort.

"Don't you think?" I hear hope and doubt in his voice. I'm not sure how he wants me to answer that.

I do think and agree it's a great deal, only if.

If you stopped looking at me like that. If you stopped fucking me with your eyes.

But I don't say that. I just nod my head. "The best of deals."

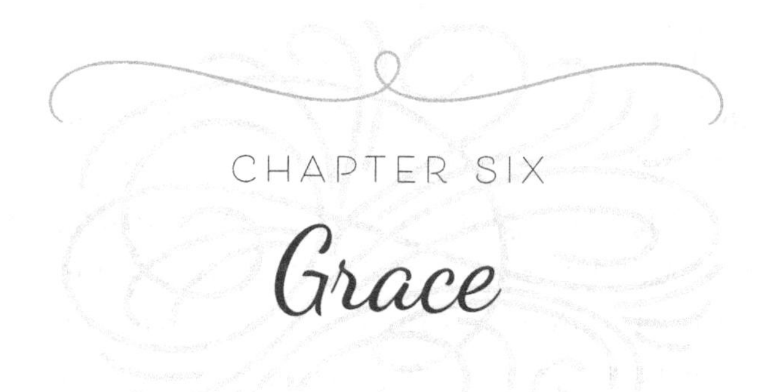

CHAPTER SIX

Grace

THE LIMO IS moving swiftly through Manhattan's hectic traffic. It's a very luxurious car. It has two bar areas with every soft drink that's available, a flat-screen TV, a wood grain floor, and fancy leather seats. Shelia and I take the center two-seater chair while Ian has settled into the seat to my left. And if there's one thing I know for sure, it's that the city always values bigger and better things. You won't become known here if you're not big or shiny enough.

If you can make it there, you can make it anywhere.

I smile, humming the lyrics in my head. That's not exactly true. I couldn't make it in my small town, and here I am, defying the old saying now. I've made it here. I wouldn't have had the guts to open any kind of store back home. I wouldn't have survived people asking me about Sam or what I did to myself.

I'm heading out to have fun. I don't need to think about Sam or how I tried to end my life. But my fingers involuntarily fly there, to press on my scar, the visual evidence of how I'd failed myself, my parents, and, most importantly, Sam.

I wonder if I would ever be able to justify what I did, or if someone like Ian would understand. I press hard on my scar. I shouldn't care about that, about him. He's not invested in anything more. But why is he so impatiently tapping his fingers near my thigh, wanting my attention, while he's having a serious conversation with Shelia? Since we got into the limo, my girl has been intent on a full-on investigation. I know she's doing it for my sake, but she doesn't know what happened earlier. I haven't had the chance to tell her yet.

"It's a waste of time working for someone else," Ian says, his fingers accidentally graze my naked thigh. I shoot him a look. Our eyes hold for a second, then his eyes and hand move away. He's finally got what he wanted—my attention. Now I'm listening as he continues, "Instead, if you put in the same time and effort, you'll finally make it on your own. It's not as hard as some people imagine it to be."

Like a lady, Shelia crosses her legs. Her shiny silver dress hitches up, showing her toned thighs. "So, should I open a modeling agency?"

I catch how Ian narrows his eyes, maybe assessing what kind of person Shelia is.

"Well, if you have a serious intent, I'd talk it through with you," Ian offers out of courtesy, or he does mean it. I cannot decide.

"Oh..." Shelia is as surprised as me. I bet she didn't expect him to offer that. Nor did I, to be honest. Nervous, my eyes jump there, to inspect his. But they're indifferent. Not that I would blame him if he'd gotten interested in Shelia. My girl is all kinds of gorgeous. And her little silver number makes it hard for any guy not to stare. But Ian's eyes don't care. And it's not like when he pretends it with me. He seriously doesn't care.

"That's very generous of you," Shelia says, but Ian's eyes are back on me, searching. Then I feel them growing intense. I know without even looking. They're intent on me, enjoying every inch of my body.

I give him a mere glance.

I'm silently warning him.

Don't do that.

Don't start in front of Shelia.

Don't fuck me with your eyes.

Don't fuck me with your eyes, I repeat, as if it's going to help, but the help comes from Shelia as she distracts him, "But if we're gonna be honest here, I don't think anyone gives his time for free, let alone offering help. Everything in the city comes with a price."

Shelia doesn't ever hesitate to say it like it is. Otherwise, I don't think she could have made it in a business as competitive, not to mention full of douchebags as hers.

And as self-assured as he is, I expect Ian to be a little offended, but as I turn slightly to study him, he's not bothered a bit by Shelia's criticism. He understands where she's coming from. "That's why I wanted my company to be different."

Ian's business was the first thing, Shelia had asked about as we settled into the limo. He went into details with her, telling her he owns a marketing company, and I was so pissed at him that I didn't catch any other details. I just sat there fuming because when I asked him about it, he answered me curtly.

He doesn't want to get too involved with me. I remind myself.

He said it clearly half an hour ago. He likes what we have—just roommates with a good deal. I need to calm my infatuation with him.

I have known him for a small amount of time. He shouldn't affect me this much.

Maybe that's what happens when one starts to live. Maybe after two weeks or so, I would become indifferent to him too. Or master it as he sometimes does.

"I didn't want to follow the same pattern as many of my competitors do, focusing only on my name. On getting bigger. Giving all my time and resources to win the next deal."

Now I'm giving my full attention to what he says. I'm genuinely intrigued about everything involving him, and maybe he wouldn't be opening up to me as he is right now.

He continues, "I wanted my success to have meaning. I wanted to give back. So, I tried to dig deep. I thought I had to be more than the guy who can sell anything."

"But that's the ultimate goal in marketing. To be the guy who sells everything," I say, only to get his attention. I'm a little envious of Shelia right now.

Stop it. Don't get affected by his passionate speech.

He won't direct any passionate words toward me. His goal is to be indifferent.

"Yes," he says, resting one hand close to me, and making me regret asking him anything in the first place.

My eyes meet the floor. I cannot gaze into his passionate eyes. I don't want him to affect me more than he has. But as his thumb starts to graze my naked thigh, I swallow hard and raise my eyes to him. I don't want him to stop. But he does stop, he only wanted my attention, and I'm willingly giving it to him even though I shouldn't.

He shifts his gaze back to Shelia, "As the truth dawned on me, that I couldn't be good at anything else, I decided to take advantage of that. If I'm that good at selling, then I'd use it to pay back. To give to others."

I look at Shelia sideways. I think he's charmed her pants off. But still, she's Shelia. She has this amused look on her face. She must have sensed the electricity in the air. And knowing my friend, she'll try to move all the strings as neither Ian nor I am willing to do anything about it.

"Pardon me," I say, knowing I'll regret getting involved soon, "but how are you using that to give back? Don't you take money for your work?"

I guess I want to find some kind of fault in him.

"I do," he says proudly. "And being so good at it has given me the ability to give back," he adds, and I have a hard time not melting in front of his passionate words. His whole body is engaged now. "I was able to consign part of my profits to give back. To make other people's dreams come true."

"I wanna hear all about that," Shelia says, and I have a feeling she's cooking up something in her head.

Ian looks at me before turning his attention back to Shelia. "You could do more than hearing. If you have an idea in mind, you could present it to our Give Back team. We choose two or three of the best ideas that go well with our company motto, and either we invest in it or present it to other sponsors."

"You mean like a charitable idea?" Shelia is quick to ask before I admire Ian's dedication to helping others. But my heart is sinking now.

She's not going to do it. I look at Shelia sideways, mouthing, "Don't."

"Exactly." Ian is all serious. "If you have one, I'm all ears."

"Well, unfortunately, I don't have any ideas right now. But guess who has?"

Ian turns to me as Shelia continues, "Grace has this great idea for helping the homeless. But so far-"

"Let me guess," Ian's eyes shine with triumph as he interrupts Shelia, "she has been looking for sponsors, but so far without any success."

I get the feeling he's found some window he has been looking for to get through to me, which doesn't make sense at all.

"I couldn't have put it any better," Shelia is quick to confirm Ian's theory.

And right here, right now, I want to pinch Shelia so hard. She's not going to play matchmaker. The guy isn't interested in me. Maybe he cannot stop fucking me with his eyes, as he's starting to do right now, but he doesn't want to act upon it.

I don't even have control over my tongue to move, before Ian says, "I'll set aside some time this week. We could go through the bold lines for a starter. I'll let Suzan send you the details."

Wait, What...!

I have to end this. Shelia has put him on the spot, and I will not take advantage of him. "That's very generous of you. But no, I will not accept anything of that sort."

Ian raises an eyebrow, glances amusingly at Shelia before addressing me again, "We're only gonna discuss the basics. I'd only accept it if I see it's suitable for what my company stands for, so it's still very early to get this nervous about it. "

I gather my hands in my lap, trying hard not to reach and pinch Shelia for putting me in this situation. "Thank you. But I will not take advantage of your generosity-"

"You're being silly here," he says in a practical tone, interrupting me. Shelia snorts with an agreement before he adds, "Most opportunities nowadays resemble this. Someone knows someone who recommends someone. There's nothing wrong or new about it. I don't see why you're getting so defensive."

My eyes leave my lap to connect with his sharp ones. They're far away from those that usually send me heated promises.

"I don't see a reason why you shouldn't give it a shot. I mean, I'm up-front with you, and there's a big chance we would not be representing you. There're lots of ideas we receive every year."

I sigh in relief. Here's my way out. "Then why bother? I'm only gonna waste your time and *mine.*" I emphasize the last word. He may have a more significant business, but my time is equally as important as his. I've spent the last two years living, sleeping, and breathing my shop.

Shelia sighs with irritation, making me want to kick her out of the car. I mean, I love that girl, but she's pushing this thing way too hard. I don't need any kind of encouragement to get involved with him.

Ian shares an understanding look with Shelia before he shifts his blue eyes to me. "You bother because you'd gain some experience. You'd gain some knowledge of how things are done. You'd spare yourself another two years sitting on your ideas."

Ian is lecturing me. His face is all sorts of pissed. Like I have insulted his intelligence or something. "You don't sit on your ass afraid to collect a no. You wouldn't make it anywhere if you didn't get tons of them. Every single no is a step closer to getting the big yes."

He sees through my bullshit. He knows I'm terrified.

But I'm not afraid of any nos. I'm scared of what I'm starting to feel for him.

I close my eyes for a bit. Then I feel Shelia straightening in her seat; his words have touched her in some way.

"He couldn't be more correct." Shelia touches a hand to my knee. "Do you know how many times I've heard that no?" She raises a finger. "Let's see… Some said my skin is too dark, and they only hire girls with a much lighter tone. Then some said I needed to straighten my hair. Then some said I have a wide forehead. Then one day, they said another thing, but I didn't listen. I don't even remember what fault they'd found in me. I didn't care anymore. And you know the rest. I got my Yes, and it was worth all the Nos."

I'm astonished. I know Shelia had faced many hardships, but I didn't imagine someone would find fault in her looks. Shelia is gorgeous. I turn to her. "Every one of these Nos had come from a place of assholeness. You know you're perfect in every sense of the word."

"You are too. I think you have more strength than you even know about."

I know Shelia and even Ian are meaning well, but I'm starting to feel uncomfortable. I'm not some kind of damsel in distress; maybe I was once, but not anymore. I work my ass off in my shop and for the homeless shelter. But as always, my scar is giving the assumption of how fragile I might be.

"So, are you ready to receive your first no? Or you're objecting for a different reason?" Ian asks, making me pissed, but I'm not going to show him how I truly feel about his offer.

"Not at all." I don't want him to figure out the real reason that I want to keep my distance till I sort out my unexpected infatuation toward him. "I'd love to. That's if I'm going to be treated equally like the others."

He eyes me carefully before resting back into the leather seat. "You have my word on that. You'd be treated no differently than the others."

My heart sinks. I'm starting to believe his lies. Because that is a flat-out lie, he's not going to treat me like the others.

Shelia claps with enthusiasm, taking me out of my reverie. "Then let's make a toast, shall we, guys?"

Ian smiles at Shelia then leans forward to pick up the champagne bottle in the nearby bar. "To...?"

He's addressing me, but I will not look into his eyes. I know he wants me to. His whole body is turned to me right now, but I glance at him before turning to Shelia. "To perfect deals," I emphasize each word. I want him to know that I will not interpret his offer as something more.

CHAPTER SEVEN
Grace

WALKING THROUGH THE front gates of Lucas's mansion, I think it's too big and too flashy. I don't care how much this SoHo mansion cost. If it lacks warmth, then count me out.

"I'll see you inside." Shelia touches my elbow. Then, as if she's racing to some finish line, she abandons me.

I shake my head as my eyes follow her steps. She thinks I need some time alone with Ian. I should have found a way to tell her the reality of our situation. But as soon as I put my coat on, Ian was by my side.

"I know I'll sound lame," I say, cutting through any awkward silence before it happens between Ian and me, "but even if I had the money, I wouldn't buy a place like this."

"Like this?" Ian questions, pausing, his hand reaches to touch my elbow, turning me to face him. He wants my eyes, my attention.

I don't want our interactions to be as intense as earlier. Still, I genuinely have a hard time connecting with his eyes before saying, "You know, the kind of place you'd have to have your private jet already parked in your backyard before contemplating the idea of purchasing it."

He gives a big laugh at my unjustified frustration. "It's bothering you that much!"

"It's just." I lift one shoulder. I want to continue talking about Lucas's mansion. It's a safe subject where I can keep my infatuation in check. But I'm lost for words.

I'm lost in his eyes. They're not intense or careless. They're full of warmth and acceptance, telling me... He's going to accept anything I say or do tonight, because deep down, he knows he's been confusing me nonstop.

"Let's have a little walk," he suggests with a warm smile.

I nod, relieved that he's not thrilled to get inside. Maybe he's like me. The affluent neighborhood is not his scene.

As we walk into the garden, away from the guests that keep arriving, I'm adamant to prove my point. "I just don't think big houses provide warmth or allow closeness. I think people buy them to run away from each other. To get some kind of fair distance. To prove they're there together, though they hardly interact at all."

Ian pauses a foot away from the huge antique fountain centering Lucas's garden. I whirl, and gaze up at him since I already know he wants my eyes. He looks down at me with soulfulness. "Maybe for some, it's a comforting distance. They don't necessarily want to run away, but they have to, at least until they figure their shit out. And being under the same roof, even if they don't speak at all, gives them that comfort. Maybe someday they will find a way back to each other."

He glances to the side before his eyes are on me again, but they're not with me anymore. "Some people cannot let go of the ones they love. They cannot fathom that they wouldn't be it."

"It?" I almost sigh my inquiry. I'm crushed by the tremendous pain that has settled in his eyes.

"Yeah..." He closes his eyes for a second, hiding. But when he opens them again, I don't see pain, just void. "It. The magical solution. The cure. Sometimes it has nothing to do with them. No matter how much effort they give. They wouldn't be it."

I don't think it's the cold breeze that makes me shiver. But I prefer to think so as a neutral smile visits his face.

I don't know how he masters this flexible change of heart. One minute he's lost in his pain, the next he forgets all about it.

I cannot judge if it was his fault, and he brought that pain to himself. Or maybe he wasn't even talking about something personal.

"Still frowning." He touches a finger between my eyebrows. I don't want to enjoy it as he starts to move it up and down as if massaging the worries out of me.

I close my eyes for a second. I need to have the courage to ask him to stop.

Stop confusing me.

Stop pretending you don't care.

Stop not wanting to want me.

"Ian, you need to..." I open my eyes to meet his intense ones. They're very close now, his whole face is, and then his lips are close. Too close.

He's going to kiss me.

"Ian..." I might have whispered or not. I don't know or feel anything but the touch of his lips between my eyes.

"You're thinking too much," he's the one whispering now, a fraction away from me. His lips are no longer on me, but his breaths are fast and hot, burning my forehead.

"Shouldn't I?" I search his eyes for help. I don't have the will to ask him to stop. I don't want him to stop. I don't even know what he wants. But right now, I don't care.

He pulls back a little, huffs a long breath before the warmth fills his eyes again. "At least not tonight."

"Why?" I hide my hands in my pockets, looking for some strength. "What's gonna happen tonight?"

His eyes slide away from me. He's looking into the void. He's still indecisive about us, even if it's only one night.

My eyes catch the fountain ahead of us. Another safe subject. "Why do people have fountains?"

He glances down at me for a second, his eyes a bit apologetic, then he turns, facing the fountain. He shrugs. "Maybe because they look pretty."

"And why do people insist on having pretty meaningless things?" I ask, secretly thanking God I didn't stomp the floor in frustration.

He shifts his eyes back to me, and, with a bit of mischief, he places a hand on my lower back. "Come on."

"What?" I don't like how I'm starting to melt under the touch of his protective hand.

"Trust me." He gently pushes me to walk ahead. To the fountain, I guess. And I secretly wish the walk there would be a hundred miles away. I want his hand to stay there, protecting me. But as we quickly reach our destination, he drops it.

He pulls his phone out of his pocket, taps it with his finger then holds it up. "I'm gonna show you why people insist on having pretty things."

"Um..." I don't know what's happening as he bends a little, puts an arm under my knees, the other on my back. He lifts me easily off the ground, and walks the little distance to the fountain before dropping me on the ledge.

I gawk as he quickly backs away, just a few steps. He holds his phone up and asks me, "Look right into the camera and say cheese."

I gather two nonexistent locks of hair behind my ears. He's going to take a picture of me. The camera flash is on, and I watch him tap on his phone, then he taps again, then again.

That's more than one picture.

That's a lot of pictures of me.

That's a lot of mixed signals he's adamant to give me.

I should be furious with him. I should get my ass off this fountain and walk away. But I do none of that.

I say cheese after cheese after another cheese. I smile from ear to ear. I love every second of this. I pause for a second, eager to know if he's enjoying it too.

I gaze up at him, and my smile grows wider. His eyes are dancing with joy. He moves here and there to find another perfect angle for another picture of me. He's loving every second of this until he approaches me. "I wanna try something."

"What?" I rub a hand over my thigh as he bends slightly, so we're eye to eye. He reaches behind me. And I don't feel anything anymore.

I'm paralyzed in his scent. I'm a prisoner to whatever lays in his eyes.

"You, too, like to have pretty meaningless things." He reaches to undo my bun. My hair falls to my back; the little pin makes a whisper of sound dropping behind me into the water.

Before I understand what he means, he pushes up, walks backward, and aims his phone at me again. He takes more pictures of me. "You keep your pretty hair long. Then you put it in a meaningless bun."

"It's more practical." My hands shoot to tidy my hair. I'm sure it's all kinds of messy right now.

"Fuck practical," he says it in the form of a command for me to stop, his eyes intense, not dancing with joy as earlier. "I don't need another practical picture. I want your truth, Grace. Not a picture of perfection. Just you, simply you."

He wants my truth now. He wants me, simply me.

Ian Skene is inventing new techniques for the mixed-signal business, and I cannot stand it anymore. Because each time, I believe he does want me.

So before I start believing again, at least until he's upfront about it, I slide off the ledge. "You don't need another picture of me. Practical or not."

There's a bit of disappointment in his eyes as I walk straight up to him. "We should get inside, don't you think?"

He glances away for a second, puts his phone back in his pocket, then he offers me his arm. "It's about time."

I don't know what he means as I loop my arm around his. We walk in silence until we reach the front steps of the mansion. "Do you always attend parties with your friend?"

"No." I look up at him, "It's a first for me."

He's kind of relieved. "Why now?"

Of course, he'd ask that.

I just shrug, and we walk up the stairs in silence. He helps me out of my coat in silence. Many guests take the same path as us, talking, joking, blowing kisses, and shaking hands, but all I can hear is our silence. It's not the silence that's tied my stomach in knots. It's the way we're peacefully accommodating to it. I'm not trying to initiate another meaningless conversation while Ian's face is content. He's not trying to get my attention, he's letting me be. Like we've done this a hundred times.

As we walk through the grand foyer, he, again, lays his hand on my lower back, my *naked* lower back. It's not a casual touch or a light one either.

He's imprinting me with his fingers. He's claiming me, labeling me as his, at least for tonight. And my mind has no window to think about how odd he's been acting. My mind has left the building, and my body is taking complete control.

The funny thing is, it has no control under Ian's touch. I'm hot and bothered. I don't trust myself to walk straight. But I need to. I cannot melt now, not just yet.

I try my hardest to focus on something else. An older woman bedizened with too much gold on her wrists passes us, and I try to imagine what life she's led, just to take my mind off his burning touch. But as his thumb starts to draw circles on my skin, I surrender. I need to let something out. Otherwise, I'll explode. So, I'm helplessly letting my shiver show. I'm shivering with each circle he draws.

"Fuck." He pauses. His thumb pauses. His breathing pauses, so does mine.

It's now or never. He's going to acknowledge what's burning between us here.

After a minute of him trying to control the air coming in and out of his lungs, he looks to the side, down at me. "Are you feeling cold?"

I shake my head. Not answering his question but fed up. He's going to pretend again.

His hand is off my bare skin, as if he cannot take it like me. He gently grabs my elbow, and we walk into the huge ballroom where the actual party is taking place.

I stop just a foot in, turning to him. "I need to go to the ladies' room, if you'll excuse me," I say and leave quickly.

I walk through the masses of elegant designer gowns, heated conversations, clinks of champagne flutes, and make a turn where I think the restroom is.

A couple of young women are heading there. They're giggling and talking nonsense, having fun.

I should be having fun too.

I follow as they push the bathroom door open. I don't need to use the stall, so I walk till I stop in front of one of the mirrors. As usual, I'm a little apprehensive of what will face me in the mirror, so I take a deep breath before I glance up.

No bloody drops, just my pale face and dark eyes that resemble what's going on inside my body.

There's heat, and there's regret. I shouldn't have shivered. He shouldn't have known how he's been affecting me. He shouldn't even be affecting me this way.

I wonder what has consumed me tonight.

I need to lighten up and have fun.

I pass a hand through my hair that surprisingly doesn't look bad. It looks like a 'made-up' out of bed look, the one done by a top stylist, but maybe it needs a little touch. I lift my hand, then drop it quickly.

Fuck practical.

I smile, remembering his words. Maybe I shouldn't be in knots about him after all. We've only known each other for a minimal amount of time. And I've only invited him to test the waters. So, he's either a bit reluctant or not interested at all. By the end of the night, I'll figure him out.

I wish I could splash some water onto my face to cool me down, but I just touch my wet hand to my neck. I take one more look in the mirror, then head out of the bathroom.

To have some fun.

But as I swing the door open, I almost jump back inside.

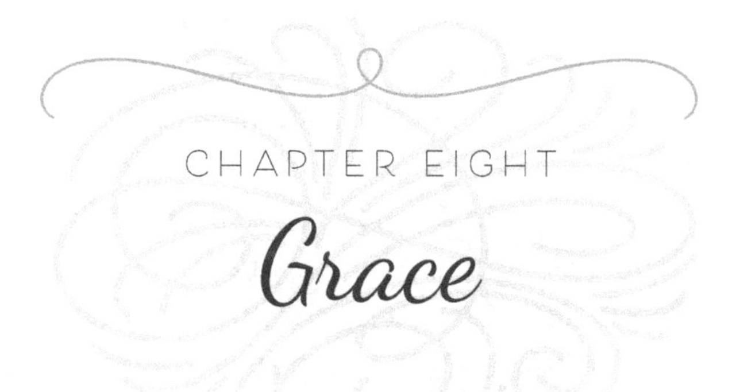

CHAPTER EIGHT
Grace

HE'S RESTING AGAINST the wall, again, waiting for me. I fight my smile. I don't want to look like an idiot in front of his mysterious ways.

The hallway is a bit dark to read his eyes, but I'm not going to obsess about his eyes anymore. "You're nursing a habit now." I walk outside into the hallway.

He returns the smile that I obviously failed to hide before he pushes away from the wall. "Lots of things could happen at these parties. I just wanted to make sure you're safe."

I nod. It's another mixed signal of his. Or he's just a gentleman.

Don't obsess about him!

As we walk back into the ballroom, there's more than enough to distract me from obsessing over Ian or his touch on my naked back.

My eyes take everything in. With its ruby walls and oriental decors, this room is a brilliant tribute to excellence—valid proof of what money can create. The three glass chandeliers alone must have cost a fortune. But what warms my heart is the rivers of flowers aligned on each large column, not to mention the lilies over every table and chair. I'm dying to pick one and lose myself in its scent, but instead, my eyes inspect the guests.

So many people are here, and still, there's room for more. As my eyes take them in, I realize I'm following the dress code. Most of the young women attending the party are wearing outfits that deliberately show lots of skin. There are too many enhanced assets, blown up lips, and nose jobs that have gone too small for my taste, but to each their own and whatever makes them happy.

As I notice a couple of stares aimed toward Ian, I end of my inspection. I'm dying to know what he thinks. Does perfection attract him, or would he have more fun with some flaws?

I stop, and his hand slides off my back as I turn to him, folding my arms. "You're not a foreigner to this scene."

He frowns. "Are you asking or making a guess?"

I miss the warmth of his touch on my lower back. "Is there a difference?"

"Lots," he says cryptically, his eyes searching mine. I guess if I'm asking, that will make me interested in him.

"Either," I say. "You're so used to this scene."

Another frown comes across his face. "What gave you this impression about me?"

I smile. He's taking this seriously, and I've decided to have fun. "Well, you have a driver. So, maybe this little detail gave you away."

"Look who's here?"

We both turn to the soft, warm voice. An older woman is approaching us.

"Lucy." Ian is quite surprised. A good surprise.

"Ian, my dear!" Lucy smiles while Ian steps forward to embrace her in a hug.

I smile too. Lucy has got the warmest face with her baby blue eyes and delicate features. Her wrinkles are untouched; her hair is an array of shining grey threads left loose on her shoulders. She's instantly gotten my admiration.

"How long has it been? Where were you hiding?" Ian asks as he pulls back beside me, his hand right on my back.

"We've been traveling…" Lucy pauses mid-sentence as her eyes shift to me. There's a quiet surprise in them before she turns her gaze back to Ian. "Not anything adventurous. Just places where we could enjoy sunny days and good food."

"That's quite adventurous for me," Ian says with yearning. "Just the idea of leaving everything behind. To not care about a thing in the world."

"I told you it's going to be a good party," an older man says, settling near Lucy while extending his arms. "Finally, a good face." He moves forward to embrace Ian in a quick man-hug.

"Good to see you, Arthur," Ian says and steps back. And I feel two sets of eyes inspecting me.

Ian's fingers are back on my skin, tapping lightly now.

There's too long of a pause where he should have said something.

Maybe he doesn't know how to introduce me to them.

Arthur narrows his eyes, a bit of doubt in them. I guess Ian's silence says much. Maybe he doesn't want to introduce me to his world tonight. Or ever! The latter thought terrifies me.

"Grace Edwards," Ian finally addresses my presence.

Lucy is quick to lean forward for a kiss while Arthur studies me in a serious manner before he says, "Nice to meet you, young lady."

I smile in return, though I know he's not warming up to me as Lucy is.

"So, you've been traveling," Ian says, his voice a little elated. He's pleased to see them. I just wonder what kind of relationship he has with the couple.

"We've been to the Middle East." Arthur gives his attention back to Ian. "We visited Egypt and Morocco. Charming people and delicious food."

"But it's good to be home again. It's always good to be home." Lucy touches a hand to Ian's arm, patting it with tenderness.

"Speaking of home," Arthur's eyes are on me again, "Is it yours here, young lady? 'Cause I get the feeling you're not a creation of this city."

"I'm not." I smile, though Arthur's tone is not encouraging. "I moved here two years ago. But I love it very much."

"Yeah. Only ambitious, driven people love it here." Lucy's smile is full of warmth. "I can see the fire in your eyes."

"Yeah," Ian interjects. "Grace has an exquisite flower shop. One that's doing very well too."

"How lovely," Lucy says. "I have an upcoming party and certainly will need some flowers. Maybe I'll drop by and see what you have."

"That would be great," I say evenly. I don't want to sound too eager to sell my shop, so I don't add anything else. I don't want Ian to think I'm taking advantage of his acquaintances. It's enough that Shelia has twisted his arm for me.

"You'd love it, Lucy," Ian says.

I'm not following the conversation as Arthur's eyes are inspecting my scar. I get the feeling he won't deter from addressing it. This man really cares for Ian. He will speak his mind if he believes it's for the well-being of Ian. I don't need to hear any of that.

I put a hand across Ian's back, smiling at the older couple. "I'll let you catch up," I say, then gaze up at Ian. "Shelia is probably looking for me."

Not walking away just yet, I stay still for a tiny second, enjoying how possessive Ian's hand is getting on my back. He doesn't want me to leave, his fingertips dig deep into my skin, but I have to. I don't need Arthur's words or another mixed signal.

Missing Ian's touch, I walk into the warmth of the room, where the young guests are starting to form some kind of dancing competition.

I smile. I'd love to watch that.

No. I'd love to be a part of it.

I have no partner, though. My eyes sway there, where I left Ian. He's still engrossed with the older couple.

I almost giggle. I don't think he would like to get into a twerking competition, as the DJ is announcing. Nor do I, to be honest. I can master a move or two, but twerking I've never practiced before.

"Come on, my girl. Let's twerk a little." I feel her hands on my waist. Shelia is a little tipsy as I turn to her. "No, I'd be the joke of the town if I did," I say, giggling. The thought of twerking really makes me laugh. I mean, what would I twerk with? I have um... little assets back there.

"You would be my partner." Shelia bends, her hands on my waist as she starts to wiggle her ass. "We'd be the Flat Butt Team."

I shake my head. Shelia is a supermodel, a skinny one too. "Stop it," I warn her between giggles. "It's gonna end up on someone's phone."

She squints her eyes at me, then straightens to her full height. "You're too sober for this. You need a drink."

I do.

I follow Shelia as she grabs me by the arm. We stop by a waiter with a tray of drinks. I pick one, so does Shelia, who asks him to wait till we've had our fill.

I know I'm a lightweight. But tonight I've decided to have fun. So, I gulp three small glasses of whatever the waiter is serving us. I don't care about what's in it. I just care to be a little wasted—a little carefree.

"Fourth one...for the best of luck." Shelia hands me another glass, and I gulp it too.

Now I'm the one dragging her by the arm toward the circle of twerking while she's shouting, "Woohoo...oooha, that's my girl."

As we step inside the circle, Shelia shouts, pointing a finger down at me. "The Flat Butt Team."

I almost cringe. But I'm too tipsy to care by now. And the music is so vibrant and alive that it shuns any thinking by me. I just want to have fun.

Side by side, near Shelia, I try to move my body with the music. There's lots of push and pull as the circle is so full. I don't think anyone would notice how awful Shelia and I are twerking. There are too many big butts here for anyone to care about us.

So, I smile and let loose. I don't even try to twerk anymore. I'm just trying to push all the pent-up energy and worry out of me.

I'm finally having fun.

Unwanted touches, here and there, occur. They're probably too drunk or just looking for a partner. But I push them off easily—nothing I cannot handle. No one is going to prevent me from having fun tonight.

I don't know how much time has passed, but it's the fifth song in a row now, and Shelia is at the other half of the circle, twerking against another girl's crotch.

A little tired, I feel another unwanted touch around my waist and I struggle to move away. His hands are firmer than the others, so if I don't act soon, he's going to think I like him or something.

"Let go!" I yell. Even at these big, affluent parties, perverts still exist.

I'm about to aim my elbow at him when his hands are suddenly gone, followed by "Fucking off her," someone growls, a familiar sound. I turn slightly to find Ian over the man on the floor.

Before Ian aims another fist at him, two guys quickly reach down for him. "Not again, Jeff." They scold him while Ian stands still, his fists clenched at his sides.

"We're sorry, he's just drunk," one of the guys says as they haul their friend up, while the latter waves a hand in a manner of apology.

I step forward to touch Ian's arm, and he instantly turns to me. "Are you okay?"

"Yeah… I guess," I say, but I'm not. I hate it when guys force themselves like that, even if he's drunk and then remorseful later.

I just want to have some fun without being disturbed.

I see Ian's eyes softening. The scorching anger slowly leaves them. "You've got some dance moves," he smirks.

I get the feeling he's teasing me. I roll my eyes. "I was just having some fun. I'm not gonna audition for the next season of *So You Think You Can Dance*?"

"Well, I didn't mean to interrupt your fun, but..." He shakes his head.

Feeling shy at this moment, I don't know why, but I am. "Um… Thanks for getting that asshole off me."

"Yeah, I felt you couldn't handle him like the others. That's why I intervened."

"Were you watching me?" I ask, rubbing my sides. I hope he didn't.

"It was good to see you having fun," he says evenly, but his eyes are so warm. Another second of this, and I would feel like he's pitying me, like he knows I haven't had fun in a long time. But then who does have a business in the Big Apple and have regular fun? Maybe we have something in common after all. I like that theory better.

I touch a hand to my neck. "What about you? Did you have fun?"

Yes. I want to know what he's been doing other than watching me. His warm eyes have brought me back into infatuation mode. I'm a little too tipsy and tired to fight my hormones. Add to that, he was about to get in a fight for me. That alone is enough to make my *get over my infatuation with him* plans go out the window.

"I'm about to." He smiles and steps forward. And I'm in La-La land as he circles one arm around my waist, reaches with the other to lay my hand on top of his shoulder. "I hope you're not too tired for another dance."

I nod my head. Then shake it.

"*Shake it* is the right answer," I mumble, then bite my tongue.

He chuckles, and my eyes jump up to meet his. They're still warm, and there's something else. Something I'm not going to obsess about now. Instead, I focus on my steps. I haven't danced in a long time, an intimate dance where I can hear his heartbeat even with all the noise around us. I hope he doesn't hear mine. It's not as cool as his.

My heart is beating fast, and I don't think it's fair that his fingers lay on my naked skin while mine meet his suit jacket. I want to have some power over this, so slowly, I travel them up to his neck. I see a quiet surprise in his eyes before they turn unfathomable. There's a vibe of danger in them that shoots straight between my legs.

I close my eyes for a second. I want to have control over this. I'm here to test the waters. To know how he feels about me.

He sways us slowly with the music, my thumb mimicking his. I draw little circles over his skin. Slowly, very slowly, and his thumb stills on me. He closes his eyes for a second, his nostrils flaring.

Knowing my touch affects him too gives me the power to ask, "Are they your friends?"

"The Browns?" he says, his voice a bit hoarse, "Yeah, they're friends of my parents."

"So, I wasn't wrong. You're used to this scene."

His steps and his touch on my skin still, imprinting me with fire. "I might be attending this party and others, but it's not necessarily my scene. Flashy phony places aren't."

"What is then?" I'm dying to know anything about him—everything about him.

He catches a point behind me. "I thought I knew that once. But now I don't have a fucking clue."

When he gives me his eyes again, I catch a warning there. He doesn't want me to ask more questions. Now a bit faster than the rhythm, he's swaying us with the music.

He's tense under my touch, so my thumb massages his neck. Up and down in slow, deliberate moves. Slow and soft as a feather. Just strokes of tenderness. I want him to let loose again. His eyes are more beautiful and less dangerous on my hormones when they're warm.

I don't feel him relax, but he does slow our steps. I push, "So you're not like any other guy. I mean, these gorgeous women would make it the dream scene to any guy."

"Do you think of me like any guy?" he asks, his steps still again. His arm tightens around my waist, and his fingertips dig into my skin. But his eyes are full of confidence. I wonder why he asked.

I hold his gaze. I'm not backing down. Even if the outcome would embarrass me later, I will not live with regret.

"No. You're different," I whisper, then I look away. He's not like any other man I've ever met. Nobody has affected me the way he does.

I feel a light touch of his lips on the top of my head. "You're different too."

My heartbeat is now out of control, making me gaze up at him. As if he's waiting for me, his eyes are intense, heated with promises, and for some reason, I don't think he'd act upon them.

"Ian..." I breathe his name. I cannot just stand still in his arms. I need more. I need a decision. A bold one that he may not be ready for as his jaw tenses.

"Um..." I want to let him off the hook. I'm way more into this than him. It's so embarrassing. Before I embarrass myself, even more, I say, "I'll go look for Shelia. It's about time we leave."

He rests his forehead against mine, but I move my head away before I lose myself in his hot breaths, his heat, and his indecisive eyes. I slip away from his arms.

I invited him for a reason. I came here for a reason. And it's not there. He's not there with me. Or he's not willing to be there. He's fighting it, and I don't want to invest in something like this. I have lots of things I need to sort out before getting into anything that is not simple.

Ten minutes later, Rick is driving us to the apartment. Shelia is leaving later with her friends. As always, she sticks till the end and probably would get back with some entourage to continue partying at her apartment. Ian called his driver, and we're in the back seat of his car. Smoldering heat fills the small space. With him. All I can sense is him. His scent. His breaths. His heartbeat.

I gaze forward at the man driving us. I want something to distract me.

He's bald, and that's all I can gather about him right now. He's bald. I cannot catch anything else. I cannot function. I'm too paralyzed from want.

I glue myself to the door. I cannot trust myself not to reach out and touch Ian. I'm a little tipsy, and my hormones are out of control. Not a good combination.

"It's not that I don't want you..."

My head instantly snaps, eager to know what he's going to reveal.

I take a look. His head is down, his elbows on his knees. "It's just... I don't think it'll work. Not right now."

I want to reach out, put his tense shoulders at ease. But I'm shivering like there's a wave of cold breeze. He does want me, and that's all my heart hears. He wants me.

But he doesn't want to act upon it.

I repeat that in my head as my gaze is adamant not to leave him. He rests back in the seat, and I repeat, he doesn't want to act upon it. I repeat it till the car pulls over to the side of the building. I gather my coat under my arm, my purse in the other hand, and hurriedly get out. I need some distance.

Walking side by side, his hand on my back, but not actually touching my skin. Like he cannot handle it like me.

I'm tipsy. And tipsy me is a total disaster. Tipsy me is going all dreamy, all out of logic. Tipsy me thinks of cheesy love movies and cheesier songs.

No. Tipsy me cannot even think. Tipsy me is only dreamy and lyrical.

We walk into the elevator, aware of our unbearable heat. We both reach to push the button. His hand covers mine, and I pray I won't whimper as he presses on my finger. The doors start to shut, and our eyes lock. Our eyes lock, and I'm terrified. His eyes are heated, intense, filled with desire and the regret that would follow if he acted upon it.

A sigh escapes my mouth.

A "fuck" escapes his.

I grasp my coat tightly to my chest. I need some shield to prevent me from reaching out to him as he looks down at me. He's pinning me with his eyes. I remain still, waiting for him to decide.

He has all the power now. I'm willingly and unwisely giving it up to him.

"Fuck..." he utters again, snatching the coat out of my hands. He throws it somewhere behind him onto the floor before he makes me a prisoner between his arms. They're on each side of me, and I glue myself against the wall.

"Grace. You don't know. You don't fucking know..." He speaks with a tormented tone. His eyes are long gone in desire before his lips crash against mine. His hands snatch me from the wall to plaster me to his heat, his lips firm and hot and taking control.

And I shiver and freeze.

I'm too excited and eager to please.

Then I don't know how I'm kissing him back. I loop my arms around his neck and kiss him back. My tongue in his mouth, his in mine. We're not following any rhythm. He's going crazy over me. His hands are everywhere. Like he cannot get enough of me, like it's his first sip of water after a long tiring marathon.

He cups my breasts then my ass. He frantically massages my stomach, then my back. He pushes against me then pulls back. His hands are eager to have all of me at the same time. Then he cups the heat between my legs, and I moan aloud, so loud I almost miss his barbaric groan.

It's so carnal and unreal.

I'm drenching wet under his touch. It's almost too embarrassing how wet I am.

Then something changes. His hands freeze. His breath halts. His lips tear away from mine. His arms prison me to the wall while he rests his forehead against mine. "I can't."

"Why?" I whisper, still shivering and wanting more. My mind has no control; it's my body pushing me now.

I don't have any dignity left. I should have let it rest.

He has feelings, and he doesn't want to act upon them. It's not hard to understand.

"There's things… I can't explain." He pulls back a little, looking down at me. With tormented eyes. No. They're *guilty* eyes.

How didn't I notice before?

There's so much guilt in his eyes.

"Are you seeing someone else?" I ask, my hands digging into his shoulders for support. Maybe he's in a relationship.

Oh my god. Maybe he is.

He pulls back from me, dropping his arms. Our eyes lock again, and I see it there.

"There's another girl?"

I almost giggle embarrassingly. She's not some other girl. She is his girl. I'm the other girl who's trying to take her place! What audacity I have.

I didn't notice, but he's resting on the opposite wall. His eyes closed. Like he doesn't want to be here anymore. He doesn't want to answer or acknowledge me.

"You're in a relationship, aren't you?" I push. I need to hear him say it. I need this slap of truth so that I can put my silly infatuation with him in the grave.

I watch as he opens his eyes. He looks right into me. And I wait. I do nothing but stare back and wait.

"We're taking a break," he finally reveals coldly. He finally aims his knife where it hurt the most. He aims it at something I truly despise.

I have feelings toward another girl's man.

Oh.

My.

God.

He's in a relationship. He has a girl. A lover. God knows for how long.

I stare at him with void eyes. I'm trying to let it sink in.

I could have lived with his *break* excuse. But not when his tongue is not even used to the words. Not when his eyes are dying in front of me. They're dying for her. For what he has done to her *with me.* That's not the eyes of a man on a break. That's the eyes of a man dying to end it. Dying to have his girl back in his arms. But instead, he's got me—the other girl who's trying to take her place. Now the guilt in his eyes turns into blame. I've jeopardized his chances with her. I've made his situation more complicated than it already is. Somehow, it's my fault now.

I shift my gaze to the floor. I want to die from embarrassment alone.

What the hell have I been doing?

I was on the verge of seducing him, throwing myself at him.

He's been trying to fight it. Fight the temptation, but I was relentless. I've almost made him lose the fight for his girl—the girl he loves.

I want to let out a cry of embarrassment. My throat tightens with guilt.

Thank God. The doors open in time.

I fly out, but he's on my heels.

I don't know where the hell my purse is, but then I don't have any keys. Not Shelia's or his. So, I stand at his apartment door. Watch as he unlocks the door. He's carrying my coat and my purse with the other hand. He's in much more control than I am.

Of course!

He pushes open the door. "Grace." I know his eyes are on me. The break is over. He wants to say some mending words, I guess.

I will the hidden power in me, the one that has let me tolerate people's nosiness and stares at my scar, to lift my eyes to him.

His are a tormented storm. But I don't care. "Goodnight, Ian," I say and walk in with timid steps. I don't want to rush my way inside. I don't want him to know how humiliated I am. I don't want him to say excuses or give me any apologies he doesn't mean. I don't want him anywhere near me at the moment.

"Grace..." He calls again. "I know we shouldn't have-"

"WE!" I spin around immediately. There's nothing timid in me anymore. I'm only angry and humiliated. "There is no we." I step forward, not seeing him, not seeing anything, not feeling anything but a big void. "It's you. You shouldn't have kissed me. You have a girlfriend. YOU! You shouldn't have."

I'm hysterical before the fog leaves my eyes, and I freeze. I put a hand to my mouth. What the hell have I done?

His hair is so out of place I almost cringe. His tie undone, his shirt half-open, the hem is out at one side, and my lipstick is everywhere on his face, on his neck. Oh my god. Is there any inch I haven't kissed?

I've done this.

I was going as crazy at him as he was at me. But there's no WE. I've gone crazy over another girl's man.

But he's the one to blame. He's the one in a relationship, not me. My brain is finally functioning right. I put my guilt aside. "You shouldn't have kissed me," I repeat at his stony face and eyes.

I want to see some remorse. To be brutally honest, not for her, but for me.

He shouldn't have let me kiss another girl's man.

He shouldn't have put this guilt on my shoulders. He shouldn't have.

But he gives only a sarcastic laugh. His eyes are so cold, so void before he walks past me. And I cannot believe he's just going to walk away without acknowledging my anger.

A minute ago, he wanted to acknowledge my humiliation. He was eager to dissolve it, but not my anger. Not the fingers of accusation I'm pointing at him.

"You shouldn't..." I turn to repeat. And he stops, his shoulders tense. Then he looks at me over his shoulder, his eyes dead.

Then he finally opens his mouth to acknowledge my anger. "More than a two fucking years' break allows me to do whatever the fuck I want."

CHAPTER NINE
Ian

THREE YEARS AGO

SHE'S BEEN TEXTING me nonstop. Telling me she's okay. As if she knew I would still be in knots about her. She's my little sister, my only sister. We talk every single day, even if I just want to tell her one of my lame jokes.

I don't know how some people go through life with just a visit or a phone call to their loved ones, and maybe that only happens on a Christmas night. I try to visit my parents whenever possible, and I constantly see Emma now that she lives in the apartment next to mine, and we hang out every weekend. Family and loved ones must come first. That's the Skene motto. My father's motto.

He grew up in foster homes, so he doesn't take us for granted. And he taught us not to take our loved ones for granted.

I hand the cab driver a wad of cash. I don't care if it's more than the ride is worth. I don't have the time or the will to count. I push open the door and sprint into the hospital.

"I'm here... where are you?" My fingers are flying to text Emma as I walk through the lobby of New York hospital.

"We're on the second floor. Second room to the left. And I'm okay, really."

Who's WE...? I'm wondering as I take the stairs. I cannot handle being prisoned in the lift's small space while I don't know what happened to my sister. I cannot stay still. I need to move.

Reaching the second floor, to the left I turn. Second room, I stand at the door. "Emma." She's on the bed, resting her back on the headboard, wearing a white hospital gown, an IV attached to her arm. My eyes are going to pop out of my head. But thank God, there are no visible injuries or any cuts.

Spotting me, she points a finger. "Put your eyes right back where they belong. I'm fine." She moves her finger in a circle. "All of this is just for precaution."

Judging by her snarky mouth and the fed-up look on her face, I know now that she's fine. Relieved, I step inside to stand by her bed. Looking down at her, I narrow my eyes. "So, what's landed you here this late?"

I follow her gaze as she looks sideways, and I notice the girl standing on the other side of the bed. The first thing I catch is her pale, fragile hands. She's clasping them over her cross bag. As my eyes travel up, I'm met by a lovely size of breasts. Further up, there's a delicate pale neck, the kind I want to travel over with my mouth, kissing lightly and lingering for bites.

Fuck...What?

I mentally shake myself. What the hell? I still need to know what happened to my sister. Family comes before any lewd thoughts.

"Meet Acacia," Emma gestures with her hand.

"Acacia." I finally meet her eyes, and they're full of mystery, as is her unusual name.

"Um..." Acacia hesitates, "I guess you're Ian."

I have an instant urge to touch her. I extend my hand. "Yes, I'm Ian."

She puts her delicate fingers in mine. But my eyes still study hers. They're calm and older than her age, which I bet isn't more than twenty years.

"Nice to meet you, Ian," she says with a timid smile. I guess she's a little skittish as she tries to withdraw her hand immediately from mine. Or maybe I've got this impression because of the way she's arching her shoulders as if she's ready to bolt at any time if necessary. I don't know. Or is it her pink hair and pixie cut that doesn't go well with her decorum personality? I cannot figure her out at this moment; there are more urgent matters at hand.

Family comes first. I gaze down at Emma. "I need to know what happened to you." I glance at Acacia. "Don't get me wrong. It's lovely to meet you. But still, it's not quite the place."

"Yeah, you're right. I'll leave you to it then-"

"No," I interrupt her. "No one is leaving until I know exactly what happened."

Emma gasps in disdain, while Acacia has the most adorable 'what the hell look' on her face.

"I'm sorry, I failed to mention, my brother sometimes belongs in the Stone Age."

My eyes jump to Acacia. She has on her poker face. Like she knows better than to get involved in sibling bickering.

"Well, this caveman asked you a question." I cross my arms over my chest.

Emma huffs. "Why did I even call you?"

Yeah. Why did she? She doesn't like how protective I am toward her. She knows I will demand all the details.

I glance at Acacia, then back at Emma. "I bet she made you do it."

Emma makes a face, and Acacia shakes her head smiling.

Yeah. Acacia definitely has made her do it.

"She wouldn't leave me be till I called someone." Emma sighs, and there's a beat before she says, "I took my shot." Emma's shoulders are down as she tells me, "Then, I made the usual mistake. I didn't eat enough. So, I found myself collapsing in front of the building, and Acacia happened to be there. She called for help and accompanied me here."

I want to be pissed at Emma for not taking precautions. She could have been in a coma if it weren't for the help of this stranger.

She was diagnosed with type one diabetes last year, where insulin shots were a must. I think it's still difficult for her to change her lifestyle. She has not adjusted to her disease.

I sit next to her on the bed, take hold of her hand, pressing lightly. "It's not that I'm blaming you here. But imagine what would have happened if you were still in the apartment. Or Acacia decided to walk ahead and not care. You need to be careful."

Emma presses her thumb over the back of my hand. "I know. It's just this thing takes lots of adjustments. I really thought I had it under control then...this happens."

"It's okay. We're gonna have it under control again. We'll find a way." I'm trying to encourage her as I feel her hand trembling in mine.

She's not going to cry. I will not let her shed another tear over this disease one more time. "You're strong. It's nothing you cannot handle. You're gonna have it under control, I promise."

I step back as Acacia drops her bag onto the floor before climbing near Emma on the bed.

She throws an arm around Emma's shoulders. "It's okay, just let it all out. Cry, even if it's for the millionth time. Cry, because the more you do today, the less you will tomorrow."

Teary-eyed, Emma glances at me before shifting her body toward Acacia.

Acacia nods at her. "It's okay, just let it all out."

"I'm here for you," Acacia says, then moves to face Emma. She embraces her in a hug. "I've heard it's not the easiest thing," Acacia says as Emma muffles her cries in this stranger's chest. "So, don't pretend it's easy or manageable until it is for you."

I like that. It's not manageable or easy until it is for Emma.

"I will not pretend," Emma says with a voice full of her cries.

"It's an ugly disease," Acacia says. "Am I right?"

"Yes," Emma pulls back a little. "It's hideous." She wipes her face with the back of her hand. "Horrible, to be exact."

Acacia nods. "Yeah, tell me how horrible it is."

Emma sniffs, a shadow of a smile on her face. "Some people lose a leg or an arm because of it. Some have sight problems, and so many side effects. It makes me so damn scared. I don't want that to happen to me."

I want to shout, 'that will not happen to you, Emma. I will not let that happen to you' as I told her a hundred times. But apparently, my words haven't made Emma less scared. I stay mute, waiting for this stranger's input.

"Yeah," Acacia says, encouraging. "I've heard about this."

"And there are the needles," Emma shakes her head, eager to share. "I have to shoot myself. Every single day. There are no vacations with this disease."

"Yeah. I can imagine how horrible that would be."

I want to object. That's not the right thing to say. But as Emma genuinely smiles, I know this stranger has touched her in some way.

"But the worst part," Emma says. "The worst and cruelest part is that I don't get to eat as many chocolates and sweets as I'd love to."

"Ah… No, no, and no," Acacia fiercely objects. "Who does? I'd be a whale if I had as many chocolates as I'd love to."

Emma is all giggles right now. Though it's beautiful to see her smiling, my eyes jump down. To Acacia's ass. I think some sweets would not harm her yummy little ass. I shake my head immediately. What the hell is wrong with me?

"So, my new friend," Acacia says, "I will not let you complain about that. We're all in the same boat. I wouldn't even consider our society as well developed till they find a way that we can eat as many sweets as we want without blowing our asses out of proportion."

"No, no, no…" Emma interjects between giggles. "You're only saying this to make me feel better because big butts are in. The bigger, the better."

"But we wouldn't be getting these perfect butts," Acacia says. "They're perfected under the best of surgeons' hands while ours would be dangling from our sweatpants and wouldn't fit in any jeans."

Joining Emma, I erupt in laughter. This girl is something else.

This girl has shown me in five minutes what I've been doing wrong. Emma knows her disease. She knows the risks and the side effects. She knows every little detail about her condition, and I bet she's heard every encouraging word that there is by now. She just needs to have a laugh at it. To mock it, to demean it. And most importantly, she needs to know she still relates to other girls her age. And that chocolate speech from Acacia has done magic.

"You're coming to my birthday party. I will not accept any excuses." Emma is threatening Acacia now, and I don't know how they got down to this.

Girls!

I'm about to insist Acacia come before I catch how tense her shoulders have gotten.

"I don't like to intrude," Acacia says apologetically. "We've just met, and you may regret it later," Acacia adds teasingly, on the surface only. I feel like she's having a hard time with Emma's invitation.

"No," Emma covers her ears. "I will not listen to excuses. You're coming. How else would I test your theory?"

"What theory?" Acacia asks, digging one hand into the bed.

"You'll be eating as much cake as you like, and we'll see… Will your ass get out of proportion or become one of these perfect ones?"

Now Acacia and I are the ones erupting in laughter. And no, I don't say she'd get the perfect butt because she already has.

I jump down from the bed before my hand touches one of these delicate cheeks. Too much talk about asses, and I'm only a normal guy. Maybe not so normal. I mean, my sister is there. It should have stopped me from imagining what this girl's ass would look like bare. Feel under my touch.

Fuck… What's wrong with me?

I shake myself as I leave the room to check with Emma's doctor.

After thirty minutes, I'm in a cab again, sitting in the backseat. Acacia is on the other side while Emma is in the middle between us.

"So, why are you living in a motel?" I ask after Acacia has us given her destination.

"I just got here. Still looking for a place."

"Oh," Emma is quick to interject. "George is looking for a roommate. You would have tons of fun living with him."

"No way, not George," I find myself objecting.

"Why, what's wrong with George?" Acacia leans forward to look me sideways.

"Nothing." "He's an asshole." Emma and I say simultaneously.

"Um..." Acacia clears her throat, preventing a sibling argument. "Thanks, guys, really, but I think I'll stay at the motel for a little while. At least till I find a steady job."

I want to know why she moved here. I want to ask so many questions. I'm so eager to know everything about her, but the cab pulls over at our building. "Wait on me," I tell the cab driver before opening the back door.

I walk Emma to the front of our building. But before she goes in, she says, "Don't forget to ask for her number." She winks and turns to walk inside.

"Emma," I call, wanting to have the last word, but she just waves her hand. "Goodnight, big bro."

As I get back into the cab, Acacia is fidgeting with her hands. "You don't have to accompany me to the motel, really, just go."

I close the door. "No. I have to, I wouldn't let a pretty little thing like you get in a motel alone after midnight, and I would love to...because you're the most pretty little thing I have ever seen."

"I'm not a little thing," she protests with the cutest pout, her palms digging into the seat while a light shade of red takes over her face.

"So, just to be sure," I side-eye her playfully, "you don't mind the pretty part, just the little one."

She squints an eye at me before traveling her gaze down. To my crotch, to be exact.

"I bet you would mind the little part too," she says, fuming.

I burst out laughing. The driver bursts out laughing. And my pretty little thing is rolling her eyes while mumbling, "Guys!"

My pretty little thing.

MY PRETTY LITTLE THING.

She is not my anything. I've just met her.

I've. JUST. MET. HER!

I've just met her, and I don't give a damn. I want her to be mine. My pretty little thing. Or anything she would like to be.

"So. You still in school?" I ask as we walk into the motel. I really like her, but if she's under twenty, I'm not going there. I'm silently praying she'll give me a hint about her age. I'm hoping she's over twenty at least.

She pauses to look at me sideways. "Um... I'm done with school."

Her answer is vague. I ask bluntly now, "How old are you?"

She whirls to face me, a smirk on her face. "This is kind of weird. I mean, we've just met, and you're comfortable asking me anything."

"It wouldn't be weird if you're over twenty. Are you?" I push. I don't care if it's weird or not. I'm into this girl, and I don't want to waste a minute making her mine.

She chuckles. "Yeah. I guess it's not then."

"Good. I'm twenty-four, in case you're wondering." I lock my eyes with her for a moment, but it's getting late, and I have a heavy schedule tomorrow. "I'll walk you to your room."

As we reach her door, I extend my hand to take her key. "Let me."

She eyes me cautiously for a second, and I throw my head back before looking down at her again. "I'm just being a gentleman. I don't look for an invitation. Even if you ask me to, I won't come in."

She taps her chin. "You won't?"

"I won't," I say firmly. I want her to know this about me. I don't play games. I'm always honest from the get-go.

She's looking me up and down. "Well, I'll choose to believe this lie tonight."

I smile. "I'm not lying. Go ahead ask, and I'd say no, thank you."

"That's like a trap. You'd have all the power then." She raises her key to her lips, looking me up and down again. "But I'll tell you what, if I do invite you and you stay true to your word, you'd have no chance to ask whatever's on your mind. The thing that you're dying to ask me. But if you accepted my invitation, you'd have a chance to ask me whatever you wanna ask, but I wouldn't give you my approval."

What the hell does she mean?

A moment, then I get it. I glare down at her. "That's not fair. It's like you're cheating to prove your point."

She shrugs.

She shrugs, and that shoots an unsettling feeling down my stomach. I can tell she's interested in me but having the power to shrug it off leaves a bad taste in my mouth.

I don't know what to think, really. But I cannot fight how attracted I am to her. So, I'll do it her way this time.

I sigh. "Okay, go ahead and ask me."

She's smiles now. "Would you like to come in?"

"No, thank you," I say firmly, and I catch her eyes grow disbelieving. "But I'd love to take you to dinner tomorrow night."

She shakes her head. "Can't… And you already know that."

"Well, I'll choose to believe this lie tonight," I say, smiling. "But tomorrow, I'm coming to pick you up."

CHAPTER TEN

Grace

IT'S BEEN A week since the elevator *rampage*, which I've kept to myself. The next day, I hurried to Shelia's. I wanted to pour my heart out to her, but I found Jack in the kitchen, preparing breakfast. The "get Jack back" was faster than I thought it would be. So I couldn't talk to Shelia about my situation.

I was seriously thinking about moving back in with her. But now, Jack is here; it's not at all appropriate. I don't want to burden them with me. When it comes to Jack, she has a *rampage* of her own. She wants to have all kinds of fun, but at the same time, she wants Jack, but he only wants her. So, I guess she has enough on her hands—lots of bold decisions she needs to make.

My roomie doesn't allow visits of any kind, so it's no surprise when, for the past week, I've been dropping at Shelia's every morning or later at night.

I lean against the counter as Jack goes through the fridge. "You know, I wanna tell you something, but please don't misinterpret it the wrong way."

"No, go ahead and say it," I encourage. My mind is far away from Jack. It's back there, at my roomie's, wondering what I should do about my situation.

For the last week, I've been pondering the idea of moving out. We haven't spoken since the elevator *rampage*. I've been ignoring him. But each morning, I check the kitchen, and he does eat the dinner I make. So maybe he still thinks it's a good deal we have. A deal that I was the one pressing all the buttons to sabotage. I invited him to that party, then went hysterical on him for kissing me. But I didn't know it was two years.

Two years!

He was full of guilt, as if he's still in a relationship. He must have loved her so much, but I shouldn't be thinking about them or their relationship. He's in love with another girl. That's enough to make me stay away. I don't need this on my shoulders.

I watch Jack close the fridge before he drops near me by the counter. He turns in his seat, and I shift to face him, smiling. "So, what's that you need to tell me?"

Jack is not a conventionally handsome kind of guy. But he's got sex appeal. He has sleepy golden eyes, dark skin, a strong jawline, shaved head, and he's tall and built. Then there's the way he carries himself. It speaks of maturity and self-confidence. That's very sexy in itself.

"You live next door, but all your stuff is still here," he says, raising a hand as he senses I'm going to explain. "Shelia thinks nothing of it, but I don't know. I think you're not comfortable living with that guy. So why not move back in here? If it's me you're worried about, I don't mind at all. To be honest, I don't think me and Shelia are ready to have this living together thing. Another roommate wouldn't get in the way of anything."

"Oh..." My heart goes out to him. He has such hope and, at the same time, realism in the way he sees their relationship. "I hope you work it out this time."

He narrows his eyes at me. We're not the closest buddies, but I'm always comfortable talking to him.

"Don't deflect. We're talking about you here. So should I help you move whatever you packed there before sleepy head wakes up?"

I'm grateful for his kindness, but I don't think me living with them is fair. They need time and space.

"Yes," I say. "I do need some help, but it's the other way around. I need you to help me move the rest of my stuff there."

Jack's given me the push I needed. It's either I move in or out. I just have to wait and see where Ian stands. I feel like he wants to ignore the whole thing and move on with our good deal. He wants to forget the whole elevator *rampage*. Maybe he has already. He told me from the get-go, he doesn't spend a lot of time in the apartment. Just a place to crash and have a meal. He might have actually forgotten and wasn't ignoring me as I thought. But me, nope.

I cannot.

I may forget the hysterical aftermath, but his touch is still imprinted on my skin.

"See, you totally misunderstood my point," Jack says, frustrated.

I lean in to pat his arm. "No, I totally get you. I was just caught up in everything and haven't had time, that's all."

He gives me a doubting look, so I say cheerfully, "Now you wanna give me a hand or what?"

"Sure," he says, defeated. "But I'm here if you change your mind."

I hop off the chair, wishing Shelia would end up with Jack. He's a great guy.

After ten minutes of packing my stuff while Jack's going back and forth from Shelia's to Ian's helping me move, I spot Ian walking up the staircase on my way back to Shelia's.

Even on weekends, he goes running. He's wearing a blue hoodie over black trainer pants and black sneakers. His hair is wet.

"What the hell is going on?" Ian stops at the top of the staircase, spotting Jack holding a box of my shoes.

I slightly turn to face him. "Jack is helping me move my stuff."

Ian has this dumbfounded look on his face now.

Oh, Oh. He doesn't want me to stay. But then he steps forward, one fist at his side. "You haven't moved your stuff till now?"

He wants me to stay! Well, I'm not going to stand there and guess.

"Why? Are you backing off on our deal?" I ask.

He gives me this pissed-off look. "I don't back off on any deals that involve you."

That's sounds good and bad. I'm frowning as Jack emerges into the hall. He looks at Ian sideways, then raises an eyebrow toward me. I step forward. "Well, Jack. Meet Ian. And Ian, this is Jack."

"Ian," Jack says, a little bothered by Ian's pissed-off face, before the latter extends his hand. "Thanks for helping, but I'll take it from here."

Jack glances at me, and I nod my head. He lets go of Ian's hand and starts walking past me. "Well, I'm here if you need anything."

Now it's only Ian and me. I touch the wall behind me. I think we should address the elevator *rampage* somehow. He's kind of looking down at me cautiously as if waiting for me to start the talk. I don't blame him. I mean, after I went hysterical that night, I'd be cautious too.

"So," I start, not knowing what to say, "I shouldn't have...you know, that night. But it's just, you gave me the impression um... like you're still with her."

"Good," he quips, then gestures with his hand toward Shelia's door. "After you."

He doesn't want to talk about it. I've been sweating for nothing.

I whirl, and we both walk inside. "There's nothing left really, just a few things here and there. Nothing to bother with."

"But I'll help you get them," he says firmly.

As soon as we walk into the room, he catches my elbow, turning me to face him. "So, I assume Jack is Shelia's boyfriend." He holds a breath, waiting anxiously and baffling me.

"Yeah. He just moved in with her."

I see his features relaxing before his eyes glance around the room. "So, what's left?"

"Um...well." I turn to my left and pick up the basket where I folded my underwear before pointing to the large box at the bottom of the bed. "Can you help me with that one?"

He eyes my basket amusingly. I involuntary cover it up with my hand, a little embarrassed. I have the whole rainbow in my underwear collection, not to mention the flowery ones.

"I've seen underwear before. I hope you know that," he says, bending to pick up the box, then he walks out of the room, smirking.

I follow him out, a little pissed. He's amused and has forgotten our kiss. I hurry my steps to meet him at his apartment door. "But you haven't seen mine," I say, fuming, then walk past him, heading to my new room.

"I beg to differ," he says, standing at the door.

He drops my box to the floor, and I, too, drop my basket near the dresser. "And how could that have happened without my knowledge?"

He crosses his arms while leaning against the door. "It was with your knowledge." He draws a teasing smile over his face. "Actually, you were flaunting it in my face."

"I did not." I take a step toward him. "If you're talking about that night before the party, my panties were not showing. You made that up so you could manipulate me to change that outfit."

"And I got a better result," he says mockingly. "That little thing barely covered anything."

"Don't change the subject." I point at him. I won't let him turn this around. "You were manipulating me then like you're doing right now."

"I'm not," he says, taking a step toward me. "You know, I have had all kinds of dreams about you all week long, where I've seen you flaunting your panties, and others without underwear at all. Just bare. Bare and wet for me."

I take a step back. I don't want to hear him, yet I'm dying for him to say more. His desire is evident in his eyes. He wants me. He's not confusing me now; I'm the one confusing myself.

"Like that night. You're so wet for me, Grace." I don't know if he's moving or standing still. All I can see is the heat in his eyes. But he's moving. He's so close now and getting closer. "I jacked off all week to that touch alone. I can't imagine what would happen if I touched your pussy bare."

I refuse to imagine that. Imagine him getting lost because of me.

He loves another girl. Tormented by his loss of her, and here, I'm standing shivering and letting him dirty talk to me.

I don't know how many steps I take back or he takes forward. I'm half leaning into the dresser while he's a breath away from me.

"Well," he says, looking at me with intense hunger. His shoulders and jaw are tense, his fists at his sides as if he's fighting not to touch me. "You wanna be bare for me, Grace?"

I nod. I shouldn't have. But damn me, I whisper, "I do."

His hunger intensifies. "Then say it, Grace. I need to hear you say it."

He's not going to snatch me into his arms like before. He's letting me decide.

I close my eyes. I cannot make a wise decision while seeing him and breathing him in.

"But you're in love with another girl," I say to myself, not to him. I want to hear it again so I can haul my ass off this dresser and move away. Or he's going to throw me onto the bed behind him and have me bare.

It's worked for him. The hungry look is gone. And here comes the void. But it doesn't work for me. I'm still aching for his touch. Hungry for him to have me here and now.

He steps back with everything in him. His eyes, his arms, his breaths.

He's walking away from me.

I inhale a breath of relief and disappointment as he reaches the door. She's won again.

After two years, she still wins.

I swallow when he pauses at the door. He inhales deeply before glancing back at me. "If you need any help, just ask. I'll always have time for you. Instead of waiting for some random guy to give you his time."

"Jack is a friend. Not some random guy." I don't know why I'm arguing with him. I should be glad he's leaving the room before I throw myself at him.

"Speaking of that." He narrows his eyes. "I don't allow any guys here. Don't let me remind you of that again."

"Why are you reminding me in the first place? I'm sticking to every rule you have so far."

"He was in your room. I didn't like that one bit." He takes one step forward before pausing again. Gritting his teeth, he continues, "You," he points a finger at me. "Bed," he points there, "and a guy for whatever fucking reason is not happening under my roof. Get that in your pretty head, and we'll still have a terrific deal."

He walks out the door, leaving me agitated.

I look around. I've made Jack help me for no reason. With Ian's attitude, I don't think it's a wise idea to stay here. But I cannot move back in with Shelia; it's not fair to her. I think I need to look for another place.

I'm not going to let him boss me around. I'm not against his rules. I mean, his deal is awesome. I can hang out with my friends anywhere. Not that I have many. And it was just a step till I had a place of my own, hopefully soon. So, I don't mind his rules, but this time, it's different. It's the way he talked about it. It has become personal for him. I don't need anything personal with a guy who's deadly in love with another girl. I need to stay away from him.

I sink to the floor.

A second later, and I'm hauling myself up, excited. My phone is ringing. It's probably Mom. She calls on weekends.

I pick up my phone from the dresser, and my face falls. It's not Mom. I don't know who it is either. Maybe a new customer.

"This is Grace Edwards. How can I help you?" I answer.

"I hope I'm not interrupting your weekend," a soft voice says. "I'm Suzan Gully. I'm Mr. Skene's assistant. I'm sorry I haven't been able to reach out to you earlier. I have set up a meeting for you this Thursday at eleven-thirty... Would that fit with your schedule, if not, I'll do my best to make something work, but it would be better this Thursday."

I'm frowning. "Why did you do that?"

"Um..." Suzan pauses. "You're one of the candidates for our charity program this year."

I cover my eyes with my fingers, getting confused. "No, it's fine. I'll be there on time."

"The best of luck then." Suzan cuts the call.

I need to find a new place away from him, but that won't affect my dedication to the homeless shelter. If it's Ian or anyone else who's going to give them a hand, I'm going to accept it for the sake of these people and for Sam.

I just need to control how I react to Ian. He, in some way, is slowly dragging me out of my numbness, making me feel things. I don't mind feeling again, but it should be with the right person. Not him. He's trouble. He's even warned me from the get-go.

I need a new place soon.

CHAPTER ELEVEN
Ian

THREE YEARS AGO

I CANNOT BELIEVE I forgot to ask for her number. What if she has left the motel? I have nothing but her name. I don't even know where to start looking for her.

I rest my forehead against the door for a bit, trying to calm my nerves.

She is here and will open the door.

I knock lightly and wait.

After a beat, she opens the door. I blink to get used to her light. She's wearing a yellow dress with spaghetti straps. It reaches just above her knees. Her short pink hair is slicked back elegantly, her eyes eager, studying me.

I exhale a sigh of relief; she's nervous and has put in an effort for me. She's interested.

"You're here," she says with a shy smile, leaning into the door.

"You were expecting me, I reckon," I say, looking her up and down with confidence. Last night, she seemed a little reluctant, or she was trying to play hard to get. I don't care if she does. I'm ready to play her game, whatever she likes it to be. And that says a lot. I hate playing games!

Her shy smile grows deeper, and a shade of pink takes over her creamy complexion as she inspects me. Wearing a white dress shirt and black pants, I'm hoping she approves. "You look nice."

I smile. "And you look nice. Beautiful. Elegant."

I expect her to accuse me of exaggerating, but she doesn't. She looks at me peacefully for a moment before I give her my arm. She glances at it, then turns to lock her door.

Linking her arm through mine, we walk the hallway to the elevator. Stepping inside, she turns slightly to me. She wrinkles her nose, releasing her arm from mine. "I like your head."

I laugh. I've never heard this line before. "You're so fucking cute."

She looks down, rocking herself back and forth. Good, she is nervous.

She raises her eyes to me. "You're not."

"What?"

"You're not cute," she teases.

I laugh again. This girl is something else. "Oh, I'm a little hurt."

"Don't be," she says earnestly. "One is either cute or sexy. I would take sexy over cute any day."

"So, you think I'm sexy." I raise an eyebrow, challenging her shyness. I'm eager to break down a wall or two of hers tonight.

After a beat, she says, "Yes, you are. I'm sure you've heard it before."

The doors open, so I instantly put a hand on her back as we

walk out into the lobby. She glances at me nervously before moving her gaze ahead.

I don't want her to be nervous. I want her to be at ease. "Yes. To be honest, I've heard it a lot." I stop at the front doors of the motel, turning her slightly to me. "Last time I heard it was while a girl was kissing me and pulling hard on my hair and telling me how sexy it looked. That's why I've been shaving my head for a while now. The memory terrifies me to this day."

She bursts out laughing. She laughs and laughs like she hasn't laughed in a while. "I find it hard to believe. I don't think anything terrifies you."

I make a wounded face, and she giggles again, all the way to our cab. I lace my fingers through hers while resting our hands between us on the seat. It's a short ride to the restaurant. I don't miss her surprised face or how she reacts to my touch. She likes my touch. I don't push for more as, silently, we arrive at Caravee.

It's a five-star restaurant. I want her to know I'm putting all my effort into this. I want her to know from the get-go that I'm serious about her, and I don't know a better way than to spend money till I get to know her better. What makes her tick, and what excites her.

Out of the cab and walking to the restaurant, I'm overwhelmed again by her beauty. Her eyes are confused, looking here and there, enticing me to take her later for a tour around the city. It's like she hasn't been here long. The dazzling lights and tall buildings seem new to her admiring eyes. She looks at me sideways from time to time.

She wants to make sure I feel the same as her, and I wonder if she's smelling the city like I do. I always smell the culture, the beauty, and the chances.

She pauses, her eyes roaming around. Mine follow her in silence.

A couple passes us giggling, another arguing, a man shouting, another sprinting, teens licking ice cream, and others licking well…themselves. She rolls her eyes before she gazes up at the sky. "I think I'm gonna like it here."

I want to ask her where her home is, but I don't want to cut her peaceful moment. I've never seen anything more beautiful than the excitement pouring out from her eyes.

I smile back as she tangles her arm in mine again while heading to the restaurant.

"Can I start this date backward?" I turn her to me before we walk into the restaurant. I envelop her hands in mine, pressuring gently.

She glances at our hands for a moment before she raises her shy eyes to me. "What do you mean?"

"I mean... One can be sexy and cute at the same time." I inhale deeply, a bit nervous about how she'd react, but I cannot help how I'm attracted to her. "And you're the sexiest thing I've seen walking on earth. I cannot wait till later tonight."

I lean forward, my intent clear in my eyes. I'm hoping she'll meet me in the middle. "Acacia," I breathe, and she sighs, raising up on her toes to meet my lips.

I brush my lips lightly against hers. I cannot kiss her like I want. Then I wouldn't have any control, and I want her to enjoy our dinner first.

"It's going to be the best backward date I've ever had." I smile, nuzzling her nose.

She giggles. "I've never had one before."

"Yeah…" I'm as joyful as she is. "Let me show you how it's done, then."

"I'm looking forward to it," she says, and we walk inside the restaurant, holding hands.

It's Italian. Nothing could go wrong with Italian food. If she didn't like my company, I hope I would get some points for my food choice, I think as I pull the chair out for her. I don't know why I'm so nervous. She likes me. I'm sure of that.

I take the seat opposite her while she rests an elbow on the table and props her chin in her hand, watching me with a quiet smile on her face.

"Why are you watching me like that?"

"I'm just wondering what plans you have for me tonight."

I'm a little baffled. She was nervous earlier, but there's peace in her eyes now, like she doesn't care how this goes.

I don't want her to be okay with it. I want her to feel nervous like I'm feeling. Nervous about what we'd be doing or where we're going to end up tonight.

"Well..." I hold her gaze. "First, we'll have dinner. I'll wine and dine you. How does that sound?"

"Sounds great."

I nod while the waiter arrives. He hands us two menus. I don't miss how his face lights up looking at my date. If it weren't going to ruin the mood, I seriously would have aimed a fist at him.

I'm already nursing a streak of possessiveness toward Acacia, and tonight I have every right to. She's just drop-dead gorgeous.

Acacia's dress pushes up her breasts for everyone to see and enjoy. She has a great set of breasts. They're creamy, round, and firm. But I don't think this dress fits her shy personality. I don't know why she's chosen to wear it tonight, on a first date.

I put my jealous vibes aside, because if I let them out, it will scare her away at this point, so instead, I ask, "So what do you wanna eat? The steaks are great here."

She puts her menu down. "Aha... I'll take a steak, well done, then."

The asshole waiter comes back, pouring us wine. Again, I don't like his eyes on Acacia. Well, she's thanking him with a big smile. Maybe the poor excuse of a waiter is reading too much into it. Shouldn't these elegant places know how to pick their staff?

I hand him the menus. "Two well-done steaks, and we would like to change the service."

Acacia forms an O with her mouth, her eyes a bit amused, while the guy nods nervously before hurrying his way back.

"That was something."

"You were smiling at him."

She pouts, resting back in her chair. "I was kind, but he took it the wrong way."

I don't want to make a rift because of a random asshole. I want this night to be all about her. I want to know every little detail I can get tonight. But I cannot let my tongue move just yet. I just stare at her, dumbfounded by her effect on me. Maybe it's the way she interacted with Emma or the fact she gave a hand to a stranger while she seems new to the city. Maybe all of that or none of it. I just like her a lot. Strange, I have never been attracted to girls with pixie cuts or short hair and not pink indeed. There's something different about her.

"Why are you looking at me like that...like you're inspecting me?"

"I wonder what color your hair is. Your complexion could go with lots of colors, and I'm having a hard time deciding. It's a bit tricky." I want to know everything about her, so I'm starting with the basics.

"Well, it will eventually start to grow. The roots will tell my truth." She takes a sip of her wine, then gazes at me over the rim of her glass. "If you stick around for a while, you'll finally get your answer."

I smile with confidence. She wants to know how much I'm interested in her. I'm not the only one feeling this strong connection. "Then I guess I'll know when I know. Because I'm going to stick around for more than a while."

She glances away for a moment before putting her glass down, her fingers gripping around the edge of the table. Either she's too nervous or at unease.

I thought she'd be happy with my answer, but I don't know. I just cannot read her well. She's starting to confuse me all over again.

I reach to catch her fingers in mine. She glances at our joined hands and smiles. "So, do you have a type?"

I chuckle. She's so forward, and at the same time so shy about it.

She pulls her fingers from mine, squirming in her seat. Maybe my chuckle has made her nervous again. But I cannot help it. She's so adorable.

I take a sip of my wine. I don't think any woman would like to hear she's not the favorite type. At least for the man she's on a date with, so I opt for a safe route. "Well, I dated brunettes, blondes, and reds. But so far, nothing worked out the way I wish it to be."

"Ah…" She's a bit disappointed. "That's lots of dating."

So, it's not a safe route after all. "I'm just like any guy."

She's studying me carefully before she says, "Can you honestly say that you remember each and every one of them?"

"Oh, now." I make a wounded face. "I'm not some kind of playboy who's intent on breaking hearts. And yes, I remember each and every one of them."

She tilts her head to the side for a moment, narrowing her eyes at me. "Okay. Time to test your words, ready?"

"Sure." I have nothing to hide. I didn't lie to her or have it in me to lie to any girl.

"Now, without taking too much time to make up a story." She raises a finger. "Spill it fast and straight. Last red. Why things didn't work out with her?"

I smile; it's an easy one. "Last red happens to be the one who pulled on my hair. That's why it didn't work out."

"Shame on her." Again, the story makes her giggle. "You look great, but I'd have liked to see your hair."

"Well," I lean forward. "If you stick around for a while, you will eventually."

She blinks, aiming her gaze down. She's a bit shy, I've figured that out, but I wonder if it's only shyness or something totally different.

I want her mysterious eyes again, so I put her on the spot. "So, you said I have a nice head, and I thought I was safe for the night, but at the same time, you'd have liked to see my hair. So, do you have a type? I sense you're hard to impress."

"Oh, me..." She gives me two innocent, wounded eyes. "I'm just a simple girl, really... Anything with ten inches would be fine by me."

"Oh, fuck." She did take me off guard with this one. I burst into laughter.

I cannot believe she's just blurted that out. Everyone is looking my way. It's not the joke itself that's making me laugh so hard. It's the way she's shy and cautious, and her eyes popping out of her face after she'd said it. Like she just wanted it to make me laugh and was waiting for the outcome.

"Oh. Come on. Stop it. It's not even that funny." I know she's a bit annoyed now, but I cannot control anything. I'll wait till my laughter subsides by itself.

I cover my eyes as the waitress, a young woman, comes with our steaks. I hear Acacia thanking her before I look back at her. She has this cute fuming face. "People are still looking your way."

"It's just that you're so worried after you blurt it out." I'm trying, but I cannot.

"Ah..." She drops her face on the table for a while, where I try to control my laughter, but when she slowly gazes up at me, I burst out laughing again. I don't want to upset her, but it's her fault.

She shakes her head. "I'll be on strike till you stop."

I see her pushing her chair back, and my heart sinks. I stop laughing. I don't want her to leave, but she surprises me again, I watch as she dives under the table, then a warning, "I will not get out till you stop."

I duck my head down and take a peek at her. "Now everyone is gonna think you're giving me a blow job."

The look of horror on her face intensifies my laughs. I cannot stop laughing as she pushes herself up again.

"Oh, God. Would you please stop now?" She rests her elbows on the table, hugging her head between her hands.

"Okay... Okay." I try to get a hold of myself. I don't want to upset her, and I'm starting to. I inhale and exhale deeply for several moments till I have some control.

She carefully lifts her eyes to inspect me. She shoots me a warning look, gritting her teeth. "Don't start laughing again. I'm gonna leave if you do."

I wave a firm hand. "No laughing. Dead serious till we eat our steaks."

Picking up her fork, she stabs into her steak. "I don't think I wanna go on another date with you ever again."

It's like a punch to my stomach.

She chews on her food before a smile takes over her face. "I mean a backward date. Backward dates are off the market."

"That was mean." I glare at her, though I feel relieved, still, I cannot shake the unease settling in my gut. I cannot imagine not having her. Well, I've just met her, sure I can.

She starts to giggle. "Poor you."

I smile at her and stab my steak. I've never gone on a date filled with so much fun. This girl is something else.

She is mine. I want her to know that as I walk her back to her motel room. She pauses at the door, smiling. "I had a great time."

"I thought you didn't like our backward date."

"Mmm..." She knots her eyebrows as if in deep thought. "In hindsight, it wasn't a total disaster. Maybe I can handle another one of these."

I want to high-five myself. She wants me to ask her out on another date. I smile, putting an arm on either side of the wall, prisoning her in. "I'm planning to. Would Thursday be cool with you 'cause tomorrow I have a heavy schedule. I won't be off till late at night."

She bites into her lower lip, her eyes going back and forth before meeting my eyes again. "Thursday would be good." She clears her throat. "And would you like um...like coming inside?"

"Acacia." I smile, touching a finger to her lower lip. "Are you asking me to spend the night?"

I look down. She's fidgeting with her hands. "Yes."

I nod my head. I'm so eager to accept her invitation, but I don't think she's ready. "You know what would happen if I walked into your room?"

"Yes...maybe." She huffs a long breath. "I don't know."

I meet her forehead with a light kiss. "You would be mine, Acacia. Are you ready to be mine now?"

She lays her hands on my shoulders while her lips meet my chin. She kisses me lightly there, before raising her eyes to meet mine. "Maybe Thursday then."

I smile. She's not ready. But I don't mind. I don't want her to do anything that makes her uncomfortable.

I make sure she locks her door before I walk back to the elevator, already preparing for the best Thursday of my life.

CHAPTER TWELVE

Grace

AFTER HIS HEATED dirty talk, I haven't interacted with Ian other than him telling me I don't need to cook for the weekend. He failed to mention he wasn't going to be at the apartment. It's Thursday, and he hasn't returned yet.

I don't allow myself to wonder where he could have spent these days—none of my business. Totally none of my business.

The idea of moving out is still in my head, though not as urgent. Maybe if I had an honest talk with him, things would go more smoothly. Like he shouldn't ever talk dirty to me, ever again.

My hands are trembling as his words start to play in my head. That was hot. Too hot to let me focus on anything. I drop the flowers in my hand, pick up my tablet, and hop off the chair. I'm not in the mood to arrange my morning bouquet or anything at the moment.

He's taken over my mind.

I don't need to be thinking of him. I don't.

I walk to the back of my shop, to the supply room. I'll prepare a list of the needed items this week. I know Mabel will do it later, but I'm not in the mood to do anything else.

I step into the room. I think we need some new vases. I've seen a couple of stores online that have beautiful warm designs and reasonable prices. I make a note to order some of these.

I'm about to type the next item we need, when I hear someone entering the shop. It's still early for Mabel to arrive.

Maybe it's a customer. I would love to interact with anyone at the moment. It would take my mind off him.

Holding my tablet, I intend to walk out and meet the newcomer, but as the steps come closer, so does his scent. It's not a customer. It's his scent. It's him.

Ian.

I hug my tablet tightly.

I so want to see him, but I shouldn't feel this way.

"Grace," he calls. His steps are closer now. Maybe if I stayed here, he wouldn't find me.

"Grace," I hear him call again. Then, he's at the door. Our eyes instantly click. I gaze at him for a moment. His eyes are calm and fixated on me. I take the chance to enjoy looking at him as he's taking me in. He's wearing a hoodie and trainer pants. He's out running as usual. I pass a hand over my long maroon dress while his eyes grow intense, inflaming the heat between my thighs.

"You left early this morning." He stops his inspection, narrowing his eyes. I did leave the apartment at five-thirty but hadn't noticed when he arrived, probably late last night.

"I went to the flower market. The earlier you go, the better flowers you get."

"You should have woken me up. I would have gone with you."

"I don't need anyone to accompany me." I put my tablet down on the shelf to my left. "Besides, I didn't know you were home."

"I arrived late." He hides his hands in his hoodie pockets as he steps into the room. "I wanted to say hello, but you were sleeping peacefully."

"You checked on me. Why now?" I narrow my eyes at him. "You thought I might have some company or breaking one of your rules?"

"No," he answers me, a bit amused. He takes two more steps toward me, then pauses as if he knows how dangerously he's affecting me. "I was just checking on you. I thought you permitted me to do that."

Yeah, that was *silly me*, and it feels like it was a long time ago. I don't need more of the silly me. "So, why are you here?"

It's not that hard of a question, as it shows on his face before he's barely able to say, "I just needed to see you."

I needed to see him too. But I'm not glad about his forced admission. He doesn't sound at ease. I keep my eyes locked with his, trying to fathom how he truly feels at the moment. But I don't need to look long. "I needed to see you," he says again as if he's come to peace with his feelings.

"Why?" It's a whisper even my ears barely catch.

I don't know if he heard it, but his eyes are fighting something. In the end, he loses his fight. His eyes are warm and yearning. "I missed you."

Don't say it back.

Shut your mouth tightly.

He's in love with another girl.

Whatever you say, just don't say it back.

"I missed you too."

He closes his eyes for a second, and I know I shouldn't have said it back. He's in turmoil now about her. Maybe he just needed me to rebuff him so he could stay on solid ground for his girl.

But he's moving fast toward me as I stumble back. I don't get far as he catches me in his arms.

"Ian..." I don't know why my warning comes out as a plea. He starts kissing me. He spreads kisses on my face, my neck, everywhere. "I missed you so much, Grace."

I'm not able to say it back again. His mouth is on mine, and I helplessly stab my fingers into his shoulders. I kiss him back. I didn't realize how much I wanted to kiss him again. His mouth is not as crazy as that night. It's possessive, controlling, leading, the taste intense, not drunk with wine. It's a bit of coffee and cinnamon. I love his mouth, his taste. I cannot imagine I would ever have enough of him.

We're moving. He pushes me to some shelf. Then he's the one leaning back into the stand as he pulls me tight against him. I'm a prisoner within his arms. He's slowing our kiss as his hands slide up and down my back. I love how he's soothing me. I need soothing. I need this so much. And slowly, so slowly, he's not kissing me anymore. He's just nuzzling me while his forehead rests against mine. "I fucking missed you."

It's the third time he says it now. As if he does not believe he has missed me. As if his absence was to test how much he can stay away. To fight the temptation.

I pull back a little. I need to look into his eyes. I need to know where I stand in this. "What do you want from me, Ian?"

He gives me a soulful look as his thumbs stroke my cheeks, "I want you to be mine."

I catch his hands. I want him to stop. I cannot think straight when he's touching me. "And what do I get?"

He chuckles a little. "Me… What else do you expect?"

I try to break out of his hold, but he ensures I wouldn't as he grabs me closer to him.

"This won't work if you run away from me," he says, his eyes intense. "You have to look me in the eye, Grace."

I give him what he wants. I look him in the eye. "But you're in love with another girl, Ian."

I feel him tense. Even his hands press on me too much. He looks at a point behind me before giving me his eyes. "Are you in love with me, Grace?"

"What?" I frown a little. I'm not in love with him. "No, I'm not in love with you. Why would you even assume that?"

He nods. "Exactly. You could want someone without being in love with them. I don't know how's that an obstacle now."

I catch his hands, and reluctantly, I push them off me. I take a step back. "What do you mean?"

"We want each other. We're both accomplished adults. I think we can control this. We can make it work. Instead of having this tormented saga, we could have what we truly want. We could have each other."

"Till she's in the picture again." I'm hurt. "You would entertain yourself till she blesses you with her presence. It's a great plan I see here."

He looks at me seriously, his eyes calculating. "Are you telling me you want the whole thing? You want a real relationship? Is that what's holding you back?"

"What if I am? What if I want that?" I don't know if I want that. Not at the moment. I think I need to be on solid ground before that. But still, I need to know where he stands.

"Then I'd tell you, it's not the time for it," he says simply without batting an eyelid. "And it's not because I'm in love with another girl."

I take a moment to let it sink in. Maybe he didn't lose the fight for her. Maybe she pushed him to lose it. To lose a bit of himself.

Maybe that girl had ruined him.

He takes a step toward me, his hands cupping my face again. "Whatever happens between us, it would have nothing to do with anyone else. It'd be a circle of me and you. Of us."

"See..." He's quick to address how I'm shivering under his touch.

"You can't deny this. You can't deny us this. It doesn't need to be complicated." His face is so close, his eyes, his breaths, and I don't think I can resist him if he keeps pushing.

This is too much to fight. I want to move, to be away from him. But he's mastering this. He's trying to seduce me to do whatever he wants. He knows how much he affects me physically. I hope he doesn't start to talk dirty to me because then I'd lose it.

He takes two locks of my hair and tucks them behind my ears. "I love your hair."

I rest my hands on his chest. If my body is a prisoner to him, maybe my tongue could do the trick. "I love my hair too."

Well, that's not what I intended to say, but somehow it's worked. My hands are shaking on his chest because he's shaking with laughter.

"You're so awkward and cute. You're so fucking cute," he says, still laughing. Maybe my tongue finally does the trick. I can win against amused Ian as his hands loosen around me. But before I pull away, my ears catch something outside.

I didn't even hear Mabel coming as she's apparently talking with someone. Probably an early customer, one who knows the flowers are fresh at this time.

"I have to go." I pull back from his embrace, but not his eyes. "Mabel is here."

"Don't run away," he says, the mirth leaving his eyes. He's kind of disappointed.

I wish I could run as he claims. "I'm not running. I have a shop to take care of, and lots of things I need to focus on, and the things you do and say confuse me to the extent that I haven't spent a solid minute for the last week not thinking about you." I spread a hand. "About this thing between us. You make it sound so simple when it's a lot more complicated. At least for me. I can't forget your eyes that night. They were full of guilt. I was full of guilt. How could that be simple? How can guilt be so simple?"

He runs a hand through his hair. "It was a mistake."

"Yeah. You shouldn't have kissed-"

"No. No." He steps to grab my shoulders as if he wants to put some sense into me. "Pulling away was a mistake. I shouldn't have pulled away. I shouldn't."

"Still... I feel it in my gut. It would be a mistake." I push his hands off my shoulders. It won't work. I've already nurtured envious feelings toward his girl. I don't imagine being intimate with him would be easy while he might be thinking about her or worse; he might prefer it would be her, not me.

"Grace. Oh..."

I turn as Mabel pokes her head through the door. Her eyes are confused before they dance with joy. "Nice to see you again, Ian."

"Nice to see you again, Mabel," Ian says back.

Mabel drums her fingers on the door frame. "I didn't mean to interrupt anything. But there's a customer that insists on seeing you in person."

I bite my tongue. Mabel is going to have fun for the rest of the day. "I'll go see him then," I tell her with a scowl on my face, then turn to Ian. He's standing like he has no care in the world. I just want to kick him out in a polite way.

"I'll hang here a little," he says before I find a way to get rid of him. "I wanna catch up with Mabel. Last time I didn't get the chance to hear her stories."

I hear Mabel chuckle before I walk, fuming, out the door.

As my eyes rest on the blond head, I want to go back and scowl at Mabel even more. He's been here for like ten minutes, and she's just remembered to tell me.

"Theodore..." I run to him, throwing my arms around his neck. "I can't believe you're here."

He embraces me in a warm hug. "Yeah. I wasn't supposed to be," he says in a soft voice, and I immediately pull back, a little disturbed.

"You didn't cut your trip because of me now." I look at his light green eyes, and I see it there. He came because he's worried about me. The last time we texted, I told him I hadn't seen my therapist for six months, and he promised he'd get back as soon as he could to check on me.

"And what kind of a friend I would be if I weren't here for you?"

Though I hate that he cut his trip for me, I cannot be sullen about it now. Even if I genuinely didn't need him to do so.

"Come here." I reach to hug him again. One hand on his back, the other reaching up to his head. "You're the best friend ever. You don't need to go out of your way to prove that."

"I'm not." He pulls away, looking into my eyes. "It's been six months. I've missed it here. I'm only using you as an excuse to take a break. These places and the things I see are tough sometimes."

"I can imagine." It does show on his face. He seems tired, like he hasn't had enough sleep. "So, when did you get here?"

He puts his hands in his jeans pockets, looking away as he says, "Just got here. Right from JFK. I just wanted to see you as soon as I could."

"Oh..." I'm a little surprised. There's something off about him. "What's going on with you, Theodore?"

"Nothing." He shrugs. "Everything. I don't know."

"You didn't come here right from the airport to tell me nothing." I give him a knowing look. "I feel something is eating you up."

"Okay." He holds up two hands. "I was so worried about you. Like really worried. That's why I cut my trip short. Then here you are, thank God, vibrant and strong as ever, and now I have to face my shit here."

He waves a hand, preventing me from asking about it. "Don't. I'm too tired to deal with it now. How about we go out for a play tonight?"

"Sounds great." I'm trying to seem excited about it, but I cannot in the face of his turmoil.

He glimpses at his watch. "All right then, I'll pick you up at seven."

I cannot wait until seven to know what's wrong with him. He gives me another hug as his phone beeps with a text.

I step back while he pulls his phone out of his pocket, reading the text. "Crap, how did they know I've arrived?"

"What?"

"Duty calls," he says, shaking his head then giving me another hug. "I have to go but be ready for us at seven."

"I will." I watch him walk out of the shop, making me very worried about what kind of situation he's dealing with right now.

I smile at the irony, because if I'm not careful, I will get myself into a situation. A situation that is right behind me, I finally gather as I watch Theodore leave the shop.

I turn to 'I don't give a damn' Ian. His eyes are careless. Like he hasn't tried to persuade me into something intimate between us minutes ago.

He gives me a mere glance before walking past me.

He's upset.

I know he's upset.

He keeps silent when he's upset.

I stay motionless while I watch him walk away. He pauses at the door to look at me over his shoulder. "Don't forget about our meeting, eleven-thirty."

Yes, right. Suzan has texted me this morning, reminding me about it.

"That was interesting."

"What?" I throw a hand up in the air as I face the amused Mabel.

"Why are you doing this to yourself?"

"Doing what?" I almost snap as I go inside to pick up a large vase to start arranging the front display.

Mabel walks toward me and pulls the vase out of my hands, puts it down, then glares at me. "He's totally smitten with you-"

"He's in love with another girl," I cut Mabel short before she tries to sell him to me even more. I'm already sold. I don't need any encouragement.

"And I'm in love with your papa," Mabel says, fed up before she bends to pick up the large vase again and starts to make it to the door.

I pick up another one and walk behind her, fuming.

"I thought he was having a heart attack when you squeaked your way to Theodore," she says as we both drop our vases outside.

"I didn't squeak." I stomp my foot on the floor. I was happy to see him, that's all.

"Don't worry." Mabel waves a hand. "I told him he's just a friend. But I don't know if that was enough. He was fuming the whole time. Like he was really jealous. You know guys get very territorial about their girls."

"I'm not his girl. He has another one." I don't know why I keep repeating that to Mabel. To convince her or to put some sense into my head.

"Lord, Satan, Iron Man, or whoever is up there... Help me here." Mabel looks up at the sky, a bit irritated.

CHAPTER THIRTEEN
Ian

THREE YEARS AGO

TODAY HAS BEEN a tough day at work. But aren't they all? Since I started my own business, not a day has passed evenly. There's always one challenge after another. But these are the challenges I like. This is the kind of life I want to live. I want to be the boss of me. I don't want my life to depend on the mercy of anyone or anything. I step out of the elevator, heading to Emma's.

Our apartments are in the same building, which gives me a lot of relief. I would always have the chance to check on her. Any day, any time, especially since her diagnosis with diabetes.

Emma lives with Matt, her boyfriend. I try not to grit my teeth at the thought. Matt is a player, and I'm having a hard time with the whole thing. But for Emma, I'm trying.

I have a key in case of emergency, so I don't knock.

As soon as I walk in, Emma jumps from the couch. "Ian, you wouldn't believe what I've found."

"Give me a sec, and I'll guess." I throw myself on the couch. I'm too exhausted for Emma's enthusiasm, which will probably be about cats or some designers' sale. But no matter what she says, I always try and listen.

She looks down at me for a moment, then opens her mouth to say something. She closes it again, then shakes her head. She's not excited, as I thought her to be. She's in knots about something. Better not be Matt, because I'll fucking kill him.

I try to be calm. "Is it Matt?"

"NO...!" She makes a hissing sound, then spins around to settle on the other couch. "You went on a date with Acacia, right?"

"Yeah, last night." I'm still apprehensive.

"So, Um, did anything happen? Um..." She covers her eyes with her hand, then clears her throat. "You know..."

"You're not asking me what I think you're asking me." I cannot believe she wants to know if I had sex with Acacia. I've never talked about anything like that with her. I talk about everything else with Emma but not my sex life.

Her head down between her hands, she says, "It's just, I want you to be safe."

"Wait a minute, let me check first." I look down at my watch, then back at her. "Oh, it's not 2005; I'm not on the verge of puberty, and..." I point at her, "You're not my father."

I'm cringing that she would ask this. And I am cringing more as I remember my father having *the talk* with me.

"Are you wasted? Did that bastard give you any pills?" That's the only explanation for her out- of-nowhere inquiry.

She rolls her eyes. "Look, Jen and I were going to set up a profile for her on this dating site. And one thing led to another, you know, a couple of sites jumped at us." She pauses, studying me for a second before adding, "And one of them is an escort site."

My heart sinks. It's like I have had a hard punch to my stomach. "How's that related to Acacia and our date?" I stand. I cannot keep still. I walk around and stand behind the couch, looking down at Emma.

"Oh..." She covers her mouth with her hand. "I didn't know you feel this strong about her."

I close my eyes. I don't want to throw a tantrum at Emma. When under control again, I say, "Don't walk around it. Just tell me."

I'm praying she wouldn't tell me what I think she would.

"I found a picture of her there," Emma reveals with a bit of sadness.

"Are you sure it's her?" I'm holding on to the last bit of hope.

Emma shrugs one shoulder, extending her phone. "You can see it for yourself."

With reluctant steps, I walk around the couch. I take Emma's phone and pray she's wrong. After all, she's only seen Acacia once. Maybe it's a girl who looks like her.

I take a long look, and it's like a hard slap to my face. It's her. Acacia. She's looking into the camera with a bit of innocence and shyness. Or is it only an act? To get more hits. More money. I bet her inbox is filled with all kinds of perverts.

"She seems like a good girl." I hear Emma talking, but my eyes stay glued to the screen. She's wearing that yellow dress, the one she wore on our date.

I want to punch something so hard.

"You know, we should talk to her. If it's about money, we could help her get a job. She said she was looking for one."

I look at Emma, who's running a hand across my back. She feels how angry I have become.

"She might be dealing with the wrong people."

"You're right," I agree with Emma. I put my anger aside. I've only known her for hours. I have no right to be this angry with her.

"Yeah..." Emma keeps a hand sliding up and down my back. I'm still pissed. Even in this short amount of time, I've grown strong feelings for Acacia. I have to act. To do something.

I hand Emma her phone. "I have to go."

"Oh, no..." Emma warns. "Just let me change, and we'll go together."

"No," I say firmly. "Just text me this website, and I'll deal with it. I think it'll be embarrassing for her to know that we all found out about it."

I head out. I don't listen to Emma telling me to think about it for a minute. I don't think at all. I don't know when and how I've developed this streak of possessiveness and protectiveness for this girl. I'm going crazy at the thought she might be dealing with these scums who visit that site. She cannot be. There's some explanation.

After the longest ten minutes of my life, I arrive at the motel. At her door, I knock, terrified that she would be with one of these perverts.

Fuck.

I knock again. Harder.

"Coming..."

Finally, I hear her soft voice, and some relief washes over me.

The door pulls open. "Ian." She smiles and opens the door wider. She looks me up and down with giddiness, like she cannot believe I'm here. My eyes cannot help it. I'm eating her up and down too. She's wearing short shorts and a white tank top.

I'm speechless for a moment, so is she. But while I'm terribly upset, she's looking at me with dreamy eyes. "Come in." She steps aside, and I walk in.

I close the door and rest my back against it. I don't know how to start this. She seems so innocent and pure for this kind of thing. But that's what attracts the perverts, or maybe she's just good at the act.

"I can't believe you're here-"

"I need to ask you about something," I cut her off.

Her eyes become wary; she nods.

I step away from the door and reach for her hand. I lead her to the bed, where we sit next to each other. Her hand is still in mine while I dig the other into the mattress. My throat tightens with the idea that one of these perverts had already visited her bed.

I give her hand a gentle squeeze and ask, "When did you get to the city?"

"Um..." She has a calculating look on her face before she answers me, "About two weeks ago. Why are you asking?"

I glance at our joined hands, then at her eyes. I need to study her eyes. "I saw your picture. On that website."

I feel her hand tense in mine, and her eyes grow a little terrified. "What are you talking about?"

I pull my phone out of my pants pocket. I don't want to give her time to make up a story. I click on the site Emma has sent me. "Here." I flip the phone to her.

"Um... Yeah, that's my picture." I notice how her fingers are digging into the mattress. She's cooking up a lie in her head. "But I don't know how it got there."

She looks me in the eye now, a bit calmer, a bit more confident.

"Yeah, I'm wondering too." I try to sound sincere, playing it her way. "Do you have any idea?"

She shrugs. "Maybe someone copied it from my Facebook account or something like that and then posted it there. I don't know."

"Listen, Acacia," I say, trying for a calm voice. "If you've got yourself into trouble, I could help you. So please…just be honest with me. You don't know how dangerous it is dealing with this kind of stuff. You could get killed."

She shakes her head and pulls her hand from mine. "I can't believe you think I could be one of these girls."

I don't…but you're lying.

The way her hand tensed in mine gave her away. Now she's in more control, I guess.

Accusing her won't work or make her open up to me. I try anew, "I hope you know you can trust me with anything. I'm not gonna judge you, Acacia. We all have our ups and downs, and as much as I love it here, the city can sometimes be cruel to us, make us do things we couldn't imagine ourselves doing."

She sighs, irritated. "I told you. I'm not that kind of girl. I would rather die from hunger than imagine myself doing any of these things."

"But it's your picture." I stand, looking down at her. "Fuck. I feel like you're not telling me the whole truth."

"The whole truth," she says in a bitter tone. "I have just met you. I hope you understand that. I've known you like what…a couple of hours. So, what whole truth are you asking from me, because I don't think I owe you any."

"Then you owe yourself," I say calmly. "You have lots of things going on for you. I don't know why you're not even considering my help. If you need a job, I could help you get one. You don't have to sell yourself, Acacia. You're better than that."

"Oh, God." She puts her head between her hands. "Just stop."

"I can't," I almost yell. I can't let her do that to herself. I can't. "I can't stay still, knowing I could help you. You just have to let me. You don't know where most of these girls end up."

"I don't," she says calmly. "And I'll never know. Because I'm never gonna be one of them, and if you don't believe me-"

"It's not about that," I interrupt, taking a step toward her.

"No," she cuts me off completely, edging away from me. "Let me tell you this little detail about me. Something you might have ended up knowing by tomorrow night."

I know she's trying to find a way out or to save face, but I'll give her the benefit of the doubt. "Know what?"

"I'm..." She touches the base of her throat, looks down at her feet before locking her eyes with mine. "I'm...I'm a virgin. I've never done anything sexual with anyone or even close to what these girls offer. So, I don't know how the hell you'd think of me like that."

I'm speechless for a moment. She's turning all kinds of red, and I'm still speechless. She's a virgin, and I know she's not lying. Her eyes glance everywhere around the room, waiting for me to speak, but I'm speechless. Not because she's a virgin, but what she said right before that.

I was going to find out tomorrow. I was going to be her first lover. I've ruined everything because of a picture.

But she did lie about how it got there. She knows, and she's not going to tell me.

"You're a virgin." That's all I can utter at the moment. I don't know how to fix this.

"Yes," she says, a bit disappointed. "I'm a virgin, and you need to leave now."

"Why?" I'm stalling for some time. "You've just told me this big revelation. I think we need to talk about it."

"Talk about what?" She's fuming. I need to find a way to fix this. I need to think of something.

"I want you to move in with me," I blurt.

Yep, right. That's going to fix things smoothly.

She looks at me like I'm out of my mind. But I'm not. That picture is there for a reason. And until I shake the doubt out of me, that she's not the one who put it there, I need to protect her, even from herself. That won't happen till she's under my eyes.

I look her in the eyes but don't move. I don't want to affect her physically. Or for her to feel I'm going to intimidate her. So, I keep my distance. "I live in a two-bedroom apartment. I had a roommate, but I didn't need anyone to help me pay the rent. So, two months ago, I finally had the place to myself. There's a spare bedroom, and I'm sure a little thing like you wouldn't get in the way, so why don't you leave this fucked-up hole and move in with me."

She covers her face with her hands, then uncovers it again. She looks at me for a second, then turns around till she's at the door, turning again to look back at me. "You're still here, and you're real, right?"

I chuckle. "I know how that sounded-"

"Unreal, not normal, um.... Too much. Too fast."

I raise two defensive hands. I need a chance to explain, but still, I stay in my spot, giving her the space she needs. "Yes, that's true. But I've never felt this strong about any girl as I do about you."

"Ah..." She looks up, shaking her head. "That's so lovely and so scary at the same time. I want to believe this, and I'm so scared to believe it."

"Don't you feel the same about me?"

She nods, smiling shyly at me.

"Then, we should follow what we feel. Not what we're supposed to be and how we're supposed to act. You need a place to stay, and I have one. If I'm not going to help you, then who's supposed to?"

"But I'd be taking advantage of you. That's not healthy for any relationship."

"Well," I say, knowing the next words would be hard for me. "We will take things slowly. Till you get a job, a place of your own. Consider me a friend till you're comfortable for us to be something else."

"Just like that?" she says, a bit apprehensive. "You're going to offer me this without anything in return?"

I curl a fist at my side. Thinking about that escort site and yes, there's still doubt in me about her intentions. "Yes, Acacia. When people help each other, they don't expect something back. That's what normal people do."

She wraps her arms around herself. "Yeah...but still, it's too good to be true."

"Some people have that, Acacia. Some people are blessed with a good truth," I say, "You know what, you could take any precautions you want."

She nods.

"Okay." I'm willing to accept anything just to get her under my eye where I could protect her. Now knowing she's also a virgin, God... I don't need to think about how innocent she might be.

"I do feel the same about you, but that doesn't allow me to act impulsively as you do. You know I've heard enough of these stories where the good guy turns out to be a Ted Bundy. "

"Ted Bundy, seriously?" I repeat, acting repulsed, but deep inside, I'm happy she's taking her precautions with me because it means she'd take them with everyone else.

"Yeah." She sighs. "Girl finds his truth, girl wants an out, but Ted Bundy knows everything about her. He stalks her, doesn't leave her alone, till he ends her life."

"Wise thinking, but I'm not gonna lie; I'm a little hurt."

"I'm sorry." She smiles shyly. "A girl has to be cautious."

"So, I'm listening. What are your precautions?"

She flinches. "I was just saying… I'm not gonna actually move in with you. I'm totally not."

"I'm sorry," I say, smiling. "I'm not gonna believe this lie tonight."

"I'm not moving in with you," she almost yells.

"You're moving in with me, so let me hear your terms."

"I'll pay the rent. That's if I move in with you."

"You're not going to pay any rent. And you're moving in with me."

She rolls her eyes, then points a finger. "That's a sign of a Ted Bundy."

"Take your precautions then. What do you want me to do to prove I'm not this horrible guy?"

She gazes at her feet for a moment. She looks back at me now. "You're serious?"

"Dead fucking serious," I say firmly. "I want to help you, Acacia. You're going to be my girl, and I'd move hell and earth for my girl. I would not be the man my father raised me to be if I let you stay at this fucked-up hole while I have a two-bedroom apartment."

"Okay…" she barely whispers. She's kind of dumbfounded. I've talked to her from my heart, and I hope she can trust me now.

"With you, I feel things I have never felt about anyone before, but..."

"The precautions." I raise a finger. "I'm ready to hear all about them. I'm so glad you have them, actually."

She smiles. "Well, I don't want you to ask me any personal questions where you could know things about me. Like about my family, my home. Anything of that sort. Till I feel comfortable telling you…you know the Ted Bundy theory. This way, you wouldn't be able to track me down if you turn out to be the bad guy."

"Sounds sane to me," I say, knowing it'd be a short time before I make her trust me, and then I'll know everything I need to know about her.

"Do we have a deal now?"

She smiles. "When am I moving out of this fucked-up hole?"

Right away.

CHAPTER FOURTEEN

Grace

IT'S ALMOST ELEVEN, and I'm already dreading the meeting with Ian. I don't know if it's a wise idea to open another path with him. But I'm trying to think of the big picture, of the homeless people. If he did accept my proposal, there would be a good chance for these people to have some kind of dignity till they can afford to have a place of their own.

"Hey, sugar," Mabel approaches me while I rest my elbows on the design table, zero ideas in my head. I'm just staring at a couple of purple lilies and pink roses, wondering if I would be making a big mistake today.

"There's a car waiting for you outside," she says as I eye the man she was talking to, who's standing at the door.

I know this guy. It's Rick, Ian's driver.

I think the decision has been made, not by me.

I stand, picking up my tablet, then walk around the table till I'm before Mabel. "I have to go." "Be careful. He's sending the big guns now." She wriggles her eyebrows at me.

I roll my eyes, and she leans in to give me a peck on the cheek. "Just for good luck, though I don't think you need it. Your man is already smitten."

I wish. He is not my man, and he's smitten with another girl.

Me, he just doesn't want us to live in this *tormented saga* and loves to talk dirty to me. I shouldn't be thinking about his dirty talk. I shouldn't ever.

At the door, I pick up my coat and smile at Ian's driver. "How are you, Rick?"

"I'm fine, thanks, Miss Edwards." He smiles back at me then looks down at his watch. "Mr. Skene is expecting you in half an hour, so we must get going."

I nod, slumping my shoulders, then walk outside to head to Mr. Skene's office. I try to refer to him officially in my head, to put a little distance between us, but it doesn't help as much I thought it would.

Mr. Skene.

This is already putting things in my head. Twisted, dirty things. I should have listened to Shelia a long time ago. I should have gotten laid.

I'm heading toward a disaster, I think.

Here I am, riding in this fancy elevator. Heading to meet not Ian's staff as I thought I would, but Ian himself.

When Rick pulled up to this huge building, I thought Ian's company would occupy only one of its multiple floors. But no, Ian owns this building.

Rick confirmed that as he accompanied me on this fast elevator ride. As the doors open, Rick gives me the second gesture of his hand today, and I step out of the elevator. He, ever the gentleman, walks behind.

It's huge. His office is huge. And there he is, bent over a large desk, writing something with a phone pressed to his ear. There's no reception, no assistant desk. I just stepped into Ian's office. I glance at Rick, who's standing with his hands behind his back, as if waiting, like my state.

So now what? I glance back at Ian, who's still bent over the desk, but his eyes are on me. He puts a hand over his phone before shifting his eyes to my left, "Thanks, Rick."

I feel Rick turn to walk back into the private elevator.

Yep. I've lost my friendly companion while Ian motions for me to come in.

With calm steps, I walk inside this large space. I knew Ian had a big business, but I didn't expect it to be this big. I'm impressed. He's like what...? I'm sure he's still in his twenties!

I wait near the large windows. From up here, I get a marvelous view of the city, reminding me why I love it here. Everything seems so small in comparison.

I press my fingers against the glass while I feel a presence behind me. For a moment, I hold a breath, afraid there would be tiny red drops, but it's not the case. Ian is right behind me, and I inhale deeply. I don't think I'm ready to meet the lion in his lair. It's kind of nerve-racking actually. I don't know why, though. Maybe I'll be meeting a different Ian, and I'm not prepared.

"Thanks for coming," he says in such a practical tone, and I guess it's time I become professional and turn to face him.

"No, thanks for offering me this opportunity." There, I hope that's professional enough, but when I gaze up at him, there's nothing professional in his eyes.

He's still pissed. Making me pissed too.

"I thought I'd meet up with your staff first. You said you'd treat me like the others. But I don't think the others get to ride with your driver, nor do they walk right into your office," I throw his lie at his face. If he's going to be pissed at me, let me give him a valid reason to be.

He raises a careless shoulder. "It's not my fault you chose to believe that lie."

I bite my lower lip. I want to control how pissed I have become. He's back to blaming me. Like I'm the one who pushed him to be attracted to me. To make his situation with his girl more complicated than it is.

And remembering his situation....her, I become more and more pissed. I shouldn't care for a guy whose heart would never be mine.

"And do you want me to believe you will not try to harm yourself again?"

I snap my eyes to his. What the hell is he talking about now?

He brings a finger to touch my lower lip, pressing, just a light touch before he holds it up to me, tainted with my blood.

I bit my lip till it bled. That doesn't mean I would try to harm myself. I don't like that he keeps doubting me.

I raise my left arm, then flip it over. "I'm more than this," I say, totally pissed at him. "I know people will always judge me and make assumptions about what kind of person I am. But I don't expect that from you."

He glances to the side. He's become really tense. He's running away from my eyes. He's afraid I might catch any emotions as he asks, "And why is that?"

"It's very simple…" I pause, silently asking him to look back at me. I want him to look me in the eye when I confess.

A beat, then he gives me his eyes.

It's a pivotal moment for me. It's the moment that would let me measure his true intentions. So, I hold his gaze. I don't want to miss anything. "You could ask, and I'd try to tell you. I've already tried to tell you once. You'd understand, and then you'd never doubt me again."

I let a moment pass. I want my words to sink into his soul. Maybe then he'd think twice before trying to drag me into his mess. I already have a ton of my own.

"If you want to talk, then you should give a call to your therapist."

His calm, distant words stab my heart. He doesn't want to get too involved with me. He doesn't want to know because then he would care.

He could want me. He could kiss the hell out of me. He could easily play me with his dirty words and heated stares. But he couldn't emotionally betray her. She's still imprinted in his soul.

"Glad you brought it up… I had every intention to call her," I say blankly. I was looking for a clue where to go from here, and I should be grateful he's honest with me.

"Let me help you out of this coat," he says evenly. He's not pissed at me, he's not staring at me, he's not anything at me. Whatever he suggested us to be is dying in his eyes. He knows I would, at some point, want more, and he wouldn't be able to give it to me.

After helping me out of my coat, he leads us to the large glass table. That's probably where he usually meets with his staff.

Seated to his left, I try to shrug off whatever happened between us and focus on why I am here. I lay my tablet on the table, ready to show my case. I've already contacted many organizations, and I have a clue or two how to present the homeless people at the city shelter.

I swipe my tablet open, but he waves his hand. "I don't need a full presentation. Unlike what you accused me of a minute ago, at this stage, I only require knowing three basic points."

I entwine my hands together across the table. "That makes me relieved," I say, though I doubt it. Maybe he's done it because he's back to his *don't care* attitude. He wants to prove something to himself, I guess.

He opens a notebook across from him and holds a pen. "So..." he looks at me, his eyes holding a practical approach, "In three words, can you give me a summary about your cause that would entice me to promote it for our annual donation this year?"

In three words. I try to think fast, but it's hard when my traitorous eyes are dying in front of his rolled-up sleeves. That's too sexy. Ian, in his office, is sexy as hell. Mr. Skene is too damn sexy. Too damn unapproachable, I have to remember that.

Maybe emotionally, but physically, I'm allowed to admire. Or perhaps he's right; I like to harm myself. Emotionally, at least I can admit now.

He's tapping his pen on the table. The slight noise wakes me up to my situation.

Three words.

Ugh.

"A flowery safe haven."

"I like that." He draws something in his notebook before shifting his practical eyes back to me. "But for whom?"

Wow, I didn't expect him to come back this fast. They're really cut-to-the-point inquiries. Well, of course, he doesn't have time. He has a big business to run.

"For homeless people," I say, starting to get nervous. I've taken this lightly, but it's an actual opportunity I'm having right now. "I know there are houses for the homeless around the city. But what they always lack is warmth—the feeling of being welcomed. And most importantly, of being safe. Tons of shit could happen there, especially to women and children. We just need enough resources to make that happen. Hire more people to help and renew these houses into a more welcoming home till they can afford to be on their own."

I'm a bit in awe as I look back at him. He's smiling, a tender smile. Like one a father gives to his daughter. "What if they like it there? It sounds too pretty for one to leave. Especially someone who doesn't have another place to go."

"That's the point. To feel they're welcomed and loved. And they can stay as long as they want. This positive energy would eventually lead them to pick themselves up and do something about their situation."

The tender smile is still on his face as he closes the notebook. He drags a laptop from across the table and presses a key to turn it on. "Would you please give me the file with all the details? I'll study it later."

I immediately hand him the tablet. "It's under the name The Flowery House."

As he takes the tablet, our eyes meet. "You're too sweet for this world, Grace."

Is that a no to my ideas? I don't ask. I stay mute till he hands me back my tablet.

Well, I guess this meeting is over. I push my chair back to stand, and he does the same.

Looking down at me, he says, "You'll get a response if it's accepted."

I nod, a polite smile on my face. "Thanks again."

I turn to leave, but he catches my elbow, pointing to the private elevator, "This way."

I eye his hand, then look back at him. "I'll leave the formal way," I say, then head toward his office door, where I'm sure there's an assistant desk on the other side. I walk ahead, not caring about his pissed eyes. He's back to being pissed.

If he allows himself to be pissed at me, then he'll give me the illusion he cares. But he doesn't want to care. So, I don't care that he's pissed.

As I'm about to grab the doorknob, he takes my hand in his. I pause while he presses his thumb into my palm.

I won't turn around.

I cannot. I cannot let him see how his touch affects me. I cannot let him play me like this. He only wants something physical, and, apparently, he's adamant to use my weakness toward him to get what he wants.

"You still seeing him tonight?"

I don't know what baffles me more: his so wary tone or what the hell he's asking about. And damn him, he makes me turn. I look at his unfathomable eyes. There's this look of fret in them.

"That guy... Theodore," he says, fed up. "Are you seeing him tonight?"

"Oh." I frown. Is he jealous, as Mabel has been telling me? For a moment, I'm tempted to piss him off even more, but I'm not that kind of person. Besides, I love Theodore, and I don't want anyone to hold any sort of hostility toward him, like what I'm reading in Ian's eyes. So, I calmly say, "Yes. He'll get us tickets to a play. I don't need to tell you again, Theodore is a dear friend of mine. Just a friend."

He glances to the side, exhaling a breath, his hand tightly pressing on mine. "Why are you doing this?"

I have his eyes. They're more pissed than I have ever seen them. What the hell?

"I need to get going," I say, not feeling enough energy to put him in his place.

"To prep yourself for him?"

Calm down, Grace. Just calm the heck down.

"I have a shop to run if you don't know. A meal I need to prepare when I get back to the apartment. So, I have plenty to do instead of standing in this meaningless situation."

"You're going out with another guy." His tone is louder now, his eyes flaming with anger, and his jaw clenched, but still, his hand is kind of protective around mine.

I shake my head. "I told you, Theodore is just a friend. Besides, you don't have any right in this, even if I'm seeing another guy on more than friendly terms. We're nothing, Ian. You don't even have the slightest interest for us to be anything."

"Friend, my ass." He lets go of my hand, gritting his teeth. "He just came from the airport right into your arms. That's not what a friend would do."

"I'm sure he needs me in some way. Sometimes a friend is more understanding than anyone else." I don't know why I'm explaining, but I don't like seeing Ian this agonized about anything even if he has no right to.

He takes two steps back, nothing in his eyes. He looks at the floor for a second before he gives me his careless eyes. "You know what, maybe that's what I need. I don't know what I was thinking."

I take a moment to let this sink in. He was pursuing me into something he didn't even know whether or not he's ready for.

But I'm standing still. I want to go and reach out to him. I know him well now. He's using the *don't care* shield to protect himself. I'm aching to step forward and take him in my arms to soothe all the worries out of him.

I know it's not only physical attraction, at least for me. I do care about him. I care about him a lot, and I cannot stand seeing him tormented.

A phone rings somewhere, and he turns away from me.

I turn and open the door.

There's a quiet surprise on the petite blonde's face sitting behind the very occupied desk. I knew there was one.

She stands, "May I help you with something?"

I bet I look lost, so that's why she's asked. I smile at her as my eyes catch the lovely vase on the edge of her desk. "Nice flowers."

She shifts her gaze there. "Well, Mr. Skene has them delivered here every day from a nearby shop. He's the best boss ever."

It's not a nearby shop. It's my shop. I know my flowers.

Yeah. Like I needed to know that. Another thing to make him irresistible.

CHAPTER FIFTEEN
Grace

I EXPECT THEODORE ANY minute as I walk into Shelia's. He doesn't know I moved into Ian's apartment, so he'll be knocking here.

Crossing the living room, I wave at Jack, who's sitting near a guy friend watching some game. I walk around calling for Shelia.

"I'm in the kitchen!" she shouts, and I head there.

I cannot believe my eyes as I witness this one-time rarity. Shelia, wearing tiny shorts and a tiny tank top, bent over the oven, pulling out a tray of cookies.

"You didn't make these!"

Shelia doesn't cook anything, doesn't mix anything, and definitely has no idea how to make cookies.

I slump on one of the kitchen chairs, resting an elbow on the counter. Shelia turns, holding the tray, and walks ahead to set it on the counter.

"I didn't," she says out of breath as she takes off her oven mitts.

"Jack made them and asked me to keep an eye on them while he watches the game."

"I did as he asked." She raises a frustrating hand, then drops it back to her side. "I did, because this man makes me do things I can't imagine myself doing. Or even wanting to. All I want is to please him."

I thought I'd come here to pour out my frustration with Ian to my bestie. I clasp my hands over my knees. Maybe I'll talk about it with Theodore. Now I have to know what's going on with Shelia. "I thought that's what you want. You want it to work out this time."

"Yeah," she says, defeated, while taking the chair next to me. "But I wish I could have some control over how I feel about him. Like…not doing things I don't like to do."

"Well, you love him. I think that's expected when you love someone. You can't really be completely true to yourself. From time to time, you'd do something just to please the other even if your heart isn't in it."

I talk from experience. I just think of all the shopping trips Shelia's made me take, just because she's my bestie, and I don't want to upset her.

"It's not just love." Shelia's eyes are intense, like she's figuring something out right at this moment. "It's an addiction. I'm addicted to him."

"You're addicted to him." I measure the words in my mouth to figure out why a shiver ran down my spine as soon as I heard them.

"I can't call it just love," she says, still figuring out something aloud with me. "I mean, I met some guys who I liked and cared about, but nothing is even close to the way I feel about Jack."

I smile. "Well, maybe because he's the one for you. Your soul mate."

Shelia chuckles. "Does anyone believe that shit anymore?"

I don't know why her cynical approach makes me wary. She's talking about herself. I have nothing to do with this. I still value normal stuff. Like I'd never agree to what Ian has offered me. I want the whole thing.

"You know, when we broke up, I knew I'd feel a little hurt. I'd cry for a couple of nights," she continues, unaware of how wary I've become. "But then I knew I'd be over it. And I was. I was having fun, doing this and that. Making money, making my dreams come true. Making my wildest fantasies come alive, but there was always something missing, and that scares the shit out of me."

I think I'm witnessing a rare moment of honesty. I cross my arms, listening.

Shelia has this mischievous smile on her face. "I fucked a married man, fucked two men at the same time, and had a blast doing that. They were so erotic, so out of reach, but riding that bastard's cock is way more thrilling than all of that."

"God." I'm cringing all over. "Could you be more subtle about it?"

Now Shelia is the one cringing in some sort. "God, you're such a prude."

"Dump me then," I stick out my tongue at her.

"Trust me, I've tried," she teases. "But you're like a lost little kitten who I need to put on the right path."

"I think you're in denial here. You're the one who was lost a minute ago," I say, knowing she needs to talk more about it.

"Yeah…" She sighs, then inhales deeply and has that serious face again. "They all say…what matters is how he makes you feel. But nah…it's not all about that. It's the way you make him feel. It's the way he responds to you."

I would never make Ian feel the same way he feels about his girl. Thanks, Shelia, I have to remember that.

"It has to be mutual." I shrug one shoulder. "It's common sense."

"No, it's not." Shelia licks her lips while picking up a cookie then hands it to me. "I have had five orgasms in one night, and Jack wasn't the man behind it. But I did make him come five times one night."

"TMI." I pick a little at her cookie, not knowing where she's heading with that.

"No. It's a necessity to let you know. I make him feel better than he makes me feel sometimes. But the joy I get from the way he feels is way better than those five orgasms in one night."

"Okay…" I'm really curious right now. "Did you make him come five times in a night? Or are you exaggerating?"

Shelia has this smug smile on her face. "The night of our reunion."

"So," I giggle, "what could go wrong?"

"We become selfish," she says bitterly. "I want him to be a little wild, and he wants me…" She waves a hand around the kitchen. "To cook stuff, I guess."

I know what that implication means. "So why are you going through it again, Shelia? Why are you doing this to yourself and him?"

"Have you been listening?" She eyes me firmly. "It's the addiction."

Addiction makes us reach out to things that would only harm us. I need to remember that. I don't need to hurt myself as Shelia is doing. I don't need to start anything with Ian, no matter how tempted I am. Because just one taste, that's all it takes to become addicted.

Hours later, after leaving the theater, I know my friend is still in knots about something. The stolen innocence and the outstanding performances of the actors haven't eased his turmoil.

"I always prefer the book, as you know by now," I say as we step onto the sidewalk. "Still, the show was great. The actors were phenomenal."

I did like it. It was amazing seeing *To Kill a Mockingbird* live. I want to talk in detail about it as we usually do after watching a play, but Theodore isn't here with me. Like, he didn't sit with me through the whole thing.

"Yeah...definitely the book." He's finally back on earth with me. He smiles, adding, "Nothing could top the original feel, the first glimpse, the driving thrill of expecting things while they wouldn't turn out the way we wish them to be. Seeing it alive is kind of fun and entertaining, but not as thrilling as the complete ignorance of what would happen."

I stop in my tracks as he stops, turning to me. I'm taken aback by the look on his face. He's sad. "What's wrong, Theodore?"

He shakes his head, looks at me for a moment before revealing, "I didn't see that coming. I didn't even have a clue. And I don't know what I'm supposed to do. I was hindering coming here, scared to face it, but then you texted me about your therapist... I had to come and check on you. But now I have to face her. I have to give myself and her some kind of closure. She wants to see me. She's texting nonstop. She's been going crazy for the past two months. I don't know what I can offer her at the moment."

Yeah. That's Theodore; he keeps it together, then bam, one minute, he lets it all out.

"You're talking about Sadie?" I ask. Because nothing is making sense to me. Theodore loves his girlfriend deeply, so I don't understand what he means.

"Even her name sounds so different now." He looks at his feet, away from my eyes. "So distant. Like I've never known her when, in reality, I know all her bits and pieces."

I don't think talking here, on the sidewalk, is appropriate for how devastated Theodore sounds. I reach to touch his arm, suggesting, "Why don't we go somewhere and talk about it."

"Let's go to Malika," he looks back at me. "I wanna eat something."

Malika is a Lebanese restaurant that serves these mouth-watering shawarmas, and after our ten-minute walk, we're seated at a table near the window.

We order our favorite rolls, then as the waiter walks away, I'm a little apprehensive about asking, "So what happened exactly?"

Theodore looks out the window. "She slept with her manager."

"Oh, shit." I didn't see that coming. Sadie is an aspiring actress, and her relationship with her manager had been causing quite a rift between her and Theodore, as he had told me.

"She said—she regretted it immediately." He cocks his head to look at me with a bitter smile before looking back out the window. "As if that would make me feel better."

"I'm so sorry, Theodore." That's all I can say. "I'm so sorry."

I'm kind of lost for words. I have never warmed up to Sadie or thought she was the one for Theodore. And to be honest, I thought Theodore was just infatuated with her big persona. That doesn't mean she's a bad person. She's just not suitable for him.

Our shawarmas arrive, and I don't think either of us has an appetite, but I say, "That looks great."

"Yeah," he agrees without any hint of enthusiasm. Very understandable.

I feel like he needs to talk about his situation, so I interfere, "So are you going to meet up with her and talk?"

Looking at his roll, he gives it a thought. "I don't know. I mean... what for? She's going to beg me to forgive her, and I don't want to see her like that. Maybe if she realizes that we're over, then I might meet up with her and talk."

"But you're thinking about seeing her."

"I was," he admits. "But I don't think I'd go through with it. Now enough about me." He gives me a genuine smile. "Grace Edwards, I have never seen you so alive before."

"I wish I could say the same about you. You look tired and miserable."

Laughing, he picks up his roll. "You're the worst friend ever. You're supposed to make me feel a little better after I told you all about my shit. But then you're so awkward, you make me laugh, and that's what I need."

"Yeah, well...shit happens." I pick up my roll and take a bite. "Shit happens, and that doesn't mean we should lie to each other when it happens. Friends don't lie to each other. We say it like it is. Awkward or not."

"Hmm..." He chews on his food for a while. "So how is it then? With Sadie and me? What do you think?"

I put down my roll and look at him soulfully. "Sadie was never right for you."

"What do you think I should do?" he asks, and I sense some kind of relief settles in his eyes.

I think for a moment. "You know, I'm no expert on this, but I'll quote what Shelia would say... When you're down, bring one to lift you, to make your wildest fantasies come true."

"My wildest fantasy is kind of embarrassing." He shakes his head, smiling.

"Wild and embarrassing...hmm. That's an interesting combination."

He rolls his eyes at me. "That's because my wildest fantasy is to have a one-night stand with a complete stranger."

"That's not embarrassing-"

"You are *the prude,* Grace Edwards," he cuts me short. "So, it's a normal thing if you don't consider it embarrassing as *a wildest fantasy.* But I'm a guy who never had a one-night stand with a stranger, so it's kind of embarrassing for this to be my wildest fantasy."

I'm trying to wrap my mind around it as he shakes his head. "You'll never get it, so what's going on with you? Who's the guy that kept glaring at me back at your shop?"

"Ian?" I take a moment before I add, "I moved in with him recently. There's something going on between us, I won't deny it, but I don't know how to label it."

"And I thought you were the wise one." There's a joyful expression on Theodore's face. Like he's happy for me even if he doesn't know all the details. It must be how I cannot stop smiling while I'm talking about Ian, totally forgetting all the stuff that upset me hours ago.

I shrug. "It just happened. I'm in such a mess."

He cracks a laugh. "Careful if he's one of these bad boys. You know what they say...They know how to play you right then dump you fast."

I take a bite from my roll, thinking about his words. "I don't think bad boys hurt the most. Because we kinda know what we're signing up for. We know we'll be getting ourselves into trouble. While with these good boys, we expect it all. The flowers, the ring, the wedding, and the happily ever after. So I think what hurts the most is a good boy who won't be good to us."

I rest my arms on the table, confessing. "So here's what I got, my friend... I met a really good boy who I'm not sure is gonna be any good to me."

Theodore chews a little, his eyes understanding. "You're right. Sadie is such a good person. She's good at heart, but look what she did."

Seeing the pain in his eyes, I say, "Then talk with her. When you feel like it, just go ahead, fight, talk... Whatever. I think you need to have a closure of some sort."

Or you would be like my good boy. Still hanging on to the past.

Ten minutes later, outside the restaurant and before Theodore hails me a cab, I ask, "So you're not calling it a night?"

He smiles, pointing to the other side of the street. "See that bar...? I'm going to get in there and make my wildest fantasy come true."

Chuckling, I'm glad for Theodore but a little sad for me. I've never even known what my wildest fantasy is or tried to figure it out.

CHAPTER SIXTEEN
Grace

HALF AN HOUR later, I walk into the apartment. I don't call it home or my place. I'm so confused. I don't know if Ian is the reason behind all this confusion after six peaceful months, or if it's the old things I still need to work on.

I'm pissed at myself. I shouldn't have stopped going to my therapist. And I'm more pissed as I head to my room. His voice catches me off guard, making me spin immediately. He's at his bedroom door. "Did you have fun? Did he do you any good?"

I don't have to look twice or even notice the small glass in his hand to know he's been drinking. His tongue is heavy, and his eyes are a bit unfocused. But drunk or not, I will not let him talk to me like that. Like he has a right to be pissed. I walk until I stand before him, raising my purse between us, "You're not allowed to talk to me like that. You're not the boss of me or anything to me."

"Why are you grumpy?" He gives a bitter laugh. "Well, I guess that's what happens after a lousy fuck."

"How about your lousy girl? What did she do to you?"

He flinches, his eyes swim in pain before he turns back to his room. And I feel terrible. I stand watching as he slumps himself on the bed, where a large bottle of vodka sits on the nightstand. He throws his glass to the floor, picks up the bottle, and tipping it up, he sips directly from it.

I just cannot. Something in me always softens my heart toward him. I walk into his room till I'm standing close enough to snatch the bottle out of his hand.

He raises murderous eyes to me before snatching the bottle back. I lose my balance, falling to the edge of his bed.

He turns slightly, waving the bottle. "This needs to be empty tonight."

I inch closer and tug at it. But his hold is firm. Turning fully to me, he waves a finger. "You cannot have it unless you wanna sip yourself."

His eyes are hooded and dark, as if he's not asking me about the vodka. I nod, taking the bottle out of his hand. Maybe I need to get loose before I surrender to his eyes. Because I cannot leave him like that, I cannot let him drink in his misery. Somehow, I cannot. But good news, I don't need to be aware to do that.

Tipping the bottle up to my lips, I take a sip and wait till it burns my tongue. Another to burn my throat. Then another to burn my stomach. And two more till it burns everything inside me. My inhibitions, my fears, my common sense, my talk with Shelia and Theodore, and my full knowledge that I'll be hurting myself. I burn everything till I feel nothing but *him*.

His heated eyes become wary. "What are you doing, Grace?"

"This bottle needed to be empty, right?" I take another sip before he snatches it out of my hand, only to raise it back to his lips.

I point a finger. "There's nothing left. It's empty as you wish."

He lowers it from his mouth, his eyes growing even darker. Darker with desire and hunger. "I know. I just wanted to taste your lips."

I swallow hard, wanting to hide my lips. I don't think I can resist him looking this hungry for them. For me.

"Don't give me your panicked eyes, Grace." He drops the bottle to the floor, edging closer to me. His heated eyes lock with mine as I feel his hand on my hair, undoing it with one touch. "I'm glad you didn't wear it down for him," he says hoarsely, his fingers spreading through my locks.

I close my eyes, enjoying his fingers in my hair. He's so gentle, so smooth, making me relax again. At the moment, I can be patient with him. "I told you, he's just a friend."

But he hasn't relaxed or stopped being pissed. His fingers are still in my hair, urging me to look at him. "You didn't fuck him?"

"God!" I flinch forward, covering my eyes and moving away from his touch. Why am I doing this to myself?

"Did you?" he asks again, and I shake my head. I don't know if it's the vodka that's making me weak, or if I'm just helplessly weak for him.

"I want your eyes, Grace," he commands, but his voice is gritty and full of pain.

I shouldn't give him anything. Not my eyes. Not my time. Not anything. But damn that tormented voice, it makes me eager to give him my soul. But for now, I just open my eyes.

"Now tell me, Grace," he says, pausing to exhale a troubled breath, "did you want him to fuck you, kiss you...touch you?"

"No," I say, not thinking anymore, just feeling his dark blue heated stare on my mouth. "I don't want him to. I don't want anyone to."

"Not even me?" He breathes, touching his thumb to my lower lip. "Because I don't want anything else in this world but to touch you, kiss you and fuck the hell out of you. I wanna be inside of you every damn minute of my life."

He wants to be inside of me every damn minute of his life.

His words play in my head and keep on playing. They are not like any I've ever heard. Because some words fly, some walk steady, and some lay thick and heavy. His, aren't any of that. His words just slap at something deep inside me. They're like the urgent sip of water you need to take after being dehydrated, but you have to be careful about taking more because your whole system might crash.

I don't take any precautions when he holds my face between his hands and plasters his lips to mine.

He doesn't even give me a sip first. He gives me his tongue, and I don't waste any time to part my lips and enjoy my risky gulp. I tangle my fingers in his hair, slide them across his back, before looping them around his neck, only to rest them on his chest. I'm trying every way possible to take the best gulp I can have. But he's better than me. He knows what he wants and how to take it.

He gathers my hair to one side and unzips my dress. He starts to lower it down and off my arms, then further down my body. He slows our kiss before I put my shyness aside and moan while he digs his teeth into my lower lip. He toys with it, his fingers unclasping my bra and wasting no time taking it off my sensitive skin. He throws it to the floor and replaces the cold breeze that hits my breasts with his palm. He kisses me again while touching, measuring, and molding my breasts, making them swell painfully.

I ache for some sort of relief. I'm not even kissing him back as eagerly as I want to. I'm so aroused that if he releases my mouth, I'd beg him to take me.

He catches one nipple and starts to taunt me mercilessly while no longer kissing me. He pulls back a little to look into my eyes. His are dark with desire and triumph.

"You're so fucking beautiful, Grace. Like an angel. My angel," he says out of breath before lowering his head to take one nipple into his mouth, sucking gently at first, then hungrily before he moves to my other breast, giving it the same attention. I just sit there under his touch, under his mercy, open for him to take whatever he wants.

Letting him have what he wants is pure pleasure. Even if I'm on the edge of frustration, I want to be whatever he wants me to be, for him.

I'm his. I may not be his girl, but I'll be his angel, at least for tonight.

When he's done taunting my breasts, his hands move to my waist, lowering me on the bed. His bed is huge, so he lays me on it sideways. I see him turn to reach for a pillow. Gently, he puts a hand under my head to slide the pillow beneath.

Then he rests on one elbow, watching me with a tormented expression on his face. One hand stroking my nakedness.

"It's gonna be okay." I hold his hand in place, pressing with assurance. "We can do this tonight. Just one time."

He gives a faint laugh. "That's not what's worrying me."

"What is it then?" I whisper, hoping I don't sound too eager or desperate.

"Let's correct some things. First," he says, pulling his hand from mine, "I'm gonna have you tonight. There's no question about it." He starts to skim a finger over my skin. "I'm gonna do you, fuck you, make love to you, or whatever you wanna call it. I'll give you that. You'll label whatever we'll have tonight the way you like. But it will not just be one time. It will be the first of many. So many, Grace."

I swallow hard, not breaking eye contact with his heated stare. His finger is not playing circles over my stomach anymore, it glides back and forth at the edge of my panties, but I'm able to ask, "Second?"

"It's not gonna be okay," he says playfully and leans in to kiss my forehead. "It's gonna be fucking epic."

"Okay," I giggle, and he shakes his head. Suddenly he's tickling me all over. "Told you… Nothing's okay here. Everything is gonna be fucking epic."

"Ian…" I'm able to warn between the giggles I cannot control.

"Epic, my angel."

"Epic," I yell through my laughs as he finally has mercy on me. I take a deep breath. Then my eyes lock with his.

He rests a palm over the front of my panties before he says, "Now, third and last."

"The third…" I try not to beg as his hand taunts me.

"Whatever happens, don't tell me to stop." He's so deadly serious. Like he's warning me that there would be no going back. Ever.

I hitch a breath, excited. "Whatever happens?"

"Do you have a problem with that?" His voice is hoarse and seducing.

Delicious fear takes over my nerves, but I'm eager to say, "No, no problem whatsoever. No problem at all."

"Can we shake to that?"

I nod, holding up my right hand. But instead of taking it, he reaches to take my left. He flips it over to press his thumb on my wrist before raising it to his mouth. He kisses my scar tenderly before sitting up and laying my hand back on the mattress. Then he's out of the bed, giving me a show I'll never forget.

He sheds his shirt, his pants, then boxer briefs. He's too quick with his stripping show, but I get a chance to stare right at his manhood before I place a hand over my eyes, feeling just a little *that's not my right.*

He joins me on the bed. One knee parts my thighs while his fingers tug at my panties to pull them off my body. Everything is going so fast, impatiently like he cannot control himself. I open my eyes. I'm going to miss everything if I keep them closed.

"It's about fucking time. I want your eyes, Grace," he says while his eyes move down to my sex. He stares, really stares, hitches a breath, then flickers his eyes to mine. "I want my angel eyes."

I lick my lips. There's nothing angelic about what we're doing. Or the way he looks at me. It would have been uncomfortable, but my body is tingling all over, I'm so turned on by the hunger in his eyes. I smile. "I'm so naked for an angel."

He chuckles, then lowers his face to give me a kiss on the lips, his eyes searching mine. "But you're my angel?"

I nod, maybe too fast, too eager, but I don't care. The way his eyes approve makes me giddy. He smiles too and presses a finger to my lips. "You're such a good girl, Grace. You're honest, forward, and you don't play any games, and for that, you should be rewarded."

I don't want to think about his words, and I don't have the chance. He smirks, and his finger leaves my lips and trails down my body, his eyes following his finger till it reaches above my sex. "Angel?"

I cannot handle his lustful and full of mischief eyes. I break the contact and huff a breath as I look at his hardness. His cock is thick, big, and I don't know how...no. I'm not going to think about that. I lick my lips before deciding his beautiful blue eyes are a safer option. "Yes," I answer finally.

"Are you ready to be rewarded?"

"With the way you look at me, I'm ready for anything," I say out of breath. I'm getting so turned on and wet by the way he keeps ogling my sex.

A tiny protest escapes my mouth as he puts his hands on my inner thighs to part me wider. I'm so exposed.

I fight my modesty as he touches my sex and spreads my inner folds. Flickering his eyes to me, he says, "Such a pretty pussy, my angel. I don't know who's being rewarded right now."

"Um..." I don't say anything. I moan as he licks a path between my folds. And I don't say anything when he takes my clit between his teeth. I arch my back and close my eyes. This is too much. I see stars.

"Fuck, Ian, fuck," I cry when his tongue penetrates my entrance.

"That's..." I try to push up, but he puts a hand on my stomach, pinning me to the bed. Our eyes meet for a second. His are full warnings before he dips his head down. His tongue is wild, moving in and out of my slit. And I cannot be anything but loud.

My entire body tingles as pleasure rips through me. I lift my head and watch Ian's head between my thighs. This is so decadent. He's fucking me with his tongue.

"Ian..." I beg now. I want him to stop. I can't come on his tongue. I can't.

I hear a laugh down his throat as if he's feeling my nervousness, then I feel his hands on my breasts, he pinches my nipples hard, and that's it. I cannot hold back my orgasm. I come apart, screaming and tugging at his hair.

"Ian, god, Ian," I cry out his name before swimming through an embarrassing climax, my juices coating his tongue.

Shit. I'm so filthy, dirty, and out of control. He's making a new *me.* A wild one. I like that *a lot.*

I'm out for a moment or more, I don't know, but I'm well aware again as he spreads tender kisses all over my body, then licks a path from my neck down to my stomach till I'm starting to cool again. He looks me in the eye. He's filled with hunger and desire.

He's done spoiling me. Now it's his time to get what he wants. He kneads my breasts, his rough hands squeezing them together. I stab my teeth into my lower lip, and he tweaks one nipple with his fingers. "Pretty tits. The girl who sells roses has matching rosy nipples."

I pant out of breath as he's rougher on my breasts, but I'm able to correct him. "I sell all kinds of flowers, not only roses."

He laughs. He throws his head laughing. Looking down at me again, his blue eyes are darker. "Well, I'm only interested in one flower right now," he says, the heel of his palm on my sex. "Is it up for sale?"

I gasp, but he muffles the sound with his mouth covering mine and breathing against, "I wanna own you, Grace, doesn't matter what price I have to pay."

I don't know what he means, and he doesn't give me a chance to ask. He cradles my face in his hand, saying, "Now, Grace. I'm gonna take you hard and fast. There's nothing I can do about it. And this is...where you don't tell me to stop."

"Hard and fast?" He's so big.

"Nervous?"

I nod.

He doesn't say anything. He just stares at me then I feel his hand between my thighs. He cups my sex, and I moan. I'm so sensitive from the shattering orgasm I just had. He leans in to kiss my mouth. I part my lips and brush my tongue against his.

I can taste myself. It's so erotic. But I don't think we're kissing right now. We're just playing *tongue*. He strokes mine, and I stroke his. And slowly, I feel his hand down there. Straight to my core, he pushes a finger inside me, and instantly I press my thighs together.

He breaks the kiss and demands in a gruff voice, "Open for me, Grace."

I open my thighs and grab his head to kiss him again. He pushes another finger inside my wetness and starts *fingering* me. Slow and teasing. I pant out of breath and move my head to the side, breaking the kiss.

His fingers move in and out, deeper and faster, and I moan aloud as he pushes a third digit inside my slit. My sex pulses on the verge of another climax. But his fingers freeze before I reach my peak. He leans in to kiss my forehead. "See, we're going to fit perfectly, angel. You're pussy is socked, wet, *for me*."

He knows what he's doing with his words. It's so arousing to hear him talking with that firm, serious voice about *my pussy*. I close my eyes for a tiny second as he pulls his fingers out, then I open them as he says, "Don't worry, angel. You're going to fit perfectly around my cock."

I nod. "Yes, but..."

"But what?" he asks in a rush like he cannot take my hesitation anymore. He's on the edge of losing it.

I push on one elbow, my eyes seductively looking at him. I want to tease him as he's been teasing me. "I wanna taste you."

He groans and shakes his head. But I don't care. I take his cock, barely able to circle it with my hand, my sex quivers just thinking it'd be inside me soon, but I don't need to think now. I look at him, I feel like he wants me to stop and doesn't want to stop me at the same time, but the second I wrap my lips around the tip, he loses it. He throws his head to the back, and I find myself on my back again.

He opens my legs wide. "Later, I let it you play with it later. Now, I need to be inside your pussy." He pauses, his eyes demanding. "And you're not going to tell me to stop."

"I won't," I whisper, bringing a hand to my forehead. I'm so ready and so not ready for this. I know it's going to be hard for me. I cannot even pinpoint when the last time was, and he's really endowed. But still, I'm eager for it. For him to lose control. For me. He will not be able to stop because of me.

I know he wants my eyes, but they follow his hand as he guides his cock to my entrance.

"Now, Grace." He hitches a breath, and I gaze up at him. I'm Grace now. It's like a warning, I guess. But it's a delicious warning, sending goosebumps all over my skin.

I dig my fingers into the mattress as he thrusts his hardness inside me. I'm so wet, it slides all the way in easily, but still, he's so big, filling me uncomfortably.

"Grace," he growls, stilling, to help me adjust to his size.

"I need a moment," I say, and he nods. Our eyes lock, his blue are intent, and focus and just looking at them fills me with heat. Feeling more comfortable, I move a hand up and down his back. "I won't tell you to stop." I think that's what he wants to hear before he slides out of me, only to slam back in. He holds himself there.

"Fuck..." He places a hand on my stomach, knowing how uncomfortable I've become.

"You know what was worrying me, Grace?" He holds my gaze fiercely, his forehead sweats. "You being this fucking tight. I want to stop; then, I'm too selfish to stop. But still, don't tell me to stop."

"I won't tell you to stop." I hold onto his shoulders as his hands lift my butt. He pulls out then surges back in hard and fast. He doesn't hold back anything now. And pure pleasure surging in every atom of my body. I'm under him, under his mercy, to fulfill his needs.

"Don't you ever stop," I say, getting really tight around him, making him uncomfortable now.

He slides halfway, then slams deep, holding my gaze. "Your pussy feels so good, angel."

I put a hand over my face. His words make me excited and shy.

"Don't shy away from this," he grunts. "Tell me, angel. Do you like my cock inside your tight pussy?"

"Yes..." I breathe.

"I wanna hear you, Grace," he demands harshly. "Be a good girl and say the words."

I close my eyes, my sex squeezing his cock tight, maybe painfully. I don't know, but I want him to move again, so I give him what he wants. "I love your cock inside me, Ian."

"Only mine."

"Only yours."

That's it. He starts to move, then suddenly stills again, locking gaze with me and revealing, "When I found you at my door that night, looking at me with your doe eyes and asking to be my roomie, I felt so guilty. I just wanted to grab you inside and fuck you against the door. You were so innocent and trusting. You had no clue why I needed that shower."

I want to smile. I want to say I wouldn't have minded that at all. I would have even joined him in the shower, but I can't when he's going crazy again, stretching and filling me with his big cock. Then he becomes totally unhinged, slamming deeper and faster.

"Ian..." My sex pulses around him like crazy while he hits my most sensitive spot.

"Yeah...you like that." He's out of breath but able to tease, and suddenly he goes slow. His cock slides out, then in with delicious slow strokes.

I wither under his heaviness, filled with his manhood, on the verge of coming, but he holds back now. He continues slowly. "Now, show me, angel. Show me how much you want this."

I wrap my legs around him, and before I find my clit, he catches my hand. "No cheating."

"Then harder, Ian. Fuck me, harder."

He doesn't need more encouragement. He slides out, then dives in until he's balls deep, and my sex pulses around him as I shatter and come. I moan and scream. I'm so freaking loud. But still, the sound of his slamming in me deafening my ears. I could come again just listening to his cock slamming in and out of me, hearing his grunts, and smelling his manly sweat while he *fucks me.*

"God, Grace...you're so fucking tight," he utters, throwing his head back, his cock spasming and pulsating his hot cum in me. He's gone and shattering because of me.

"It was fucking epic," he mummers with a hint of a smile as he falls on top of me, his face in my neck, his body hot and heavy.

It was epic. It was so unreal. It was magical.

It was everything I have ever dreamed of and never even dared to dream of. It's the most beautiful thing I have ever experienced. I hope it's the same with him.

I think it's the same with him. He was really out of control because of me.

"Ian..." After a while, I bring my limp hands to move up and down his back. I love how we're this close right now, but he's really heavy and probably not aware of my state, because, like me, he's a little drunk.

Immediately, he rolls over to his side while reaching to tuck me under his shoulder. "I'll make it up to you in the morning. I promise." I feel his lips on my head, leaving a tender kiss. "It'll be everything you've ever imagined, angel."

He thinks he was too rough with me. He thinks I would have liked it a little less intense. But he doesn't know a thing. I didn't even know. As he dozes quickly, I lie near him, unable to shut an eye. I'm watching the ceiling with amazement. Finally knowing, finally figuring out my wildest fantasy. I have just made it come true. I had rough, out-of-control sex with the most intense man I have ever met. With the only man I'd ever want to rest naked tucked under his arm.

But I cannot stay here enjoying his embrace. I'm afraid I'd sleep before I clean myself up. I slide out of his embrace, only for him to catch me and tuck me back under his arm.

"Stay here, Acacia."

Acacia…

So that's her name.

Drunk or not, he called me by her name. He called me by her name, and my damn heart doesn't sink or skip a beat. My stupid heart is just fine. My breathing is also calm—no adrenaline-pumping to help me out of my shock. My body is not shocked; it is functioning right. Like I have been expecting the letdown.

He called me by another girl's name after he fucked me hard and fast, and I'm just resting peacefully in his arms. I wish I could master a tear or let out a cry, but I just lie there. Looking into the void. Waiting till he dozes completely so I can leave.

As soon as I make sure he is, I slide from under his arm, sit up, and let my feet hit the floor. Standing, I bend to pick up my stuff and leave his room with two disturbing facts.

First: I like to harm myself. If not physically, then emotionally. Because he cannot call me by another girl's name, and I feel nothing but numbness. There's something seriously wrong with me. And I know exactly what I should do first thing in the morning. I'm going to set up an appointment with my therapist.

Second fact: I'm totally and helplessly in love with him, and I don't know what the hell to do about that.

CHAPTER SEVENTEEN

Ian

THREE YEARS AGO

IT'S BEEN A month since Acacia moved in with me. We don't interact a lot throughout the day because I'm buried at my office. It's not an easy task to run a business, no matter how small it is, and my marketing company is small but thriving. My last deal for a new shoe brand got me some serious calls—one in particular from another shoe brand with a huge name. I'm crossing my fingers to seal a deal with them.

When I come home, Acacia tells me about her day, which usually includes hanging out with Emma or filling out job applications, or doing girly stuff. I don't ask about that. I don't ever get it. But those two have gotten really close. Emma says she's never met such a supportive girl like Acacia.

Today is no different. I walk into the living room, and there they are, snuggling up on the couch, Emma's head dropped on

Acacia's shoulder while watching some romantic movie playing on the flat screen. I smile. Emma is so content in Acacia's presence. After graduating this year, she had a hard time with everything, especially her diabetes. She's taking a break for a while, and I'm glad she has Acacia now. Because the rest of her friends are busy moving forward into the real world.

"Hey." They both smile at me as I take one of the arm seats. "How was your day?" Acacia looks at me sideways before shifting her eyes back to the screen.

"Busy, that's if you care to know." I'm a little grumpy. She's not giving me attention as usual.

"Don't scowl at her," Emma says, "it's a pivotal moment for Penelope."

"Penelope?"

Pointing at the screen, Emma says, "The redhead. She's going to decide whether to forgive him or not."

"What did he do?" I ask, noticing how sad Acacia is watching this Penelope.

Acacia tilts her head to look at me. "He broke her heart. She gave him everything, and he chose to break her heart."

"You…stupid. Don't take him back," Emma fumes, and my eyes shift there, to their Penelope. She's crying while taking some blond dude into her arms.

"God, why do I keep watching this shit," Emma stands as the credits start to roll. She puts her feet into her flip-flops, lifts the veggie bowl from the coffee table, and says, "I'm leaving. I don't want to argue with this one." She points a finger down at a smiling Acacia before walking out of the living room.

My gaze travels to Acacia, who's stretching her arms. "What's wrong with her now?"

Acacia giggles. "We don't always see eye-to-eye when it comes to these movies. I wanted Penelope to forgive him while she didn't. If she stayed, we'd be arguing non-stop about it."

I frown a little. I never thought I'd be discussing romantic movies, but with Acacia, I'm a little intrigued about her opinion. "But you said he broke her heart. Why do you want her to forgive him?"

"It wasn't his intention. He just wasn't ready for her. For them to be. That's something he couldn't control. So, he's not the bad guy here."

Whatever.

I don't get a word of Acacia's serious explanation, and frankly, I shouldn't have asked. It's just she was so sad watching it, I thought she, too, would be on team 'don't forgive the blond dude.'

She gazes at me for a moment waiting for my take on this before some knowing expression takes over her face. "You don't give a damn, do you?" she says and starts laughing. I shrug, and she laughs even more.

Acting a little hurt, I say, "Glad I'm making you laugh."

Putting a hand on her stomach to control her laughs, she hauls herself up. "I'll heat dinner for you while you get over your grumpiness."

I stand and catch her hand as she edges around me to leave. "Acacia, you don't have to do that. I don't want you to feel obligated to do these things for me."

"I don't feel obligated, Ian." She looks down at her feet, as usual, a bit shy. "I just love to do things for you."

I won't lie. I feel a little like I'm using her generous nature. Since she'd moved in with me, my life has gotten easier and better. The place is always spotless, there's always something to eat when I come back home, and all my clothes are clean and tidy, not to mention her adamant attempts to make me feel better after having a shitty day. She would tell these embarrassing jokes just to make me laugh, even if she felt ashamed afterward. Like the one at the restaurant. She's always so attentive to me. And with Emma, there's those little bits and pieces. Like earlier, instead of eating the usual snacks, she made that veggie bowl considering Emma's diabetes. She's that caring to the people around her. She's the kind of person who gives a hand to a stranger as she did when Emma collapsed a month ago. She does all that while there's turmoil inside of her. I can feel it whenever she's not aware I'm paying attention to her. Something is eating her up. Maybe like any young woman her age, she has a lot of things to discover about herself and what she would like to be and the things she wants to achieve.

As difficult as it was, I've stayed true to my word. I didn't pressure her to tell me anything about herself. The most challenging part was to keep my attraction to her in check. I haven't even kissed her since. But like now, when she's giving me her caring eyes, I'm having a hard time not wanting to take a taste.

"You're so beautiful, Acacia." I brush the back of my hand across her cheek. I cannot resist touching her anymore. "You're beautiful, inside and out. You're the most beautiful woman I have ever met."

"And you're just perfect, Ian." She smiles at me, leaning into my touch, and I cannot. I think I've reached my limit of tolerance. I need to kiss those pink lips. Right here, right now. It's just a kiss. I wouldn't be breaking any big promises.

"Ian," she whispers, probably figuring out my intent as I cup her face between my hands, my mouth falling on hers in a soft touch at first. As I look into her eyes, I know for sure it's different with her.

I drop my hands at my sides and recognize... Kissing is not the same with Acacia, and it's not about the kiss itself. It's the moment before I gather her closer to me, my hands on her waist, my eyes locking with hers. There are all kinds of emotions: trust, fear, excitement, nervousness. There's no pretense in how she feels about this.

Now, we're kissing like two crazy teens. My hands are eager to touch every inch of her, and hers are frantically all over me. I love that. I love that she's there with me, as desperate as I am. I wonder if she loves my taste as I love hers. She's like vanilla and vintage wine. She's so sweet, and sweet has become my new favorite taste.

But, fuck, I've promised her. I have to keep my promise.

I rest my forehead against hers. "I'm sorry. I didn't mean to push you for more."

"It's okay," she says, nuzzling me. "We can do this now."

"We can?" I smile against her forehead.

"Yeah," she breathes. "The men's clothing store called back, and I'm officially an assistant store manager."

"That's great," I say carefully. "But that doesn't mean we have to change anything. I want you to take all the time you need."

"I need you." She loops her arms around me. "I don't need any more time."

I pull back to look into her eyes. Does she mean what I think she means? I don't have much time to think about it as she circles her arms around my neck, lowering my head for a kiss. I kiss her back. Soft and warm at first, then deep and demanding. I want to know if tonight will be it. If she's ready for me as she says. I gather her closer. I want her to feel how hard I've become. I'm rewarded instantly with a soft moan.

I break the kiss, some logic settling in. Maybe she just thinks she owes it to me.

“What?” she asks, out of breath, her delicate fingers digging into my shoulders.

I try to do the right thing as much as I can, and it’s pure torture with her pretty pink lips and the hazy look of desire in her eyes, but I’m trying. I clear my throat. “I don’t want you to think you’re obligated to do anything with me. You’re a virgin.”

“And?” she says, amused while her arms loop around my neck again.

“Acacia,” I warn as she glues herself to me, my hard erection poking against her stomach. And with her barely-there tank top, I feel like I’m poking against her naked. Her tiny shorts don’t help either.

“I want you, Ian,” she whispers while her light kisses trace my jaw.

“I want you too,” I whisper back, but my arms are firm. I push her off me gently. I put some distance between us. “But I want you to be sure. I don’t want you to feel pressured. I think we should wait a little longer.”

“What if…I believed this lie?” She steps to erase the distance between us. “How would you spend the night?” She raises a hand to caress my cheek. “You’ve been imagining how it’d be between us for like what…more than a month?”

“Acacia.” I don’t know if I’m warning her or losing the last bit of control I have. The one that separates a good man from a lousy one. Because I’m becoming very lousy. I need to do the right thing. And the right thing is not taking her virginity tonight. I want to give her more time. But I’m losing all control as her lips move closer to mine, “You know I’ve been dreaming of you since that night at the hospital.”

That’s all it takes. I quickly lift her in my arms, walking us out of the living room. I’m feeling every bit of nervousness radiating from her body. Maybe she's starting to have second thoughts, or these are the good nervous vibes; I hope it's the latter because I'm done waiting or being the good guy.

In my room, I flick the light on before putting her down on her feet. I waste no time. My lips seek hers in a hungry, no-going-back kind of kiss. When I feel she's asking for more, I break the kiss, pull my shirt up over my head and throw it to the floor.

I try to inhale and exhale. I hope she likes what she sees. Through my teens, I struggled with my weight. I was a big, fat kid. I couldn't reach my weight goal till after I finished college. I have a routine now. I try to eat healthy all the time, and I run every day. But with the work stress, I haven't been paying attention lately. So, I have put on a couple of unnecessary pounds. I'm not as ripped as I want to be. But I'm not fat either. My stomach is still flat, there's no fat there, but there's no six-pack either.

I'm nervous as if I'm fifteen again.

What the fuck?

I'm not fat anymore. I shake my head. I'm over that.

Acacia is watching me with desire. So, I guess she has no problem with how I look.

"Take your top off for me, Acacia," I say urgently. I don't want to lose control. I want to be patient with her. I want her to show me that she's sure of this.

She eagerly nods, her hands reaching to take it off, dropping it next to my shirt on the floor.

I stand, staring at her white bra. "Take this off too."

She bites her lower lip, her eyes growing wide with indecisiveness.

"For me, Acacia." I'm hardly able to speak. But I need the confirmation that she's one hundred percent sure of this. "You want to do things for me. Am I right, babe?"

Touching her neck, she holds my gaze. "Everything you want."

Clumsily, she reaches behind her back, unclasping her bra and sliding it off. Her creamy breasts spill out as she lets her bra fall to the floor. I'm staring at the most beautiful woman I've ever seen. I'm getting harder and harder. Her breasts are complete perfection, and I want this to be perfect for her. Because she's perfect.

"You're so beautiful," I say, lifting her in my arms again. I walk us over to the bed and lay her there.

"Now, you're gonna be mine forever, Acacia." I'm on my knees, bending to brush a hand over her cheek. I let it slide down to her neck. I slip my fingers around it as I lean in to thoroughly kiss her lips, her neck. Then I take one nipple into my mouth. I nip and suck, then nip and suck at the other. She whimpers and moans with every touch. And I kiss and touch till the little fabric of her panties stands in my way.

I easily rip her panties off. She gasps, then giggles. I smile at her before my eyes travel down.

I hitch a breath.

Her pussy is so pretty and so wet. And bare, making my cock throb painfully. I want to be inside of her now. My eyes shift to hers. But she's covering them with the back of her hand.

She's shy.

"Acacia, did you do this for me? Are you bare for me?"

"Yes. For you," she whispers, still hiding behind her hand.

"Acacia, babe." I want her eyes.

Slowly she moves her hand away, her eyes growing apprehensive.

"Having second thoughts?" I ask while I try to control my hands, my mouth, and my cock. I want to touch her little pussy, taste it, and be inside her tightness.

"No," she says mysteriously. "I just want you to kiss me first."

I'm relieved, but as I lean down to kiss her mouth, she shakes her head. "There," she says, smiling with mischief, and I try not to look like an idiot as she points a finger down to her pretty pussy.

There's a moment where I close my mouth, take hold of my painfully throbbing cock, and then that's it. I kiss her there. My mouth is on her, tasting her sweet virgin pussy.

Her moans are the best melody to my ears as I open her lips. I let my thumb strum her clit while I slide a finger inside her tightness.

"Ian." She flinches. She's *fucking* tight. I wait till she gives me her eyes again, and they're full of approval. I start to move my finger in and out of her tiny slit. She breaks out of her shyness under my touch, under my mouth, under my hands. It doesn't take as much time as I thought it would before she's on the verge of climax, I lower my mouth to take her clit between my teeth, and I hear the most erotic sound. She's coming apart in my mouth, her hands on my head, scratching my skin, but I don't care. I'm in another world. I feel like I'm on the verge of dying. I need to be inside of her now.

I'm so fucking hard. But she's a virgin, and I need to have some control.

I leave the bed to take off the rest of my clothes. She watches with amazement, her eyes taking in my nakedness. I think at this point, she's decided to let go of her shyness.

"That's really something," she says, giggling while eyeing my hard cock.

I smile as I dip near her on the bed. I don't know if her words are flattering or not, but I'm glad she's a bit relaxed.

"You don't approve?" I say, hoping I can master some seducing tone because I'm the one getting nervous now. I'm going to be her first, and I have never heard someone enjoying it the first time, but I hope she does.

A heated promise enters her eyes while she's licking her lips in a seductive way. "I *so* approve."

"Well, who's getting out of her shell," I say, teasing before I lose it completely. I put on a condom, then I put a knee between her legs and lock my eyes with hers. "Ready, babe. Ready to be mine forever?"

"Yeah," she breathes, holding her hand up for me. I take it in mine and lace my fingers through hers before resting our hands next to us on the mattress. Then I take what's mine. What she's giving me. What she's not going to give to any other man.

I enter her. She flinches in pain, and I still. She's so fucking tight.

"Tell you something?" she says out of breath, her head resting on one side as she slowly adjusts to my size.

"Anything, babe," I say, a bit apprehensive that she might ask me to stop.

"You're ten inches," she says, shaking her head and closing her eyes, already feeling a bit ashamed of her joke, and I cannot help it. I throw my head back, laughing.

"And you're mine," I say as I recover from my laughter. My eyes and hers are intense. It's the moment we've been waiting for. I hold her gaze as I start to move. I slide in and out of her slowly, but when she wraps her legs around me, urging me for more, I go wild. My thrusts are hard and fast, and I'm taking her with me. She digs her nails into my back, screaming her second climax. She's coming around my cock, taking me to the edge. I thrust one more time, while her pussy pulses around me before I lose control. Then when it's all over, I collapse on top of her. And that's my heaven.

"I love you, Ian," she whispers into my neck as I tuck her under my arm.

"I love you too, Acacia," I say back. "I fucking *love* you."

Hours later, I extend my arm next to me on the bed. I want to reach out for my heaven, but I only feel a void. She's not here. I dozed a little, and she's not here.

Maybe she's in the bathroom. I leave the bed and walk there to check. But she's not there either. Something tells me where she will be exactly, but I don't want to know. To know that she chose to go back to her room. To sleep alone in her bed after what we just had. But I go there and slowly open her door.

I stand there, staring as she's so sound and asleep. In her bed, not mine.

She's shy, maybe that's it. But the fat kid in me is playing with my head, telling me there's something more. A girl as perfect as Acacia would not find me enough. Trying to ruin this. To ruin us. But I just shake my head. She's just not used to sleeping with someone, that's all.

I close her door and rest there for a while. Because out of nowhere, the thing lurking all the time in my mind is coming back. That escort site jumps at me now. I've never felt at ease with her explanation, even when I convinced Emma of it. I shrugged it off as she told me. But now it's coming back. I shake my head again. I'm just overreacting. After all, she was a virgin. I settle on that thought as I go back to my room. Without her in my bed.

CHAPTER EIGHTEEN
Grace

I HAD WOKEN UP to so many horrible mornings, and still, life went on. Today is no different; life must go on. Maybe I don't have Sam with me now, but I have a better and stronger version of myself. So, life must go on for me. I have already called my therapist and set an appointment with her. I may not be in the steady place I want to be, but I don't want to step back either.

I will not admit that I'm heartbroken. Maybe my therapist would wring out such an admission from me, but I'm not doing it on my own. If I did, I wouldn't be standing here in my shop, taking care of my business for five hours or so. It's almost noon, and I haven't heard anything from him. He was still asleep when I left the apartment. I shouldn't expect much from him.

It was just sex, one night where he could get a taste. But that's what I wanted too, just a taste. I try to calm myself.

I don't know if I'm in love with him as I thought last night.

I was drunk enough to admit it to myself, but now, aware and sober, I don't have the guts to acknowledge such feelings for a haunted man, haunted by his love for another girl.

I don't need all that baggage.

It's about lunchtime as I see Mabel grabbing her coat. I told her I'm staying in the shop. I want to have some alone time with my flowers. I need beauty to pass this day. Otherwise, I'd be crawling to the nearest corner and crying my eyes out. I don't think I can master any numbness like I did last night. So, either my flowers or crying. I'm also wearing my favorite flowery dress. It's a long-sleeve maroon dress with tiny blue flowers print. It reaches just above my knees. It's so pretty, and I need all the pretty things in the world right now.

"Sure you're fine?" Mabel says, her hand on the door handle. Like she knows better than to leave me alone. But I'll be fine. I have my flowers.

"What's the real reason we do things?" I don't want Mabel pressuring me to reveal what's wrong with me, so I deflect. "What's the real reason you don't want a serious relationship, Mabel?"

Mabel is a single mother. She does date a lot, but only seeks casual stuff. She says she doesn't want to confuse her daughter till she's at a stable age to understand things.

She looks at me for a second, a 'what the hell' look on her face before her eyes soften a bit. Like she knows it would help me if she talked.

"Because it hurts so much when it ends. It hurts when we don't have that backbone anymore. It hurts because we get used to the support, but then suddenly we wake up doing it all alone. It's peachy and worth a million kinds of things when it's happening, when we're living it. But when it ends, nothing is more horrible."

I inhale her words. I want them to become part of me. I want to remember the pain in her eyes and act better for myself.

"But if you ask for any advice, then... Go for it. Maybe you will be one of the lucky ones."

I give a laugh. "*Me,* one of the lucky."

She doesn't know. I didn't even have a great start. Our first time and he called me by her name.

"Yes," she says firmly. "I get the feeling you're not having a happy start. You're having an awful heart-wrenching one, and you're still here and fighting. You know what you're getting yourself into. And the lucky ones always know what they're getting themselves into. They know what they're going to pay, and that's what makes them ready to conquer every obstacle they face, not blinded by all the sugary stuff."

Mabel pulls open the door, a full smile on face. "Love is just a long road, Grace. It's not a gift or a thing falling from the sky. It has to be earned."

I rest my elbows on the table and rub my eyes with my fingertips as Mabel finally goes out for her lunch date. I try not to think about anything till I meet my therapist. I let multiple ideas about my shop run through my mind, but I cannot concentrate. Everything calls me to that moment. When he called me by her name. Every cell in my body is aching for an outlet, like they are all arguing for me to let something out. Cry or scream, anything other than the numbness I'm swimming in.

But I don't swim for long. My head snaps as I hear the door open. I thought Mabel put on the closed sign. But someone enters despite that.

As I lay my eyes on the visitor, my heart sinks.

It's Ian.

I instantly stand.

It's Ian with wet hair and a casual jacket with a blue shirt over dark jeans. He's showered, and he's well put together. He's got what he wanted, and he doesn't care for real now—not pretending as usual.

I know his eyes are on me. I have to be brave and look him in the eye, not caring like he is. But when my eyes connect with his, I lose sight of everything around me. The cries I tried to suffocate are eager to show right now, in front of him. The tender look in his eyes doesn't help at all.

He feels sorry for me.

God.

"God…"

I didn't say that out loud. It's him.

I feel his arms around me from behind. He's enveloping me with his arms, scent, and strength. With everything that is him. My unshed tears didn't let me see him walk around the table to embrace me from behind. He's hugging me tightly. His head buried in my neck, and I cannot hide my cries anymore. I don't have any control over them. I cannot be numb around him. He makes me feel. He makes it okay to feel, so I cry hard and ugly. I cry because he called me by her name.

"I was really drunk," he says, apologizing as he turns me slowly to him, one arm around my waist while a hand is on the back of my head, laying it over his heart. But I don't want to listen to his steady heartbeat. It makes me cry even harder, yet it makes me feel safe. I don't know how he's making me feel both at the same time.

"I'm sorry, I should have stayed with you all night. I should have cuddled you to sleep, telling you how beautiful it was."

His soothing voice makes things worse. I cannot stop crying. He's soothing me again, "But I'm telling you now. You were beautiful and amazing. I cannot even describe how great it was. I should have told you that right away. I'm so sorry."

Suddenly my cries are a little weaker. I want to hear him clearly because there's something seriously wrong with what he says.

"I shouldn't have fallen asleep after what we had. But I was drunk, if that's an excuse. I didn't mean to make you feel like this, like I have used you."

Oh, my God.

He doesn't know. He thinks I'm heartbroken because he fell asleep, not that he called me by her name. He thinks all this crying is because he didn't cuddle with me afterward.

I feel really embarrassed. Mortified, actually, that he might think I want something more out of our night. I know it was just one night—a one-time kind of thing. True, I'm deeply hurt he called me by her name, but still, I knew deep down it was a one-time thing. Now he thinks I wanted some cuddling stuff. That I would push him for more.

God.

Managing a steady voice, I pull back a little from his arms. Wiping my tears away, I look up at him. "It's okay. I don't know what has gotten into me."

He doesn't know he called me by her name, and I will not tell him. What's the point? He loves another girl. I should just step back.

Soulfully, he looks at me for a moment; then his thumbs are rubbing my cheeks. He's wiping away all my tears. I cannot let him this close to me anymore. I raise my hands and place them around his, but before I can pull them away, he kisses me. It's a tender kiss. Soft and comforting. I know I shouldn't kiss him back, but my hands are gripping his tightly. I'm eager for this tender moment, for this comfort, and I slowly open my mouth to welcome his tongue. His strokes are soft, beautiful, and reassuring. I'm drawn completely into him, his arms around me, mine around his neck. We're hungrily kissing each other. I should stop, but I cannot. I cannot pull myself away. But the dread of him calling me by her name again makes me break our kiss.

He rests his forehead against mine. "I know I fucked up big last night. But I'll make it up to you, Grace. I promise."

I shake my head and take a step back as his arms tighten around me.

"I think you-"

"Shh…" He puts a finger on my lips, smiling. "Don't say anything before I tell you how beautiful and sweet you are. How good you were to me last night. How patient and wonderful you were with me."

I shouldn't stand still and let him charm his way back to me.

But foolish me is taking control, and I just stare at him as he continues, "I was a total ass last night. I don't only mean falling asleep. I shouldn't have talked to you like I did about your friend."

"Theodore?" I let his name out, amazed he's talking about that.

He nods uncomfortably. "I'm not comfortable with you being close to him. But I'm also thankful for your patience with me about it. Maybe you felt I needed to hear it constantly, that you're just friends with him, and I'm grateful for your tender care towards my jealous state."

"You have no reason to be jealous. Theodore doesn't think about me like that." I shrug one shoulder. "Nor do I."

But you do about someone else. You called me by her name. But I don't say it.

"I believe that," he says, exhaling as he looks to the side before he gazes down at me. "But I'm not comfortable with it."

Okay, we're talking like we're an actual couple. So, I should tell him how I feel about the idea of us. "I'm seeing my therapist today," I say, trying to hold his gaze.

His eyes become wary before he says, "It's about time."

"You know why…because you've been confusing me, because my world has turned upside down since I met you."

"I know," he says calmly, his eyes unreadable as he keeps them intent on me. "I wish I could change that right here and now, but I think with some time, I will."

"Some time with lots of um…sex. Is that what you mean? Because if it is, I need you to know that I'm not interested in that. Last night was just that, one night. I don't want to indulge in anything that's just sexual with you."

"Neither do I," he replies instantly. I won't lie, my heart sinks. He doesn't even want sex.

"I want more, Grace." I'm glued back against him as his arms pull me closer. I raise my eyes to his smiling ones. "But I want lots of sex too."

Involuntarily, I let out a laugh despite the slight tug at my heart after what happened last night. Maybe he was just drunk. I didn't feel him making love to another woman. He was with me the whole time. It was just a slip of the tongue. Because his eyes are so sincere right now, he does mean what he says.

"I want more," he says again with more confidence. Probably since there's a goofy smile on my face.

Keep it together and ask…

"What does that mean?" I ask nervously. But I have to ask. "We'll be a couple? Like you're my boyfriend, and I'm your girlfriend."

There, I cannot be more precise than that. I don't want to walk into this blindly. I need to know for sure, because he is a master in the mixed-signal department.

"I like that. I'll be your boyfriend." He gathers me closer to him, leans in to kiss my forehead, and breathes, "But you're more than a girlfriend to me, Grace. You're my piece of heaven on this earth."

Oh my God.

My eyes get teary after this. I don't want to cry again. So, I hide my face in his chest. I don't know a worthy comeback to his beautiful words.

We stand for a while in comforting silence. My head is on his chest, while his chin rests on the top of mine.

"I wanna ask you something?" He breaks the silence.

I pull back a little, smiling. "What?"

"We're throwing a party for my mother," he says, observing me. "It's her birthday tonight. Just the family and a couple of friends." He pauses for a second, his hands getting firmer on my waist, "I want you to come with me."

"Where?" Isn't that the stupidest question ever? But I'm amazed he's asking me to his mother's birthday party.

"To my parents," he says calmly, but I feel how nervous he is. He's now detaching himself from me, one hand going behind his neck. "I know it's a last-minute kind of thing, but I really want you to come with me."

I'm back to being confused. Now he wants me to meet his parents.

This is moving too fast and very unexpectedly as well.

I was wallowing in misery the whole morning, and now I'm excited and daydreaming about a life with him. I should think wisely.

He does seem honest and sincere with me. He's trying to move on from her, and I don't think that's going to be an easy road for him and us. But if he's willing to give us a chance, I'm more than willing to try. I do love him; there's no question about it. He was drunk when he called me by her name. It still hurts, but it was a slip of the tongue. He was with me the whole time, not her. I'm sure of that.

"I don't know. You're right. It's a last-minute kind of thing," I say, nervously. I don't want to let him down, but I'm still confused. Though I'm willing to try, I prefer to take baby steps. "I don't know if I'm ready to meet your parents."

"They're very nice people—the sweetest on earth. You shouldn't worry about anything," he says in a rush. He's in a hurry to convince me to do it.

I rub my arms, as if I want to take the sudden excitement out of him being this desperate to move us into the next step. But still, this is too fast, and I don't want another letdown like last night. But I'm not meeting his eyes when I apologize, "I'm really sorry. I just don't feel this thing. I mean, meeting your parents."

He hides his hands in his pockets and looks down at his feet. I feel how nervous he has become before lifting his eyes back to me. "When do you finish with your therapist?"

"I have an appointment at three. So by four, I'll be finished." Unless my therapist decides to give me extra time if she thinks I need it. She's great with me.

"I'll call you then," he says, a bit of hope in his eyes. "To hear your final decision. Talk about it with your therapist if it helps," he adds with a tender smile.

Am I a total wreck? I need to talk about a party with my therapist? Or did I lose my sense of humor?

"Why do you really want me to come? You were going without me anyway. Why the sudden urge to have me tagging along?"

"It's my mother's birthday party. I'd be gone like the whole night," he says and starts to rub his neck. "That's too much time without you, Grace. I don't think I can be away from you after last night."

Oh, God. I can't now.

This good boy keeps surprising me with good news. I'm literally speechless. I thought he'd be wary about me, about us being a thing, and now he's pulling all the strings for us to become one.

"I don't think I can either," I say, smiling. I cannot contain my happiness at his words, his confessions, and his heartwarming nervousness about us. I decide to leave the worrying to my therapist. For now, I'll accept this happy moment.

I'm in his arms again as he asks, "That means...it's a yes?"

I nod. "It's a *yes,* and now I need you to tell me a little about your mother so that I can bring her a gift."

"I'll bring one for the both of us," he says, kissing my nose. My heart is over the moon. We're going as a couple where we'll share a gift.

"But she has never met me or even knows about me or about us." I'm reluctant to say this, but I have to. It'll be weird for his parents. We've just happened.

"Um...not exactly," he says. "I've told her about you."

"Really?" I jump back from his arms. I'm totally surprised. "What did you tell her about me?"

"That you're gonna be good for me," he says cryptically. I sense he's not going to divulge anything more.

I wish I could ask... *Are you gonna be good for me too, Ian?*

But I offer, "I'll arrange a bouquet for her then, just tell me what her favorite flowers and scents are."

"I think you should arrange one of your favorites. That way, she'll get to know how wonderful and amazing you are."

And just like that, after this miserable morning, my good boy has made me the happiest girl alive. My goofy grin doesn't leave my face, even when I arrive at my therapist's office. I have a lot to tell her. For the first time, I'll be giving her good news, and I hope she will approve.

CHAPTER NINETEEN

Ian

THREE YEARS AGO

LIFE HAS ALWAYS been good to me. Except struggling with my weight throughout my teen years, I haven't had big issues to deal with, I have lovely parents and the sweetest sister in the world, and our home is always filled with love. But now, life is better than ever because of Acacia.

I've landed the contract with the well-known shoe brand, and all I can think of is how to break the news to Acacia. I left my office half an hour ago and headed to the store where she works because I want her to be the first to know.

I'm standing with a stupid smile on my face in front of the store. Before I pull open the door. I look inside, and there she is in front of the counter, interacting with a customer. As soon as she finishes with him, I pull open the door and walk inside.

It's not long before she tilts her head to the side, and our eyes lock. Her mouth forms an O before she hurriedly walks around the counter toward me.

"Ian," she says nervously, before looking over her shoulder, then suddenly she grabs my hand, dragging me toward the glass doors.

"Acacia." I need an explanation as she pulls open the door and drags me behind her and out onto the sidewalk.

"I'm sorry." She lets go of my hand while we stand facing each other. "I'm not allowed to entertain anyone here. I'm still in the three-month trial, and I don't want to break any rules."

"I'm sorry." I bring a hand to my neck. I didn't even think of anything before coming here. "I just wanted to tell you my big news and couldn't wait till we get home."

She looks back nervously at the store. "I wish I could stand here with you and hear all about it, but I have to go back. Customers are coming in."

"I understand," I say, disappointed. I think she's exaggerating. "So, I'll tell you when we get home."

"Yeah, I'm sorry," she says, raising up on her tiptoes to brush her lips against mine before she sprints back into the store.

I stand there watching her till I see her back behind the counter. She told me she was accepted here because they liked her edge. At the time, I really didn't think she had an edge. She's just my sweet Acacia, but times like this make me wonder. Do I really know her? I mean, the way she just ignored me. I don't think five minutes to tell her about my news would make any difference. My mind goes back to the escort site. I don't know why it's still in the back of my mind. I know she put that picture there, but I don't know why, which still causes doubt in me.

I don't want to keep questioning my luck. Maybe the store has strict rules, and it's the fat kid in me who tries to ruin Acacia and me.

The fat kid doesn't believe his luck. Yes, from time to time, I still think of myself like that. It's not something I can get rid of all the time. So maybe it's just some insecurities that keep poking that doubt in me about her, like how I could be enough to such an amazing, beautiful girl.

Going back to the office, I try to forget these thoughts. I try to focus on my work, my ideas, and creating the next one. To be honest, I want to stay late till I know Acacia will be sleeping when I get home. I don't want another encounter where it'd make me question my luck.

It's not until twelve-thirty that I leave the office and head home. I try to walk in quietly, so I don't wake her up, but she literally jumps up from the couch as soon as I walk into the living room.

"You're finally home." She throws herself at me, her arms behind my neck and her legs around my waist. I welcome her with a spin. I like that she was worried about me, but she also knew I needed a little space. So, she didn't text or call. That's what makes Acacia great with me. She gets me most of the time and gives me the space I need.

"I landed that contract." I finally get the chance to tell her my news as I spin her around the living room.

"Oh, that's so great!" She brushes her lips against mine as I slowly settle her on the couch. Her eyes are full of anticipation and worry. But she's so damn beautiful. I shrug off my worries as I pull back from her, not breaking our eye contact. "You know how much I want you, Acacia."

She's looking at me with heated eyes as I start shedding off my clothes. I'm hungry for her, for confirmation that what we have is real.

I lean in to give her a kiss before I feel her fingers unbuttoning my shirt. I pull away and shrug out of it, my pants next. Acacia looks at me with pure excitement. As soon as I connect my lips to hers, she doesn't hesitate to show me how much she wants me.

We kiss, we make out, we fuck, I make her come, and she makes me come alive. We fuck again then we make love on the couch not once or twice. We just do it, and do it, then do it again. I know she's telling me how sorry she is about earlier at the store, and I want to believe there is nothing to make me worry.

"I'm gonna make a ton of money with this contract," I say as I pull her on my lap after our sex marathon. She runs a hand over my chest while my hand runs up and down her back. "I'm already planning where our house will be."

I feel her hand still on my chest before she starts drumming her fingers on my skin. She's become nervous or excited. I don't know which as she says, "Yeah, tell me about our house."

"It's gonna be everything you ever dreamed of." I kiss the top of her head. "But first, you have to tell me about your dreams, Acacia."

She looks at me for a second before gazing down again. "I never knew I dreamt about you. You're the most beautiful dream I never asked for."

"Acacia." I don't like that. I don't like it at all. "If we're moving too fast, just tell me. I'll do whatever I can to make you comfortable with us."

"It's too late now," she says cheerfully. "You'd never change exciting into something comfortable. I like your fire, Ian. I like the urgency you have for everything you do, for us. I like that you're making us unique. We don't follow any patterns of what couples are supposed to do or how to act."

Then why do I feel like there's something missing for you? Why do I feel I'd never make you happy or content no matter what I do or how hard I try?

I feel these little things, like earlier at the store and a minute ago when her hand stilled on my chest. Those little things worry me, but I don't tell her how I feel. I will not allow that fat kid to come to the surface anytime soon.

"I think I proved myself. I'm not a Ted Bundy," I counter, hoping she'll get the hint. So far, she hasn't really told me anything personal about herself. I respected her need to be sure of me. But after two months of closeness, of her opening up physically to me, I think it's time she opens up about herself. I'm already planning for a house and a future with a girl I hardly know anything about, but at the same time, I feel like she's closer to me than anyone else.

"I grew up in Tendaville. It's a small town near Seattle," she reveals, and I sit there and listen. "I'm an only child. So, my parents pampered me to death. That's why I decided to be on my own for a while. To discover myself without the protection and guidance of my parents. So..." I feel her smile against my neck, "I'm a pretty normal girl, and I just wanted a little edge. That's why I dyed my hair, I guess, in case you're wondering about it too."

Okay, maybe she needs some time to figure herself out. That's why she's reluctant about us sometimes. I don't blame her. I know I can be too much at times. I have a strong personality that might shadow her in some ways.

"You know what," I'm going to say it for her sake. I'll say what she's holding back. "I'm ready to wait forever till you find your true passions and desires. We don't have to do the big house and big commitment anytime soon. Until you figure everything out, I'll just hang in here and support you as much as you need."

She spins in my lap till she's looking down at me, her hand cupping my jaw. "What did I do to deserve you?"

"No..." I move her till she mounts me. "It's what did I do to deserve you?"

"Well, I can tell you a thing or two," she says hoarsely as she lets me into her entrance slowly. "For starters..." she starts to giggle, and I know she's going to tell me one of her jokes, "you're ten inches," she says, still giggling.

I burst out laughing. "I'm not."

"You are to me," she says, sliding down on me. My cock feels deep inside her, warm, and at home. In heaven.

"God," she moans as I close my mouth around one nipple, then she starts riding my cock. "If that is not ten inches, I don't know what..." she moans, unable to say more.

"I'll tell you what it is, babe." I take hold of her hips, lifting her, then slamming her down on me. "It's the only cock your pretty pussy is gonna ever have." I lock my eyes with hers. There's no question there. I'm the only man for her. I just wish I could hold onto this moment forever. But there are always these things that I try hard to ignore. But they are there.

I'm not surprised when I wake up the next morning to an empty bed. I carried her there last night. But she again, as always, went back to her room. She says she needs some space. Even after last night, she still needs space from me.

While I'm trying to break all the walls between us, she's still hanging onto hers.

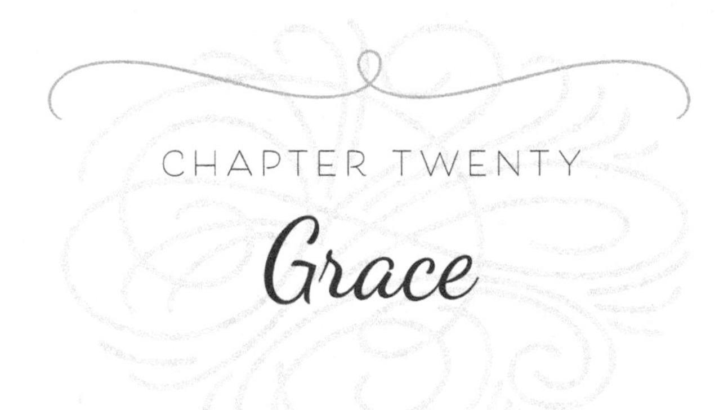

CHAPTER TWENTY
Grace

I'M SITTING ACROSS from my therapist, Dr. Cooney Griffin. She has this look of intrigue on her face. "There's something marvelous happening with you."

I entwine my hands and rest them in my lap, a bit giddy and nervous. "I've met someone. His name is Ian. He's a great guy, really one of the good guys. Like, he's ambitious, successful, donates to charities regularly, very close to his family." I huff. "I mean, he's almost perfect."

"Almost?" Dr. Griffin taps a finger on her desk. "We're gonna talk about that then. Why is he *almost* perfect? I know no one's perfect, but why does it bother you?"

I glance at my hands for a moment, then back at my doctor. "He's in love with another girl."

"Do you think you're doing it again?"

"What do you mean?"

"Trapping yourself into something that would only make you unhappy. Unsatisfied." Dr. Griffin sighs. "You still feel guilty, and you're going into this relationship because, deep down, you cannot picture yourself deserving any real happiness. You still think you owe it to Sam."

"No," I say. "It's not about Sam. This time it isn't about Sam."

"But you said this guy is in love with another girl. Why would you invest in this relationship with that knowledge? It's like you're going after hurt and pain, not moving forward with your life and seeking the things you deserve."

"I feel like he wants to let go of her. Of her love. Maybe I can help him with that. Maybe I can truly show him what he deserves."

"Did he tell you anything about her? Or why did they end their relationship?"

"No, I don't think it's an easy topic for him, and I don't want to push it." I pass a hand over my dress before meeting my doctor's firm eyes. "I mean, we've just happened, and it's too early to talk about these things."

Dr. Griffin rests back in her seat. "I understand. But you have to be careful, Grace. Maybe on some unconscious level, you think you don't deserve real happiness."

"I don't know. Thinking about Sam doesn't bring any guilt to me anymore, but..." I take a long breath. "Like three weeks ago, I saw that scene in the mirror again. I don't know what happened. I wasn't stressed or anything. Like, out of the blue...I was passing a mirror, then it was there. Ian was a great help when it happened."

Leaning forward, Dr. Griffin gives me another sigh. "I don't need to tell you again, but I will. You have to open up about that night, about what made you do it. It's not enough to say you're not going to harm yourself again. On some level, you're still haunted by that night. Building walls around it won't help. Because if you don't feel any guilt anymore, why do you choose to disassociate yourself from everything that would make you feel again?"

"Not with Ian. With him, I'm not numb," I say. "He makes me feel. He makes it okay for me to feel things. Sadness, anger, hurt. I don't know. He makes me feel safe to feel anything."

"I don't want to sound like a downer here," she says. "But you should know by now. It has to come from within you. It's great he can help, but you have to be able to do it on your own."

"I know." I press my lips together. "But I'm glad I have him now."

"So, that means…" Dr. Griffin squints an eye at me. "Did you talk with him about that night?"

"I wanted to," I say honestly.

"But?"

"At the time, he didn't want to know," I say, squirming in my seat.

"Now I can honestly say, you're doing it again," Dr. Griffin says firmly. "He doesn't want to know about this important event in your life. In my book, that means he doesn't care."

"Or he just can't deal with it. He can't get deeply involved with me, at least for now," I counter, praying it's true. "He told me he needs time. I'm willing to give it to him."

"While he's in love with another girl?"

"It's not what you think." I hate her words, even if they're the truth. I want to give him the benefit of the doubt.

"Then tell me how this guy is going to be good for you?"

"He makes me feel," I say, wishing I would get the okay from my doctor. "He has this ability to break my numbness. And most of all, he makes it okay to open up about that night. He makes it easy to face it again because he makes me feel safe. Like, whatever

I might find about myself, he's gonna be there for me, supporting and not judging."

I know that my guilt had driven me to cut my vein. It's a thought that played in my head for a while. That was led by other dark thoughts over the years.

I was adopted, while Sam paid the highest price to protect me.

I was the one who lived to get the life of my dreams, and Sam just died in such a horrible way. Why did someone as courageous and selfless as Sam not get anything good in life?

All these thoughts had driven me crazy, until I finally couldn't live with that guilt.

I take a long breath, feeling uncomfortable. "Um... I think-"

"I understand," my doctor interrupts, knowing I cannot divulge anything more today. "But next time, we need to dig deeper than this."

My doctor still wants me to dig deeper. And telling her about Ian, she thinks I'm starting to follow a pattern, to hurt myself. As deep down, she thinks I don't believe I deserve anything good.

I don't think my talk with Dr. Griffin helped with my confusion, but it was good to talk and open up again. Especially about Ian. Maybe I can think wisely about him now.

Two hours later, I'm back at the apartment and getting ready for the big night. I'm going to meet Ian's parents.

I feel a little nervous, and wonder what to wear.

I choose a blue dress with flower print, short sleeves, and pleated ruffle trim around its V neckline. It looks pretty and elegant with my dark hair loose around my shoulders. I apply concealer under my eyes to hide those dark circles, then some lip gloss and eyeliner, and I'm ready for the night.

I heard Ian close the front door a while ago, and now he's knocking on mine.

I grow nervous as I open my bedroom door, and the deliciously handsome Ian is waiting for me. He's not wearing a suit, so I guess the party isn't formal. I want to high-five myself since my simple dress will go well with Ian's dark blue shirt and dark jeans.

After the quick body sweep, my eyes connect with his. He smiles tenderly. "You're breathtakingly beautiful."

I think I'm tongue-tied at how he's the one breathtakingly beautiful or just because of the heat in his eyes before I catch on fire as the back of his hand travels the neckline of my dress. He's drawing the V with his fingers as he says, "Flowers and ruffles, that's very you, Grace. Elegant, beautiful, and angelic."

I put a hand over his. I need him to stop. First: I cannot stand with dignity while he's touching me like that. Second: "I'm not angelic, Ian. I don't think I've done anything of that sort in my entire life."

He catches my hand in his, raises it to his lips before dropping them at our sides. "You've filled my heart again, Grace. That's very angelic to me."

I try to breathe. I cannot handle his words or the tremendous emotions in his dark blue eyes. If I don't act soon, *I love you* would come next from his sexy lips.

But it would be from the man who called me by another girl's name last night. I don't think he's ready to say these words. Or I'm even ready to accept them. So, I squeeze his hand. "Let me show you the bouquet I arranged for your mother."

He blinks, taken aback and disappointed. But I have to.

He looks to the side for a second before he looks at me again, saying, "I have something to give you first."

Walking me out of the bedroom and into the living room, he says, "I hope you like it. I got it while buying a gift for Mom. I couldn't resist buying you something."

I smile as we sit on the couch. Two velvet boxes are on the coffee table.

He picks one up and flips it open. "This is for Mom."

"It's beautiful." It's a vintage diamond necklace with three-stone drop pendants. I'm sure his mother will love it.

After putting his mother's gift aside, he picks up the other box and flips it open. "I hope you like this one too."

Blinking twice, I cannot believe he's bought me a diamond bracelet. I've never worn one or even been this close to any diamonds. I look up at him, and there's anticipation in his eyes. He's giddy, waiting for my response. As much as this gift is scaring me, I cannot disappoint him. "It's very beautiful," I whisper while my eyes drop down to the box. It's a beautiful bracelet. It's wide and filled with tiny pink flowers. I cannot stop smiling. He chose flowers; he's put a lot of thought into it.

He lifts the bracelet out of the box. "Let me," he says, dropping the box aside, and before I hold out my right arm, he reaches for my left.

"Does it bother you?" I ask after he clasps the bracelet around my left wrist, thinking he doesn't want his parents to see my scar hidden under his diamond bracelet now.

With warm eyes, he reaches to take my hands in his. "Of course not. I just want you to feel comfortable tonight, not worrying about anyone questioning what you did. I want you to get to know my family and have fun."

"But I've gotten comfortable with it all," I say, as we're looking down at our joined hands. "You know, the questions, the surprised looks, even the pettiness. I don't shy away from *me* anymore."

"I'm sorry. I'm not going to believe this lie tonight."

"I'm not lying." I try to pull my hands away from his, but he doesn't budge as he looks me in the eye. "Remember the night at your friend's party? As soon as Arthur looked at your scar, you ran away, and I don't want you to run away from me tonight."

"I was doing it for you. I was saving you from me."

"And knowing you…you might try to save me tonight too," he counters, unconvinced.

I clench my teeth. He has a point. I don't want to cast a shadow over his mother's birthday party. I look at our joined hands while his thumb starts to draw circles over my skin. "At some point, I'll tell them everything. But not tonight. I don't think you're even ready for it."

"They're very protective of you," I state, fearing how they'd react if they knew their son is in a relationship with a girl who tried to kill herself once. That would scare the shit out of any loving parent, or that's what I think at the moment.

I guess *his girl* is not the only obstacle we're going to face.

"Very protective," he agrees.

"Well, my parents are finally giving me some space," I try to share. "I mean, after I moved here into the city, they were calling nonstop and taking monthly trips to see me. Not that I was complaining, I just didn't want them to worry about me constantly."

I cannot put my finger on what came over his eyes at the mention of my parents, but before I figure it out, he smiles, "I'd be a very protective dad too. Especially if we had a girl like her mom. Sweet and too good for this world."

My heart is going to jump out of my chest. He's talking about having a baby girl with me. It's too soon and too good to be true.

Like he's pushing all the buttons to move on from his girl. Because I don't think we're even close to getting a pet together, not to mention having a baby.

He almost said *I love you,* and now is talking about a family. I think he's a little dreamy tonight. I want to believe that, but I know better.

I inhale deeply before I get to my feet, pulling him up with me. "You said we should be there at eight. It's about time we leave."

"Yep." Standing, he bends to brush his lips against mine; his eyes read my confusion. "I wish it was not my mother's birthday tonight. Otherwise, I'd be buried deep inside you, convincing you how good we're going to be."

"Ian..." I want to say so much. I want to inquire about the sudden changes he's showing me, but it's not the time. "We're gonna be late."

Nothing is said after that. We're in his car, and he's driving us to his parents' house.

"So, how's it been growing up in the big city?" I ask, enjoying watching him this carefree. "Is everything twice bigger, twice larger, and more dramatic?"

"Small or big, life could be twice bigger and more dramatic for some than others. It's not the place. It's the people around us who make the difference."

"Wise words." I agree with him, but... "We don't get to have these big ice cream cones to make the drama less dramatic, so the city does have some points."

He gives a laugh. "I thought that would make your ass blow out of proportion."

"Yep, I think so too," I say with a timid voice. I don't know why I just get the feeling he's sharing one of those inside jokes with *his girl*. He didn't even know he was doing it. It came naturally out of his lips. But I shake my head. A minute ago, he was talking babies with me. He's serious about us.

But serious doesn't necessarily mean it's the right thing.

At the threshold of his parents' house, I decide to abandon thinking and enjoy the small party as the door is open by a smiling young woman. She has light brown hair that is loose on her shoulders and bright green eyes, wearing a knee-length white dress.

"Oh, finally." The cheerful young woman throws her arms around Ian's neck, and her voice is a bit tearful. "You don't know how much I missed you."

"Yeah…" Ian hugs her tight. "I think I have an idea or two. Actually, I have hundreds of texts to prove it, little sis."

My heart is relieved. She's his sister.

The sister pulls back a little. "You've read them?"

"Oh, I read them," he says dramatically. They both crack up laughing before he gathers her in his arms again. "It's good to have you back," he says as he pulls back from her and turns to me where our eyes connect. For some reason, the mirth leaves his. At the same time, his sister turns around, her eyes land on me, and her smile disappears.

"What are you doing outside?" An older woman walks out the front door, her mouth forming an O when she spots me. She gives me a smile before turning to Ian. "I didn't know you were bringing someone."

She turns to me again. "He didn't tell me he was bringing a date." She's walking my way, then pauses a foot away from me, looks me up and down before shaking her head. "Can you believe it? He hasn't brought a date here since ever. And when he does, he didn't even bother to tell me. I don't even know your name."

Her words make me think. He told me she knew about us. I glance up quickly at Ian before I smile at his mom. "I'm Grace." I extend the bouquet I brought for her. "I hope you like them."

"Grace," she says in shock, then turns to Ian, then back to me. "You do exist then. When he told me about you, I thought he was just saying... You know, to get off his back about dating again."

So he did tell her about me. But why didn't she believe him?

"Happy birthday, Mom." Ian steps from behind her, lays a hand on her shoulder, and bends to give her a kiss on the cheek before saying while smiling at me, "As you can see, Grace really exists, so why don't you accept her beautiful flowers."

His mother taps her head. "The flowers, oh how lovely." She takes it from my hands, babbling, "I can be clumsy sometimes."

"Sometimes!" Ian and his sister mock in union, but when my eyes land on the latter, I feel like she's not warming up to me like her mother.

"These two," Ian's mom shakes her head, then grabs me by the arm. "Come on. Brad will be thrilled to meet you."

"Brad?" I question as I'm led inside the house by Ian's mom.

I'm not yet out of earshot as his sister says, "I cannot believe you've brought her here."

Oh, oh...

So, his sister knows about me too, but she's not as thrilled as her mother, to say the least.

CHAPTER TWENTY-ONE

Grace

WE'RE IN THE living room where I comfortably sit between Ian's parents, Catherine and Brad. The family album lay on my lap as they take turns flipping through the pages. I'm having a blast with all the jokes and the stories they're sharing with me.

From time to time, I glance where Ian and Emma are having quite the talk near the French windows. A tough conversation is going on between the two of them. Ian's handling it calmly while a storm shows on Emma's face. I wonder if it's about bringing me to this family event.

"Now the horrible teen years," Brad says as Catherine flips the page, bringing my attention back to the album between my hands.

"In a big city or a small town, teen years are tough on us all." I smile back at Brad, who is an older version of his son. He's got the same dark blue eyes while Catherine has bright green like her daughter.

"I see a very wise girl here," Brad tilts his head to look at his wife.

"She has a peaceful energy. I think she's going to be very good to him. She'd put the brakes to his urgent soul." Catherine bends to communicate with her husband as the two of them act like I don't exist, which is so adorable and quirky.

I clear my throat, pointing two fingers down. "I'm right here."

Both crack a laugh. "We're grateful that you're here."

Catherine pats my knee. "Very grateful."

I don't want to read too much into their words, but I cannot hide my smile. I feel giddy and content. "Thanks for having me."

"It's our pleasure," Brad says, then taps his fingers back on the album. "He was chubby. Just a little bit, but at the time, he thought he was the fattest kid on earth. Thank God those years are over."

I'm taken aback. Brad is pointing at a picture of Ian. He might have been fifteen or a little older and a little fat, if I might say. My heart aches for him, after hearing his father talk about his struggle.

"Yeah, those were hard years for him," Catherine shares. I look at her sideways, saying, "Well, he was a little chubby, but still, he was very cute."

Brad snorts. "No fourteen-year-old boy wants to be chubby but cute."

I want to ask more about teen Ian, but the doorbell rings, and Ian says, "I'll get it."

I guess the party is about to start.

Brad and Catherine stand to greet their guests, and I also, watching the newcomers. I'm a bit surprised to see Arthur and Lucy, who I met at Lucas's party. I guess I shouldn't be. Ian said they're friends of his family.

"They're Ian's therapists." I didn't notice that Emma was standing by my side. I'm genuinely shocked she's sharing this with me.

And more shocked that Ian has not one, but two therapists.

I turn to Emma. She has this calm look on her face. I cannot read much into it, but I don't have to as she's willingly sharing her thoughts with me, "Don't take it the wrong way, but I don't think he's ready for you."

Like I don't know this already.

I want to excuse myself because it's wrong standing here having this conversation. It's as if I'm stealing something Ian's not ready to share, but Emma is intent on telling, "He's gonna be mad as hell at me if he knew I said anything." She huffs a worried breath, glancing over at her brother, then back at me. "But for the sake of you both, stay away from him."

"I don't think you have the right to say that," I say calmly, though my heart is swimming in unbearable pain. I feel it in my gut. Her words, I felt them long before I had met her.

"Tomorrow at seven." She looks nervous, as Ian and the guests head in our direction. "Meet me at the Yoldi bar, and I'll explain everything."

I don't get the chance to respond as Ian and his therapists walk toward us. "Oh, Grace," Lucy says, approaching us while I catch the shock on Emma's face. She's probably surprised I've already met Ian's therapists.

"It's so nice to see you again," Lucy says, leaning in to place a kiss on my cheek.

"It's very nice to see you too," I say, smiling.

Arthur nods his head. "Grace." He's still not as thrilled about me as Lucy.

Ian slides an arm across my back as we walk into the dining room. I feel a bit relaxed. I try to shrug off his sister's words. He's a big boy who can decide for himself.

I'm not going to care what his sister thinks or let her words affect us. We have enough going on, and I will not add his sister to the mix. I understand she might know more about him than me for now, but that doesn't validate her meddling between us as she did a minute ago. Even if she's doing it for his sake.

I'm more confident in my decision as Ian pulls me into him, his arms looping around me from behind. His chin rests on the top of my head as we chant *Happy Birthday* to his mom.

He holds me through it all. The candles blown out, the wish made, jokes and laughter fill the room, and I become more relaxed.

I know what I've gotten myself into, and I'm not leaving Ian's side till he tells me to. I feel like he needs me in his life to get over what's keeping him unsettled.

"Lucy and Arthur seem like really good friends of your parents." I turn to Ian as everyone enjoys the cake.

"Yeah," Ian says, "they used to live next door before they moved. Unlike my parents, they're a bit adventurous, and not having any children helps a little."

"Are they teachers like your parents?" I want to test Emma's words.

"No, they are psychologists." He's not looking my way now. His eyes travel the room. "I'd say they're the best in their field, but recently they've retired and decided to travel all around the world." He glances at me calmly before looking away again, "They helped me deal with lots of things, actually."

I can feel that's all he wants to share with me right now, so I don't push for more, though I'm dying to know everything about him.

For a moment, we stay silent, neither of us knowing what to say before he asks, his voice near a whisper, "How did things go with your therapist?"

I smile. I think that's a start. He's genuinely interested in knowing me better. "It was good to talk," I pause. "I told her about you too."

I know he's not ready to know everything about me, so that's all I share.

Turning to me, he has a giddy smile on his face. "You did, huh?"

"Yeah," I cannot help but become giddy too. "We did lots of talking about you, actually."

He looks at me soulfully for a moment, his eyes traveling over my features before he gathers two locks of hair behind my ears then lets his fingers go through them. "I love your hair. I love how long it is. I love the color. I love how dark it is against your pale skin. Just like an angel."

I reach to ruffle the front of his hair. "I love yours too."

"I wanna take you somewhere." He grasps my hand and starts guiding me toward the door.

I don't know if everyone's oblivious to us as we walk out of the dining room and to the stairs where Ian gushes, "I'll show you all my hidden skeletons."

"That would be your room."

"You're right, angel." He's so giddy and thrilled, making me giddy and thrilled, and whatever his sister said is thrown down the stairs as we reach the top.

We turn to the left, walking down a long hallway before Ian pauses at the first door. "Are you ready, angel?"

I don't know why he's calling me angel, but I don't mind it.

"Never been this ready." I press a hand on his shoulder. I don't know why I feel him getting nervous.

He nods before reaching to turn the doorknob. He opens the door, steps inside, and turns on the light. "I hope I'm gonna see yours too."

"Of course," I immediately say. I know he's not only asking to see my room. He wants to know me better, to understand what I have been through.

It feels like he's talking to himself, wishing he will have enough strength to get to know me better. To make me his girl.

Moving to the side, he gestures with his hand for me to step in.

Excited, I walk inside.

As soon as I walk in, he closes the door and rests against it. "Don't look at me. Look around and try to find me here."

A hand touches the nape of my neck. A cloud of yearning, joy, and nostalgia fills his eyes, making my heart pulse with so many emotions.

I spin and look around. His room is quite large. The bed is under a large window, where there must have been lots of sneaking going on.

My eyes travel to his desk, where there's a crystal snow globe. "Let me guess," I say, a bit cheeky, walking there and picking up the crystal ball. "One of your girlfriends."

I'm a bit jealous.

"No, it's Emma. I had gotten very sick one time, and she insisted it'd make me less grumpy. And what Emma plants has to stay."

"You're so close to her." I put down the crystal ball, and I'm nervous all over again. Maybe she's right in some ways.

"Yes, we are." He folds his arms, looking me up and down as if assessing how much he should tell me about them. "You know, while growing up, I thought I was her rock, and she was just my sweet little sister. But for the past two years, she's the one who had my back. She was my rock, not the other way around."

I nod, wondering if that was the case, why she tried to reveal some things about him. I think Ian would be very disappointed in her if he knew.

My eyes scan the desk one more time, and I take a minute to stare at the siblings' picture. Ian is laying his arm protectively over Emma's shoulders.

"That was 2008. I'm fifteen years old." Suddenly Ian is by my side. A heavy breath escapes his mouth. "What do you think? Would you have dated me back then?"

I frown, then it hits me why he asks. I didn't even notice he's heavier in this picture. I've only captured his younger soul and beautiful eyes.

I tilt my head to look at him. "You were fifteen then, and there's a four-year age difference between us, so I would say that would have been impossible."

I'm not going to say I was shallow as expected of any teen girl when it comes to dating, where looks played a huge factor. But that's not the case with me because dating hadn't even crossed my mind back then. I had a lot of heavy stuff to deal with, and Sam was still alive. "But I see a very cute guy right here. I'm sure lots of girls wanted to date you."

"No, not really," he says lightly, as if the memories don't hurt anymore. "I had lots of friends, and I was outgoing and did this and that. But anything related to dating and girls was a total disaster." He inhales deeply before sharing, "What I'm telling you here...is that fat kid sometimes shows up here and there. I can't control how he acts or what he says. It's really hard to get rid of him. So, sometimes I'd act or say things out of his insecurities, and that doesn't mean I'm targeting you in some way."

I think he's talking about how he usually reacts to anything *Theodore-related,* but I don't say it. Instead, I ask, "Why do you want to get rid of him?"

For a beat, discomfort shows on his face before he smiles. "I don't want a kid controlling me. Things could go dramatically wrong."

"Well." I smile too. "Let's say he's here, and somehow I'm here too... I mean fifteen-year-old me." I lock my arms around his neck. "How could anything go dramatically wrong?"

Laughing, he wraps his arms around me. "He would totally ruin this."

"Cute Ian would ruin nothing. I think he'd ruin it only in Sexy Ian's head." I tap a finger on the side of his head.

"Oh, how delusional you are." He chuckles, and I'm a little irritated. "Don't laugh at Cute Ian."

"Don't defend him," he says. "The things he would want to do to fifteen-year-old innocent Grace would make you want to strangle him."

"Oh, not really. Teen Grace has hormones too."

"Is that so?" He raises a doubting eyebrow.

"Yes, indeed."

"Don't think like the Grace you are now," he says firmly. "Think like a fifteen-year-old Grace, and this huge kid convinced you, somehow, to be here and wants to have sex with you. What would you really do?"

"Well," I say, thinking deeply about it, "if I'm really attracted to him, if I really liked him, and he'd take all the precautions, I might go along with it."

"What if he doesn't have any protection? What would Teen Grace say?"

"Well, now... I don't think Teen Grace would risk a pregnancy."

"See, now this Ian kid would totally ruin it."

"How? He's not gonna force himself on me. I know Cute Ian would never do that."

"But he would suggest doing it in your ass."

I jump backward, away from him. My hand goes dramatically over my chest. "How dare he? That's so fucked up."

"I told you. He'd ruin it somehow. He's a horny teen boy who had never even kissed a girl."

"Ruin it?" I yell. "He destroyed every little chance he might have in the future."

"Well, thanks for the heads up." Ian rolls his eyes dramatically.

I squint my eyes at him. Would he want...? I want to ask him, but I just wave a hand and spin around. "We're not even...like ever, ever gonna talk about that, not to mention doing it."

I hear him laughing before he envelopes me from behind. "Yep. I kinda figured it out on my own."

"Yeah, don't even try, like ever." I stomp the floor. That's so not in my books, like never ever.

He laughs against my neck. "I'm not into that, so relax. I'm all into your little kitty."

"Shut up. You're not talking dirty to me now." I dig an elbow into his ripped stomach. "I don't even call it that."

"Oh..." He says hoarsely, one hand starting to massage my stomach in circles, "what do you call it then?"

"None. Of. Your. Business." I try to sound firm as his hand starts to move down.

His hand stills. His breaths get hotter on my neck. "It is my business," he says possessively, turning me to him suddenly. My chest clashes against his, my nipples dig right into the fabric of his dress shirt. "It's the only fucking business my mind could think about all day," he says before his lips crash against mine. And as if I was waiting, my lips open for his tongue, and he's showing me how much he wanted this business, as he claims. He kisses me thoroughly, before I feel his hands reach for the hem of my dress. With difficulty, I pull back from him. My eyes blur with desire. "Your parents," I hope he gets what I mean. Because I cannot do anything of that sort at his parents' house. I cannot control how loud I'd be.

He presses his hand over his eyes before he steps toward me, grabbing my hand. "Then, let's say our goodbyes."

I barely keep up with Ian as he drags me by the arm out of his room and down the stairs, and back into the dining room, where we indeed say our quick goodbyes.

I feel a little ashamed in front of Ian's parents' knowing smiles, and Catherine's heartwarming, *"Oh they're so in love"* before we're out of earshot.

After fifteen whole minutes of Ian racing to get us out of our frustrated misery, we reach the building. When the doors of the elevator close, I'm pushed against the wall. Ian kisses me like he's never kissed me before. His mouth is possessive, frantic, and hungry, but mine is barely there. I don't know how to deal with his urgency, but as I hear a deep groan down in his throat, I feel like I'm doing something right or um...south.

Jeez.

I'm grabbing him down there. And he's hot and thick and hard in my hand.

He groans again, and I drop my hand while the doors open wide.

He drags me out of the elevator toward his apartment door. He pulls out his keys, opens the door, ushers me in, and slams the door shut as I walk inside. Then suddenly, I'm carried in his arms, his steps racing to reach his room. He lets go of me, and I stand watching. His hands are frantic on his clothes while his eyes glare at me. "What are you waiting for?" he utters urgently. "If you love this dress, you better take it off before I rip it off with my hands."

"I love it, I do," I nod. But I'm still frozen in place, my eyes watching in amazement how he's losing all control.

"Grace," he almost yells as he shrugs off his shirt and throws it to the floor before stepping toward me. "Take this off. Now." He gestures with his eyes as he unbuckles his belt, then unzips his pants, his eyes glaring at me.

I nod again and reach with trembling hands to the hem of my dress. I pull it all the way up and above my head, leaving me in my maroon strapless bra and matching lace panties while Ian only has his boxer briefs on.

When I gaze up at his eyes, he shakes his head. "I can't believe you." He shakes his head again, his eyes heated and intense. "You're going to kill me, aren't you?"

I look down at myself, then up at him, then I'm in his arms. He's kissing me again while his fingers are working my bra. A beat, then I'm braless, my nipples meeting his hard chest, and I moan.

"Ian..." I break the kiss, pleading, the sensation is too much to take.

"I know, angel...I know," he says before his mouth is hot on my nipple, sucking, licking, and driving me crazy and wet.

I'm so damp, my panties are a dripping disgrace.

"You're so fucking wet," he says, shocked, his hand resting down there, on the fabric of my panties. He hasn't even touched me bare yet, and he knows how wet I am.

"Ian," I whisper. "I need um...."

"Need what, angel?" He pulls back a little, giving me some air.

"Um..." I don't know words. Words fail me now. His eyes are concerned, but his hand is still on my panties, burning the shame out of me. As a cloud of doubt fills his eyes, I only find these four words on my tongue. "I need you, Ian."

He huffs a breath of relief before he rests his forehead against mine. "You want slow, angel? If so, you gotta help me a little before I lose all control."

Words, words, words. Where are they? I nod my head. I don't particularly want slow, but I don't mind slow or fast or hard or anything. I don't mind anything from him at all. I only wish I could form some words. But my lips don't know a thing, only to reach and kiss him back. He's kissing me slowly, tenderly, one hand palming my breast while the other reaches for mine. He places it on the elastic of his boxer briefs, whispering, "You wanna help me here...?"

"I definitely wanna help you here." I giggle, and I'm not sure it's an appropriate thing right now, but he's smiling too. I waste no time and dip my hand inside his boxer briefs, and all the mirth leaves his eyes. I plant a kiss on his lips as my hands close around his shaft, pulling it out.

Oh.

He's so perfect. So male. So hard and thick and pulsing non-stop. He's so mine.

"Grace," he says with agony as I still stand, amazed by his manhood. His eyes are full of warnings as I give him my best innocent eyes; he knows I'm going to make him lose all control. "Grace," he warns before I drop to my knees.

"No...no, I didn't mean that." He's shocked and sincere, but I don't care what he wants. I so want to take him in my mouth. See him lose all control because of me.

He's big in my mouth, in my hands. But I try to focus on giving him the best pleasure he's ever had. Him, groaning, guiding, hissing, tells me he's in another world. But then, too soon, too fast, he taps my head. But I don't care, I want to taste him in my mouth, but he taps and taps.

"Grace, don't."

With his firm voice, I pop his hardness out of my mouth. Maybe he's not into that. Still on my knees, I watch as his hand closes around his hardness. He wants to finish what I've started, but I still want him to lose control because of me, not his hand. So, I arch my breasts forward and, locking my gaze with him, and I guide, "Here."

He shakes his head, but his eyes are eager to comply, his eyes don't believe what I'm offering. So, I say again, "Come on my breasts, Ian."

"Fuck," he growls, and without any help of his hand, he comes shattering all over me. It's so erotic and hot as hell.

After calming down, he bends to capture my arms, hauling me to my feet before he reaches to grab some tissues and starts wiping his come off me.

After making sure I'm clean, he throws the tissues into the trashcan before picking me up in his arms and walking us over to the bed, where he lays me in the middle.

"You're such a wicked angel," he says as he slowly lays himself on top of me, watching his weight. He spreads wet kisses over my face and neck, then, with a smirk, he eases his kisses further down. He flicks a nipple between his fingers before he starts sucking on it. I spread my hands in his hair, urging him to move faster.

"Oh, you want it fast now?" he says in a taunting voice before working his tongue between my breasts and down to my stomach. There, he raises his heated, full-of-mischief eyes to me, his fingers playing with the elastic of my panties. "I want to rip this thing off…but when you dropped your dress, it was the most fucking beautiful sight I have ever seen. *You* in your matching bra and little panties. I want to see that again."

"I'll buy another set," I quickly say. I want him to tear them off me. I'm throbbing thinking about it.

He seems surprised. "You bought these for me?"

I make a face. "Maybe."

"Cock tease," he says playfully before I gasp as my panties are no longer covering me. He throws the torn panties to the floor, his blue eyes taking me in, every inch of my nakedness.

And I'm staring too. He's so beautiful, so male.

He fists his cock with one hand and strokes himself from the base to the tip.

I cannot take my eyes away. I'm blushing. I'm squeeing inside. I feel like a pervert watching him do that, but I cannot take my eyes away.

He smirks, his eyes smoldering with heat. "That's what I did when I thought of you."

A moan escapes my mouth. The heat between my thighs is becoming unbearable.

He doesn't miss a thing. He nudges his chin forward, his features becoming more intense. "Now, touch your pussy while telling me how much you want my cock."

"Ian..." A small protest surges out of my mouth, despite how hot and bothered his bossy attitude is making me.

He doesn't budge, his strokes becoming faster, his eyes challenging me to surrender. As the heat between my legs intensifies, watching him stroking himself is a big turn-on.

Bashfully while my cheeks flame with heat, I part my folds and slip two fingers inside. Just to lick off some of the frustration I have.

"Wider, open wider," he says gruffly, coming forward, and a loud moan escapes my mouth as he starts to rub the tip of his cock against my clit.

"Ian..." I cry out. My fingers aren't bashful as I am, slipping in and out of me in a frenzy while he's rubbing his cock mercilessly against my bud.

This is so intense. He's so intense. I can't tell if he's even breathing. I don't hear anything. The only sounds to be heard are my fingers slipping in and out of my wetness.

Before I start to get bashful again, he takes my mouth in a kiss, his hand reaching down to replace mine.

Now easily, he slips in three fingers at once, asking roughly against my mouth, "Are you ready to take me?"

"Yes. God, yes." My heart beats loud in my chest. I'm still nervous. I don't think I would ever stop being nervous. He's so big.

"Relax," he asks the impossible as he puts a condom on. Done, he presses a kiss to my lips, his eyes gazing at me tenderly. "Gentle and slow, is that what you want?"

I nod and hold a breath as he pushes the tip inside. Our eyes lock. I'm so mesmerized by the intensity in his beautiful blue, while slowly, he slides all the way in.

I gasp, and he stills, his hot breaths burning my neck. "You feel fucking amazing, angel."

"You're amazing too." I push a hand in his soft hair. It's the softest thing about him. I touch the softest thing about him while he pushes his rigid member inside me. I smile at my own joke, and he starts to move.

He pulls halfway, then pushes in again, starting a slow rhythm. "You want it like this?" he barely utters, one hand digging into the matters to restrain himself.

I reach for his hand to entwine our fingers together. "I want it like this, and I want it any way you're willing to take me."

He loops a hand around my neck and thrusts deeper, filling me to the hilt.

"Oh my god." I moan, my walls tightening around him. Really tight. I move a hand up and down his back, feeling how tense he's become.

"Tell me, Grace," he says out of breath, riding me with slow deep thrusts, "when you were at my door the first night, did you know you're gonna end up here, under me, my cock buried deep inside you?"

"Worse," I say hoarsely. "I ached for it. For you, your mouth, your eyes and..." He sucks in a breath, and I let out one, the intensity in his eyes encouraging me. "I ached to be under you like this, your cock buried deep inside me."

"Fuck..." He lets out in an agonized voice, and something in him flips. Taking me slow and gentle is out the window now. He's thrusting hard and fast.

And I wither and whimper. It's pure torture and pure pleasure what he's doing to me.

"Ian, God, Ian..." I'm so close, his thrusts somehow have become deeper. "What are you doing to me?"

He leans down to kiss my mouth deeply. "I'm ruining you for anyone but me. You're mine, Grace, fucking mine."

With urgency, he slips a hand between us to touch my clit. I cannot take it anymore. My walls tighten more around him, making him groan. "You're so fucking tight, Grace. So fucking tight."

"Ian," I cry his name, everything inside me shattering. I close my eyes while he rides me through my orgasm. His thrusts now are faster and harder. Though limp and liquid, I swipe the sweat off my forehead and open my eyes. I want to watch him while he loses control.

But I'm not ready for the emotion in his eyes. He looks down at me with amazement, and I know he's going to say *those* words. He's going to say he loves me, and I have to act.

"Don't go easy on me now," I say urgently. I don't want to hear those words. "Harder, Ian. Harder. I know you want to."

I don't miss the flash of disappointment in his eyes before he surrenders to the hunger inside him. Hunger for me. To take me harder and wilder. He slides all the way out of me before slamming back in, and it doesn't take him long. I watch in pure satisfaction as he throws his head back, groaning his own release.

My favorite part finally arrives as he collapses on top of me.

I love his smell, his sweat, and his weight on me. I feel like I'm his home, his sanctuary, but it doesn't last long. He needs to get rid of the condom that I haven't even noticed he's put on.

After a moment, he rolls to his side, tucking me under his arm. "Grace?"

"Yeah," I say sleepily, already closing my eyes.

"You know you're not gonna get any sleep tonight, right?" he says, assertively, making me giggle.

"I'm serious," he adds, annoyed.

"Yeah, right," I tease.

"It's so fucking right," he retorts fiercely as I feel him slipping his hand from under me, then I gasp as he easily flips me over on my stomach.

"Ian..." I'm so excited and terrified of how aroused this is making me.

"Angel," he says in a knowing voice before he grips my hips, helping me onto my knees.

Breathe, Grace. Breathe

I'm on my knees.

Then I'm on all fours.

I'm panting and excited—drenching wet, excited.

He slides a finger in me, testing if I'm ready for another round. "You don't need to test anything." I look at him over my shoulder. "Wet and ready for you anytime."

He throws his head back, laughing. "What am I gonna do with you now!"

"You're not going to let me sleep."

"Oh…" he places his hands on my hips, his lips near my ear, he whispers, "but if you had any…. I want to wake up to you. Smelling you while your hair spreads over my pillow, and your soft body entwines with mine. 'Cause, you're mine, Grace. You know that, don't you?"

"Yes, I'm yours." I'm barely able to breathe, and I feel his smile before he murmurs, palming my ass cheeks, "I know your pretty little ass is not fuckable, but is it lickable, my angel?"

"It's *outable.*"

"Outable," he repeats, shaking with laughs.

"You know… Nothing goes in, only out."

"I can live with that. But what I can't live with is waking up in a bed without you." I feel him poking at my entrance, before his voice is out of control, "Promise you'll be here when I wake up. Promise I'll wake up to you."

"I promise," I'm barely able to whisper as he slams into me, and any decent thought is out of my mind. "I promise," I say again.

CHAPTER TWENTY-TWO

Ian

THREE YEARS AGO

WITH THE NEW deal, I spend more time at the office and less time with Acacia. On the surface, things are going smoothly. She's so supportive of me. I haven't heard a complaint about us not spending enough time together during the last month. She still makes everything easier for me. Everything's perfect. When I get home, there's always a smile on her face, welcoming and missing me. No complaints are made. But with all of that, I feel there's something wrong. Like my existence or lack of it does not affect her.

I only wish I knew for sure. Is it the fat kid tricking me into his old ways, or should I really be worried about it? Maybe there's something seriously wrong in our relationship.

I don't know. But tonight, I'm going to have an honest talk with her.

I've done everything possible to get off work early, to have decent time for what I'm planning to do.

At six, I arrive at the building. I take the elevator to my apartment, unlike what I do every day since I prefer to walk up the stairs. I want to be as calm as I can when I face her tonight.

But when I open the apartment door, I freeze in place.

What the hell?

I hurry into the living room, where I hear Acacia arguing with some girl, and before I step in, something inside of me decides to stay out of sight and listen.

"Just give me the cash," the girl says, irritated.

"I'm done giving you money. You're a pathetic liar. All you do is lie to me." It's Acacia. She's scolding the girl, but what breaks me inside is the layer of hope still evident in her voice.

"All right," the girl maliciously says, "but blame no one but yourself."

At this point, I cannot just stand still listening outside. I cannot let anyone mistreat my sweet Acacia. I walk right into the living room to put that girl in her place. Even if Acacia is hiding this whole thing from me, I cannot leave her in danger and do nothing about it.

As I walk in, the girl is walking out. As much as I want to make this scum pay, I cannot lay a finger on a girl. I just block her exit to let her know what could happen if she comes close to hurting Acacia.

"Please, Ian. Let her leave," Acacia says as my eyes connect with hers; I'm already feeling the lie she's planning to explain this whole situation. She's nervous, but she's ready with her lie. I can tell. I have come to know her very well.

I step out of the girl's way, shaking my head. I just stare back at Acacia, wondering if I will let myself believe her lie tonight.

But I don't think I can. I don't have it in me anymore. I cannot pretend just to keep her by my side.

"I will not ask," I say, folding my arms as we hear the front door slam shut. "I know you're making up a lie in your head. And tonight, I have no intention to believe your lies, Acacia. So, when you're ready to talk and tell me everything, I'll be in my room, more than ready to hear you and offer my help."

"Ian," she desperately calls as I turn, walking away. "Please, don't be like that."

I spin to face her, spreading my hands in frustration. "Like what? Just spit it out." I yell. I cannot help how frustrated I've become. "What is so wrong with me that you won't open up about anything? Why do you hide things from me? Why don't you trust me enough, Acacia?"

"I'm not hiding anything from you." She takes a step back, till her behind hits the couch. But she's standing still, not blinking an eye.

I cannot believe my eyes. She's just staring at me with dead eyes. With liar's eyes. She's looking at me, spilling her lies, not caring that I know. And damn it, I know she's just told me the biggest one of her lies.

She's hiding everything from me and doesn't even blink when she lies anymore.

I shake my head, miserably laughing. "How about that escort site, which I'm sure that girl has everything to do with." I take a step toward her, my hands curling into fists. "How about that? How about hiding the fact that you're the one who posted your picture there?"

She winces, and I know that I'm right. The girl and that site are related in some way. I push my anger aside, fearing for her safety. My heart is exploding in my chest, but I try to be calm. I need to be calm to save her from whatever she's gotten herself into. "Please, Acacia, if in some way you've gotten yourself into trouble, just tell me, and I'll do whatever I can to help you. Things like that could be very dangerous."

She raises a hand, then drops it down and turns around, her hands gripping the couch so tight, her back shaking, everything in her is shaking. "There's nothing to say. There's nothing you could possibly do. I swear there isn't."

"Yes, there is." I step forward till I catch her elbow and turn her around. I plead with my eyes, with everything in me. I want her to trust me. I don't know why she doesn't.

"Why is it so hard to share, Acacia? I would never judge you or think less of you-"

"But I would think less of myself," she cuts me off, her eyes looking everywhere but at me. "You've already given me so much. I appreciate everything that you do and what you're able to offer. But for some things, I need to be on my own."

"No, you don't," I say firmly, bringing a hand to cup her chin. I want her eyes. I want her to look right into mine and believe how sincere I am. "People get together for lots of reasons. One is to support each other. To help each other deal with shit. I'm dying here while you're leaving me in the dark."

She closes her eyes for a moment, leaning into my touch, before she brings her hand over mine, pushing it away. "You've promised to give me space. Time to figure myself out," she retorts, and I don't know who's more frustrated, her or me, as she continues, "I need that. I could do that while we're together if you stay true to your word. If you give me enough space and time..." She pauses, her lips trembling, her eyes hopeless. "Or do I need to find another place, Ian?"

"Yes," I say, sarcastically. "Let's make things simple. Black and white. Either I keep my mouth shut, or you leave. Either I keep a blind eye on how much you might be in danger, or you leave."

"I'm not in any danger-"

"But I don't know that for sure," I cut her off. I cannot stand her lies anymore. Worse, I don't know her truth from her lies anymore. "You know what? I don't know for sure either. I don't know if you truly want us to be together. Or if you're just passing the time till you land someone better."

"Ian..." She looks at me like I've broken her heart into a million pieces. Her eyes are full of tears. But I cannot help it. I cannot help that I'm doing everything, and it's not enough for her. I cannot silence the fat kid in me. I cannot help but feel broken. I'm not enough. I'm not worthy of her truth. I'm only worthy of a tiny part of her. Or maybe worse, I'm just the guy who helped her out of her shell. I'm just the guy who took her virginity, and that's all she's willing to give me. And that's where my role should have ended.

I cannot deal with it.

"How could you say that?" She's in tears, shaking her head.

"Because you're lying to me," I say, my voice full of hurt and doubt. "All it takes is one lie—just one lie to destroy us. And I've tried to believe your lies, but not anymore. Not when I feel you might be in danger."

I exhale a long breath. "So you're not in danger, my ass. It's now, Acacia. I need to know why the hell your picture was there on that shitty site. Why that girl was threatening you, and why the hell you freaked out when I walked into your work."

Now everything is catching up with me. She didn't want me to go in there for a different reason than she'd explained.

"I don't want to lose you, Ian." She looks at me, pleading for me to understand her. But how can I understand anything when she's keeping me in the dark?

"Then, tell me. Open up and tell me everything," I say with everything in me to convince her to talk, to trust me.

"I can't." She spreads a hand. "I'd be cheating myself if I did. I know the minute I tell... everything would change for me. Everything."

I fight every feeling I have for her, every weakness I have toward her, and say, "I can't be in the dark anymore. I can't, not while I feel you're jeopardizing your safety. I can't be part of this."

She nods. "I understand."

I know it's the end.

"I hope you do, Acacia," I retort. "I hope you understand how much I care about you. I hope you understand why I can't accept this."

Rubbing her arms, she nods again. "Um, I'll pack my stuff, and by tomorrow morning, I'll be out of here."

I catch her arm as she edges past me. So that's it. She's simply walking away from me, from us. Things get tough, and she walks away like I'm not worthy of a fight.

"Is it that simple for you?" I place my hand around her elbow. We're standing side by side, facing away from each other. I don't even have the will to look at her. If she had asked, I would have tried to give her the moon. "You're just walking away."

"It's not simple." I can feel the turmoil in her body. "But at the same time, it wouldn't be fair to you. I'm not being fair to you."

I cannot accept only a glimpse of her, and she cannot accept me as a whole. It's that simple, after all.

I inhale deeply, time to get to the facts. "Where will you go?"

"Um... Martha, the owner of the store, is offering me a place to stay. I'll be rooming with the other girls working with us."

I nod. But I'm not sure if it's true or if she's just making this up to lessen my worries. "I'll help you move." I turn to her, raising a firm hand as she's about to object. "Just don't." I don't want to argue with her.

She nods, her eyes tearful. Then just like that, everything is over.

I cannot help to yell my frustration as she's walking away. "Why is it so easy for you?"

She pauses, one hand on the wall before she turns to me with nothing but desperation in her eyes. "Because you're right. It'd only take one lie to destroy us, and um…" She puts a hand over her mouth, maybe trying to control how shaky her voice has become. "I don't want to lie to you anymore. You know, I imagine that one day… I hope it doesn't take us too long… One day we'll find each other again, and then I hope you'll find it in you to give me another chance. So, I better leave now before I ruin us for good."

I want to step forward. Take her in my arms. Tell her I'll give her all the chances in the world, she just has to be honest with me. But I know now. I know I'm not enough for her. I'll never be enough for her, to let me hold her hand while she's crossing this hard road in her life. I'm not enough, no matter how much I try or how much effort I'm willing to make.

I'm not fucking enough.

CHAPTER TWENTY-THREE
Grace

I LIE ON MY back, not knowing why I left Ian's bed. I should have stayed as I promised. It would have saved me the awkwardness this morning. But I couldn't help the fear that had settled in my heart. I'd become so scared I might hear her name again, and I couldn't tolerate that after how wonderful he'd been with me, after all his heated touches and sincere promises.

After he made me believe in us.

I toss the covers aside and leave the bed to head to the bathroom, see to the necessary needs, then hightail it back to my room.

I put on a black blouse and dark blue jeans. Of course, I left my hair down. He likes it that way, and I need him to like me more than any moment we've had so far.

I've let him down, and I don't know how to explain it.

At the kitchen door, I inhale deeply. He's in front of the coffee maker. Disappointed or not, he cannot function without his morning coffee. I know this little detail about him, and it makes me smile, but still, I'm nervous. I broke my promise to him last night, and I'm always nervous whenever I face his naked back. It's mine now, and I can step in and print all the kisses I've always wanted while staring at it. But my smile doesn't last for long. I know he feels my presence; his back becomes rigid before he relaxes again.

"Morning." I demand he acknowledges me.

"Coffee," he says nonchalantly, while retrieving two mugs out of the cabinet.

"Sure," I say, walking cowardly to slump myself on a chair.

Holding two full coffee mugs, he turns to the kitchen table. He drops one in front of me without any eye contact then turns to walk the little distance to the counter. He drops an arm over the back of a chair while resting against the counter, facing me.

"You slept well?" Finally, he locks his eyes with mine. Pissed. His voice is calm, but his eyes give everything away.

He takes a sip from his coffee, his eyes narrowing at me, waiting. I take a sip myself before shaking my head. "No."

When I look up at him again, I can feel for that chair. He's gripping it so tight that if he gripped it any tighter, it might shatter into pieces. "No," he repeats sarcastically. "Are you aiming to please me with this answer or to piss me off even more?"

I rest my elbows on the table, my hands on each side of my face before I dare to look up at him and be half honest. "Neither. It has nothing to do with you."

"Great," he says. "Just fucking great."

"Don't be like that." I don't know if I'm warning him or pleading with him to understand. "I just felt I needed to leave, that's all."

"I hope you know what you're doing then." There's a disappointment in his eyes. He's not pissed anymore. Just disappointed.

I circle a finger on the rim of my mug, watching him as he carelessly drinks his coffee, his eyes in another world, not with me anymore. "What do you think I'm doing, Ian?" I ask urgently, fearing he's back into her world, at least in his mind.

Briefly, he looks at me before shifting his gaze to the side. He exhales a long breath, closing his eyes for a second before I have his eyes again. "You're building a wall between us, Grace. And if you want me to be honest, I'm done breaking walls."

I push my chair back and stand, my hands curling into fists. "I'm not building any walls, at least not intentionally. So please don't throw her shit out on me. I'm not her. I am *me,* and if you're not ready to start all over again with *me,* with all that's *me,* with all my walls and shit, then we should end this before it begins."

"Finished?" He spreads a hand dramatically, but his voice is calm.

I nod, slowly slumping my ass down on the chair. I don't think he's as calm as he seems right now. I think there's a battle going on inside, but at this point, I don't care. I want him to know I'm not an echo of her, even if some of my actions say otherwise.

I'm not her. I want to scream, but of course, I don't do that. I just look down at my lap, fidgeting with my hands and watching him without making any eye contact.

He puts his mug on the counter and doesn't utter a word before I give him my eyes. Then he speaks, "I told you before, and I'm telling you again. We're in this together, only the two of us, nothing less and nothing more. There's no third party between us and never will be, Grace. If I'm interested in someone else, I wouldn't be standing here tolerating all your mercurial moods."

"Me," I retort, stunned. "Mercurial!"

"Yes, you are," he says penitently. "That's why I wanted us to be a casual thing for a while. But what did you demand? You wanted more than that. More than sex, more than casual. I'm trying to give it to you, but I can't when you start hiding behind walls."

I'm really having a hard time understanding what he means. I shake my head. "So, I'm the one to blame again. Of this, whatever we're arguing about, I don't even know what we're arguing about."

"I'm not arguing or blaming," he says firmly. "I'm trying to understand what you want. I want us to be, Grace. I so want us to be. But nothing will work out when you don't even know what you want. When you keep having second thoughts."

I'm speechless. He's just turned the tables so easily on me while he's the one who was fighting us from the get-go.

He sighs heavily, calmly assessing me, like he knows how I truly feel, and is just waiting for me to articulate it to him. But I'm just disappointed and hurt. He's blaming me again. I watch as his eyes soften a bit, and he starts to break our silence, "I knew this would be hard. I wanted to give you the time you needed 'cause I know you're dealing with lots of shit, but then you would look at me with those doe eyes, like I'm going to turn your world around, like I'm this sort of superhero who's gonna save the world for you and I fell for that, against my better judgment, I fell for that. Thinking that you're ready for us, but whenever I'm taking a step forward, you take a step back."

"I'm not," I almost yell. Being prudent doesn't mean I'm backing away from him, from us. I'm so sick of this. He's adamant about blaming me.

"Let's see," he says, challenging me with his eyes, "you didn't want to meet my parents. You didn't want to hear how I feel about you last night. And you said over and over you didn't want just sex but guess what... The two times you visited my bed, you took your orgasms then ran back to your own shell. So how do you want me to interpret all that? Please tell me what you really want, do you even want me?"

I'm squirming a little because he has a point. But only a point.

"I want you, Ian," I say as I read doubt and some insecurity behind his words and in his eyes. "I want us to be more than anything I've ever wanted."

"Then what's the problem?" I know he's lost, but I'm lost too.

"There's no problem," I say, trying to get through to him. "It's just that things are moving too fast. You're moving things so fast for me. A week ago, you were in another world, fighting us, fighting your attraction to me, and suddenly you're pushing at every corner and at any chance to pull us together. It doesn't make sense to me."

"I only act how I feel," he says simply. "Last week, I was in turmoil. But after the last two nights, I have no doubt about us. We're right for each other, Grace."

"So, sex changed everything for you. Is that what you're telling me?"

"Not just the sex," he says, smiling. "It's just the last two nights told me lots about you. How you respond to me, how you're opening up to me, wanting to tell me everything about yourself, and how you're patient with me about my insecurities and doubts. You didn't get angry or, worse, give up on me when I wasn't making any sense. You didn't run away when I wasn't nice to you." He inhales deeply, pausing as if the following words would be hard for him. "You tried and tried to make me understand. You wanted me to understand your world. That means you want me to be a part of it. It means that I'm enough for you."

"God, Ian..." I put a hand over my mouth before I stand, walking in crazy steps toward him, my heart aching for him, for what that girl made him feel. "You're more than enough." I stand before him, taking his face in my hands. I cannot believe he'd doubt that for a minute. "You're more than I ever asked for. You make me feel safe. You make it safe for me to feel anything. Anger, hurt, guilt, but most of all, you make me complete. Content. You make it okay for me to be happy. To have the things I deserve."

He presses his hands over mine. I cannot read his eyes, but I feel how rigid he's become. Did I say too much? Is it too much for him at this point? I don't know, but he just keeps staring at me with those unreadable eyes. I bite into my lip as he slowly pulls our hands down, bringing his forehead to rest against mine. He exhales into me before he opens his mouth, "I love you, Grace. And it's not too fast. It's too fucking late."

I know he's waiting for me to say it back. I can feel how nervous he has become. I know it's too soon, but it feels so right. "I love you too, Ian. I. Love. You."

Breathing in relief and pulling back from me with a smile on his face, he looks down at me. "And I. Love. You."

I smile, and I don't know who goes for it first, but we're in each other's arms. His arms are hugging me tightly while I move a hand up and down his back. I do believe in us now, but still. "I love you, Ian," I say again, but I also have to say how I truly feel about other things. It's better to say it when he's in my arms. "Because I love you, I want to be honest with you." I can feel him grow rigid, his arms growing tighter around me, but I have to. "We know how we feel about each other now, and let's leave it that way for a while. No pulling big stuff on me. I mean, last night you talked babies."

I can feel his smile before he pulls back from me. "Yeah. I understand this one."

"So, no big stuff for a while. Slow steps. Just me and you." I bring a hand to the side of his face, stroking him tenderly.

He nods. "I promise. No big stuff. Just me and you." He clears his throat, smiling with mischief. "And your little kitty."

"Ugh..." I pull away from him, folding my arms. "Don't call it that."

"You squirm when I say pussy, and you don't like kitty, so what do you want me to call it then... Lady Pink!" He folds his arms. There's so much smugness in his stance. He knows I'm no match to his dirty mouth, and he is flaunting it in my face.

I so want to take that smugness off his face. For once, I wish I was the smug one. But I can't.

I can't, but Shelia can.

Thanks, Shelia.

I lock my eyes with his, grateful for all these TMI moments with Shelia before I shock the life out of him and retort, "How about...your cock hole."

He's literally gawking. "How am I ever gonna go slow after that?"

I press my fingers deep into my skin. "I don't know if it's the feel of moving things fast that pokes my worries, or it's just a thing deep inside of me that telling me this won't last."

Dr. Griffin tilts her head to the side as if she needs a moment to concentrate on her thoughts before facing me again. "I don't want to dictate what you want to talk about, but I think the key to all of this is that moment." She glimpses briefly to my left wrist before continuing, "I hate to say it to you, but I think keeping it all in won't help you in the long run, and it shows now. You decided to be in a relationship, and you're nervous for no obvious reasons. It seems to me this guy really loves you."

"It's just… I don't have anything to say." I exhale a long breath. "It's all in me. I'm feeling it all inside, but I can't face it again."

"But you said you wanted to talk about it with Ian. Am I right?"

"Yes," I say, "somehow, he makes me feel safe about it. Like nothing would happen if he knew. Everything will be fine, but now I feel I'd be the one moving things too fast if I started to talk about heavy stuff. I'm so confused."

"Well, since he seems okay with moving things fast, why don't you take that step?"

"But then, I'm afraid he'd be obligated to tell me about her. I don't think he's ready to do that. I don't want to pressure him into anything."

"Then…" Dr. Griffin gives me a knowing look, "I have to see you more."

I nod. I think I need to see my doctor for longer than I thought.

I had an honest talk with Ian, a good one with my therapist, and a lovely time at the shop, but still, my day isn't over. I need to see Emma. So, I head to the bar to meet up with her. But for a totally different reason than she asked for.

I've already texted Ian and asked him if we could meet up there, and of course, I didn't tell him about Emma.

Minutes later, I'm at the bar, seated at a table and waiting for Ian. I don't wait long; I see him walking through the front doors, his eyes doing a quick scan before they land on me. He's worried, and I hope I can explain myself before Emma arrives.

"Hey..." He's at the table, leaning down to press a kiss to my lips before pulling back a little to look into my eyes. "Is everything okay, angel?"

I smile. "Fucking epic."

He breaks a laugh, straightens to his full height before he takes the seat next to mine.

I guess he knows me well as he pushes, "But, I feel there's a talk we need to have."

"Kind of," I answer, glad he wants to know. Emma is arriving any minute. "Not about you and me, though. Emma asked me to go out for a drink, and you know, I'm really apprehensive that things are moving fast in our relationship, so I decided you should join us to ease my nerves a little."

I catch some kind of surprise on his face, but he instantly neutralizes his features. "Yeah, Emma would love to know you better. I guess at Mom's party there wasn't enough time for that."

"I'd love to know her better, too," I say, sensing he's worried about something like whether his sister and I will get along. I'm worried too. And neither of us is hiding the discomfort that suddenly envelopes us.

My eyes and his fixate on the front doors, and we don't wait long as Emma walks in. She runs her eyes over the place till they rest on us. There's a pause before she adjusts her purse tightly over her shoulder. Of course, she didn't expect me to bring Ian. I hope she gets my message.

I won't go behind his back. If she has something to tell me, she must say it in front of her brother. I won't feel comfortable talking about stuff he doesn't want to talk about behind his back. That would be like betraying him. And I would have just ignored his sister and not bother to come, but the way she was intent on telling me has made me do this *in-your-face* act. I want her to understand that I will not accept her meddling.

And yes, a part of me is scared of what I might find out. But it's just a tiny part.

As she reaches us, she leans in to kiss my cheek before turning to give a kiss to her brother. "I didn't expect you, but I'm glad you're here too." She slumps herself on a chair facing me, then rests her arms on the table and smiles, running her eyes between Ian and me. "This way, I can enjoy how cute you are together."

I thought she'd be a little pissed or uncomfortable, but she seems like she doesn't care, or she's bluffing.

For a moment, there's a bit of uncomfortable silence before Emma breaks it, "Ian told us about your floral shop, and I'm dying to check it out."

A phone rings. It's Ian's. He pulls it out of his pocket and rises. "I have to take this." He leans down to kiss my lips, then turns toward the front doors.

"Good call, you know," Emma says before I get the chance to tell her anything

"You think so?" I say, skeptical as I still feel that she's nervous somehow.

Resting back in her chair, she sighs, running a hand through her hair. "I'm sorry. It's just I felt I need to tell you, but now..." Her gaze travels across the bar to where Ian is taking his call. "I think he's in good hands. He didn't have it easy in the past, but knowing you'd go this far to protect him, even from yourself, has told me all I need to know about what kind of person you are." She smiles. "And I know you're dying to know stuff about him. You're in love with him, it shows."

I touch my neck. I feel kind of embarrassed that she knows how much I love her brother and how I'm agitated about his past, but suddenly she's nervous again—or embarrassed as her eyes land across some point behind me.

She covers her eyes with the back of her hand, and I cannot fight my curiosity anymore. I look over my shoulder, and I'm surprised myself for a different reason. Theodore is standing at a distance behind me. There's an intense look on his face, and of course, he's not directing it toward me. He doesn't even see me. He's looking at Emma. He's fixated on her.

Oh, oh.

What's going on?

"Theodore," I call, waving as his eyes finally land on me.

"Oh, God," Emma gasps from behind me, and I turn immediately to her.

Her eyes plead with me. "Don't tell me you know this guy. Please don't."

I open my mouth to say something, but then Theodore is standing at our table, clearing his throat. "Um...hey."

I cannot help it, my eyes travel the scene between him and Emma. Emma is swallowing while Theodore's eyes are fixated on her. Intensely, like he doesn't believe he's seeing her.

After a moment of this, I pat the chair next to me. "Come on. I assume you two know each other?"

Neither of them says anything. Theodore just looks at Emma for guidance, like how much he should reveal before he takes a seat. I know without a doubt, these two share a juicy story.

"Kind of," Emma finally acknowledges my question before looking back at Theodore, who doesn't like her answer. She smiles nervously at me, pointing a finger back and forth between Theodore and me. "And how about you two?"

"I've known Theodore for about two years now," I say cheerfully. "He's one of my best friends."

"Yes. Grace is one of my best friends." Theodore looks at Emma for a moment, then taps his fingers on the table, looking at me sideways. "But you never told me about Emma."

"Well, Emma is Ian's sister."

Theodore nods at me; then, his eyes are back on Emma while the latter, I think, wishes to be anywhere but here. I gaze across the bar where Ian is walking toward us, and there's an angry look on his face.

I think these two need a moment alone, so I push my chair back. "I'm going to the ladies' room."

I wish I could be a fly around them to enjoy how adorably uncomfortable they are, but there's Ian, and I sprint to him, catching him midway.

"What is he doing with Emma now?"

I tug at his arm. "They need a minute." Then I drag him behind me to another table. "Please, let them be."

He settles on the chair, his eyes over there, on Emma and Theodore. "I don't like that guy."

I laugh at how adorable he's being as the protective brother. "You don't know him."

He looks back at me, gritting his teeth. "I know he wants between your legs."

I roll my eyes, then point a finger across where Emma and Theodore are seated. "I think he wants between your sisters'."

Ian seriously glares at me. I smile. I like his glare.

I shrug one shoulder, giving him my best doe eyes. "What, do you prefer him wanting between mine?"

"God…!" He shakes his head, a smile on his face. "He better be the best guy ever then. Emma doesn't need another douche."

I know Theodore isn't a douche, but a minute ago, he was mourning his girlfriend. True, she wasn't the one for him, but still, it's too fast. I mean, the way he looks at Emma tells me he has intense feelings for her.

And my eyes are back on Ian. It's taken him forever to forget about her.

No!

Not after this morning. I will not think about her anymore.

CHAPTER TWENTY-FOUR

Ian

THREE YEARS AGO

IT'S BEEN A month since Acacia left. I don't try to contact her, though I'm aching to. We've reached a dead end and, being very practical and busy with work, I haven't had any spare moments to change my mind. But deep down, I know why I haven't tried. I want her to come back to me willingly. Since this whole thing started, I've been the one making all the first moves, pushing at every corner, and I'm not sure if she's as into me as I'm into her, despite what she says.

I need validation that what we have is real.

I step out of the elevator, and midway to my apartment, I change my mind. I don't like my place anymore. I don't like the void in my heart when I walk in, knowing she won't be there. I turn and walk to Emma's. As I open the door, everything becomes blurry. I shake my head; this has been happening for a while. I probably just need to eat. I haven't put anything in my stomach for the last ten hours. Plus, I've been suffering horrible flu, and working like a maniac doesn't help. I guess everything is catching up with me.

Emma isn't here. Two weeks ago, she dumped loser Matt and decided to join our parents and the Browns for a trip around South Asia.

Now I'm without my two favorite girls.

I head to the kitchen. I need to put something in my stomach before I contemplate the idea of swallowing any pills. But I stop partway.

Someone's in the apartment.

It's quiet here, so I easily recognize the hurried footsteps down the hallway toward the front door.

What the hell?

I hear the front door open and shut quietly, and I sprint there, an unsettling feeling in my gut. I open the front door and head to the staircase, where there's someone hurrying downstairs.

My eyes blur again, but I recognize her pink hair. It's Acacia. She's running from me.

Fuck.

"Acacia, wait," I call with all the power in me as waves of worry hit me in the chest. I hurry down the stairs as fast as my shaking legs will let me.

"Acacia." I'm able to stop her, catching her elbow. "What the hell?" I turn her around, and I don't know who gasps louder as dollar bills fly down the stairs.

We freeze for a moment before she tilts her head, looking at me horrified. "They're mine. I swear they're mine. I told Emma to keep them for me at her place."

"Fuck!" I yell. "Do you think I'm gonna accuse you of stealing or something?" Shocked and exhausted, I let go of her elbow and lean onto the railing before I drop down on the stairs. I don't know if it's my body giving up or my mind. I press my fingers over my eyes; my vision is blurry again.

"God, Ian. Are you okay?" I hear her panicked voice before I feel her drop next to me, her arm resting over my shoulders.

"I just need a minute."

"Okay, I'm right here," she whispers, her fingers rubbing my shoulders.

After a minute of me trying to breathe normally, I open my eyes, tilting my head to look at her. She gives me a half-smile. "You need to take it easy on yourself, Ian. I know how you're passionate about your work, but you'll drive yourself into a wall if you keep going like you are."

Turning to face her, I run the back of my hand over her cheek. "Worried about me?" I don't need proof. It's all in her eyes. I don't know how sometimes I doubt her feelings for me.

Her eyes look away from me. She's becoming nervous, so I catch her hand in mine. "I worry about you too."

"Now isn't the time for this. You're tired." She squeezes my hand, her eyes so soft, so pure. "Why don't we go back to your place, and I'll fix you something to eat."

Smiling at her, I nod. "Sounds great, but pick up your money first."

After climbing up the stairs, it's clear I've done a number on myself. I'm barely able to reach the top. I'm barely able to breathe, but I try not to show it to Acacia. I don't want her to feel obligated to spend time with me. I want her to do so because she wants to.

In the kitchen, I take a big gulp of the juice Acacia hands me before she goes back to the fridge, trying to find something to prepare for dinner.

"How come you cook so well? I don't mean edible. You cook like a professional chef," I ask, recognizing, as much as I have these strong feelings for her, I haven't really taken the time to know her better.

After rummaging through my empty fridge, she turns to the cupboard to bring out the only bag of pasta that's there. She turns again with a peaceful smile on her face. "Mom was protective of me, so instead of letting me indulge in after-school activities, we'd spend our spare time together. She's fond of cooking, so I learned a lot from her."

She walks to the sink, opens the pasta bag, and drops it in a pot. "I know how to sew, knit, host a family event, and even take care of a baby." She sighs, gazing at me over her shoulder. "There's a hidden housewife inside of me."

Maybe that's the road her parents drew for her, and that's why she's running away from them. Because I get the feeling she's running or breaking away from something.

"Is that what you want to be, Acacia?" I try for a normal tone. I don't want to sound eager to know. I don't want her to get nervous again. "A housewife? Stay-at-home mom? Or you haven't figured things out yet?"

Placing the pot on the stove, she's silent for a moment before shaking her head. "If I only knew, things would be much easier."

"Not knowing and not deciding is way better than starting something you're not passionate about. Take all the time you need, Acacia. And whatever you choose, I'll always be here for you."

"Always?" She's smiling, but not looking at me, her eyes on the stove.

"You don't believe that?" I know how I feel about her, but somehow, she doesn't totally believe me. "Why, Acacia? Why do you prefer to run away?"

I don't know why I'm asking again. I know I won't get an honest answer. But my heart cannot let it go, not when she's in front of me, taking care of me. I cannot resist how I feel about her. How much I want her in my life.

Sighing, she shifts her gaze back to me. "This is always hard." She huffs a long breath. Her eyes are pleading with me to understand. "But it's not you that I don't believe. It's all me, Ian. I hope you understand that. I mean, if I'm capable of this, of being completely with someone, by giving everything in me, it'd always be you."

"But you're not." I don't want to sound pissed, but fuck I am. "It's always hard to hear, Acacia. It gets harder every time you say it."

"I'm sorry." She lifts a finger to wipe her unshed tears. "I'm so sorry I've put you through this again. That's why I tried to run earlier. I don't want to hurt you."

"You're not putting me through anything." I don't want her to have any doubt over where I stand. "I want to be here. I want you to be here. I want to spend time with you." I wait till she locks her eyes with mine. "And I want to eat whatever this delicious thing is that you're making," I add lightly. I don't want to spend this time convincing her of something her heart isn't in. Instead, I'm going to show her how good we can be together. That's the way to get her back in my life.

"It's just pasta," she shrugs like it's nothing. Like she does every time I compliment her. She's selfless. No matter what she does for others, she thinks nothing of it. My heart squeezes. How am

I going to walk away from her? Even if I could, I don't think I'm going to stop loving her, *ever.*

For the next fifteen minutes, I sit there and enjoy her going back and forth to prepare dinner. Deep down, I feel it'll be the last time I do, but I'm still hopeful.

My hope intensifies as she sets two plates on the table. She's not leaving just yet. She's having dinner with me.

"Delicious and spicy and everything I need," I say after the first taste of pasta. Her giddy eyes make me ask, "We've established you're a good cook. But do you like to cook? Do you enjoy yourself, or is it just a chore you're good at?"

There's a perplexed look on her face like she's surprised. "I haven't ever thought of that." Her eyes grow focused, and she adds, "I don't know really, but I love cooking for you. You're always excited and appreciative."

I know why her answer draws a silly smile on my face. I like that she's figuring herself out with me. Or this tiny bit about herself.

I take another bite before saying, "I must return the favor. You know what, I'll cook dinner for us tomorrow."

Flinching back in her seat is not the response I'm hoping for, but that doesn't deter me from pushing, "It's the weekend. Surely, you don't have lots going on, and I'm too tired to go out and eat."

"But–"

"No buts." I place my hand on her knee. I know my touch will affect her somehow. "It wouldn't mean anything big. Just a day we'll spend together, that's all."

"A day? You said dinner!" she says in a hoarse voice, and a hand goes around her neck.

"So what?" I push her short skirt up, my thumb moving in circles over her knee. "Surely you won't leave this late."

She shivers under my touch, and I know I have her now. Though it's not the only way I'd like to affect her, it's better than nothing.

"Like, just a day?" She purses her lips, barely able to make eye contact with me.

I smile. "Just a day."

"A day…ha?" Shaking her head, she giggles. "I'll believe this lie tonight."

"Do you wanna believe another one?" I slowly hitch my hand up her thigh.

"Yeah," she barely whispers; her eyes hazy with desire and want.

"If…" I say, then put an arm under her knees and one around her waist, standing to lift her from the chair, "if I carried you to my room now, I wouldn't eat your little pussy till you beg me to fuck you hard and good."

"Don't let me beg," she whispers against my neck as I indeed carry her to my room.

I'm so tired as I wake up the next day way past noon. Every cell in my body aches, but that's not what concerns me. As usual, Acacia is not on the other side of the bed, but this time I fear she might not be in her room or the apartment either. So, I leave my room, running around the apartment calling for her. She has definitely left. I want to go back to my room and text her, but what would I say? Beg her to come back? She wouldn't. I know she wouldn't, and last night was just a weak moment for her. Instead, I head to the kitchen to have some coffee before I do something stupid.

And there, near the coffee maker, I find her note.

<I'm out for a walk, sleepy-head ;)>

I smile. She knows the first thing I need is my coffee; that's why she left her note there.

Two minutes and I drink my coffee, thinking I can do this. I can make us happen. I only have to take things slow with her.

She needs time for herself, for whatever makes her indecisive about everything in her life. It has nothing to do with me, but it's still hard to deal with when she keeps rejecting opening up to me. But to be fair to her, I barely have time for our relationship. I'm always busy with work.

I hear the front door open, and I quickly drop my coffee mug in the sink and hurry to see her. I've already missed her. But I pause around the corner. She's looking into the mirror near the front door, wiping her eyes with her sleeves.

She was crying and trying to make sure I wouldn't know.

I contemplate what to do for a moment. I decide to give her time and space, so I turn and walk back to the kitchen and wait till she can gather herself.

"Morning," she says cheerfully, too cheerfully, as she walks into the kitchen. And my heart aches. She's trying to hide another thing from me.

"Yeah, morning," I say sarcastically as it's past noon. "I promised you a day and slept through half of it."

"It's okay." She walks to me, reaching to stroke my jaw. "You needed some rest."

I wrap my arms around her and lay her head against my chest. Even if she doesn't admit it, I think she needs some comfort, a hug at the moment. I hold her for a while before she wraps her arms around my neck. "I've missed this," she whispers into my chest.

"You don't have to miss anything," I say, my lips next to her ear. "You can have it all the time. Every day, Acacia."

I pull back a little to look into her eyes. "We'll take it slowly this time. I won't be asking things you're not ready to tell me. Things you're not prepared to face with anyone yet."

I know I'm lying through my teeth, and I hope this time more than ever she believes my lie. I'm dying for her to believe this lie. Because now, I've got a plan for her, for us. A plan I can finally afford. What made me determined to go through with it is the fact that she keeps her cash at Emma's. She doesn't trust her new roommates. She is not safe, and I have to make sure she is.

"But that's not fair to you. I've seen how it affects you-"

"Look," I say, cutting her off, "despite what I've been saying, I really don't have time for anything serious. I'm busy with work, you know, with all these new deals. So that suits me, and being causal is a thing I need. I just need to see you every day and make sure you're safe and doing well. I don't have time to bother you with my questions. And I think you won't mind seeing me every morning."

"I don't mind that," she says, but still, I feel she doubts me.

"So, we'll have this arrangement. Casual for as long as we both need. Till we're both ready for more."

She rests back on my chest, sighing in relief. And I feel guilty for what I have in mind for us. But I cannot do nothing when I feel she's not safe.

I hug her tight, still feeling tired. I think I'll take a nap, and I'm sure Acacia won't be leaving me this time.

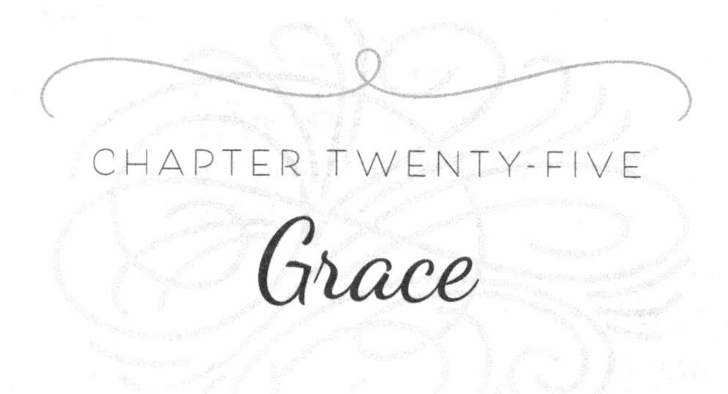

CHAPTER TWENTY-FIVE
Grace

I'VE SPENT EACH night of the last week in Ian's bed, where every morning, I moan my delight as he slips a finger inside of me. It's our ritual to indulge in a quickie before we get up to start our day.

He slips another finger in while his thumb strums my clit. "What do you wanna ride, angel? My fingers or cock?"

"I'm indecisive," I tease him.

"Oh, how about some anal play then," he teases back, knowing how I squirm whenever he mentions this subject.

He pulls his fingers out of me and runs the tip of his cock along my backside.

I clutch the sheets tightly. "Ian..."

"What, angel?" he mummers. "It's a win-win situation, you're becoming wetter, and I'm harder than steel."

"Oh, stop it." I bury my face in the pillow, embarrassed how wet this makes me.

"But you like it." He doesn't stop, his hard cock nestles against my butt, and his hand finding my hard nipple—embarrassingly erect— he toys with it. "It doesn't turn you on, ha!" He nips my neck, pushing his hardness more into me.

"Ian." I reach for his cock. I give it a tug, hopefully, a painful one.

He laughs. "You know I'm not really into that, it's just you're making it so taboo, it burns my brain cells."

"Poor you."

"Are you making fun of my fantasies?"

I giggle and turn to cup his jaw. "Oh, I'm sorry. How can I make it up to you?"

"Well," he counters, his eyes getting darker. "You could do something for me."

"Sure," I say huskily, eager to know what he wants.

He eyes me suspiciously, and I lick my lips. This is so arousing. I can feel he's nervous about it, which only means one thing. He has a sinful, filthy, dirty fancy, and just looking at his eager blue eyes is turning me on.

I dive down and trace his happy trail with my tongue.

"Jeez," he hisses out, and I look up at the fire burning in his eyes. I shiver. The anticipation is killing me.

I run the back of my hand up and down his length. "Come on, tell me what you want, baby."

"Grace." He puts a hand over mine, calling me with that firm voice that drives me crazy. I like how bossy he's become. I look up at him and edge closer, my hard nipples pressed to his hard chest. "Yes."

He loops a hand around my neck, squeezing gently, his eyes burning as he says, "I want you to ride my cock, while I watch your ass bouncing up and down."

Filthy. Dirty. I knew it. I swallow hard, my body shivers, my clit pulses painfully, just imagining I would be exposed like that. But I'd be exposed to him. He wants to watch me like that, and suddenly it's too hot. Ian's blue eyes watching me riding his cock while my ass...ah... Now I'm the one with burning brain cells.

He arches a thick dark-brown eyebrow. "Too much?"

I sigh, my nipples getting so hard. "No, too hot."

His eyes gleam with excitement, and I waste no time. I set up on my knees. I'm so turned on by this, and hopefully I can deliver.

"Condom," I say.

He grabs one from the nightstand and tears the foil packet open with his teeth while his eyes study me like he cannot believe I'm going to do it.

I grab the condom from his hand, my fingers looping around his hardness, I throw him a smile, and he shakes his head, knowing that I'm going to tease him. I roll my tongue around the tip, tasting his precum.

"Goddammit..." he groans, fisting a hand in my hair as I take him in my mouth.

I start to stroke the base while I suck on him, and he hisses, "Yeah, just like that."

"Is that so?" I pop his hardness out of my mouth, and he glares at me.

"Salty." I wink. Still holding him, I roll the condom down his erection, aware that his breathing is out of control.

"Fuck, you're doing it," he utters, disbelieving as I place my legs on each side of his thighs, giving him *my back*. It's so adorable how excited he is.

I look at him over my shoulder and smile. "Should we use a safe word in case you passed out over this?"

"A safe word!" He acts shocked. "You've heard of that?"

I roll my eyes, and he smiles, circling a finger. "Turn and let me enjoy that yummy ass of yours."

I do turn to business.

I take his cock in my hand and position him at my entrance. I let out a breath before sinking down on his length. And holy shit, from this angle, he's even bigger. I try to push further, feeling myself stretching to accommodate him.

"Kill me now," he grunts, and I gaze back, his eyes are right on where we're connected.

I take a moment to adjust to his size while I feel him push up. He presses a soft kiss above my ass then nuzzles my back. "I love you, Grace."

My sex pulses around him, goosebumps spreading everywhere. I'm Grace, and his voice is rough, and that means he's going to fuck me hard and fast and hot as hell.

"Ian…" I plead. This is not like anything we've done so far. I feel pleasure, mixed with the pain that comes from him filling me like that, and the filthiness of this position.

My head falls back as I feel him swelling. He's getting harder. I can't take any more of his length.

"I've got you, babe," he holds my hips and slowly glides me down on the rest of his cock. When he's buried deep, I moan, and he groans. His teeth nipping my back, he asks, "Does it hurt?"

"Yessss," I breathe. "It hurts really good."

I can feel his smile against my back. I love how attentive and considerate he is, and I do love his *dirty mind*. I reach back and place my hands on his shoulders as I start to move. I want to bring his fantasy to life. I slide halfway up, then slide down, slowly

"I'll get there," I promise, out of breath, knowing he would like it hard and fast.

"We'll get there," he utters gruffly, and I have no control anymore. His hands are on my hips, guide me up and down, slow and steady at first. And before I pick up this pace, he urges me faster. I try to catch a breath, but he demands, "Ride me faster, harder, I need you that way. I need your ass bouncing."

A moment ago, I wasn't a big fan of this position, but hearing him needing me this way switches things. Lust licks at my skin, and I start to obey. I move up and down his hardness, moaning as I ride his cock. Hard and fast.

I like this very much.

He likes this very much.

I hear his moans of pleasure. "You're my little plaything, Grace. You like being played by me. Fulfilling every dirty fantasy I have."

"I do," I say, my clit throbbing painfully and my skin tingles everywhere just hearing his dirty words. I'm so close. So fast. My sex is contracting around him.

"Yeah, clench your pussy around my cock. It's yours." He feels it too.

"Ian." I grind down on him one last time; my pussy squeezes his hardness painfully as I hear a deep grunt, an animalistic one from him. It's a pure pleasure and pain for both of us.

"Now, babe. Now. Scream my name while you come all over my cock."

"Ian." I close my eyes, crying his name as he demanded, his rough voice mixed with his rough strokes inside me, tickling me over the edge.

"Ian...god..." I scream his name one more time, my body shivers reaching its peak,

For a moment, I stay in place, trying to normalize my breathing. Once having a bit of control, I try to climb off him, but he holds me in place. Before I gaze over at him, he brings us onto our sides. "I'm not done yet."

He grazes my ear with his teeth, and I gasp aloud as he starts to move again. He's still hard.

"This time, wait for me, babe," he roughly demands.

He only calls me babe during our quickies. Otherwise, I'm either his angel or Grace. And to be honest, I don't like to be called babe. Unlike angel, I feel he might have called her that. But any thought about her disappears as his fingers toy with my clit. I don't know how many partners he had, but I don't think any of them reached their peak as fast as I do. Each quickie we have, he asks me to wait till we shatter together, but *me*...nope, I cannot. As my breathing grows heavy and my moans get out of control, he knows I'm close. So, he stops toying with me down there and gives me his hand as he thrusts into me deep. And that's it. I dig my teeth into his palm as a second climax explodes throughout my body.

Now I'm limp and helpless as he keeps his hard thrusts. "You're mine, Grace. Only mine," he says, then his teeth mark my shoulder. He pounds into me one final time before his body spams and shudders while multiple grunts escape his mouth.

"Fuck, Grace. Fuck," he says into my neck, his body relaxing behind mine.

Yes, fuck. Ian climaxing is so fucking hot, making me feel very feminine, pretty, and wanted.

For a tiny moment, I enjoy his hot breaths over my shoulder. Just a tiny moment before he pulls out of me. I know he's getting rid of the condom, but I wish he wouldn't break our contact even when I know he's coming back to envelop me from behind as I lie there motionless where he left me. My head on the pillow, my arms limp on the mattress, too satisfied and too exhausted to even breathe.

"Did you enjoy it, angel?" He's spooning me, and I feel his smile against my shoulder. I know he only asks to tease me about how fast I climaxed.

"Yeah, but it's too quick, even for a quickie." I try not to giggle, but I'm so relaxed and happy. Silly happy.

"Whose fault is that?"

I know I'm the one to blame. But I'm not going to admit it. "Your talented fingers," I answer, breaking into a laugh. I don't know why I'm laughing or why he's joining me. We're both shaking with laughter, and this is the happiest I've ever been in my life.

We're happening, and we're good. He doesn't even try to initiate anything big after our talk. We're just happening slowly and deliciously. Without worries or big plans and I like that a lot.

He recovers from his laughter, resting a hand over my stomach and nuzzling my neck.

"Do I make you happy?" he whispers into my ear before grazing it lightly with his teeth. The hand on my stomach becomes possessive.

"Very." I put a hand over his. I don't like the bit of doubt in his voice. "Happier than I have been in a long time."

He inches closer to me. One leg slides between mine. "Satisfied?"

I tap on his fingers. "You can smell my answer here."

He gives a mere laugh before I'm suddenly rolled over to face him. He playfully looks me in the eyes as he tucks a lock of hair behind my ear. "That's because you didn't have sex for a long time."

I shake my head. I don't think he's affecting me that way because of that. I'm seriously in love with him.

"You haven't had sex for a while, Grace?" He's calling me Grace, and his hand lays possessively over my back. He seriously wants to know. I guess the light talk is over.

"That's true," I say, still locking my eyes with his, as we lie facing each other. "How about you? When was the last time you were with someone?" I'm asking because it would bother me if he stayed celibate after her.

"More than two years," he answers clearly. Not blinking, not breaking eye contact with me. Like he doesn't care if I figured out how much he'd been loyal to her, how much she meant to him, or still does. The fact that I'm the one who broke her spell on him doesn't make me happy either. Because I might be just that, just breaking the spell for a while.

A bit uncomfortable, I want to get up, and apparently he does too as he places a kiss on my lips, saying, "I have a hectic day ahead of me, so I better leave this bed."

He gives me another kiss, looks at me soulfully for a moment before leaving the bed and walking to the adjacent bathroom.

I roll onto my back before I stretch my arms and sit up. I bend to pick up my nightie from the floor and put it back on. Listening to the running water in the adjacent bathroom, I'm usually the one using it first, after fleeing from his arms. But the mere mention of *her* made him want to leave.

I shake my head. We're just happening. It's too early for me to get possessive and jealous over his past. He needs time. Everyone does after any relationship.

Baby steps, Grace.

For him and me, it's better if I don't dig deeper. I still need to fathom many things about myself before I even start to share with him. At least, according to my doctor.

I press a thumb over my left wrist, worried. He's never asked me about it, and I should be grateful he's giving me time. I don't even know how to talk about it or about Sam. But there are these worms in my head telling me if he genuinely cared, if he's that intense about me as he shows over and over, he'd want all the details.

Doubt, doubt, doubt. Only doubt. I shake these thoughts out of my head. I need to believe in us, and he just needs time. And for that, I need to be patient and understanding.

Showered and wrapping his lower body in a towel, he walks into the room, and I smile. He looks my way, returning my smile before he walks over to the closet. And I just sit and watch as he unwraps the towel from his waist and starts to dress. He's giving me his back, but I can see the amused look on his face in the mirror.

His pants on, he pulls a hoodie over his head then locks his eyes with mine. "You do that every time." He knows I like this scene.

"What?" I give him my best innocent eyes, and I know how innocent my eyes can look. They're big and dark, a good combination to play the part, but he shakes his head. "You know what I'm talking about."

"It's just…" I rest back against the headboard, a bit embarrassed. "I like watching you get dressed. It's intimate and so sexy."

He smiles tenderly, and for a moment, our eyes stay locked through the mirror before a cloud of something I don't understand visits his eyes. Then he whirls, dropping himself on the bed. "And when do I get to see that?"

"What?" I frown, not sure what he means.

"What?" he repeats the word as if giving it a thought. His eyes visit the floor for a second before raising them to meet mine. "I thought we agreed to share this room, but all your stuff is still hanging in the other one. You do everything there, and just come here to crash."

"Oh..." I push away from the headboard and seek his lips with a kiss. "That's because I have so much stuff. It wouldn't fit in this room."

"That's all?" he asks, doubting me. But honestly, that's why I don't bother to move my stuff. The other room is just a step away from this one. I don't see a big deal.

"Yep," I say cheerfully, hoping to erase the doubt in his eyes. "That's the only reason." I link my arms around his neck and start spreading little kisses all over his face.

I feel him tensing under my touch, and I stop my kissing spree. I pull back to look into his eyes, but he shifts his.

"Well." He's reluctant about something before he reaches to spread a hand through my hair. "I want to suggest something, and I don't want you to get tense about it... it's just a practical thing, that's all."

My heart sinks. He's going to pull another big move on me. I feel it in my gut.

"Grace," he says, "don't give me your panicked eyes. Just listen to me first. We wouldn't be doing anything you're not comfortable with."

"What's that exactly?" I pull away from him, crossing my arms. I thought I had Urgent Ian under control for the past week, but it seems to me that's about to change.

"I think we need to move into a bigger place," he says evenly. "So, your stuff and mine can fit in one room. That's all. Just a practical idea."

"And how big is this place?" I ask, hoping he won't say what I think he would, because that would be a whole new situation.

That would raise all my doubts about us, and why he's pushing so much.

"As big as you would like it to be," he says carefully as if he's sensing my refusal before he edges closer to lay a hand over my knee. "Everything is gonna be as you wish, angel. Actually, I think you might enjoy checking out houses with me."

"Houses," I try not to yell. "So, you've already made this decision." I'm frustrated. It's like we haven't talked about slowing things down a little.

A hand goes through his hair before he presses it back on the mattress. "We're living together, and we would be moving into another place. There are no new decisions made."

I don't know what to say or how to get to him without hurting his feelings. He seems really disappointed by my reaction. "Can we talk about this later? You just threw this one at me, and I need some time to process it, and we both need to get going."

"Sure," he says, leaning to press two kisses on each of my knees. "We're not going to do anything that would make you uncomfortable. I want you to know this for a fact."

I don't want doubt to play in my head again, but it's like he has decided and wants to make sure he'll follow through with his decision.

He's made a decision to let go of her. Now, he must find another girl to fall in love with, introduce her to his parents, then buy her a house. He's even talked about having a baby. It's like boxes he needs to check.

But that's just my doubt again. My heart feels how sincere he is about us. I'll believe my heart. I leave the bed quickly before I start doubting him again.

Hours later, after I close my shop, I arrive at the shelter. It's always hard for me to visit, but I don't let that deter me from giving the people here a hand. Something I wasn't able to do for Sam. And knowing Theodore will be here tonight helps a lot. I know I won't be drowning in Sam's memories while I'm here.

Living in a place with so many people you've never met a day in your life is tough and sometimes dangerous.

In this particular city shelter, there's a lot of families, and our number one concern is to provide a safe place for their little ones. I've introduced Theodore to the people who keep on changing around here. One day you visit, and the next, their faces are gone, but new ones are here. We all hope the ones who leave find a permanent home for themselves. Theodore helps a lot, publishing multiple stories about the place and the people around here.

But tonight, Theodore is not coming to capture stories. Tonight, we're going to hang out with them where there's food and a movie to watch, just to give them the feeling that they're amongst family, to provide them with a sense of home.

I cross the hallway to meet up with Theodore, hoping he's here by now, but something feels different. The place is different than the last time I visited.

It smells unusual too.

It smells new.

As I walk into the foyer, I almost gasp. Instead of the minimal one couch and two-seater, there are different seats and new furnishings all over the place.

As my eyes glance up, I'm shocked. There's a new flat screen hanging on the wall, where it's already playing the movie Theodore and I had arranged for the night. Even the faces tonight are different. A bit of joy vibrates from the people taking the new seats here. There's a totally new face here also, but not a homeless one, I suppose.

I'm kind of nervous as I see Emma approaching me. I didn't catch her earlier, but she was standing in a corner with the staff having a talk.

"Hey..." Her fingers curl around my arm as she leans in to kiss my cheek.

"What a surprise," I say as she pulls back, a giddy smile on her face.

"Ian hasn't told you?" She digs the pen she's holding into her lower lip.

"About what?" I don't need to ask.

Emma wrinkles her nose, becoming nervous like me. "I had no idea he didn't tell you. But I'm in charge of the office's charity programs. Recently Ian decided to donate to this shelter. He said it means a lot to you." She spins, waving her pen around. "And we usually make sure the money goes where it should. That's why I'm here."

"You work with Ian?" These two are close then.

Lifting her shoulders, she thinks on it a moment. "It wasn't planned. It's just...he was going through some heavy stuff, and I wanted to be by his side. Then I really liked working with him, so here I am."

Heavy stuff.

Pointing her pen back, she suggests, "Why don't we take a look at the kitchen? I want you to meet someone."

I follow Emma to meet this someone, and as we get closer, I can smell it. Someone is cooking dinner.

"How is it going, Gabriel?" Emma asks as she walks into the kitchen, where there are faces I haven't seen before. Two guys and a woman.

This Gabriel smiles. "Very well, Miss Skene. We're cooking lasagna tonight. The equipment here is great to work with."

I run my eyes around the kitchen. There are tons of changes here—a new stove, a new fridge, cups, bowls, lots, and lots of new stuff.

Ian is definitely serious about the shelter.

I exchange pleasantries with Gabriel and his two assistants before Emma reveals as we stand by the counter, "We hired them to cook every night for the people here. And we'll see how it goes."

"What do you mean how it goes?"

"You know...in a place like this, different kinds of stuff could happen."

I get her. This chef and his team are professionals, and of course, not all the people around this shelter are pleasant to deal with. That's also what deters me from visiting on a regular basis, but I always donate money; it's the least I can do.

"Grace... here you are." Theodore is at the door, a smile on his face. Then it disappears as his eyes shift to my side. To Emma.

I feel Emma now. She's getting nervous as Theodore comes closer.

He stops a foot away. "Emma," he acknowledges her with a simple nod. But his eyes are not simple. They're heated with all kinds of emotions. They're not light green anymore. They're dark.

"Um..." Emma is out of words. "Um, nice to see you again, Theo."

Theo.

I look at Emma sideways as she stabs her pen into her lip again. "I need to go back to check the rooms."

And like a haunted soul, she walks past Theodore and out of the kitchen, leaving the latter agitated.

"Oh..." I wait till he's back on earth with me. "I didn't know you were a *Theo.*" He glares down at me, but I don't care. "I thought you hated being called Theo. But you know, it sounds different from her lips, I guess."

He shakes his head, smiling, then looks around. "What's going on here?"

I know he's trying to escape me teasing him about Emma, and for a while, I do the right thing. I introduce him to the new staff and tell him all about what Ian has done here before grabbing him by the arm to stand near the counter again. "Are you going to tell me what this thing is? I mean between you and Emma?"

He sighs. "I'm not sure."

"Why?" The question flies from my lips. I'm this curious about them.

"Because she's not sure." He shrugs. "She has a point. We weren't supposed to meet again."

I totally don't get what he's talking about. "So, how did you meet in the first place?"

There's a huge smile on his face. "She's my wildest fantasy."

I gasp. "That night. That bar."

He nods. "Yep."

He leans against the counter, crossing his legs. "I haven't been able to stop thinking about her since. So, when we met again, I thanked my lucky stars. But as you can see, she's not as thrilled about it as me."

"But you just ended it with Sadie," I say, concerned about him and more about Emma. "How did you even develop these strong feelings for her?"

He spreads a hand. "I don't know. It just happened. You know, sometimes one night can tell you more about a person than a whole year."

Wise words, but not realistic, which is why Emma is reluctant about getting involved with him, I guess.

But I don't need to be concerned about this. I need to make a decision about that house Ian wants to buy.

God.

An idea pops into my head, not the wisest, but I should give it a try and see how it goes. As I look around me, Theodore has already left the kitchen, so I walk out, heading down the hallway. I want to find Emma and casually tell her about it. Maybe her reaction would tell me something.

I walk down the hallway, shifting my eyes right and left, looking for her. But apparently, I'm not the only one looking.

With an open mouth, I watch as Theodore grabs Emma by the arm and pulls her against him before she wraps her arms around his neck, and I don't know if they're kissing or attacking each other's lips.

I close my mouth and turn with the silliest smile on my face. As I round the corner, I pull my phone out of my bag and text Ian.

> **ME:** I think I'd like to check out houses with you.
>
> **IAN:** You're such a wicked angel.

Why? I text back, adding a grumpy face.

> **IAN:** You've left me hanging all day, and for that… I'll pull another big move on you when you get home.
>
> **ME:** No, you're not.
>
> **IAN:** I so am.
>
> **ME:** Seriously, don't.
>
> **IAN:** Seriously, I am.
>
> **ME:** Stop it.
>
> **IAN:** Not gonna.

I'll go to Shelia's tonight. This one I send with a tongue sticking out emoji.

> **IAN:** I'll pretend to believe this lie till I get my hands on you.
> **ME:** You're not gonna get your hands on me. I'll be at Shelia's.
> **IAN:** Keep lying, and I'll keep believing.
> **ME:** I'm so spending the night at Shelia's.
> **IAN:** You're so wearing my ring tonight.
> **ME:** God, Ian.... Don't kid about these things.
> **IAN:** I'm not kidding. Besides, we don't kid with each other; we only lie.

I don't lie. I never lied to you. I type this, agitated. He's comparing me to her. I have never lied to him, but apparently, she had.

> **IAN:** Look who's getting nervous.
> **ME:** I'm not nervous. I'm mad.
> **IAN:** Mad Mrs. Ian Skene... so musical.
> **ME:** I'm seriously so mad. Stop it. Then, if you're serious, I'm more mad that you're giving me your ring via text. So cheap.
> **IAN:** But my ring isn't. It's five carats.
> **ME:** You didn't buy me a ring.
> **IAN:** I so bought you a ring.
> **ME:** Ian... Say it's a lie, and I'll forgive you for scaring me.
> **IAN:** Not a lie. Here, see for yourself.

I open the pic he sends me, and gawk. He bought me a ring.

ME: It's a ring.

IAN: I know. I bought it, my silly angel.

ME: When and why?!!!!!!!!!!!!!

IAN: Now, don't scream at me. And when... same time as the bracelet.

ME: You didn't answer why?

IAN: Hang in with me...

ME: Why...?

IAN: Cuz I'm in the car....can't bend on one knee to answer your why.

ME: You're not gonna bend on one knee.

IAN: I'm gonna bend on one knee... here... I'm out of the car now.

ME: Ian... Don't.

IAN: I'm bending on one knee. Ready?

ME: NO!

IAN: Will you marry me, Grace...?

ME: Not. Gonna. Marry. You. Crazy You.

IAN: I'll believe this lie right now, but when you get home, you're so gonna be my fiancée.

I sigh, heading out of the shelter. What am I going to do with him?

Well, first thing, I need to stop smiling.

CHAPTER TWENTY-SIX
Ian

THREE YEARS AGO

MY THROAT BURNS, my chest hurts, and I barely walk because of the flu. But things need to be done. I have to help Acacia, and dig deep to know what she's gotten herself into. We spent the weekend together, and she's considering the idea of moving back in with me. But what resurrected all my worries was the phone call she took late last night. It left her shattered. She didn't want to talk about it, but for the first time, she went back to my bed and spent the night there, spooned by me. That's why I'm meeting Ridge Colman at the coffee shop around the corner from my office despite being sick. I need to act before it's too late.

Ridge Colman is a former FBI agent who has a private investigation bureau. With my last deal, I can afford to pay for his services.

"I need to know everything about her," Ridge says in a practical tone. "If you could get me any of her formal documents, that would be a great help."

"Consider it done. But I really need to know what kind of people she's hanging with. She's new to the city and is kind of innocent, and I'm afraid she might have gotten herself into an awful situation."

I hate this. I hate that I have to rely on a total stranger to protect her, even if he's the best in his field. But I have no choice. Time isn't on my side.

Ridge takes a moment to sip from his coffee before saying, "Sometimes, that's not the case. Some people aren't what they seem to be, and part of my job is warning you to be ready for what we might find out about her."

"I'm not worried about that," I say firmly. "I'm worried about her safety. Whatever you might find out won't change how I feel about her. I just want her to be safe. And if she's in any kind of danger, I want to be able to help her."

Ridge gives me a slight nod. "Then I'll contact you when I get my hands on something, but please do send me those documents as soon as you can so we can check her background. But don't worry, from this moment on, we'll keep an eye on her."

Ridge Colman stands to leave, and I feel bad about this meeting and what I have asked him to do. But there are worms in my head that won't stop nagging me about how Acacia might be in danger. She might not even know it herself. With her background, I don't think she's street smart enough for this city.

To confirm my doubts and validate hiring Ridge Colman, I find myself heading to the store where she works. I wonder if she'll react the same way she did last time.

I don't know how I find the power to go all the way there as my body aches everywhere. I'm exhausted. But when I arrive at the store, I'm alert again. Another girl is standing at the counter where Acacia was last time.

My immediate reaction is that she might be out on her lunch break, though it's early for that. I pull my phone out of my pocket and text her.

ME: Where are you?
ACACIA: At the store.

Fuck. She's lying again.

With tremendous pain, I walk out of the store and text her again.

ME: Can I drop by and take you out for lunch?
ACACIA: That would be awesome, but today we have a hectic schedule, and lots of things to do.

There's nothing hectic in that store. And she's not there.

She. Is. Not. There.

Shaking my head and trying not to get upset about her lie, I drop down to the pavement. I really need to rest. Otherwise, I won't be able to see the last of Acacia's situation. I have to be strong for her. I take multiple deep breaths, and all the time I need till I'm finally able to push myself up again and head to my place. I need to take my medications that I forgot this morning.

After thirty minutes of non-stop coughing, I unlock my apartment door. I need to take my pills and have some rest before I find some of her documents. I don't know how to do that just yet. Acacia took all her stuff out of my apartment, but I'll find a way.

I need to find a way.

Closing the apartment door and before I walk two steps inside, a text beeps on my phone. Although challenging, I pull it out of my pocket to take a look.

It's Acacia. I close my eyes and open them, fighting the blur to read her text.

> **ACACIA:** I wish I could have lunch with you, Ian. I wish I could have so many things with you. I really do. But I'm… I'm leaving for good this time. Please don't look for me. Trust me. It's best for you.

I don't know what happened to her in these last minutes for her to send me this text. I'm shocked and tired. I cannot even start to fathom what's happening. My heart is going to explode from pain. I drop down to the floor. My hands shake. I cannot even dial her number. I know she won't answer, but I have to try. I curl my fingers into a fist, helpless.

After a shaky, grilling moment, I'm able to dial her number. Now I wait for something I'm sure won't happen. She will not pick up. She thinks she's doing the right thing, but she's wrong. I try to reason with her, for the last time, I have to try. My fingers fly to text her back.

> **ME:** Acacia, please...don't pull this on me. You could leave, you could do whatever the hell you want, but please let me know you're safe.

I wait a minute, then two. She doesn't text back, and I don't have time. I knew she wouldn't, but it doesn't matter. I could get her back here. I close my eyes for a second to wash away all the blur, then text her again.

ME: I'm not feeling alright, Acacia. I need you here by my side. I need to go to the hospital. I think the flu is morphing into something serious.

I don't think it's a lie. I cannot even push myself up from the floor. Something is happening with my body.

ACACIA: Don't lie about this stuff.

I cannot believe she's texted this fast, and my fingers type on my phone.

ME: It's up to you, babe. Maybe it's the last lie you're going to choose not to believe of me.
ACACIA: Hang on. I'm coming.

I want to high-five myself. I knew how to get her to come. I know her well, despite everything she hides from me. I don't know her details, but I know her truth.

I'm praying she comes soon.

I think I'm going to lose consciousness. My eyes fight against my mind. I'm dying to shut them and have some rest, but I need to know if Acacia is truly coming or not. Not only to make sure she's safe, but I need someone to take me to the hospital. I'm seriously sick.

I don't know how many minutes pass when I hear her using her key to open the door, and my body gives up. I slump my head against the wall and close my eyes, aching for this moment of relief, physically and emotionally. But still, I'm not totally unconscious. I can hear her voice.

"Ian," she says, urgently. She's probably inside the apartment now. I feel her cold hand over my forehead. She doesn't say anything else, but I know she's calling for help. Then after a minute, I hear her hurried steps inside the apartment, then she lays something cold over my forehead. She's telling me something, but I cannot figure out what it is. Probably some comforting words.

After a while, everything fades away. I feel nothing or hear nothing. Nothing till I feel myself lying on my back and attached to tubes, white stuff everywhere. It feels like a moment has passed, but I'm sure it's more than that. I'm in the hospital. I figure this out.

"Ian." I feel her soft hand on my forehead before I tilt my head to the side where Acacia is standing by the bed, her eyes terrified. "Tell me you're here with me, Ian. It's been hours now. Please say something."

Hours, it felt like a moment.

I blink more, trying to let her know I'm awake as I try to find my voice. I cannot speak yet.

"You have to fight this, Ian. You have to pass this night. Please, stay strong."

"I can fight anything with you," I'm finally able to say before my eyes shut again. I don't know what's wrong with me at this stage, but I think my flu has morphed into a phase of pneumonia.

I heard someone say that a while ago. Maybe a nurse or a doctor.

I feel her hand on my head. "I'm here with you, Ian. I'll never leave again. I swear, just get better, and I'll do whatever you want."

"Do you mean that?" My eyes suddenly snap open. I cannot believe how sincere she sounds, and I have to make sure because the truth will be in her eyes. But I cannot keep them open to take a good look. They shut again.

"Yes, I do."

I hope she does mean that. That's my last thought before I black out again.

CHAPTER TWENTY-SEVEN

Grace

I THINK I'M AT that moment. The moment that precedes either greatness or dumbness. Either it'll be the best decision I ever make, or it'll be the biggest letdown of my life. I don't think he's kidding. He's serious. He wants us to get married.

Nervous, excited, and terrified, I step out of the elevator. It's the moment of truth, I guess. I left the shelter half an hour ago, dreading this moment. I know he's already inside the apartment, and I know what's waiting for me. He's going to bend on one knee.

God.

I wish it was easy. I wish I could sit down with him and have a serious talk, but I know he won't listen till he gets what he wants. I'm partially at fault. How am I going to convince him with a goofy grin on my face? I cannot help how excited I am.

But is it for the right reasons?

Maybe the idea of being legitimately attached to him is calming my fears.

What if she came back and asked for a second chance?

He loves her. I know he loves me, but he loves her too. It's why I should say no. I should wait till she's not in his heart. Out, far away from him, from us.

But he said over and over, there's no one else for him. He *only* loves me. I should listen to my heart and stop these meaningless doubts. Everyone has exes. Look at Theodore. He was madly in love with Sadie, and now he cannot even keep it together around Emma. This makes me a little less nervous.

The apartment door is open. I take a deep breath. This is happening. I take another deep breath and walk inside.

It's a bit dark, but I blink as I look down where candles form a path. This is so happening. He's going to propose. I'm on the verge of tears. I put a hand to my mouth, too early to cry. I need to make a decision first, and I haven't made up my mind.

This is so beautifully hard.

I shrug off my coat and shut the door behind me. I follow the candle-lit path. I know I should think wisely. I should put my big girl pants on and stop listening to those butterflies. It'll get worse when I lay my eyes on him. I cannot be indecisive in front of him. I cannot risk walking to him without a firm decision.

I'm still walking down the path. I cross the living room and make my way to the bedrooms, and there he is. Bending down and lighting a candle. He's in a white dress shirt and black slacks, and it doesn't take a second before his eyes clash with mine.

I'm at the head of the hallway, and he's at our bedroom door. Probably where the candle's path will end.

I entwine my hands and press them to my stomach. I don't like how I'm starting to shake. He has this bashful smile on his face before he straightens to his full height. He takes a moment to work his eyes over me. Up and down. I'm glad I decided to wear this pretty dress. It's dark green with long sleeves, a high-rise waistline, and a tiered skirt.

"Always beautiful," he says, glancing up to meet my eyes. "Always taking my breath away." His eyes shift down again, spreading a hand. "Sorry, I couldn't complete the task in time." He gives me his eyes again. "But those candles are quite the work."

I nod. I don't know what I should say, but he knows. He takes two steps toward me and pauses. "I wanted it to be pretty, like a fairy-tale proposal. But time wasn't on my side, and I felt I had to propose to you tonight. So, I hope this unfinished path of candles will be enough."

"More than enough." I don't know how I got those words out as quickly as I did, but I hate it when he doubts himself, that he's not enough for me.

I hear his sharp intake of breath. He's so nervous, so unsure of himself, and I don't know how I can say no to that. My heart squeezes at the sudden hope settling in his eyes.

With firm steps, he walks toward me, pausing two feet away. "Grace," he says my name with hope and fear, "I know you might think this is too fast, so before I say anything, I want you to tell me. Take all the time you need and tell me if you imagine yourself with someone else. If you can imagine yourself with someone else, then it might be too fast. But if you're like me, I cannot imagine what life would be without you-"

"I cannot imagine myself with someone else." I don't need to hear the rest. I cannot stand here and let him doubt us. "You're the only one for me, Ian."

My heart jumps at the relief washing over his face. He moves forward; then nothing separates us but thin air. He looks down, taking my hands in his before he drops to one knee. "Grace," he says as I connect my eyes, which are full of passion. "Will you be my wife? Will you spend the rest of your life with me? Will you marry me, angel?"

I know why girls cry their hearts out in moments like this. It's so beautiful. The love in his eyes is so beautiful. I'm the only one for him. I have no doubt now. It's all in the way he's gazing up at me. Like his life would shatter if I didn't say yes.

"Yes, and yes...and yes." I swallow as my throat tightens. I don't want to cry. I have to tell him how I feel. "I want to be your wife. I want to spend the rest of my life with you. I want to marry you, Ian."

"Oh, angel," he murmurs, and I let my happy tears jump out of my eyes before he stands up, and I feel myself in his arms. My face is buried in his chest, his arms around me, hugging me as if he wants to imprint me onto his soul.

I stand in his arms, crying. Crying out of happiness, and all these years of guilt and fears. I even let myself cry for Sam. I'm crying for Sam for the first time in two years. I'm crying for my past, looking forward to a future with Ian. The only man who could finally make me feel again. Make me safe again.

"I love you so much, Ian." My tears choke my voice, but I have to tell him, I have to thank him.

"I love you too, angel. I. Love. You," he says with such peace like he's just crossed a hard path.

I know now I'll never doubt him or doubt my luck again. I'm glad I was lucky. I'm glad that fate gave me so many beautiful things. I don't even feel guilty about what happened to Sam. It's not my fault. I cannot be held responsible for what these scums do to helpless children. All I can be is grateful, but I'm also ashamed I almost wasted what Sam did for me all those years.

Sam wanted me to live.

"Angel?"

"Yeah?" I pull back a little to look up at him though I want to be in his arms forever.

"The ring, I should give you a ring." He shakes his head, smiling that he forgot this little tiny detail!

"Yes, where is your ring?" I giggle, wiping my eyes with the back of my hands.

"It's your ring," he corrects, reaching inside his pants pocket. He pulls out a small red box, opens it, then takes the ring out. He takes my hand in his and easily slides it onto my finger. "Now, you're a step away from being officially mine."

"Mrs. Ian Skene." I play the words on my tongue; my eyes cannot get enough of his ring. It's beautiful, elegant, and sparkly. It's a round-cut diamond, but what I love the most is the band. Rose gold blended with the little pink flowers that run the circle. So much thought in his choice.

"Okay. Can I get some attention too?" He folds his arms.

I squint at him. "Too demanding. That's not a good quality in a husband."

He playfully glares at me. "You better know from the get-go then, I'm gonna be a very demanding husband and…" he points a finger at me, "it's too late to change your mind, you already said... Yes and yes and yes."

"And…" I jump, wrapping my arms around his neck, "another yes and yes and yes," I say against his lips before I brush them over his.

"And," he says with intent as he lifts me from the floor, "it's time to know what she thinks about this whole marriage thing."

"She?" I ask as he carries me to the bedroom.

A grin tugs at the corner of his mouth. "Your little kitty – slash- my cock hole."

I smack his chest. "You need a new mouth."

"And you're perfect as you are, my angel."

I nuzzle his neck as he carries me over to the bed. "You're so full of it."

Scowling, he places me down on the edge of the bed. "I need a new mouth, and my personality sucks." He folds his arms, still scowling down at me. "Why are you marrying me exactly?"

He waves a finger. "Don't think about it. I want a quick, honest answer."

"Well," I say, looking him up and down. "You're six feet and *ten inches,* aren't you?"

I'm on the verge of giggling when I notice how his whole demeanor has changed. He tries to lift his lip in a mere smile. But it's like he's taken aback. Like he's shocked.

No, he's paralyzed.

Isn't he familiar with these jokes?

"What?" I ask as I'm genuinely baffled by him.

"Nothing," he says, a hand in his hair. "I'm just..." He shakes his head. "I'll be right back."

What the hell?

He disappears inside the bathroom, and I'm still shocked. I don't know what happened to him. But I'm not going to sit wondering what's wrong with him. I stand and walk around the bed, but stop at the bathroom door.

No, no reluctance. I need to know what's wrong with him. I open the door he quietly closed a second ago, and I don't like what I see.

He's standing at the faucet, his head down while his hands grip the edges. "Ian," I call. I don't know who's more agitated, him or me as he turns his head to look at me with lost eyes.

"What's wrong with you?" I ask, dreading to know, but I have to. "It's just a lame joke. Haven't you heard it before?"

"Um..." He slowly pulls his hands down and turns to face me.

He closes his eyes for a second before a hand goes around his neck. "I just need a minute."

"For what?" I take a step inside, folding my arms. This man will be my husband, and I'm not going to let him leave me in the dark about anything.

He presses two fingers to his eyes. And I just can't take it anymore. I walk to him, reaching to grab his hand. I need to know. I need to look into his eyes. "Ian, please, tell me. You're the one who said you don't want any walls between us."

He pulls his hand from mine, then takes a step back. "I just need a minute. Is that hard to understand?" he snaps at me, his eyes full of anger. I'm making him angry.

God, I'm not going to cry.

He snapped at me. He shouldn't have snapped at me. He just proposed to me. No one snaps at their girlfriend after a dreamy proposal. I want to cry. I don't know what to think or how to feel. I just want to curl in a corner and cry. But not in front of him.

I'm trying to stay strong, unaffected. "Take all the freaking minutes you need," I say, pulling his ring off my finger. "And take this too." I drop his ring on the faucet and hurry outside. I will not let him see me crying.

I stumble with each step. My eyes cannot see anymore. They are full of disappointment and confused tears. I don't see, but now I feel. He's made me feel again.

I feel his arm trying to stop me before reaching the front door. "Acacia, listen, please."

I freeze in place. He called me by her name.

No, it cannot be. I slowly turn.

My mouth is hanging open, while he doesn't even know what he's done. He's destroyed my whole world, and he doesn't even have a clue. My heart slowly bleeds.

But now, his whole demeanor changes.

I put a hand over my mouth to cover how it's stupidly still hanging open, watching as it hits him, as he recognizes what he's done. He knows it's the end of us now. It's in his eyes.

"Fuck..." he mutters, closing his eyes and shaking his head.

Yes, fuck.

I cannot handle this. I cannot breathe. I cannot stay here. I have to run from him. I whirl as he calls, "Grace, please."

"Grace!" I turn again, yelling. "You got it right this time!"

He shakes his head, pain and remorse in his dark blue eyes. I can barely stand as he cuts the distance between us, his hands on my shoulders as if he wants to shake some sense into me. I fiercely push them down and turn again to the door.

"Grace, wait." He gathers me into his chest. His arms tighten around me more than they've ever been while shaking at the same time. He knows like I do, it's over. We're over. There's no *we* anymore. He cannot forget her. He cannot let her go.

"Ian." I try to be calm and firm. I need to leave and now. It's like my whole body is shutting down. Nothing is functioning the way it should. "Let me go. I can't even breathe right now. So please, just let me go. I need to breathe."

He rests his chin on the top of my head, his chest against my back, thundering with his rapid breaths. He's desperate to make me stay. "Just listen to me first."

"I'm serious, Ian," I say, my voice helpless and pleading. "I can't breathe. I need to breathe. So, let go of me."

"Promise not to do anything foolish."

I don't think I've ever heard such a tormented voice.

"I promise," I say, not understanding what he means. But I'll say anything if it means I'll be able to walk away from him. I'll be able to breathe again.

As soon as his hands loosen around me, I open his damn door and stumble to Shelia's apartment. I open her front door, then step inside, closing the door behind me. My legs cannot hold me up anymore; I slide down against the door.

I sit on the floor, hugging my knees, my eyes full of tears. I don't know if I'm crying or not. I cannot feel or sense anything. I'm literally in shock. My mind and body are closing in around me, shutting every window for me to feel or know anything.

"God, Grace, what happened?" I hear Shelia's panicked voice before I feel her drop next to me, her arm around my shoulders. "Please, Grace...calm down."

I'm crying then. I just hope I'm not ugly crying.

"You're scaring me. Please, please, tell me what's wrong?"

Oh, I'm ugly crying, then.

Yes, I'm crying loud and ugly. I can feel this now. I'm sobbing with every bit in me, but the loud knock against the door makes me flinch.

"Open this fucking door."

Hearing his urgent voice, I instantly snap my head, shaking it restlessly. I don't want him in. I cannot be around him anymore. I just cannot.

"It's okay, honey." Shelia rubs my shoulders. "I'm not going to open it for him."

I nod, not looking at Shelia. My teary eyes look ahead of me, into the void.

"Go the fuck away!" It's Shelia yelling now.

Thank God, Shelia gets me. I don't want to see him.

"Please don't let her cry," Ian says from behind the door, his voice agonized and helpless.

It's too much hearing his voice, so I push on my hand. I want to get up and run away from his voice. But before I can, Shelia takes me in her arms.

"He loves her. He still loves her." I bury my face in Shelia's chest; I start to sob all over again.

"Oh, God, baby. I'll kill him. I swear, I'll kill him." Shelia doesn't even know the whole story, and she's ready to kill for me. I'm a bit relieved. I have Shelia, and everything is going to be okay. But I'm still sobbing and shaking in her arms.

"Please, Grace... don't cry. Just let me in." It's Ian again, but his voice makes me cry even harder.

"Go the fuck away!" Shelia shouts with evident anger, and I hope he listens this time.

"I'm not going away till she stops crying, or you open this fucking door!" Ian yells back.

No agony in his voice now. He's determined, and I know what a determined Ian can do. He'd convince me everything is fine.

I pull away from Shelia and plead with my eyes, as I cannot form a decent word. She nods and helps me up, muttering a curse. She walks me to her bedroom, away from his voice.

In her room, I walk over to the bed, pull the covers aside, kick my shoes off, and just lay there, pulling the covers over me. I want to hide. I want to go numb again. I cannot deal with this pain. I need to feel nothing.

"Shh..." Shelia passes a hand over my hair while sitting right next to me. "Everything is going to be fine. I promise, baby."

I give her a faint smile, swallowing the remaining sobs inside my throat. "He called me by her name. He still loves her, Shelia. He can't let her go."

"Then it's his loss," Shelia doesn't hesitate to say. "It's his loss, and you're gonna be just fine without that asshole."

A sob escapes despite me trying my hardest not to cry. "He's not an asshole. He's not. He just can't let her go. It's not something he can control."

"Fuck." Shelia looks down at me helplessly. Like she cannot think of anything to say or do to ease my pain. She keeps stroking my hair, and I'm trying my hardest not to cry again. I close my eyes, hoping some sleep will ease my pain before I snap them open as I hear him knocking on the door again. Loud and desperate.

"Don't worry." Shelia pats my arm, standing up. "I'll deal with him. Trust me on this."

I nod and just close my eyes, hoping I'd be able to open them in the morning and would feel nothing. I doubt that, but I have to hope. Hope is all I have right now.

I don't have Sam or Ian anymore.

CHAPTER TWENTY-EIGHT

Ian

THREE YEARS AGO

I'M NOT ALONE. The hot breaths whispering against my neck confirm my suspicions. I bring a hand over the one resting on my stomach. It's delicate and soft. I fight my fatigue and open my eyes. It's Acacia's hand, Acacia's breaths, and Acacia's pink hair. She's sleeping right next to me. She's curled into a ball.

"Acacia," I whisper, rolling over on my side.

"Hey." She opens her eyes, smiling. "Welcome back."

"Welcome back?"

She props herself up on an elbow, looking down at me. "You've been knocked out for two days now. They said your body needed the rest, and there's nothing to worry about."

I want to lift my hand to touch her face, but I'm still too tired. "And you've been here by my side. The whole two days."

She makes a face. "It's just two days."

I remember what she told me when I arrived at the hospital. "Did you mean it? Are you going to stay with me forever? Did you mean what you said, or you were just saying it to make me feel better?"

She nods. "Yes, that's what I want." For a moment, she just smiles down at me with so much content in her eyes before she brings a hand to my face, caressing it tenderly. "I'm sorry it took me so long to make this decision."

"Are you sure?" I place my hand over hers. I cannot believe how sincere she sounds.

"Positive." She rests back on the mattress, placing both her hands under her head.

We lie side by side, facing each other. I lift my hand to caress her arm. "But that's not enough, Acacia. I still need to know everything you're hiding from me."

She sighs. "I will tell you everything. But I need to know that you will understand me, give me a chance to explain some things, and I need you to forgive me."

My fingers curl around her arm, involuntarily. I'm becoming nervous. "What do you mean, forgive you?" I take a deep breath and exhale slowly. "Were you involved with another guy, Acacia?"

She shakes her head, fiercely. "No. But would you forgive me if I was?"

"I will not answer this," I say as firmly as I can. "And there's no need for you to ask such a thing either. We don't need to talk about such stuff. We should start talking about you. About all the things that made you wary of me and the idea of us."

"We will, just when you get better." She smiles, tapping my nose with her finger.

I want to protest when we hear her phone ring. Instantly, she rolls over and jumps down from the bed. She walks toward the chair in the far corner of the room. I watch as she pulls her phone out of her bag, then shakes her head. "I need to leave," she says, locking her eyes with mine. "But I'll be back soon."

"Where are you going?" I immediately ask, all sorts of nasty stuff running in my mind.

"Um..." she hesitates, "it's one of the things I'll tell you later. But now I need to go. There's no time to explain."

"Acacia," I almost yell, wishing I could be a little stronger so I could go with her, but I'm beaten. "Don't do this. You just promised me."

She throws her bag over her shoulder. "And I promise I'll come back soon. But I have to do this to be able to come back and spend the rest of my life with you, Ian. I hope you'll be ready for me."

I drop my head back to the headboard, watching her walk out of the room. I cannot trust her to come back. I hope Ridge Colman is still watching her because I don't feel like this call will bring any good to us.

It's been two days since Acacia left the hospital, promising to come back. But she didn't. She didn't answer any of my calls either. For the past forty-eight hours, I've held on to the hope that she would come back. Hoping she'd stay true to her word. That she was finally choosing me, choosing us over everything else. But apparently, I was wrong to hope and to believe her.

It's over. We're over forever.

And with all that, I'm still worried about her safety. I need to call Ridge Colman and see if he found out anything about her. I haven't been able to give him what he wanted, but I need to make that phone call, maybe later today.

I feel helpless in this hospital bed. My body is not allowing me to do anything. I'm so sick, and according to the doctors here, it'll be a week before they even think about releasing me.

My phone rings beside me, and hope suddenly jumps into my heart. I pick my phone up from the nightstand and check the screen.

It's not her.

It's not Acacia.

It's Ridge Colman, and my heart sinks.

He's found something. Why else would he be calling me?

I'm so hesitant to pick up and know her truth.

No, I know her truth. I'm just scared of her secrets.

I'm scared to know something that would end every hope for us to be together.

I swipe my finger over the screen. My throat tightens, knowing it's the end for us. "Have you found anything?" I can barely utter the words. Everything in me is dying. Every hope has left me.

Ridge gives me this horrible sigh as if preparing me for his atrocious news. I glue the phone to my ear, listening to what I'm sure will devastate my world.

CHAPTER TWENTY-NINE

Grace

I KNOW SHELIA HAS been checking on me nonstop. I know it's past ten in the morning, and I need to leave this bed. But that's not what makes me pull the covers to the side. I can hear the argument outside between Shelia and Ian. It's not fair to let her deal with him again. I know she's been doing it the whole night. I need to face him and end everything. I cannot hide forever.

I walk to the adjacent bathroom and stop at the mirror. A thing that once resurrected all my fears, but not anymore. I don't even need to take a deep breath. I just look right into the mirror, but I don't recognize myself. Not my features, though. My big eyes, with their dark circles, are the same. My white face is the same. My long dark hair is all sorts of messy, but still, it's the same. It's my soul that I don't recognize and the desperation that settles in my eyes. I'm lost. I don't know where to go from here or what to do.

What should I say to him?

I don't know how I'm going to face him again. Is he my man or hers?

He is hers.

Because he couldn't have been so passionate about us, about me, as he was and still be able to call me by her name, mistake my name with hers. Things like this don't add up.

I turn on the faucet and let the water wash away my tears and messy eyes. But nothing can wash away the pain in my heart. This pain is not only for me but for him too. I'm aching for him, that his attempt to let her go has failed. It's so heartbreaking to think of his situation too. This is so messed up at every angle.

God, Ian.

I turn off the faucet and grip the edges of the sink tightly. I'm not going to be weak. I have to think of myself and what another incident like the night before will do to me. I cannot risk hearing her name again. I have to be strong in front of him. I know he'll try his best to win me back, and he can easily do that, so I have to keep the pain of hearing her name alive in every bit of my soul.

Acacia...

I have to remember that name.

I have to remember he still loves her, and no matter how hard he tries, he cannot let her go.

I take another look in the mirror before walking back to the room. I change out of my dress and pick up a green blouse and jeans from Shelia's closet.

After getting dressed, I pass the brush through my hair, then gather it in a messy bun before heading out to the front door, where Shelia and Ian are still arguing.

At the end of the hallway, I take a moment to run my eyes over him. Dressed in jeans and a dark blue shirt, he seems disoriented, like he didn't have enough sleep. There's so much intensity in his eyes, but that intensity is soon gone as he spots me. I can see the relief that washes over his eyes before he says, "Fuck, finally."

"Grace, you don't have to talk to him." Shelia turns to me, her back to Ian but still blocking him from getting inside.

I nod. "It's okay, Shelia."

"Are you sure?" Shelia asks, worried while Ian sighs in relief.

I cross the hallway and stop near Shelia, touching her arm in an assuring way. "I'll be fine."

Shelia hugs me, then looks back at Ian with all sorts of warnings before she leaves us alone. Now, the inevitable. I can feel him vibrating with impatience. He knows I need to have the first say in this, and I know it's killing him to be patient.

I'm not ready for him. I don't think I'll ever be, but I turn to face him anyway. "Why don't we go to your place," I suggest, and immediately I notice the annoyance in his eyes.

"Our place," he retorts firmly before taking a step back, giving me space to walk past him.

Once inside his apartment, I think we should have our last talk in the living room, where we had our first. I don't want to sit. I don't want this to linger, so I stand, letting him know I prefer to have this talk as fast as possible.

We stand facing each other. He's silent, letting me have my silent wish to be the first to start. My heart tugs a little. He knows me well. I shrug off that thought. I don't want to make this harder than it is. But I don't know how to start. I don't want to sound pissed or vindictive. I know it's something he cannot control. And knowing he tried his best to move on from her makes no room for me to be angry at him.

"I can explain everything, Grace," he says, determined to win this, to make me believe in us again.

My hesitation has let him have the first word, but not the last.

I shake my head. "I don't want you to explain, Ian. There's nothing to explain."

He exhales, then looks to the side for a moment before looking back at me. "So, everything is fine between us. Is that what you're telling me?"

"Ian..." I frown, shouting his name with bitterness, tremendously gutted that he could think like that.

How could he think I'd be fine after he called me by her name? Or is it just a desperate wish of his because deep down, he knows he couldn't do anything to change my mind.

He takes a step toward me. "Then listen to me and let me explain."

"I don't want you to explain," I say, trying to sound firm, but my emotions take the lead in this scene. My heart is bleeding, and I cannot hide it. I cannot stand strong in front of my beautiful dream. A dream I didn't know I had, that would never come true. "I don't want you to explain," I repeat. This time I will not hide anything. I want him to know exactly how I feel, how any attempt of his would only break my heart all over again.

With utter desperation, I say, "I want you to lie, Ian. I want you to give me the best of your lies. The one you, yourself, wished to believe so I can believe in us again. I want you to lie till I believe in us."

He shakes his head, and I don't think I can control my emotions anymore. I let my crying voice be heard, "Lie to me, Ian. Lie till I believe. Can you do that? Because nothing would explain what you did. Nothing but a pretty lie."

I bring a hand to my mouth. I don't want to sob in front of him, but my teary eyes still see how hard he's trying to stay in control.

He curls a hand at his side, walking till he's able to circle one around my arm. "I never lied to you, Grace," he says every word as clear as day, his fingers digging so hard into my flesh before he retreats. He whirls, pressing a hand to his neck before turning again to look back at me, his eyes holding nothing but blame. "I've tried my hardest. I fucking tried my hardest to stay away from you. To give you all the time you needed-"

Now he's the one pissed. He gets to shatter my heart into a million pieces, and still be pissed at me for trying to protect myself. Instantly, I cut him off, "Don't you dare start blaming me." I let a bitter laugh reach his ears, remembering how hurt I felt the night before, and our first night together, "I didn't call you by another guy's name. I didn't, Ian."

"I didn't." I take a step till I stand in front of him, poking a finger at his chest. "I didn't, but you did. You called me by her name. And I'm not talking about last night. It wasn't the first time."

He does seem surprised. Of course, he was wasted that night. "Yes, that's right. Last night wasn't the first time. It wasn't the first time you broke my heart. You broke it the first time I opened my heart to you. The night I knew I was in love with you. The first time you made love to me. It was supposed to be special, but I'll always remember how it ended. You wished it was her. You asked her to stay by your side. Not me, HER."

I don't want to cry again, but I cannot help my tears or how my throat starts to tighten and how it's hard to breathe. The soft look in his eyes doesn't help either. I don't want him to pity me, but I cannot seem to control how broken I am.

"Don't cry, angel. Please don't cry." He steps closer to wipe my tears; his touch is so tender I just want to stay there, soothed and comforted by him. He's the only person who can make me feel safe. But then I get terrified.

What if he calls me by her name again? I flinch back from his touch.

Wishing I could stop my tears to speak decently, I speak anyway, with whatever voice I have. I don't care.

"So," I clear my throat, my teary eyes glued to his. "I don't want you to think I'm angry at you. I know that's something you can't control, and I should have known better. It was too good to be true. I was just eager to believe your beautiful lies."

"I never lied to you," he retorts in a murderous voice, looking down at me with unbelieving eyes, his breathing out of control.

I bring my arms around myself, preventing them from reaching out to comfort him because he seems lost and devastated. "Not intentionally. I know you wanted to believe those lies too."

"Oh, just fucking stop." He raises a hand in the air and makes a semi-spin, like he cannot look at me anymore. He's back to being pissed, and that makes me pissed too.

I let him hear my bitter laugh. "So, you don't want her back. You don't wish it was her standing in your living room. Just look at me and tell me you don't wish to have her back."

He utters a fed-up sigh before turning to look me in the eye. "I'm only in love with you, Grace. I only love you. There's no one else for me." He spreads a hand before saying sarcastically, "Happy now?"

"Happy now?" I yell my broken heart, my anger, and my frustration. He's so in denial. "I'll tell you what makes me happy. I'll be happy when you at least admit it, when you start acknowledging your true feelings, when you're able to admit that she's still imprinted on your soul. I have seen so many signs, but I ignored them like you're doing right now."

"Are you for real?"

There's so much contempt in the way he speaks, in the way he's looking down at me. Like what he did doesn't even deserve my outrage.

"You. Called. Me. By. Her. Name." I don't know if I'm shouting or not. But I hope he knows how much he'd hurt me. "You called me by her name, and it wasn't a mistake. It was your hidden wish. A wish you don't want to admit." I pause to take a breath. I'm so angry at him. "You called me by her name," I repeat for the last time before I walk away from him, fighting my disrespectful desire to stay and let him convince me again.

"You know why I called you by her name?" His harsh voice stops me from turning away. It's the moment I've been waiting for, or dreading; I don't know. But I can see it in his pissed eyes. He doesn't care anymore. He's going to tell me what's going to destroy all my hopes.

"Yes." I walk back to stand in front of him. My eyes have no tears, they're bravely gazing up at him to hear the truth. I want to listen, so I can act better for myself before he goes back to convince me of us again. "I want to know why."

"Because…" A sarcastic laugh escapes his mouth. "It's the only fucking name you gave me." I frown at him, and he nods his head. "Yes, you didn't even tell me your real name."

I bring a hand around my neck. I don't think he's stable enough or even knows what he's talking about. It's like he's with her. Talking to her, not me.

I close my eyes, sad. Sad for him and me. So sad, I cannot even stand straight. I'm shaking from head to toe. There's a battle inside of me. To stay and do the right thing for him or walk away and do the right thing for me. I need to make this decision fast.

"Goodbye, Ian." I open my eyes, nothing in them but love and best wishes for him. I think he needs to heal himself from her, and I hope he succeeds. That girl ruined him, and I hope it's not too late for him to pull himself together.

But I cannot be here while he's doing it. That would be like trying to kill myself again. It's too painful to stay.

"Goodbye," he repeats, disbelieving. "Goodbye, ha?" he says again. And I turn to walk away. No matter how devastated he sounds, this is not about me. He's all about her. I wish I could keep thinking like this till I'm able to walk away. I only hope.

"Why is it always easy for you?"

The pain in his voice stops me despite my determination to protect myself. I know that pain isn't about me or us. But damn my stupid heart, it makes me stop.

With clenched fists, I turn. I don't know why I turn, but I cannot leave him in pain alone. I don't intend to stay either, but for now, I just cannot walk away. And when I look up at him, when my eyes clash with his, I immediately flinch two steps back. There's so much pain and hurt in them. There's so much desperation too. My heart breaks again—this time for him. But there's something else, something that erects a hidden fear inside me.

It's not the first time I've witnessed this. It's not the first time he's asked me this. It's not the first time I decided to walk away from him for good.

It's not the first time I have seen these pained dark blue eyes.

I put a hand at the base of my throat. Fear clenches around my heart as an image crosses my mind. Ian is standing with the same look, asking the same painful question, but he's a little younger with a shaved head and a couple of pounds heavier. And I'm different from the way I look now. I had that stupid pink hair. The hair I woke up with after recovering from trying to kill myself.

It does seem so real. The pain is alive there. Like I've met this younger Ian for real.

"Ian..." I utter his name, my hands trembling, "is there something you're hiding from me?"

"Me, hiding stuff." Ian throws his head back, laughing. "I don't know. It's your specialty."

I gasp. This cannot be true. I didn't do that to him. I didn't. "Did you ever shave your head?" That's the first thing I ask as image after image of shaved-head Ian visits my mind. I'd met him when he had that shaved head. I know now for sure.

"Have you ever dyed your hair pink?" he retorts bitterly, taking a step toward me. "Did you give me your virginity?" He takes another step, his eyes boiling with anger. "Did we meet three years ago?" his voice breaks, his whole body breaks while my mind is in utter chaos.

Image after image crosses my mind, filling those empty months I lost after waking up in the hospital recovering from trying to end my life. Bits and pieces of Ian and me, making me flinch and wish to run away.

But my legs cannot run. I just walk backward till I hit a wall. Then I look back at Ian, and I've never seen him like this. Like his whole world is turned upside down before he shakes his head. "You just forgot me," he reveals, his eyes pained and haunted. There's so much darkness in the way he's looking down at me.

"I was forgettable. You remembered everything but *me*." Now his voice is as dark as his eyes. No, his voice echoes death and despair.

Oh, my god.

It wasn't her. There was no other girl.

It was me.

I was the girl who ruined him.

But why didn't he tell me? I sink to the floor as my mind and body become too exhausted to think or do anything.

Why didn't you tell me, Ian? Why?

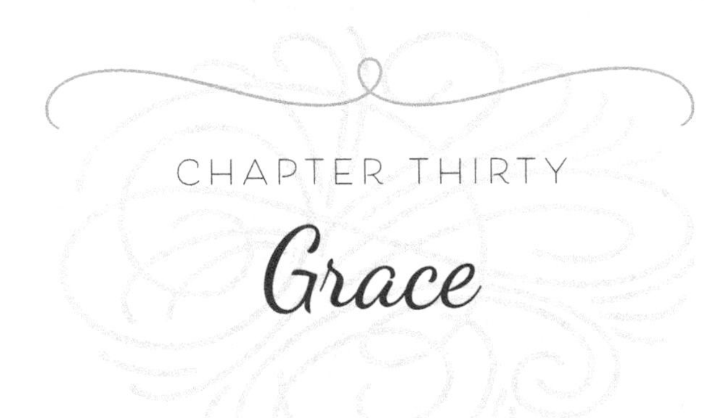

CHAPTER THIRTY

Grace

IAN PICKS ME up from the floor; his muscular arms carry me to the couch. I'm not helpless, but maybe my body is right now.

I swallow a cry as he puts me on the couch. "Relax, Grace," he whispers against my mouth before backing away from me.

How could I relax when a fire burns inside me? A lot of anger too.

How could he do this to me?

I sit straight. "Why didn't you tell me?" I glance over at him, where he's at the far end of the room, resting a hand against the wall, staring back at me.

I feel ashamed of the way I handled everything three years ago, but that doesn't give him the right to hide everything from me.

"Why did you do what you did?" he throws back with a calm voice. "Why was it hard for you to open up to me? What was going on with you, Grace?"

I open my mouth, but nothing comes out of it. I don't know where to start. Everything seems so raw and new for me. I'm still trying to tie all these bits and pieces together.

He sighs. "See… It's not easy to answer all the whys. It's not fucking easy, and it wasn't easy for me either. It was fucking hell."

I don't know what to say. I just stare back at him; my mind is busy with all the details that keep coming back to me. When we first met, when we went on our first date, when I moved in with him, when he wanted to know everything, when everything collapsed around me, and when I couldn't stay. Because if I stayed, I would be betraying Sam.

I see him calming a little before he walks over to me. He settles to my right but doesn't initiate any physical contact. Like he knows his touch wouldn't ease anything for me. I'm so messed up inside. This is so messed up. I don't know who's more in the wrong, him or me.

"If you think you're ready…" He pauses to take a breath. "I'll tell you why."

I guess he's more courageous or less at fault than me. I don't know where to start explaining what I did three years ago.

I turn slightly to him, nodding my head. "Why didn't you tell me we knew each other? Why, after all this time, you decided to be in my life again?" I don't know how to wrap my mind around this, but I have to ask. "Has anything between us even been real? Because everything seems so planned right now, but the question is why?"

"Do you remember when I was at the hospital? When you left, saying you'd come back?"

I don't think I want to remember how I'd let him down, but what other choice do I have? Either I talk about this with him or be a prisoner to the myriad of thoughts that are making terrifying chaos in my mind. "I was sincere. I was going to come back. I was."

He nods. "Well, I was worried about you, but since I didn't believe what you said, I thought you weren't going to come back. But then I got a call from Ridge Colman…" he hesitates to reveal more.

"I don't remember that name," I say, wanting him to clarify more. Maybe I don't remember everything, after all.

"He's…" He brings a hand to cover his eyes, hesitant again.

"Ian…" I wait, a little apprehensive of this Colman guy.

"I was worried about you." He shakes his head, maybe remembering how awful I was to him. "You wouldn't tell me anything, so I hired a private detective to find out what kind of trouble you were getting yourself into."

I gasp. I cannot believe he hired someone to watch me. "I wasn't in trouble. How many times did I tell you that?"

"It doesn't matter now," he says sarcastically. "Anyway, he called two days after you left. He told me that your real name wasn't Acacia. He pretty much gathered all the information he could about you. But that wasn't the thing that shocked me. I knew you were hiding stuff, and I was hurt that you even lied about your name, but that was nothing compared to what he told me later."

I don't want to think of the obvious. I bring a hand to my neck. "What was it? What did he tell you?"

He looks at me soulfully for a moment before saying, "He appointed someone to watch you. He said you had gotten into the city shelter, stayed there for a while. But when you were gone for too long, this guy went inside asking about you, and that's when they found you bleeding." He huffs a long breath then mutters a "fuck" before continuing, "You cut your wrist that day. And as soon as he told me, I jumped from that hospital bed and went out like a lunatic to be by your side. I didn't even ask him if you made it. If you were still alive. I didn't wait to hear any details or ask where you were. My mind was going crazy, but my body was going crazy too. I think I collapsed in the hospital hall and was tied to the bed for a week or so after that."

"I'm so sorry, Ian." I cover my face with my hands. I cannot look him in the eye, knowing what I had made him go through. "I'm so sorry."

"It's okay." He edges closer to me, wrapping an arm around my shoulders. "The worst is over. I promise you, angel."

I don't think it is. I still don't know why he hid everything and worse.

Did he intend to hide everything forever?

As if he feels how tense I've become, he edges back to the corner of the couch. When I glance over at him, he starts to talk again. "After I was well enough and able to function, I called Ridge, and by then, he knew you were in a coma for five days, and your parents decided to continue your treatment back at your home. So, I headed there, I took the first flight to Seattle, and from there, I took a cab to your town and the hospital you were admitted into."

"Um..." I sigh. "I woke up from the coma, not remembering what happened exactly. Why did I have pink hair and what happened during my stay in the city. I didn't even know where my phone was. So, I knew nothing. But I knew why I came here in the first place, but I didn't remember what happened." I don't tell him I was able to remember what happened to Sam. "I remembered that moment when I tried to kill myself. The doctors said I bled a lot, and after a coma, it's expected not to remember things, but they said with some therapy, I'd be able to put the pieces back together. Obviously, I couldn't till now." I dare to look him in the eye when I ask, "But I don't remember you coming to visit or even asking about me."

He seems a little irritated before saying, "I'm not lying, ask your parents. When I asked about you at the hospital, they said I couldn't visit without your parents' permission. And when I met them, they wouldn't let me see you. They said the doctors warned them about anything or anyone who might trigger you to do it again. To try to take your own life because no one knew why you did it. And since you didn't remember what happened, everything was a *no* till you gained your memory back. But that didn't deter me. I visited every day trying to convince your parents. Your father was a bit more understanding while your mother wasn't at all. She even got a restraining order against me."

"Oh, shit." I know my mother will do anything to protect me. I've told her every little detail about the horrifying things Sam and I went through. But still, this is like a slap in the face, considering how I made Ian suffer.

"But that wasn't going to deter me either," he says firmly. "I was ready for all the consequences just to be able to see you again. Until your father talked me out of it."

There's a bit of pause, much needed for him and me before he continues, "He sat down with me and tried to explain where they were coming from. He told me how sensitive your situation was, and that any trigger might cost them your life. He told me you suffered from depression before you moved to the city. So, he begged me to wait. To give you some time, to let you do your therapy, and he promised me that when he felt the time was right, he would allow me to contact you again."

"Did you promise him?" I whisper, hoping he didn't give up on me back then.

"Yes," he says without hesitation. "Though it was hard for me, and I was dying to see you, I promised him because I didn't understand myself what you were going through. What led you to do what you did. So, I've put my feelings aside. I tried to make the best decision for you. Since I didn't even know your real name, I thought I was in no place to make any serious decisions considering your state. So finally, I listened to what your parents thought was the best for you."

I feel a little disappointed. Why did he wait more than two years before trying to get in touch with me again? Did he, at some point, give up on me completely, and why did he decide to be in my life again?

Knowing what I made him go through doesn't allow me to express my disappointment. I cannot start to blame him when I was the one who destroyed us in the past.

"Why did you wait so long to come back to me?" Despite everything, my mouth doesn't hesitate to ask.

I don't care how teary my eyes look as I glance up at him.

"Trust me. It was hard. But I had no other choice." He smiles tenderly. "Even when I knew you moved back to the city, your father didn't allow me to contact you. He wanted to make sure you were in a stable place before allowing me to walk back into your life. He told me your therapist had advised that it'd be risky to face you with something your mind chose to ignore, to wipe away from your memory. They were afraid of the risks because no one knew why you did what you did. So, it was the rational thing to do."

We're silent for a couple of moments. Ian's body vibrates with a lot of emotions; it must have been hard for him. I've made everything hard for him. I dare to bring a hand over his nervous knee, and when he lays his hand over mine, I'm comfortable enough to ask, "So, did my father give you permission to contact me finally?"

I can feel his smile, though my eyes stay glued at our joined hands. He presses on mine, tenderly. "Yes. That's why I moved in here. I wanted to be close to you. I was wondering if you could just remember me. But since we bumped into each other a couple of times and nothing triggered your memory, an idea popped into my head. I put that sticker up, asking for a roommate who can cook. Just like the old days when we were living together, and you used to cook for us. I thought that might trigger your memory to remember me."

"Oh…" I feel a bit embarrassed. "So, it was just a trap. You didn't want a roomie."

He laughs. A small laugh. "Well, I wasn't complaining when I saw you at my door asking to know the terms. My trap has succeeded way beyond my original intentions."

"I guess." I circle a thumb over his hand. I'm too exhausted to explain myself. I know he still wants the answers he wanted three years ago, but now I'm terrified he won't find it in himself to forgive me. To start again. To give me another chance.

"Angel," he says in a soothing voice, pressing his other hand over ours. "It's okay. You don't have to explain anything right now. I know things are still raw for you, so take your time. I'm not going anywhere. I'll be here for you no matter what."

I dare to look up at him, and when I see how vulnerable he is, I wrap my arms around his neck, clutching him tightly before my river of tears starts to flow. He instantly pulls me onto his lap, resting my head against his chest while wrapping his arms around me tightly. "It's okay, angel. The worst is over. We're going to succeed this time. We're gonna make it. No matter what, we'll fight everything together. I won't let anything come between us again, I promise."

But nothing came between us three years ago. It was me and my guilt that prevented us from being together. It was only me.

I wonder if he knew he could be this forgiving and willing to give me another chance. But I'm not going to wonder or keep him in the dark anymore.

I have to tell him everything. I have to tell him what my love for Sam made me commit. I hope he'll find it in himself to forgive me.

"Ian." I pull back from him, wiping my tears with the back of my hands. I don't want him to feel sorry for me or obligated to give me his forgiveness. I want him to know I'm strong enough now. I'm strong enough to accept any decision he'll make. "I'm ready to tell you everything."

CHAPTER THIRTY-ONE

Grace

IAN INSISTS WE have breakfast first. So, here I am, sitting at the kitchen table, eating the eggs he prepared. I don't know what kind of eggs he's made, but I'm eating them anyway. I need a full stomach to have some strength before I spill my worst and darkest secrets.

"I can't believe it's over," Ian says with tremendous relief. "I don't have to keep anything from you. It was hell to be always on guard."

Nothing is over till I tell him about my past and why I hid everything from him. I don't know if he will be as understanding as he seems now. "Is that why you never asked about my scar, why I tried to end my life? You were following my father's advice?"

"To be honest." He circles his fork through his food. His eyes search mine for a moment before saying, "I didn't know how to handle anything. At first, I was thinking I just needed closure.

I needed to know why you kept running away from me, but you didn't remember anything about us. So, I decided to wait for you till you figured your shit out, but my feelings toward you got in the way. Your feelings got in the way too. I was amazed by you. How you were responding to me, how you were willing to open up to me. At first, my mind took control. I chose to stay away, afraid of getting hurt again. I was willing to wait till you were on solid ground, till you remembered me because I was afraid of the old you. The old you would easily outcast me from her life. But you kept surprising me about how you wanted us to be, how you stayed by my side even when I didn't know what the heck to do, and that made me eager to make you mine again. So as you know, I've finally given up and pursued you relentlessly."

He grabs my hand in his, lacing our fingers together. "I didn't care if you ever remembered me or not. I knew I couldn't live without you, and I'd take you any way I could."

I smile nervously. I think it's my turn to reveal everything. "Since you talked to my father, you must know that I'm adopted. They're not my biological parents."

He nods. "Yeah, I know. Your father told me lots of things about you."

"Um…" I'm reluctant to ask, but I have to, "did he tell you about Sam?"

"No. He didn't." I feel his hand tense in mine.

Slowly I unlace our fingers and rest back into my chair. It's time to answer all the silent questions in his eyes.

"Sam was my big sister." I know words fail me when I remember Sam, but the soft look entering Ian's eyes helps a little. He has a sister, so he might understand why I did what I did. Hopefully, he will.

"She's my only sibling." I huff a long breath, trying to prevent myself from crying. Ian reaches again to take my hand in his, giving me some strength.

"She wasn't just a sister to me. She was my protector." I want to tell him how much Sam meant to me, but I cannot without crying my eyes out, so I fast forward to the facts. "Our father died when we were little. Someone shot him; he was dealing with the wrong people. Our mother wasn't any better. She was a drug addict, but she could provide for us till she wasn't anymore. But I had Sam. She was like a mother to me. She took care of me, gave me everything I needed. But she was only thirteen at the time, and I was too young to wonder how she did it. I didn't have a clue about anything till I got a little older. That's when everything changed for me."

"Oh, fuck." Ian spits and reaches to cup my face tenderly. "You don't have to tell me anything, Grace. I don't want you to go through that horrible shit again."

"I have to," I say, slowly pushing his hands away. I don't want him to feel sorry for me. I want him to have his answers. "You still want some answers. You still want to know why I lied to you. I have to tell you everything so you can trust me again."

Despite what he says, I know there's a part of him that doesn't trust me. That's why he kept doubting I wouldn't try to hurt myself again.

He rests back in his chair, and I keep eye contact with him when I say, "My mother was… selling Sam to any man who would provide her with any kind of drugs. I guess Sam was smart enough to keep part of the money for us, but she never told me anything till my mom was planning to start selling me too. I was old enough in her opinion, but thank God I had Sam. She threatened to go to the authorities, and for some time, it worked. With Sam, I felt safe and protected."

I try to calm myself. I don't want to cry while I feel Ian boiling with anger. "I hope that fucked up woman got what she deserved."

I laugh bitterly. "I don't think so. She died of an overdose, not feeling any remorse for her crimes."

"Yeah, that's like a bullet of mercy to a creature like her."

I'm glad Ian agrees, but I wonder what he would think of me after I tell him the rest. "So, Sam did what she could to protect me from mom and her outrageous plans for me, but she couldn't control the men that usually hung around our house. They were scary, addicts, all sorts of bad. And I was constantly molested by them. I didn't understand that at the time. I thought it was the norm for big guys to touch you in places. But nothing as bad as what Sam had to endure because she knew how to protect me." I huff, and so does Ian before he mutters a curse.

I never thought I'd recall that night again, but with Ian's presence, I feel safe enough to tell him about it.

"But one man, in particular, a guy that my mother considered her boyfriend, was much smoother than the others. He kept giving me his attention. You know, he was a little attentive to me, he'd buy me stuff, hug me constantly. At the time, I hated anything related to any man, and with a mom like ours, I hated grownups in general, so he couldn't succeed to seduce me as I think he planned." I clear my throat; it's still hard for me to remember those events.

"One night, he was going to have what he wanted. He was going to force himself on me. My mother was out, and he thought Sam wouldn't mind since he knew she was doing it with other men. But thank God I had Sam that night. She heard my screams, and the next thing I knew, he was off me. She stabbed him in his back. She knew that was the only thing that would stop him. Sam was there for me. Always protecting me. Always there for me."

"Sam was always there for me." I repeat hysterically.

I don't know how I got into Ian's lap. But I like how he's cursing now. I'd never cursed at my biological mother or the horrible men she dealt with and the awful things they did to Sam and me.

Resting my head against his chest and with his steady heartbeat, I feel calm enough to continue, "After that, Sam called the police and told them everything. We were put in a foster home where, after a while, I got lucky, and my parents decided to adopt me. But at first, I refused to go. I refused to leave Sam behind till I woke up one morning and Sam was gone. She knew I wouldn't leave her, so she left to let me have a stable home and loving parents. She was selfless."

"Just like you, angel," Ian whispers, comforting me.

"My parents tried to find her because of my desperation to see her again, but she was out of town. She was seventeen at the time. And after a while, I stopped looking." I stop at that, wondering what he would think of me. "I became selfish. I was so engrossed in my new life, and with my parents' love, that I decided to bury my past for good. It wasn't easy trying to deal with everything we went through, so it was the safest option to block it out."

"So, what happened to your sister?" Ian asks.

"I got so sick one time that my parents admitted me to the hospital, and that was when I saw Sam again. She came to check on me." I don't know how I manage to keep talking and telling him about my sister, but he makes everything easy to share. He's listening without an ounce of judgment. The way he's holding me and touching me is comforting and supporting, nothing else. Like he understands.

"I was really surprised. It'd been four years since the last time I had seen her. And to be honest, I was scared shitless. Seeing Sam after all those years of love and safety had erected my old fears, and poor Sam, she totally felt it. So, when I asked her to stay, when I told her my parents would help her, she refused. She told me we'd become so different, belonging to totally different worlds, and being by my side would only hinder me from moving on. From leaving the past behind me, and that's all she wanted for me. She wanted me to live without any fears, away from our sick past."

"Now, listen to me." Ian pushes me away gently, so he can look into my eyes. "None of that was your fault. You were a victim yourself. Even if you didn't go through the same things as your sister, you were constantly in danger. So, your reaction to seeing her again was totally normal, and I bet you cried your eyes out trying to convince her to stay, but that was her choice, Grace. She went through a lot, she needed professional help, and that's what you offered her. You did what you could, so don't blame yourself."

I nod. I pleaded with her to stay. To accept my parents' help, but like a ghost, she walked out of my life again. But that doesn't erase the guilt I felt. I should have controlled my fears. I shouldn't have let her feel them. I shouldn't.

"After that, I kept looking for her, asking whoever I thought would know anything about her. But I couldn't find anything. I didn't even know which town or city she was in. I kept going with my life. I graduated from college, and that's when I finally got a lead about where she was staying."

"The city," Ian says as a matter of fact. Without telling him, he figured out why I came here in the first place.

"Yes," I confirm. "Someone saw her picture on that escort website, and I instantly packed my bags and headed to the city. I didn't want my parents to worry about me, so I didn't tell them I was going to look for Sam. My aunt had already passed away, leaving her shop for me, so I told them I wanted to open the shop and start my own business. They were thrilled, and I felt a bit guilty because, at the time, I had no intention of opening the shop. I just wanted to find Sam."

"And then we met," Ian says with a tender smile.

"Yep." I smile, placing a kiss on his lips.

"So, will you tell me now? Why was your picture on that shitty site?" Ian asks, and though he tries to be supportive, he cannot hide how apprehensive he is.

I sigh. "It was the only way I could reach out to Sam. I thought if she saw my picture there, she might try to contact me. I know she was so protective of me, so seeing my picture there would entice her to reach out to me."

"I understand now." Ian's eyes are full of relief and curiosity. "But why didn't you tell me your real name?"

I feel a bit embarrassed, remembering how easily I kept lying to him. "Last time I saw Sam, she said we were in totally different worlds, so that's why I dyed my hair pink and wore different clothes than I usually do. I was copying her look, and that's why I changed my name. I know she'd changed hers into a more enticing name. I wanted her to believe that we were still close. We didn't belong to two different worlds. That's the only way I thought I'd be able to bring her back to my life. And for this to succeed, I had focus, I had to have that look and that name to become me. I had to try my best for Sam as she did for me."

"Did you find her?"

"Remember that girl you saw me arguing with at your apartment one time?"

"How could I forget?" Ian shakes his head. "You left me after that."

I cup his face between my hands. "I'm so sorry. But at the time, I had to put Sam before anything else. I couldn't just be happy, not knowing what kind of life Sam was living."

"I understand," Ian says. "So, what about her?"

"Well, I contacted her at first because her picture was also there on that escort website. I contacted lots of them, but she's the one who kept giving me tips about where Sam was. But eventually, none of it led me to my sister. So, I thought she was just extorting me for money and would never give me real information about Sam, so that's why I was arguing with her at the time."

"So, did you ever find her?"

"No, she kept running away from me," I say what I think had happened. "She didn't want me to help her… Every piece of information I got led to a dead end."

"I could have helped you if you just told me," Ian says with desperation as we cannot change anything right now.

"I felt it was my obligation to do things on my own. And honestly, I didn't know how Sam would react, knowing I was happy and in a relationship. I thought that would make her stay away from my world. Like she would think that she would bring darkness to my life."

"So, if you found her, you still would have left me?"

"I don't know," I answer honestly. "You know, when I met you, I thought we'd be having a short-term kind of thing. I mean, look at you…."

"Seriously??" Ian snorts.

"Well," I say, "I didn't know we'd get this serious. I never had a boyfriend or been in a relationship. So, I didn't think we'd develop such strong feelings, and that's what made it okay to hide things from you at first. I didn't think we'd last, but as time went by, as our feelings grew, my guilt intensified. I know I wasn't fair to you, but I couldn't walk away… and I felt guilty finding a perfect guy to love me, having all these wonderful things while Sam was still suffering. So, it was a decision made out of guilt to walk away from you. I had to do it to be able to find Sam and convince her to accept my help."

"But when I was in the hospital, you said you'd come back. Did you mean it at the time?"

"Yes." I sigh. "Seeing you in that state made me weak, made it okay for me to stay, and not making Sam my priority. Like I had found the perfect excuse to stay. You needed my help. So, it was about you, not me, or my happiness."

"So, why didn't you?" Ian asks, his eyes sad, and I feel he wants to know everything.

"When I got that phone call…it was from that girl," I say, clearing my throat. I don't want to cry. "For two days or so, she kept calling me, but I didn't answer her. I thought she just wanted more money without any lead to my sister, but I picked it up after she sent me a recent photo of Sam. So, I thought I had nothing to lose, I'd see her, and if she was lying, I would come back to you as fast as I could… But she wasn't lying. Now I don't think she lied at all. I think Sam knew when I was coming to see her, and she'd made sure not to be there."

I don't know who's more tense, Ian or me, as his hands dig into my flesh. I don't think either of us needs to hear the rest, but at the same time, nothing would go smoothly between us if I didn't clear that once and for all.

"This time, Sam didn't run because she couldn't." I inhale deeply. "She was at the city shelter. The one you decided to help. But it was too late when I arrived."

I let a bitter laugh escape me. "Just like that sick woman, she died of an overdose. I called for help, but she was gone when I got there. I couldn't stop blaming myself after that."

"The ifs started to take over my mind. If I had picked up, if I had answered that girl two days ago. I felt so guilty. I didn't answer her because I, again, was selfish. I was so engrossed with you. I was so engrossed with you I let my focus stray. If I only had her in mind, I would have been able to help her… But I chose you over her, I chose my happiness over her, and I couldn't wrap my mind around that guilt. I mean, she did everything possible for me, she went through all that shit for me, and I was selfish, thinking only of my happiness. So, I went to that shelter again to be close to her, and I don't know… I just couldn't bear being guilty anymore. I just wanted it to end."

"Don't, Ian." I stop him from saying anything. I don't want him to feel sorry for me. I want him to know my truth, to know I'm strong for any decision he will take. "So that's why my mind blocked you out. I mean, I woke up remembering how Sam died. I remembered I cut myself out of guilt. I even remembered at some level that I'd met a guy, had sex for the first time. But my mind tricked me into believing it was just a random, non-meaningful thing. I didn't want to feel that guilt anymore, so that's why I blocked you out of my memory. I didn't want to feel guilty about what happened to Sam. I think I'm still selfish because of it."

"No," Ian objects firmly as I'm about to stop him. "No, I'm not going to sit and let you blame yourself all over again. You did what you could, Grace. I was there, remember. I saw the turmoil you lived through. I saw you breaking time after time for her. But sometimes, we just cannot help how things turn out. Your sister was haunted by her past, and for some reason, she couldn't accept any help. So it's not your fault, angel. None of it was your fault."

"So…" I'm hesitant to ask, but I don't want to wait either. "You're not angry at me?"

He smiles tenderly. "No, I'm relieved you finally told me everything. And to be honest, I was never angry with you. Even knowing you lied about who you are, I couldn't be after you tried to end your life. I didn't have any details, but I knew how deeply you were suffering. I knew you went through a lot, and I was ready to forgive you for hiding everything from me. But now I understand more. You did what you felt was necessary for your sister, and I'd have done the same for mine."

He smiles, and I jump to ask, "What?"

"I know now why you freaked out when I walked into that store. You were going by your real name there, weren't you?"

I laugh. It's strange that he remembers this now. "They wanted my ID, so they knew my real name. I couldn't be Acacia there."

"Yeah." He sighs, and I feel there's something he wants to ask, but I don't know why he doesn't just go ahead and blurt it out.

"What?" I cup his jaw. "You can ask me anything now. I will never hide anything from you ever again."

"Well," he starts, really getting tense. "After you left the hospital and when things started to become stable…you didn't… you know…"

"What?" I frown.

"I kept an eye on you and kept in touch with your father, but these kinds of things."

"What kind of things?" I'm getting frustrated here.

"Have you been with any other guy?"

I laugh, throwing my head back, then lean in to press a kiss to his lips. "No, I hadn't been with any other guy." I pause, internally sighing. "Is that why you had that rule? Forbidding me to bring anyone here?"

"Yes," he retorts firmly. "I wouldn't have survived if you brought any guy here. So, I made up that rule to protect myself and whatever guy you might bring."

I glare down at him. "How about you? I hope you haven't been with any other girl."

"You already know my answer."

"Yep," I whisper against his lips. He did tell me it was more than two years for him. "But why did you make me believe you were in love with another girl. That was pure torture."

He smiles, apologetically. "I didn't mean to. When I kissed you in the elevator, I really freaked out. I mean, your father said it was okay to contact you again, but still, I felt you were still too vulnerable to get involved with me. So, when you asked me if there was any other girl, I gave you my honest answer. I was still attached to you, but we weren't together either. It was wishful thinking from my side to consider us on a break. But then you wouldn't let it rest. And that's something I didn't expect or know how to deal with without lying to you. I didn't want to lie to you. I felt that might trigger your memory to remember us, but, jeez, you took it the wrong way."

"But you didn't mind suggesting a casual thing?"

He seems a bit ashamed. "Well, that was only to protect myself. I thought if we had something causal, I wouldn't get hurt if you decided to leave me again."

"Ah..." I'm the one ashamed now. "I'm sorry for what I made you go through. You went to therapy because of me."

"It was good to talk because I was going crazy not being able to contact you."

"And Emma, is she angry at me?"

"Not angry. She wasn't on board with me getting in touch with you again without telling you about our past. But not angry. She was concerned for you and me."

"But, I bet Mr. Brown is?"

Ian laughs. "Maybe a little. You know I hadn't told my parents anything about us at the time, and he felt he was obligated to take my father's position, and I had a hard time after what happened, so he didn't want me to get hurt again."

I start spreading kisses on his face. "So, where do we go from here?"

"Set a date for the wedding," he says simply like it's the most normal thing to do.

"Seriously," I gasp. "You're still on that fast boat. I think we should slow things a little. Take some time to figure things out."

"We're going to set a date and wed as fast as we can, Grace," he says in a *cut the crap* voice. "I can't bear the idea of not being anything to you. I lived through hell for more than two years. Only because I don't have any legal attachment to you, I couldn't see you, contact you, make any decision considering you, and I want to be everything to you from now on. I don't want anyone to doubt to whom you belong. You're mine, Grace."

"I'm so sorry you had to go through this." I rest my forehead to his. "I made you suffer for nothing. After all, I couldn't give any help to Sam."

"Well, I don't know about that." Ian seems to bein deep thought as I pull away to look into his eyes.

"What?" I ask, a little apprehensive.

"Did you tell Theodore about your sister?" he asks in a serious manner. "Does he know about Sam and what you went through?"

I frown. Is he going to be jealous again? I'm baffled why he's even bringing that up right now.

"Just tell me, does he know about Sam?" he pushes again.

I sigh. "No. He knows I went to therapy. That I went through some shit, but I haven't told him about Sam. I couldn't. Because even if he's one of my best friends, he's still a guy, and I've never felt comfortable bringing up my past with any male. Even my father. I haven't opened up to him about it. I only told mom, Shelia, and my therapist. I never felt comfortable talking about this stuff with any guy but you. You make me feel safe, Ian. You're different."

I hope that will erase any jealous vibes toward Theodore, not only because he's my friend but also for Emma.

"Have you read all of his articles?" he asks. "I mean the local stories he usually reports."

"Not all his work. But since we met, I have been reading everything he writes about," I answer, still not fathoming where he's going with this.

"Okay." Ian nods his head. "I need to show you something."

"About Theodore?" I jump to ask.

"Yes and no," he says, but doesn't even seem sure of it.

"I don't understand."

"Well," he says, touching a hand to my neck, gently squeezing. "Since Theodore is your friend and a potential boyfriend for my sister, I had to do some research on him. To know what kind of guy he is."

My mouth falls. "Did you make that guy, Colman, watch him?"

Ian shakes his head, laughing. "No, angel. But I did. I read the stories he reports. His work is really captivating, but one story in particular just popped in my head."

"And?"

"I think he met your sister. I mean, what are the odds? But it's just a feeling I can't shake. There's so many similarities between your story and hers."

"What do you mean hers?" I ask. My heart is jumping out of my chest.

"Let me show you," Ian says, and I jump from his lap as he stands to pick up his phone from the counter.

I stand by his side as he goes through Theodore's page.

"Here." He proffers his phone to me after a while of searching.

With shaky hands, I hold his phone, my eyes already tearing as I see some girl's right arm in the cropped picture showing on

Theodore's page. She has a unicorn tattoo on her arm. Just like the one on Sam's arm, but no face or name, as most of the stories Theodore reports, and as I preferred too. And this girl didn't want to show her picture either.

Could it be her?

I inhale a deep breath before I'm ready to read what this girl said. "She thinks she's the lucky one. She thinks she had it easy while I took it all. But she's wrong. I was the lucky one. Unlike her, I had a purpose. I knew why I had to suffer. I was there to protect her. But that poor little thing. She had to endure everything, not knowing why. Every time a new man came, her eyes would pop out of her head, like a little helpless rabbit, wondering what he would do to her this time. That poor thing hated everything, not knowing why. And worse, she felt obligated just to sit and take it. She didn't know any better. She doesn't even acknowledge her own suffering. True, I did my best to protect her, but I knew those scums always found a way to hurt her. She's trying to contact me again. She wants me back in her world. But I can't. I can't be near her and not remember all these horrible things we went through. She thinks I'm doing it for her sake, but I'm not. I'm doing it for me. I'm at peace right now, finally knowing where my next trip will be. I just need to see her happy, like really happy, then everything would end for me. I'll finish my purpose on this earth. To be honest, this earth isn't for me. I know there's a better place waiting for people like me. Much better than this one. I hope she doesn't feel sad when it comes. The minute I see her happy, like really happy, I'll go on my next trip."

"Who's she?" Theodore asked her.

"My doll."

I have no doubt now. It's Sam.

Shaking to the core, I turn to Ian. "She used to call me that."

"See, angel." Ian wipes the tears that are streaming down my cheeks. "You did everything you could for her. I don't want you to feel guilty anymore. I mean, the way she described what you went through...it makes me feel so helpless." He pauses, closing his eyes and resting his forehead against mine while his hands cup my face. "I'm sorry, I'm so sorry you had to go through that," he says, hardly able to maintain a steady voice. "I'm so sorry and so fucking helpless. But I'm so proud of you, Grace. I'm so proud of the woman you've become, for not giving up on your sister, for being this selfless human being after all that horrible shit that happened to you."

He takes a deep breath before he pulls back a little to look down at my teary eyes. "I'm so glad you chose to make me the happiest man alive."

Still cupping my face, I grip his hands tight. I want him to know how much he means to me. I want him to know how much I value what he has done for me. "I'm so glad you didn't give up on me. I'm so glad you believed I deserved your time. You put your life on hold for me, after all the things I did, after all my lies."

"You weren't lying, angel," he says with tenderness. "You were just trying to find a way to survive. I think you just wanted to run away from yourself. From your past, so you could be able to help your sister. Because on some level, you believed Grace wouldn't be strong enough to help her. And Acacia, this mysterious girl, can. You just didn't know how strong you are, Grace."

"I will never lie to you again." I kiss his mouth. I kiss it hard. "I hope you know that."

"Well, since you're this vulnerable." There's a hint of a smile on his face, before he playfully says, "I'll choose to believe this lie today."

I smack his chest before he takes me in his arms as we both erupt in laughter. I have never been any happier.

In his arms, I feel safe.

In his arms, I don't feel guilty.

In his arms, I'll never be numb again.

In his arms, I'm happy.

I'm happy, Sam. Like really, happy.

"She's at peace, angel," he whispers, always figuring out how I feel.

"I know now." I pull back a little to look up at his eyes. "Because of you, I know now. Because of you, I'm able to talk to her. I'm able to tell her everything. I'm able to have her back in my life. All because of you, Ian."

"And because of you, I know now. I know I'm enough. I know I can be unbearable and don't make sense, and you still want me in your life," he says, ending his sentence with a kiss.

And I was wrong.

I was wrong, Sam.

I'm not happy. I'm the happiest girl alive.

EPILOGUE
Ian

THREE YEARS LATER

I'VE MADE SURE to make her officially mine right after she remembered everything about us. I've made sure she had the wedding of her dreams. I've made sure to take her on the most thrilling honeymoon around the world. I've made sure she had as much carefree time as I could. And after three years, and after we're blessed with our little boy, Sam, it pops in my head to ask, "Why did you have so much faith in me? Why did you keep in touch, telling me about her progress and the life she was building for herself? Why didn't you act like her mother?"

Noah, Grace's father, frowns as he sits next to me on the couch while his wife, Fay, is on the floor playing with Sam.

"I don't know why I never asked, but I'm seriously curious right now," I add amid the surprised look on Noah's face.

His features relaxing a little, he sighs. "You were our secret."

"What?"

"Grace really never opened up to me about anything. It took her a while to warm up to me. That's understandable, considering the men that she hung around when she was little. So, before she moved into the city, I made her promise to share a secret with me. A thing that only I would know about her. I was a bit jealous since her everything was with Fay, so you were our secret."

"She told you about me?"

"She told me she was in love. But she didn't go into details. So when you showed up, I thought you might be that guy. But still, I needed to be cautious for her sake. After all, we didn't know for sure why she tried to end her life." He takes a moment before adding, "And actually, I would like to thank you."

"Thank me?"

"Yes," he says with tremendous seriousness. "We've grown closer. She constantly reaches out to me, telling me things, asking me about things. That didn't happen until you came back into her life. You've made her feel safer. I'm grateful to have you in our lives."

"I've never apologized," Fay says from across the room, and my head snaps there. I didn't know she was listening. She has this soulful look in her eyes before adding, "I was just trying to protect her. I swore the day she came into my life, that I would not let anything hurt her again. I couldn't take any risks."

"And I've told you this a million times, but I'm gonna say it again," Grace says from behind us, and like a magnet, she makes our heads snap back, as she adds with giddiness, "I'm more than grateful to have you all in my life."

Later, when I take my angel in my arms, grateful isn't sufficient to describe how I value my wife. She makes everything more beautiful and easier, and now she's whispering in my ear. "Ian..."

I instantly roll over on my side. I want to look into her eyes when she tells me her secret because I know this tone. It's just like the one she used to tell me the first time. Her voice is full of joy and a bit terrified.

"Angel?" I smile. I have come to know her very well, so I'm already giddy before she even utters, "I'm pregnant."

I want to shout. I want to jump out of bed and spin her in my arms. I want to let her know how she makes me happy and alive, but she puts a finger on my lips. "Shh...before you say anything, promise me not to tell your parents right away. I don't want to steal Emma's thunder. I want her to enjoy the spotlight like I did the first time."

I nod. Emma and Theodore tied the knot two years ago, and last month, they announced they're pregnant. "You're a true angel. Always thinking of others," I say as soon as she lifts her finger from my lips, and I don't waste any time telling her how I feel.

"I'm the happiest man alive to father another child with you," I say, kissing her lips hard, our bodies entwined. There's no beginning or end between us. We're just embracing each other in the middle. In the life we've created. I hug her tight, whispering how much she means to me. I try to do that every night.

"You're my piece of heaven on this earth."

"And you're my serenity after a prayer," she whispers back.

The End

Thank you so much for reading Checking Boxes

It is my debut novel, and it would mean a lot to me to know how you felt about the story and the characters. So, if you would like to share your thoughts with me, I would be delighted to read them.

Reviews are really appreciated.

And if you want to read a bonus chapter about Ian and Grace

Join my mailing list
https://www.magdolineward.com/about-3-1

Keep in touch with me

Magdolineward.com

My Instagram:
https://www.instagram.com/magdolineward_author/

My facebook personal page:
https://www.facebook.com/profile.php?id=100073477187491

Sing up for my mailing list to receive
exclusive updates and content.
Sent only when I have a new release,
or free content.
https://www.magdolineward.com/about-3-1

About the Author

I write steamy contemporary romance novels. I love to write about strong characters that face difficult choices.

My father named me after the heroine in 'Sous les tilleuls' by Alphonse Karr. So, I've been bookish since zero years old.

CPSIA information can be obtained
at www.ICGtesting.com
Printed in the USA
LVHW052150010722
722611LV00008B/288